# Loyalty's Web

# Other works by Joyce DiPastena

**Poitevin Hearts**

*Loyalty's Web (Book 1)*
*Illuminations of the Heart (Book 2)*
*Loving Lucianna (Book 3)*
*Dangerous Favor (Book 4)*

**The Loves of Lyonstoke Castle**

*Courting Cassandry*

**Stand alone titles**

*The Lady and the Minstrel*

**Short Stories**

*An Epiphany Gift for Robin: A short prequel scene to The Lady and the Minstrel (1)*
*The Girl by the River: A short prequel scene to The Lady and the Minstrel (2)*
"Caroles on the Green," in Timeless Romance Anthology: Winter Edition *(2012)*

**Non-fiction**

*Name Your Medieval Character: Medieval Christian Names (12th-13th Centuries)*

Some of my titles are listed in separate series, but have interconnecting characters. If you are interested in reading these books as they take place chronologically, here is their order:

*Loyalty's Web: Poitevin Hearts 1*
*Illuminations of the Heart: Poitevin Hearts 2*
*Loving Lucianna: Poitevin Hearts 3*
*Dangerous Favor: Poitevin Hearts 4*
*The Lady and the Minstrel*

JOYCE DIPASTENA

Cover design by Roseanna White Designs
roseannawhitedesigns.com
Cover images from Shutterstock
shutterstock.com
Sable Tyger Logo by The Write Designer
thewritedesigner.com

ISBN: 978-0-9892419-4-6

Sable Tyger Books
Mesa, AZ
sabletygerbooks@gmail.com



This is a work of fiction. All the characters, names, places, incidents, and dialogue in this novel are either products of the author's imagination or used fictitiously.

Printed in the United States of America
First Sable Tyger Books Edition: 2014

022020

*To my parents, without whose support this book could never have been written.*

*And to Dr. Thomas Parker, professor of Medieval History at the University of Arizona, who with passion and wit, fed my history-hungry soul.*

# Cast of Characters

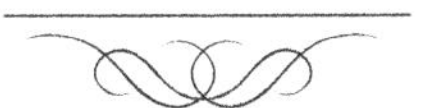

*Fictional Characters (in alphabetical order)*

**Audiart**: a serving girl at Pennault Castle

**Aumary de Laurant**: father of Heléne de Laurant, Therri de Laurant, and Clothilde de Merval

**Brandon de Vexin**: squire to Hugh de Bury, Earl of Gunthar

**Challons**: highest ranking vassal to Hugh de Bury, Earl of Gunthar; a member of his council

**Clothilde de Merval**: older sister of Heléne de Laurant; widow of Fulbert de Merval

**Damien de Brielle**: a rebel knight who sided with the princes during their war with their father, King Henry II of England, known as the Great Revolt (1173-74); crippled by Hugh de Bury, Earl of Gunthar during an assault on his castle; master of Vere Castle

**Edmund de Muncey**: secretary to Hugh de Bury, Earl of Gunthar

**Etienne de Brielle**: younger son of Damien de Brielle

**Flora**: a serving girl at Pennault Castle

**Fulbert de Merval** (mentioned): deceased husband of Clothilde de

Merval; one of the rebel barons who sided with the princes during their war with their father, King Henry II of England, known as the Great Revolt (1173-74); defeated by Hugh de Bury, Earl of Gunthar

**Garoux de Rousillon**: a mysterious knight who blackmails Heléne de Laurant

**Gwenllian de Laurant**: mother of Heléne de Laurant, Therri de Laurant, and Clothilde de Merval; of Welsh descent

**Heléne de Laurant**: younger daughter of the former rebel baron, Aumary de Laurant, and his wife Gwenllian; is blackmailed by Garoux de Rousillon who claims he has evidence that her father has joined a new plot against the king

**Hugh de Bury, Earl of Gunthar**: an English supporter of Henry II during the Great Revolt with the princes of 1173-74; led the king's campaign against the rebels in Poitou and Aquitaine during the Great Revolt; sent by King Henry II in 1176 to ensure the defeated barons of Poitou are keeping their oaths of peace with the crown; sits on the king's high council

**John Heywood** (mentioned): an English baron who wishes to marry Heléne de Laurant

**John Lee**: best friend of Hugh de Bury, Earl of Gunthar

**Julian Parr**: squire to Hugh de Bury, Earl of Gunthar

**Sir Oliver**: leader of mercenary knights at Vere Castle

**Osanne**: second wife of Damien de Brielle

**Roger Tollerton**: marshal to Hugh de Bury, Earl of Gunthar

**Stephen Goldingham**: an English knight sent to arrange the marriage of Heléne de Laurant with John Heywood

**Sybil**: an old woman who was once nurse to Heléne de Laurant and Clothilde de Merval

**Therri de Laurant**: son of Aumary and Gwenllian de Laurant; brother to Heléne de Laurant and Clothilde de Merval

**Thomas Enslye** - one of Hugh de Bury's knights

**Triston de Brielle**: elder son of Damien de Brielle; brother to Etienne de Brielle

*Historical Characters:*

**Eleanor of Aquitaine** (mentioned): Queen of England, wife of Henry II; mother of Richard Plantagenet; encouraged her sons to rebel against their father

**Henry II**: King of England (mentioned): rules over large sections of France, including Poitou and Aquitaine, the homeland of Heléne de Laurant; defeated his sons in the Great Revolt of 1173-74; surnamed Plantagenet; sometimes known as "the Angevin" for his original homeland of Anjou

**Jean aux Bellesmains** (John aux Bellesmains): Bishop of Poitiers

**Richard Plantagenet**: second son of Henry II of England and Eleanor of Aquitaine; rebelled with his brothers Henry the Younger and Geoffrey in 1173-74, demanding more power and respect be granted them by their father; defeated by Henry II. By 1176 (the setting of *Loyalty's Web*), Richard had been made Count of Poitou by his father. In order to avoid reader confusion with the Count of Angoulême, who also participates in this story, I have chosen to refer to Richard as "the prince."

**Thomas Becket** (mentioned): Archbishop of Canterbury 1162-1170; quarreled with King Henry II over the jurisdiction of the secular courts over the English clergy; when Henry II in a frustrated rage shouted, "Will no one rid me of this turbulent priest?" four of his knights crossed the English Channel and murdered the archbishop in his own cathedral.

**William of Angoulême**: a Poitevin count who sided with the princes in the Great Revolt of 1173-74

# Prologue

The young lady struck his hand away. "It is a lie!"

He caught his breath at the transformation anger worked upon her. He had thought her drab but curious a moment ago, decked out in what he imagined must be some squire's cast off clothes. Although her hose-clad legs were nicely turned, the too large, knee-length tunic completely swallowed up any hint of womanly curves. He might well have taken her for a tall, lanky youth had it not been for her pale gold braid. Even tumbled over her shoulder as it was, its thick, feathery end brushed against her hip.

Now tiny flecks of fire set her silvery eyes ablaze. The way her cheeks glowed, he thought the whole of her might burst into flames. A calm, critical survey confirmed a sad lack of her sister's bewitching charms. But drab this young lady most certainly was not.

"I assure you, my lady—" he began, only to be cut off.

"Nay, you lie!" She leaned forward, hands on hips, challenging him as stoutly as any battle-hardened knight. "My father has not betrayed his oath to the crown. How dare you slander my house like this!"

"'Tis no slander," he insisted. "I have proof. A letter. One with your father's seal."

He had seen her wariness when he first approached her on the riverbank, fishing with a pole he suspected she had swiped from the same squire whose clothes she now wore. She had dropped the pole when she flared into anger at his initial accusation. Now, though that anger remained bright, the veriest hint of doubt stole into her face.

"A letter?"

He smiled and raised his bone-thin hand to toss back his long, crimped curls. Hair even paler than hers shone white rather than gold in the spring sunlight. But not the white of age. He guessed himself not more than six or seven years her senior. Yet at times, he felt almost ancient. The corruptions and debaucheries he had once found so thrilling had now grown little more than tedious. Gluttony, theft, seduction, even murder. He had tasted, nay, he had gloried in them all.

Only one earthly pleasure—revenge—continued to elude him. Continued to madden him. But with this innocent's help, he would finally glory in its fulfillment as well.

He said nothing more for a moment, allowing doubt to work its way deep into her mind. Then: "Aye, a letter. You might have it, for a price."

Her hostile eyes narrowed. "I do not even know your name. Why should I believe anything you say?"

"Because it might well be the truth. And if it is, your father is courting disaster, thinking he can play both ends against the middle. The earl is no fool. He will discern the false faith behind this marriage agreement. He will learn, as I did, that your father's oath of fealty already lies broken in the dust."

The lady's long braid swished with the fierce shake of her head.

"I do not believe it. My father would not swear an oath he did not intend to keep. He would not place his family in danger of the king's retribution again."

"Ah." He smiled sympathetically. "It was most unpleasant for your family, was it not, when the earl besieged your castle?" Her bright cheeks paled. "Or perhaps frightening would be a better word."

Her sharp little chin jutted out at that, whether in defiance of him or her memory of the earl, he did not know. He hoped it was the latter. If he could but focus her hostility from himself to the earl, the risk of meeting her here in the open would have gone far to accomplish his purpose.

"Come, my lady, I do not ask so much. A little information is all.

If you could only tell me when the earl is due to arrive, perhaps a few other details. . ."

He trailed off. Drat the lass. Her eyes surveyed him too shrewdly. And her defiant chin lifted higher.

"Your name, sir. Your house. And how this dark secret of my father has come to your knowledge. Tell me all of that and then, perhaps, I will see fit to tell you what you want to know."

His admiration of her stout heart abruptly turned to annoyance. He had not time to joust words with her. If he were seen and recognized, his life would not be worth a copper coin.

His voice hardened. "I have the letter. If you do not wish it to come to the king's knowledge—"

"Then show it to me, if it exists. I will know my father's hand and seal. Show me your proof. Otherwise, be on your way."

She faced him boldly. The tension visibly slid from her body when he did not reply.

"I see. Then I shall be on *my* way."

She picked up her fallen fishing pole and turned to leave.

"My lady."

He touched her arm to stay her. She gasped and jerked away so hard she nearly lost her balance. In that instant he saw the fear in her face. She had masked it well until now. But seeing it assured him of the power he needed.

"I have the letter," he repeated, and this time he allowed some menace to slip into his voice. "Meet me here again in a week's time. Only come at night, when the moon is high. Bring me the information I require and I will surrender the letter to you. Fail me, and your father will find himself in chains. And you and your family will learn the ugly fate that awaits a traitor's kin."

He reached out for her again, hoping the strength of his hand about her arm would press his warning home. But before he could touch her, she swung her pole at him. He ducked just in time to avoid a crack to his head, and felt the *whoosh* of the rod in air.

"You are a liar, sirrah! And if you dare to step foot on our land again a week-night hence, you will be met, not by me, but by my father's guards."

She turned and ran away from him.

He let her go and smiled. Seven days to let the doubts he had sown harrow her mind.

Aye, she would be back.

# One

## Poitou ~ Spring 1176

"Can you see him yet? What does he look like? Is he tall and slender? Is he as handsome as they say? Oh, tell me, Heléne, tell me quickly! I am like to die from trepidation!"

Heléne glanced at her sister, waiting anxiously beside the bed. Agitation only deepened the bloom in her glorious cheeks, while an almost feverish dread lent a dazzling fire to her brilliant eyes. Clothilde de Merval was a heart-stopping beauty. Golden hair streamed o'er her shoulders in shimmering, luxurious waves, and her chemise of fine lawn graced a figure so tantalizing as to have driven men to distraction for miles around.

She stood now, her fair hands clasped to her shapely bosom, her tender face a tortuous mirror of hope and fear. She looked, Heléne thought, more like a maid awaiting her bridal night than a twenty-one year-old woman who, not eighteen months past, had seen her husband's body laid in the grave.

"If you are so curious," Heléne said, "why don't you come and see for yourself?"

Clothilde shrank delicately from the thought. "Oh, I could not. It would be so bold. What if he saw me? What would he think?"

"He would think you as curious about him as he must be about you. Do not be such a goose."

Clothilde's bow-like mouth drooped at her sister's chiding, but she made no move to join Heléne at the window. Heléne tried hard not to feel impatient with her, but she, herself, felt no compunction at all about spying on events in the bailey below. She knelt on the cushioned window seat in the bedchamber they shared, heedless of her own state of undress, and leaned forward again to look through the recessed opening looped into the castle's thick stone wall.

Dozens of men had ridden into the yard below. Heléne saw the colorful flash of rich mantles, a flurry of yellows and blues and reds. At least thirty knights mingled with the men of her father's court, but even amid this miscellany of aristocratic rank, she easily singled out the Earl of Gunthar. She had glimpsed him once before, arrayed in full battle armor in her father's hall. He had been oblivious to her presence then, and she had been hastily bustled away by her mother before he could become aware of her. But even though he wore no armor now, she had no trouble recognizing him.

He stood head and shoulders above the others and even from the distance of her second story window, she saw the proud loftiness of his stance. She watched with scorn as her father acknowledged the earl with a low, self-effacing bow.

"Heléne . . ." her sister's voice floated once more across the room ". . . please tell me what you see."

"I see a yard full of knights come to pay court to our father."

"But the earl? Can you tell which one is he?"

"Of course. He is the one Papa is groveling before."

It had been over a year since the Peace of Montlouis wherein the king had made peace with his sons, and her father, like the other rebels, had renewed his oath of loyalty to the crown. Heléne dismissed with disdain the accusations made by the strange young man she had encountered near the river a week past. His suggestion that her father intended to break his oath was absurd. Her father was a man of honor and it was unfair that the king should continue to punish her family for their support of the princes.

Her voice took on a crisp note of anger. "It is not enough that the king has ordered Gunthar to take our brother away and make him little better than a hostage. He insists on humiliating us with this insulting offer of marriage."

Offer? It was a command devised by the king to ensure their family's loyalty. And her father simply bowed and consented!

"Were the king to bear such a dictate to me, I would—"

"Heléne, is he fat?"

Heléne turned her head, biting her tongue on an exasperated response. What on earth had that to do with anything?

Clothilde gave a despairing shudder and too late Heléne understood the urgency of her sister's question.

"No, no," she said quickly as Clothilde raised trembling hands to her face. "He is just as you hoped. He is very tall and lean and . . . and handsome." She added this last though in fact she had not yet seen his face. "Come, Clo, see for yourself. He will never know we are looking."

She turned back towards the window and leaned out over the courtyard once more. Only then did she realize the inaccuracy of her last statement. The Earl of Gunthar had turned away from her father and, as if sensing her gaze, suddenly glanced up at the window.

Heléne expected to feel again the rush of hatred she had known when she had seen him in her father's hall, his features concealed by a fearsomely crested helmet. Instead she gasped. His face, exposed to her now, was hawkishly proud, though not exactly handsome. His eyes, grey and piercing beneath thick, lowering brows, met her contemptuous stare with a powerful, probing regard. For a moment it transfixed her so thoroughly that she felt as though she had ceased to breathe, frozen into some curiously fashioned image laid open, every favor and flaw, to his uncompromising gaze.

Then one of his heavy eyebrows lifted and his cold, unyielding mouth curved upwards into a quizzical smile.

With that first glimmer of unexpected charm, Heléne remembered her awkward state of undress. Like her sister, she wore only a sleeveless chemise, with her pale gold braid spilling over her shoulder. She drew back with belated modesty and leaned against the cold stones that ensconced the window seat. She pulled up her knees and twisted her arms around them, trying desperately to quiet the wild thudding of a heart that had but a moment ago been so inexplicably still.

The chamber door clicked open. "Dear me, what is this?" her mother's voice sounded. "Why have you not begun to dress? The earl has come and your father will be sending for us any moment."

The Lady Gwenllian de Laurant stood on the threshold, her pretty mouth drawn down in displeasure. Twenty-three years of living among her husband's people in Poitou had softened but not entirely erased the lilt of her native Welsh accent. Though a few strands of grey glistened in her pale gold hair, there could be no doubt whence Clothilde had inherited her profusion of graces.

"Where is your maidservant? I sent her to attend you hours ago. If I find she's been sporting again with that pretty stableboy, I shall have the pair of them soundly whipped."

The Lady Gwenllian sailed across to her daughters' wardrobe. To Heléne's relief, she came alone. More often than not the old nurse Sybil was at her heels, ever ready to employ that stinging rod she carried.

"Heléne, come quickly. Take this to your sister and begin helping her dress."

Heléne scrambled from the window seat and took the smock and costly kirtle from her mother's arms. The clothes smelled of sweet violets and felt soft against her skin. With a wistful sigh, she slid the straw-colored smock over her sister's head, an easy assistance as she stood several inches taller than Clothilde. The luscious blue silk of the kirtle followed.

"See you lace that up tightly," her mother called, as she searched her daughters' clothing chests for the appropriate accessories. "We shall give the earl something to dream of tonight. Mayhap he will prove the more amenable in his negotiations with your father on the morrow."

Heléne saw the unhappy blush that stole up into her sister's cheeks. Clothilde's beauty had snared the rich, fat, twice-widowed Sir Fulbert de Merval when she was scarcely sixteen. But Merval, after persuading their father to join the princes' rebellion against the king, had died suddenly at the height of the war, leaving their father to face the royal wrath alone.

The king had sent Hugh de Bury, Earl of Gunthar, to pacify this particular corner of Poitou. Gunthar had employed the same sort of lightning tactics for which his master, the king, was famous, and with the same devastatingly successful results. After a few token weeks of resistance, Laurant had surrendered his castle and thrown himself and his family on the earl's mercy.

What took place at the actual moment of her father's formal capitulation Heléne did not know, for her mother angrily whisked her away from spying on the proceedings. What she *did* know was that the earl imposed a humiliating oath of surrender upon her father, an oath that spared Pennault Castle and salvaged for his family a tenuous security.

Secure, she knew, so long as her father abided his oath and obeyed the dictates of the king. She thought again of the young man beside the river, and frowned.

"No, no, Heléne, I said *tightly*." Her mother pushed her aside and finished lacing up Clothilde's gown herself. "When one is so perfectly formed as your sister, one need not be ashamed to display it. The modesty of Clothilde's manners will provide an appealing counterpoint to her provocative figure."

A vivid blush flooded Clothilde's cheeks as her mother tightened the gown, but while her delicate hands clutched at the flowing folds of her skirt, she made no protest. Heléne knew their mother's spirits, so cruelly dashed first by Merval's unexpected death and then by her husband's defeat, had soared at the king's decision to cement their father's new-found loyalty by marrying Clothilde to the Earl of Gunthar.

No one had considered consulting Clothilde's feelings in the matter, but Heléne had no doubt that she would go to this marriage as meekly as she had gone to Merval. Heléne would never have done it. Her parents might have whipped her daily and locked her in the loneliest tower, and she still would not have—

"Heléne, where are your wits?" her mother's sharp voice broke across her thoughts. "I asked you to—"

"Yes, Mama." Heléne hastened to preempt the scolding by fetching the semi-circular cut of fine white linen her mother had already requested twice.

She placed the veil in her mother's waiting hand. The Lady Gwenllian arranged the veil skillfully about Clothilde's head, fastening it into place with an elegant gilt circlet, which drew the cloth into a becoming frill against her daughter's brow. The snowy folds floated softly to Clothilde's shoulders.

"Heléne, fetch me that girdle I left on the bed."

Once more Heléne obeyed. She carried the silken band with its colorful adornment of embroidery and beads to her mother. She waited while her mother passed it about Clothilde's slender waist, crossed it at the back, then brought the tasseled ends to the front once more and knotted them loosely below Clothilde's hips.

"What am I to wear, Mama?" Heléne asked breathlessly then. Hopeful visions danced in her mind of some ravishing silk such as Clothilde now wore . . .

"You shall wear your green smock and your surcote of saffron wool."

Heléne bit her lip, dashed by the mundane choice. But her mother's indifference to her appearance did not come as a surprise. To her mother's frequently voiced despair, Heléne had failed to inherit even the lowliest of her sister's graces.

Three years younger than Clothilde, Heléne stood a full head taller, her figure as boyishly slender as Clothilde's was generously curved. Heléne's hair, sweeping below her waist, tended towards the flaxen, insipid, her mother never tired of saying, beside the vibrant sheen of her sister's glorious mane. The blue of Heléne's eyes paled almost to silver against the deeper hued sapphire of Clothilde's. Her mother repeatedly bemoaned Heléne's imperious little nose, together with the wide mouth she had inherited from her father. And that chin of hers was far too pointed and decisive to ever permit anyone to take her for some frail and delicate maid.

Heléne did not need her mother to remind her that such deficiencies accounted for her still unmarried state at the embarrassingly advanced age of eighteen. Not that she wished to be used as the kind of pawn Clothilde had been made to play at a much younger age when her parents had betrothed her to Merval. Still, sometimes when she saw men staring at Clothilde with such enraptured admiration . . .

"Tush, girl, don't look so downcast. Tonight is your sister's, but your turn will soon come."

The Lady Gwenllian's rare expression of sympathy startled Heléne. "Why, Mama, what do you mean?"

Her mother responded with a thin smile. "Your father has had a letter from Lord Heywood. That land we inherited last year from your father's cousin in England apparently marches alongside one of Heywood's manors in Northumberland. Heywood desires to purchase it from us. He is a man of respectable wealth, holding substantial estates which he has shrewdly enlarged since his father's death. What is to our benefit is that he remains a bachelor. I have suggested to your father that we offer Heywood the land he seeks as a portion of your dowry."

Heléne gasped. "But Mama, he has never even seen me. He cannot possibly wish me for his wife."

"That he has not seen you can only be to our benefit," her mother answered coldly. "Not every man can wed a beauty like your sister. Heywood is determined enough to gain the land that he has agreed to overlook a few flaws of face and figure. Be grateful, Heléne. You've no idea how humiliating it has been for your father and me to admit the likelihood that you were destined to remain a spinster."

Heléne bit her lip again, this time against the sharp twinge of pain her mother's callous words inflicted. To be bartered off for a piece of land! She knew she was not beautiful, but she would sooner have died a pitiable maid than be sold like a piece of chattel. Defiance hovered on her tongue, but before she could blurt out what her mother would have viewed as a pert reply, the door flew open.

"Milady," a flustered voice exclaimed, "milord is demanding your attendance. He is below stairs with the earl and says you are to bring your daughters at once."

"Does he?" The Lady Gwenllian's chill voice cut like a knife across the serving girl's excitement. "And where have you been this past hour, when you were told to prepare your mistresses for this very summons? Or need I ask? Your shameless countenance speaks volumes of what you have been about."

Audiart's pretty face puckered, but Heléne knew that her mother had judged the cause of the servant's delinquency aright. Telltale strands of hay clung in Audiart's dark hair and her bright cheeks still glowed with the lingering passion of a stolen tryst.

"'Tis no time to speak of this now," the Lady Gwenllian said. "Be assured you shall taste the rod for your disobedience before the day is out. Aye, and your shiftless stableboy, as well. Now see to the Lady Heléne. If she is not prepared in a trice to attend her father, I shall have Sybil replace the rod with the whip."

The servant's eyes widened in fear. Heléne did not blame her. Sybil had once served as Heléne's and Clothilde's nurse and still had the whole castle in terror of her rod. Clothilde was the only person Sybil doted upon, and her mother the only one she obeyed.

The pretty servant moved quickly across the room to fetch Heléne's smock and surcote. She helped her young mistress dress in silence, but when Heléne thanked her softly and smiled, she warmed responsively.

"I'll brush out your braid if you wish it, milady. 'Twould look so lovely, your long tresses—"

"Leave it alone," the Lady Gwenllian said. "There's no time for such nonsense. The earl will not be looking at her anyway."

"At least," Audiart insisted, "let me fetch a fresh ribbon—"

"Come, Heléne."

Her mother's voice was a crisp command. Too abashed to meet Audiart's gaze again, Heléne followed her mother and sister out of the room.

Heléne's spirits quickly revived as she trailed her mother and sister down the winding circle of deep stone steps that led towards the tumult of the hall. She recognized her father's robust laughter and the nervousness that cracked it. But the other voices intrigued her more. The strange, foreign ones belonging to men she did not know. Heléne's feet twitched with excitement. Had she not been trapped behind her mother's languid movements, she would have run ahead to peer around the final twist in the steps. Fortunately for her impatience, she was tall enough to see over the Lady Gwenllian's head as they made the final turn that brought them full into the hall.

The great hall of Pennault Castle where the Baron de Laurant had assembled his guests gleamed handsomely in the slanting rays of the afternoon sun. A huge, sprawling chamber with a vaulted ceiling two stories high, the freshly whitewashed stone walls sported bright tapestries attesting to the weaving skills of generations of Laurant women. A banner bearing the emblem of their house, a double-headed phoenix rising from the flames, draped the wall opposite the stairs behind the dais.

Dozens of men, knights, squires and pages, mingled in the hall. Heléne identified some of them as members of her father's house, but most belonged to the earl's retinue. She knew them from the blue and silver livery they wore and the badges on their shoulders—a stallion embroidered in silver, prancing on a field just shy a royal blue.

Gunthar she recognized at once. He was the tallest man in the room, though a plain but amiable-looking gentleman standing beside him nearly rivaled him in height. Still, the latter seemed oddly dwarfed beside the earl's powerful presence.

Gunthar's close-fitting tunic strained at his broad, square shoulders, the dark brown cloth dulled by the dust of travel. A wide band of gold embroidery formed a belt from which hung a jewel-hilted sword, and a silver brooch worked in a Celtic knot sprinkled with sapphires and diamonds clasped at his neck a red silk mantle, tossed negligently over one shoulder. Beneath a stylish round cap he wore his dark hair neither cropped too close at the sides nor flowing in elaborate curls to his shoulders, but in a soft, natural wave cut to the nape of his neck.

But his style of dress, quite unobtrusive in itself, did not account for his unmistakable aura of power and strength. No, Heléne realized, it was something in his face. The hawkish cast of his features, the implacable set of his lips, the piercing grey eyes that cut one to the soul. She remembered her brief meeting of that unnerving gaze from her window and for a moment her heart thumped anew.

But as her mother had predicted, the earl was not looking at her.

He had tilted his head towards her father, listening to one of Laurant's tedious jokes. Laurant ended with a roar of self-appreciative laughter, then choked a little when the earl showed no other response than a lift of his heavy brows.

Heléne felt an uncomfortable tightening in the pit of her stomach at the sight of her father's nervousness. Did he anticipate trouble over her brother's absence? Or had the man beside the river been right? She remembered his challenge to meet him again if she would know the truth. She had not considered doing so . . . until now. Watching her father fidget before the earl, Heléne found herself wondering . . .

Laurant caught sight of his wife standing at the foot of the steps and hastened to summon her forward.

"My lord, allow me to make known to you my wife, the Lady Gwenllian de Laurant."

The Lady Gwenllian dissolved into a curtsy of perfect depth and grace, her head bowed modestly before the earl. When she rose, her face glowed with a soft and delicate smile so that it seemed impossible a hard or calculating thought could possibly lie behind it.

"My lord," she murmured in her most musical tones, "we are overwhelmed by this honor. That you should condescend to rest in our most humble home—"

"My lady, the pleasure is mine," the earl interrupted, not curtly, but with an evident desire to preempt whatever fulsome abasement the Lady Gwenllian had intended to make. His deep, vibrant voice intrigued Heléne, for though he spoke a flawless French, there lingered on the words the faintest ring of a foreign timbre. "I am most appreciative of your hospitality while I attempt to discharge the king's commission."

The Lady Gwenllian offered him a coy smile. "I trust your duties will not prove too demanding, my lord. We have many pleasures to offer you here at Pennault. Pray allow me to present to you our daughter, the Lady Clothilde de Merval."

Clothilde came forward at her mother's gesture and sank into an elegant curtsy. The earl bowed over her delicate hand.

"My lady, rumor has failed to do you justice. The whole realm speaks of your beauty, but the bards have sought in vain for words to describe such grace as I see before me now."

Clothilde blushed and made some whispered reply, but Heléne felt a stir of anger. Though her mother looked delighted at the prettily worded compliment, Heléne failed to detect any hint of the sort of ardor that normally accompanied such flattery to her sister. There was not a man within a hundred miles of Pennault who had not been genuinely smitten by Clothilde's beauty and would consider it the fulfillment of a dream to claim her for a wife. Yet this man whose privilege it would be to wed her, stood smiling now rather vacantly, his grey eyes no longer piercing, but merely looking bored.

"Our poor Clothilde is but recently widowed," the Lady Gwenllian informed him, striking a sorrowful pose. "A most unfortunate marriage, as it turned out. Of course, we had no notion when we succumbed to Sir Fulbert's offer where his sympathies lay. Had we realized he harbored treason in his heart, we would never have delivered our innocent daughter into his hands."

The earl looked politely skeptical of this obvious attempt to distance herself and Laurant from their son-in-law's politics. "Indeed," he said dryly, the smile now gone from his face.

Heléne felt a frightful fluttering in her stomach again. Laurant's hurried attempt to divert the earl from his wife's unfortunate words did little to reassure her.

"My lord, you have not yet been made known to my younger daughter. Come forward, girl. My lord, the Lady Heléne."

Heléne finished descending the steps. She stiffened her back as she confronted the earl. Her parents could bow and tremble in fear of this man's displeasure, but she would have him know there was at least one Laurant whom he could not awe. Tall enough not to be intimidated by his height, she met his eyes with an unveiled challenge.

He surveyed her coolly for a moment, his level gaze lowering from her face to sweep the length of her dull saffron gown, then traveling slowly back up again. Heléne somehow managed not to blush at this insolence.

"But, my lady, have we not met before?"

The mildly voiced query took her aback, momentarily checking her anger. "Why—why I do not think so, my lord."

His brows rose, faintly incredulous at her reply. "Are you sure? I am quite certain I have seen you . . . somewhere."

She was about to protest again when she saw his eyes flicker to her pale gold braid. His haughty mouth twitched and when his eyes swept back to hers she saw a distinct twinkle in their probing depths. This time some heat did steal into her cheeks. Surely he was teasing her, remembering her inquisitive face at the window?

Her mother's pretty laughter floated across Heléne's embarrassment. "I assure you, my lord, it is quite impossible. Heléne has not set foot off Pennault since she was eight years old."

"Then it must have been some other vision, or perhaps a dream," the earl murmured in his deep, subtly accented voice. He spoke quite gravely but there was no mistaking the amusement with which he observed Heléne's discomfiture. Then he seemed to take pity on her, or perhaps he merely grew bored with the game. He turned to her father. "My lord, my companions and I are weary with travel. The crossing from England was less than pleasant for a few of my men, as the waves were high and uncooperative. If you would be so good as to direct us to our chambers?"

Laurant promptly bowed. "But of course, my lord. I trust you will find your accommodations here more than adequate. We know how to enjoy our comforts here in Poitou. And perhaps a bit later you will consent to partake of a few of our more humble dishes? After you and your companions are rested, of course."

This, Heléne knew, was Laurant's way of informing the earl that a lavish banquet was being prepared in his honor.

"We should find such refreshment welcome," the earl said. "My thanks to you."

Laurant nodded, warming to his theme. "Aye, a fine, hearty meal and a good night's sleep will set you up right. And tomorrow I'll show off to you my park. Well, King Henry's really, but my father won grant of vert and venison there. You'll not be disappointed. The deer are in plenty this year . . ."

Laurant rattled on happily now, for hunting was his passion. Heléne knew he could continue such a discourse for hours. The earl listened, then betrayed a shared interest in the subject by inserting a question when Laurant paused for air. They were soon deep in the throes of discussion, arguing the rival merits of the red versus the fallow deer and the hunting of deer in general versus that of the wild boar. Heléne occasionally enjoyed participating in the sport herself and was generally accounted a good huntswoman, but she dared not enter the debate while her mother stood by. The Lady Gwenllian would consider any remark on this masculine subject by a daughter of hers unforgivably bold.

Precluded from joining in the lively discussion, Heléne soon grew bored with it. She allowed her attention to wander by taking stock of the men who formed the earl's court. The hall teemed with unfamiliar faces. She guessed those standing nearest the earl to be the most important. Not all wore the badge of the stallion. Some wore distinctive emblems of their own or no insignia at all.

Among the latter, one gentleman interested her for his extravagant dress. He wore a bright red tunic slashed up the front to reveal yellow hose banded about with green stripes embroidered in gold. A tangle of gold and silver chains, some with jeweled studs, adorned his breast. Clearly, she thought, a man of wealth and one, moreover, who enjoyed displaying it. Of medium height, he had a round, smooth face and a mouth full of good humor. Heléne saw that he was not attending in the least to the discussion taking place between her father and the earl. Rather, he stared like a man bedazzled at Clothilde.

He was not alone. Heléne counted fully a dozen other gentlemen gazing at her sister with the same bemused expression. Clothilde stood with her eyes modestly downcast. The earl must be a cold-blooded man indeed to be so impervious to her sister's charms. How could he stand there speaking of stags and hounds when so exquisite a creature waited nearby, trembling for his approval? No wonder Clothilde looked so pale. If only he would speak one genuine word of warmth to her—

Heléne realized she was glaring at the earl. She forced herself to look away before her mother caught her, and almost gasped at seeing amid the company a face that clearly did not belong. She knew him instantly: Etienne de Brielle, the younger son of their neighbor, Sir

Damian. His presence filled her with apprehension, for the family was in disgrace and held a bitter grudge against the earl.

She thought Etienne looked pale, uncertain as he stood for a moment, watching the earl. Abruptly, he edged his way past a ruddy-faced knight, then stopped again. His green eyes narrowed on the earl, still conversing with her father, both of them oblivious to the youth's appearance.

She wondered if she should call out a warning. Etienne's hand disappeared inside his cloak, but came out again a moment later, empty. She told herself not to be ridiculous. Etienne could not possibly intend any mischief in the midst of this crowd of armed knights, all of whom owed their allegiance to either her father or the earl. Surely simple curiosity had brought him here, for he had not been present at the battle that left his father crippled. Etienne had been sent away with his stepmother before the earl's siege of their castle began.

Etienne stood quietly now, gazing at the earl through thoughtful, narrowed eyes. If resentment burned in their normally teasing depths, surely that was understandable? His soft dark curls, tousled by the wind, formed a wild halo about his handsome countenance. He was but a year older than Heléne. They had played together as children. She still counted him a friend, but she sensed with some disquiet that it was not mere curiosity she read in his face. He kept reaching beneath his cloak in an odd way. But if she cried out and it was nothing—

Then he moved. His expression changed in an instant from quiet resentment to desperate resolve. His hand flashed out and this time, Heléne saw a glint of steel.

She screamed, but it was too late. The earl turned as Etienne closed the distance between them and flashed his dagger in a deadly arc towards the earl's chest.

# Two

The Earl of Gunthar threw up his left arm at the blur of movement and felt the sting of a blade cut its way into his flesh. He shot his right hand out to grasp his attacker's wrist. The man cursed as Gunthar forced the steel clear of his arm. Gunthar swept both their arms into an upward arc, then abruptly snapped them down again, at the same time giving his attacker's wrist a sharp twist. A loud crack sounded and the dagger clattered to the floor. The man fell to his knees and Gunthar finally saw his attacker's whitened face.

Nay, scarcely a man at all, a boy no more than nineteen, at most, twenty.

Gunthar's men belatedly swarmed to their master's defense. His marshal, Sir Roger Tollerton, hauled the youth to his feet, while the others closed in around him, blocking him from Gunthar's view.

Gunthar heard shouted oaths of anger. At least a half-dozen fists raised, a few of which fell with resounding thuds before Gunthar shouted, "Enough. Let him be. Stand back, I say!"

His knights dispersed at his command, all save Sir Roger who continued to hold onto the struggling youth.

"Who are you and why did you attack me?" Gunthar demanded.

The youth glared at Gunthar from his one good eye. An ugly purpling bruise had already swollen the other shut. The youth looked angry and defiant and a little scared. But he pressed his lips obstinately together and refused to answer.

"My lord," Laurant said, rather nervously, "he is Etienne de Brielle, the younger son of Sir Damian."

"Ah." Gunthar eyed the youth with comprehension. "Then your father sent you here."

"Nay," Etienne spat. "English dog! My father is too weak and my brother has not the courage. But I have sworn to avenge our wrongs, and next time—"

Laurant stepped forward and slapped him. "Insolent whelp. There will be no next time. Take him away."

"Wait. My lord, perhaps you should see this." Lord Challons, one of the earl's vassals, spoke. His eyes were as bright as the jewels adorning his scarlet tunic. He scooped up the fallen dagger and held it out for Gunthar to see.

Gunthar examined it from where he stood, the blade stained with his own blood. On the pommel was carved a most wondrous creature. From the waist up a beautiful woman with flowing hair, the nether part twisted sinuously into the subtle, undulating coils of a serpent. A tiny, forked tongue darted from between the creature's lips and a pair of winking rubies for eyes completed an unsettling portrait of demonic evil. One knight who stood near enough to share the vision muttered an oath and crossed himself. But Gunthar recognized it for what it was.

"Where had you this dagger?" he demanded, irritation lending an edge to his voice. The youth, who had been staring slack-jawed at the weapon, snapped his mouth shut. "Nay, don't play mute with me, boy. Prince Richard makes gifts of these to those who pledge his cause. Are you one of his, then?" The youth glared at Gunthar. "Or perhaps you merely stole it—"

"I am no thief!" The youthful face reddened and his one good eye flashed.

"Then it *was* Richard. That ungrateful, iniquitous pup. If he thinks his father will not recognize this assault upon my person for what it is—"

"I've never even met the prince," the youth interrupted hotly. "I came of myself, and it was for myself and the honor of my house that I wielded that blade. And had *she* not screamed, I would have had my revenge."

Gunthar followed his furious glance to Laurant's younger daughter. She colored but lifted a defiant chin to meet the youth's anger.

"Well that she did scream," Gunthar said, "else 'twould be the headsman's axe which awaited you rather than our good host's tower."

He jerked his head towards the stairs and Laurant bade one of his men show Sir Roger the way. Laurant turned back to Gunthar. "My lord, I am appalled—! How the boy found his way in here— This negligence by my guards shall not be overlooked, I assure you—"

"Enough," snapped Sir John Lee. His height allowed him to hold Gunthar's gaze squarely for a moment. Gunthar saw the worry in his friend's plain, pleasant face before Sir John turned back to Laurant. "We can deal with the boy later, and with your guards as well. But the earl has been hurt. A physician must be found at once."

Gunthar glanced down at his arm, as if only just remembering his wound. The blow had fallen on his left forearm and a dark wet stain had spread on his tunic's torn sleeve.

"Nonsense," the Lady Gwenllian said. "My daughter Clothilde will serve you far better than the fumbling Jean Chovet. He calls himself physician but is as like to bleed you to death as heal you. There is no one else within a day's ride."

Sir John looked dubious at this news. "Your daughter—"

"Both of my daughters are thoroughly skilled in the art of herbs and healing. You need not fear your lord's safety. Clothilde—"

Her smile faded as she turned towards her elder daughter. Clothilde was being delicately supported by one of Laurant's squires. Gunthar guessed she had swooned at the youth's attack. She appeared somewhat recovered now, but looked ready to succumb again if her mother spoke so much as another word. To Gunthar's relief, the Lady Gwenllian turned to her steady-faced younger daughter.

"Heléne, go with the earl and tend to his needs. I will send Audiart along to help."

"Yes, Mama." Heléne dropped her first curtsy to Gunthar. "Pray, my lord, if you will come with me?"

Sir John placed a hand on Gunthar's hale arm. "Hugh, perhaps we should at least let this Chovet fellow have a look."

Gunthar noted the offended sparkle that flashed into Heléne eyes. It lent them an exquisite luster before they returned to their own calm but unremarkable hue.

"Nay, John, I doubt but what it is only a flesh wound. We will give the Lady Helen a chance to prove her skills."

He saw the way her back stiffened when he Anglicized her name. Her skirts swished as she turned and swept her way up the stairs.

Gunthar mounted the steps behind her, trailed by a dozen of his knights, with as many squires, pages and miscellany of lesser-born servants at their heels. They climbed two flights of winding stairs and crossed a gallery before reaching their destination. Heléne stopped before a large wooden door, but before she could push it open, one of Gunthar's guards shouldered her aside. She protested this rudeness, but Gunthar's entourage ignored her and swept their master into the room.

A pair of well-trained squires flung back the dark blue bed curtains and Gunthar sank down onto the large, four-poster bed. A pageboy reverentially removed the cap from Gunthar's head. Another knelt to pull off his dust-stained boots. The room burst into a flurry of activity as several knights issued orders at once for the fetching and disposal of their lord's belongings. Amidst the confusion, Gunthar attempted to take stock of his surroundings.

The room must have been large, though it seemed otherwise now with so many warm and anxious bodies filling it. The mattress beneath him felt gratifyingly packed with feathers. There appeared to be some sort of embroidery on the bed curtains the squires had drawn, but he could not make out the design. Through the press of his men he caught a glimpse of a tapestry against one wall and a chair in the corner. He felt rather than saw the flames that emanated from a hearth someplace in the room.

At a word from Sir John, a squire with flowing, red-gold locks stepped forward bearing a keenly honed steel blade in his hand. To him fell the task of cutting away the earl's sleeve and laying bare the wound for Heléne's ministrations. Gunthar braced himself for the uncomfortable process. But Julian Parr was a gentle-handed youth.

He did his work quickly and efficiently, slicing through the blood-soaked fabric then carefully peeling it away.

Only then did Sir John gesture to Heléne.

Gunthar saw that her eyes were bright once more and her cheeks shone with a heightened color.

"I cannot work in the midst of all this commotion." She waved a hand to indicate the maddening bustle of knights and servants. "If you wish me to help, then send these people away."

There was a general gasp at this demand and Sir John began a sputtered protest. Gunthar silenced him with a glance.

"No, she is right. You are distracting to us both. Away with you, all of you save Julian. I presume, my lady, you will not object to my retaining just one servant? In case we should need someone to run errands and such."

He lifted a brow at her and she answered stiffly that of course the squire might stay if the earl wished it. The room's walls expanded wondrously as the others departed. The distracting tumult vanished with them and in the ensuing silence, Gunthar gazed expectantly into Heléne's face.

It was a most interesting face, he thought. Not beautiful, not even what most men would have called pretty, except when set aglow as now with an emotion he could only interpret as anger. At this moment, her high cheeks mantled with an indignant blush, her eyes magnificently ablaze with whatever offence she imagined herself the victim of, she radiated a brilliant allure, so unexpected that it made him blink.

At first she returned his steady regard, but then her eyes flickered and fell. The glowing color died from her cheeks and in that instant the fascinating woman he had been viewing disappeared.

"Oh pray, let me see!" she said.

She had glimpsed the wound in his arm and moved towards the bed. He saw her suddenly quite differently. An eighteen-year-old girl, boyishly slender, with a flawless but sallow complexion. Her sharp, curt features made her look younger than her years, and instinctively he moved his hand to shade the bloody cut from her sight.

But with an imperative movement, she reached out to grasp his fingers and pulled them away.

"Oh!" she exclaimed. The blood flowed freely now, dripping from his arm to stain the lap of his tunic. "Quickly," she bade the squire, "fetch me that basin of water and . . ." Her gaze darted about the room but apparently failed to find what she sought. She sank to the floor, lifted her heavy skirts and tore a strip of fabric from the lawn chemise beneath. Julian brought her the basin and held it down to her. She folded the cloth and soaked it thoroughly, then rose onto her knees. "This may hurt," she warned.

Gunthar smiled grimly and braced himself. Some of the blood had grown sticky. It matted the dark hair of his forearm and clung stubbornly there. But at last she washed away enough to grant them both a clearer view of the wound itself, a good, clean slice from a blade that might have proved lethal but for her warning and the quick deflection of his arm.

"I owe you my thanks, my lady," he offered rather belatedly. "But for you, it is doubtful I should be alive."

She did not look up, but murmured, "I do not believe that Etienne intended any real harm."

His brows shot up. "Indeed? The boy comes flailing at me with a knife—"

"Oh, I'll own he was angry. He is very close to his father, and Sir Damian certainly holds you to blame for his misfortune. Etienne blames you, too. Perhaps he meant to threaten you, to frighten you, even. But I *cannot* believe he intended to kill you."

A waspish retort hovered on his tongue, but at the last minute he bit it back. Something in her earnest, naive defense stirred a suspicion in his mind.

"You are well acquainted with young de Brielle?" he queried, with more gentleness than he was wont to show in the face of what he considered a foolish speech.

"We have known one another since childhood." She daubed at his wound with the cloth. "He was always of a cheerful temper until . . ."

"Until his father's 'misfortune'," he finished as she trailed off.

Sir Damian de Brielle, he remembered, had ardently opposed the king's claim to sovereignty in Poitou. Charged by the king with bringing him into submission, Gunthar's army had laid siege to Sir Damian's keep. At the end of three weeks, Gunthar had successfully stormed the castle. But even then the rebellious knight refused to yield.

In the ensuing conflict, he and Gunthar ultimately fought hand to hand. Forced to retreat before the powerful onslaught of Gunthar's sword, Sir Damian had renewed his stand on a portion of the curtain wall much damaged by Gunthar's siege engines. There the contest between the two men resumed until a particularly heavy blow from Gunthar's sword sent Sir Damian flying off the crumbling wall to land on the hard earth below.

The castle's garrison immediately surrendered. But miraculously, Sir Damian's fall had not proved mortal. Sir Damian continued to live, confined, Gunthar had heard, to a specially constructed chair, for the injury had left Sir Damian with no feeling or movement of limbs from the waist down. Still master in name, gossip called him a pathetic invalid, a cruel mockery of a man whose mind and tongue burned with hatred for his lot and for the man who had caused it.

Gunthar said abruptly now, "I thrice gave Sir Damian the chance to lay down his sword. No one regrets more than I the consequences of his own stubbornness."

Heléne looked up quickly. "I did not say it was your fault. Only naturally that is not the way Sir Damian would see it, nor Etienne, either."

She hesitated. He observed the compassion which now warmed her eyes, an intriguing contrast to the flashing, indignant young lady who had confronted him so short a time ago.

"Pray, what will happen to him now?" she asked.

"To your Etienne? That all depends. He must be questioned, of course. If in truth he acted only in impulsive anger, to 'even a score', as it were, with me—" Gunthar's gaze drifted over her head to the opposite wall. He sat for a moment in silence. "Aye, it is that we must determine. Was he acting individually, on a private grudge . . . or was it something more political?"

"Political?"

"Aye, you saw the dagger. But perhaps you did not understand it." He looked down at her again. "Do you not know the tale of Melusine the Beautiful who married Foulques the Black of Anjou, ancestor to our king and his perfidious sons? In what strange land he found her no man knows, but it was said her beauty was not of this world. There were many uncanny things about her, but that which troubled her husband most was the way she always vanished from mass just before the consecration of the Host."

Heléne resumed the cleaning of his wound. Gunthar marveled at the gentle skill of her touch as he continued, "She endeavored to dismiss her husband's suspicions with light words and protestations of her faith. But one day, doubt and fear overcame his trust. When the Fair Melusine rose as was her wont to leave the chapel, he commanded his men to seize her and forced her to witness the completion of the rite. They say the skies grew dark and thunder shook the walls. With a terrible shriek, Melusine the Beautiful vanished out the window, leaving behind a cloud of smoke and a tell-tale reek of brimstone."

Heléne stared at him now.

"One knight claimed to have seen a hideous, winged serpent flying through the air in fire. Whether it was the former countess's true shape or some other fiendish manifestation was pondered without resolve. Of what there could thereafter be no doubt was that the sons she had borne to Foulques were scions of the Devil, for she had been revealed the Demon's own daughter. Melusine was never seen again. But her blood still runs, they say, in the veins of her descendents."

Gunthar stopped. Heléne's eyes had grown wide. She looked very much like a child who had just been treated to a spine-tingling tale of ghosts and ghouls, and did not quite know whether to believe it or not.

His lips twitched a little. "I hope you will not let this story trouble your dreams tonight. That is all it is, you know, a silly legend propagated by the king's enemies . . . and when it suits him, the king himself."

She seemed to shake herself out of the spell of his words. She looked embarrassed. "Of course I know it is only a story. But I don't see what it has to do with Etienne's dagger."

"Why, the image on the pommel. The woman-serpent. It is well known that Prince Richard employs the figure on his servants' livery and has the symbol stamped onto daggers that he gives out to his friends. The image is Melusine, of course. Apparently he finds in the legend some vindication for his own execrable behavior. King Henry has been singularly cursed in the treacherous characters of his sons, but of them all, Richard has shown himself to be the most pernicious."

She gasped. "Are you saying you believe Etienne gained his dagger from Prince Richard and that he was sent to assassinate you?"

"It is not beyond the realm of possibility."

She shot to her feet so fast that she knocked the basin out of a startled Julian's hands and sent the bloodied water flying. "That is the most outrageous thing I have ever heard! Etienne has never even met the prince. He said so in the hall."

Those wonderful, magnificent sparks exploded once more from her eyes. Her face flushed with a furious but glowing color. Gunthar was duly impressed. But the steady throbbing in his arm prompted him to some exasperation.

"And I suppose I am to believe the word of a man whose father I have crippled and who has just tried his best to plant a dagger in my heart?"

"But why should he lie? If he was sent by the prince and knows you have seen the proof in the weapon he wielded, why should he deny it? Unless it is the truth!"

"Because, my lady, a personal act of vengeance against Hugh de Bury is one thing. But a murderous attack on the Earl of Gunthar while on the king's commission is very plain and simply treason. Even if he were a fool, de Brielle would have to know that. And the penalties for treason are far more harrowing than for any other crime under the sun."

Her color drained away and she looked abruptly shaken. Too late did he remember her youth. He cursed himself. The ugly business of treason with its gruesome consequences was hardly a fit subject for the sheltered ears of a gently bred young lady.

There was a moment of awkward silence. Then she murmured, "Your arm. It is bleeding again." She turned towards the squire and issued a sudden string of rapid orders. "Fetch me some fresh water, then go to the kitchens and find me some help. Mama said she would send up Audiart, but if she is not there ask for Flora or Hawise. Tell them to gather fresh tutsan and plantain leaves and to prepare me a comfrey poultice. I must have some good, fresh linen, too. And have them bring up some camomile tea. Your lord will find it soothing."

"I should much prefer a bracing cup of wine," Gunthar said.

She sent him a rebuking glance. "That is the last thing you should have. Unless you enjoy being feverish? Bring up the tea—"

"Julian, the wine."

The squire looked from Gunthar to the brisk, business-like young lady confronting him with her hands on her hips. Even Gunthar acknowledged that Heléne's sparkling eyes were compelling. But in the end, he had no real doubt whom the squire would obey. Julian retrieved the fallen basin, refilled it with water, handed it to Heléne and left the room with a bow.

She seemed to realize her defeat as well, for she gave a resentful sniff, then knelt once more and tore off another strip from her chemise. She moistened it in the water and applied it to the earl's arm.

"My lady," Gunthar ventured after several moments of frigid silence on her part, "my words just now regarding de Brielle— I do not wish you to think that I have already judged him. I assure you, fair ear will be given to whatever story he chooses to tell and only then will I—"

She thrust the folded cloth with quick, hard pressure against his wound.

Pain exploded up his arm like a scalding iron. *"Ow!"*

"We need to slow the bleeding," she said.

He glared at her bowed head. "You might at least have warned me you meant to do that."

She murmured an apology, but a little smile hovered at the corners of her mouth and she held her makeshift bandage firmly in place.

He could not quarrel with her procedure, for he knew it to be sound. But her none-too-subtle look of triumph infuriated him. Had one of his own servants dared to treat him with such callous disregard and then had the audacity to *smile*— His anger deepened with the frustrated knowledge that she lay safely beyond any discipline by his hand, while her ability to wreak still further havoc with his injury forced him to bite his tongue on a scathing rebuke.

Silence stretched tensely between them, neither speaking again until Julian returned. The squire brought a bottle of wine and a jewel-crested goblet. He had to fill the latter twice, Gunthar drained it off so quickly. As the wine dulled the pain, Gunthar found himself increasingly tempted to tell his nurse exactly what he thought of her methods. But before he could do so, a young, freckle-faced serving girl came scuttling in.

"Bring the tray over here, Flora," Heléne said. She finally released her tortuous pressure on his arm and stood up.

The servant came forward, staggering a little under the weight of the tray she carried. She was a thin girl and the tray was heavily laden with a multiplicity of bowls, vials, pots and jars. She said, "Sybil sent along a few simples of her own. She says they will draw out my lord's bad humors."

"I trust she managed to send a few of the items I requested, as well." Heléne inspected the cluttered tray. She gathered up a handful of fresh green leaves from a bowl and turned to lay them on the earl's arm, squeezing them first so that the juice ran into his wound.

The wine had dulled the fiery pain to a bearable throb, but that discomfort began to subside as the flesh around the wound grew numb. Gunthar watched her turn back to the tray. She ran her fingers through the powdery contents of one bowl, peeked under the lid of a still-steaming pot, picked up a jar and held it to her nose—

"Oh!" Her straight little nose twitched and she screwed up her face with a look of alarm. "Oh, but this must be a mistake!"

"My lady?"

She turned her head at Gunthar's query, as though startled by the sound of his voice. He thought he saw a faint wave of color sweep up into her face, but she answered, "It is nothing. These simples and ointments will be of no use. Here." She removed the leaves she had spread on his arm and replaced them with a different kind, gathered from another bowl. "Plantain," she explained, crushing them between her fingers as she had done before. "It will slow the bleeding, and then we will spread on the comfrey poultice to help in healing."

She followed through with this prescription and finished by binding up his arm with several strips of linen that Flora handed her from the tray.

"There," Heléne said. "Your arm should remain numb for several hours. The pain may return after that, but you may send to the kitchen for more leaves if it becomes too uncomfortable. Mind they be of the tutsan plant and fresh enough to squeeze as you saw me do. If the bleeding resumes, it is plantain you must ask for. The bandages should be changed frequently for the next day or two, each time reapplying the poultice. I will see that some be kept in readiness for you."

"You have my thanks, my lady." Now that the pain had subsided, Gunthar regretted his ill temper. Heléne stood stiffly before him, apparently ready to resume the battle if he so desired. A battle, he reminded himself, which had been far more a reality in her mind than in his.

At least one of his suspicions concerning de Brielle must he true. Her vehement defense of the youth seemed to confirm it. Gunthar wondered if her parents were aware of where her affections lay. He had taken the Lady Gwenllian's measure rather quickly and could not conceive of her sitting idly by while her younger daughter fell in love with the son of a disgraced rebel.

Heléne turned away and addressed Julian in cool, painfully polite tones. "I will inform my father of the earl's condition and suggest the banquet be postponed. Your master will no doubt wish to rest—"

"Rubbish," Gunthar said. "I am not to be undone by a little scuffle with some delinquent young hot-head. Pray assure your father that my men and I are looking forward to the feast he promised and that we shall not keep him waiting."

He was not surprised by the stiffness of the curtsy she dropped him. But the frank glitter of dislike that flashed from her eyes took him aback. The next instant, the flash was masked as she dutifully bowed her head.

"As you wish, my lord. We shall see you then anon. Come, Flora."

Her skirts swished smartly as she marched to the door. The little servant, still struggling beneath the heavy load of her tray, scurried after her.

# Three

Helène paused outside the earl's door. What a haughty, arrogant, insufferably imperious man! It took her several minutes to quell her indignation enough to ask the girl lingering beside her with the tray, "Flora, are you sure it was Sybil who made up these ointments?"

"Yes, milady," the girl replied.

"Where did you leave her?"

"In the kitchens, milady."

Helène nodded and motioned the girl to follow her.

The kitchen of Pennault Castle had been built of stone to minimize the danger of fire, and hence was one of the few outbuildings to have withstood the fiery arrows of the earl's siege. As Helène traversed the long passageway that connected the kitchen to the great hall, she remembered those frightening days of assault upon her home. The shout of the earl's army that had awaked her from her sleep . . . The relentless pummeling of the walls by the stones of his siege engines . . . Her mother's white face when one of her father's knights had ordered the women to retreat to the cellars . . .

They had huddled in the murky half-darkness for days, not knowing what destructions were taking place above-stairs, how many of their men still lived, or what fate might befall the women if the castle fell. And she remembered her mixed emotions of relief and anger when Laurant's surrender had finally brought them safely into the light again.

Those days of terror Heléne would never forget.

Nor would she forgive.

She realized she might have snatched a small piece of revenge by ignoring the discovery she had made in Gunthar's chamber, but the mistake, if uncovered by one of his servants, might be misinterpreted as a deliberate attack against the earl. The risk of retaliation against her family was not one she was willing to take.

She stopped in the doorway to the kitchen and squinted across the smoke-filled room for the figure of her former nurse, Sybil. The kitchen hummed with the activity of servants anxiously engaged in setting the finishing touches to a feast they had been preparing for days. A huge, fierce-looking boar with great curling tusks hissed and spit over a leaping fire, turned on a rod by a boy scarce tall enough to reach the tool's end.

Heléne's eyes watered, stung by the smoke. Her nose twitched at a pungent odor that included mustard and peppercorn. She wiped the tears away, then turned her head at a strident voice that carried shrilly above the clanging pots and thumping mallets.

"Wicked, stupid boy! I will teach you to be so clumsy!"

Heléne finally saw Sybil. The old woman was laying a thin but supple rod furiously to the back of a cringing scullion boy. The boy, whose crime appeared to be a tumbled basket of fish, wailed loudly and tried to shield his head with his arms.

The sight stirred stinging memories for Heléne and without pausing to think, she flew across the room.

"Stop! Oh, stop!" she cried, and fell to her knees beside the child.

Sybil, startled by Heléne's sudden appearance, was unable to check the downward swing of her arm. Heléne felt the thump of a blow that set her shoulder aburst with pain. There were horrified gasps and the distracting din that had filled the walls grew still. Heléne could not stop herself from wincing, but she pulled the terrified boy into her arms and tried hard to squeeze back her tears.

"Mistress, I did not see— It was a mistake! I was disciplining the child!"

"I know." Heléne spoke quietly, but she made no attempt to hide her animosity as she looked into her old nurse's face.

It was impossible to tell whether Sybil were truly remorseful or not. Her features were so wizened as to be almost unidentifiable. A short, stocky woman, she exaggerated her girth with layers of thick, heavy cloth. She gripped her biting rod with a blotched, gnarled hand and, to Heléne's mind, her rough, uncut nails bore a striking resemblance to talons.

Despite her cronish appearance, Heléne knew well the strength that lay behind those arms. She and Sybil had been at odds almost from the day of Heléne's birth. The old nurse had resented being forced to share the attention she had formerly lavished solely on the lovely and docile Clothilde. She had not much liked Heléne's brother, Therri, either, but he had been a boy and soon turned over to masculine hands.

Heléne remembered envying her brother's escape. Her attempts to hide in the chapel and listen to his lessons had been met with sore punishments. She had borne some woeful beatings for her obstinate insistence that she be allowed to learn to read, until her father had intervened. He remarked that he saw no harm in her being able to decipher a little French, though he drew the line at Latin.

But Sybil, though no longer allowed to rebuke the girl's inquisitive mind, had found plenty of other excuses to employ the rod. The beatings had only ceased two years ago, after Heléne had grown taller than her tormentor and her mother had finally admitted the discipline's utter ineffectiveness on her daughter's character.

But if Sybil had been deprived of one target for her shrewish temper, she had a plenteous supply of others in the hapless servants of the castle.

"There was no need to hit him," Heléne said, feeling the way the boy trembled in her arms. "I am sure it was only an accident that he dropped the fish."

"It was, milady," the boy whispered. "I tripped over that bone."

Heléne glanced at the discarded item lying nearby and then at the scattered fish. She gave the boy a cheerful smile. "Well, then, we must set everything to rights again."

She scooped up a handful of the tiny, scattered bodies, valiantly suppressed a shudder at their slimy feel, and dropped them into the basket. The boy watched with amazement as she repeated the process. Then he gave a shy smile and began to join in the task.

"Pray, milady, let me." A plump kitchen maid dropped to the floor beside the boy and scooped some fish into her red, cracked hands. The boy seemed to know and like her, for he gave his new assistant a grin. Heléne stood up, but when he went scampering under a table to where a few of the bodies had rolled, she bent down and whispered in the kitchen maid's ear.

"Take him down to the river when you are done. There are sure to be welts on his back. Ask Flora for some ointment to soothe them, then send him to bed. If anyone questions you—" she glanced Sybil's way "—tell them the Lady Heléne commanded it."

The kitchen maid nodded. Heléne straightened again. The eyes of every servant were upon her. She called to Flora, who still swayed under the weight of her heavily laden tray. Flora carried it with her as she obeyed her mistress' summons.

Heléne's memory guided her to a small brown jar with a chip along its mouth. She picked it up from the tray before giving Flora instructions on what sort of ointment should be prepared for the scullion boy's hurts. Then she turned again to face her old nurse.

"Pray, Sybil, will you come with me? I have something to say to you."

She did not wait to see whether Sybil would obey, but walked out of the kitchen into the connecting corridor. She heard the resumption of excited voices as she left, but did not turn around until she had reached the middle of the passageway. Sybil was indeed at her heels. The old woman might be a harpy but she knew her place in this house.

"The boy was clumsy and impudent," Sybil muttered, defending herself with a sullen scowl.

Heléne answered coldly, "That is not what I wished to speak with you about. Is this one of your recipes?"

Sybil glared at the jar. "What if it is?"

"That is no answer, Sybil."

The tiny, watery eyes so narrowed in the wrinkled face as to almost disappear. "I sent along a few simples of my own. I thought you would find them helpful. I taught you what you know of healing, milady, but sometimes you are careless in your preparations. It is not wise to forget the ancient ways, to disdain the spells and chants."

"Picking an herb while barefoot and spitting on it three times will not make for a more effective salve," Heléne said, "any more than pronouncing over it some gibberish string of Latin phrases. You know how Father Dominic frowns upon such beliefs."

Sybil's mouth tightened at this mention of Lord Laurant's chaplain, but she only said, "'Tis more than 'belief', milady. The practices you scorn have saved men's lives."

Heléne knew it would do no good to argue. "All I wish to know is what you put into *this* ointment."

Sybil hesitated, then dipped a crooked finger into the jar and scooped out a small lump of its contents. She rubbed it between her fingers, brought it close to her squinting eyes, then sniffed at it carefully.

"'Tis valerian," she pronounced at last, "mixed with goose fat and beeswax, with a little germander to sweeten the scent."

Heléne shook her head. "Then you did not add enough of the latter, for 'tis not valerian but cowbane *I* smell."

"Cowbane?" Sybil's tiny eyes grew wide and she shook the lump from her hand. "Never, milady! Cowbane can kill a man."

"Well, done up into an ointment like this, it is doubtful that it should kill anyone unless rubbed repeatedly into a wound. But it might have made the earl sick." Heléne frowned at the old woman. "It is you who are too careless, Sybil. However did you come to mistake cowbane for valerian? The two are nothing alike."

"It was that foolish girl from the kitchens, Gunnore. I could not find Audiart or Hawise, so I sent Gunnore out with Flora to gather the herbs."

"But when she brought them back—"

"My eyes are not so sharp as they once were, milady. And how was I to single out one smell amid all the odors floating about in the kitchen? Those heady, foreign spices your father purchased for the earl's feast are enough to set one's head to spinning."

It was a fair defense and seemed an honest one. After all, what possible reason could Sybil have for wanting to harm the earl?

"Very well," Heléne said after a moment's silent study of the old woman. "But kitchen odors or no, it is a mistake I trust will not be repeated."

"Be assured of it, milady. I shall beat the girl myself for her dangerous stupidity. You will bear my apologies to the earl?"

"He does not know, and I see no reason why he should. Only see that it does not happen again."

"Yes, milady. Will that be all?"

Heléne tried hard to read the old woman's expression, but it was like staring at a withered stone. She glanced down at the jar in her hand. "This ought to be destroyed."

"Very well, milady." Sybil extended a gnarled hand, but Heléne hesitated.

"No, I will do it myself. Thank you, Sybil, you may go."

The old woman shrugged and shuffled back off to the kitchen. Heléne watched her go, disturbed by the heavy, ominous presence that seemed to vanish with her.

# Four

The Earl of Gunthar stood while his squire, Julian Parr, turned back the cuffs of his dull yellow tunic to expose the ornamental embroidery worked along the narrow wrists. Gunthar had selected the undergarment for the roomy cut of its sleeve, to relieve his bandaged arm of unnecessary discomfort.

When Julian finished, two younger servants pulled forward a heavy, elaborately carved chair from the corner. Gunthar sank onto its crimson cushion and extended a well-turned foot towards a kneeling pageboy. It was unlikely that anyone would have a chance to admire his pale green hose, destined as they were all evening to be concealed beneath the ankle-length folds of his costly silk tunic. But, he mused, an appreciative audience might be found for his handsome red shoes, cunningly embellished with row upon row of tiny gold rings.

Sir John Lee observed the delicate care with which the page placed the shoes on his master's feet, then exclaimed, "Fiend seize it, Hugh, but you are a lucky dog!"

Gunthar raised a querying brow at his friend

"Your servants fawn over you, you've a dozen wide and prosperous estates, you sit on the king's high council, and now – now you are about to marry the most ravishingly beautiful creature I have ever beheld. Devil take me if I know what you've done to merit such exquisite good fortune as this."

"You've a beautiful wife of your own, John," Gunthar reminded him. "You outwitted a dozen suitors to win the fair Berthe's hand."

"'Twas not wits that won me Berthe Molyns," Sir John said with a good-natured grin, "but a well-lined purse. I may not be able to match your wealth, but I had sufficient to pay off Molyns debts and the man knew how to show his gratitude. Aye, Bertha's a pretty piece, all right." He gave a rueful sigh. "You'd think that would content me."

Gunthar said nothing. John Lee had many admirable qualities, but fidelity to his wife was not one of them. In spite of a rather homely countenance, his engaging manner and generous purse enabled him to satisfy his restless nature with a constant string of buxom wenches. Gunthar was not impervious to feminine charms himself, but he had never allowed passion to overrule his own good judgment.

The page finished fastening on Gunthar's shoes. Gunthar stood up, motioning to Julian that he was ready to don his surcote. He had to bend down so that the squire could pass the garment over his head, then he straightened and smoothed out his sleeves. They ended in pendulous, elbow-length cuffs designed to display the elegant full sleeves of his tunic. The dark green fabric was unenlivened by any embroidery, but there were other ways to mark one's wealth and status.

Julian brought forward a wide gold collar sprinkled with a generous studding of rubies, emeralds and diamonds. He hesitated, waiting for Gunthar to make his height more accessible again by bowing his head, but Sir John came forward and lifted the collar out of the squire's hands.

Sir John lacked less than an inch of his friend's height. He set the collar about Gunthar's neck and remarked, "I thought sure you would wear the blue and silver tonight."

He linked the gold clasp and brought his hands away. The collar slid down, weighted by the jeweled studs, to form a glittering, inverted arc across Gunthar's broad chest.

Sir John continued, "I'm quite sure the Lady Merval will be draped in the colors of *her* house and that you'll be sitting beneath a baldaquin bearing the twin images of phoenix and stallion. Before this night is over, there will be no doubt in any man's mind what the real purpose of this visit to Pennault is."

"My purpose," Gunthar said, "is to enforce the terms of the Peace of Montlouis, as commissioned by my most excellent master, the king."

Sir John flashed a grin. "As I recall—and I do so from your own lips—there was another rather imperative commission, as well. Certainly it is the one the Lady Gwenllian has her heart set upon your fulfilling."

"Then the Lady Gwenllian is a fool. I said nothing in my letters to Laurant to imply the least interest in his daughter."

"Then how do you explain this?"

Sir John turned to the bed and caught hold of one of the curtains, drawing the cloth out wide to reveal the shimmering embroidery wrought thereon. Gunthar stared at the silver-worked horse prancing on a field of deep blue silk and caught his breath on a curse.

"Devil take that woman," he swore, "aye, and Henry, too!" For he saw quite clearly the hand of the king in this.

Henry Plantagenet was no more accustomed to having his orders flouted than was his vassal, the Earl of Gunthar. The king had been frankly shocked when Gunthar had resisted his suggestion that he marry the Lady Clothilde de Merval, for there could be no question but what such an alliance would strengthen the king's hand in Poitou. It was not, the king insisted, as if he were asking Gunthar to wed some hag, for the Lady Merval was, by all reports, an incomparable beauty.

The king had dealt gently with his counselor at first, wheedling and cajoling with that irresistible charm which ran so thick in Plantagenet veins. But when Gunthar continued to refuse, charm gave way to an explosion of black Plantagenet temper. The ensuing scene had been an ugly one. Henry had shouted himself hoarse, abusing Gunthar with every curse in his vast arsenal of denunciatory and mostly blasphemous oaths. He ranted and raved for what had seemed like hours, pacing up and down the council chamber, tearing at his hair and beard, fairly frothing at the mouth in the face of Gunthar's stubborn resistance.

Gunthar had witnessed such outbursts before, but he had never been the object of one himself and it left him churning sickeningly inside. But he stood mute as a stone, refusing to bend, until the king finally ordered him out of his presence, with the parting shot that he expected to receive a betrothed Lady Merval in his court within a fortnight of Gunthar's arrival in Poitou.

Gunthar had done his best to forget the offensive scene. Deep in his soul, his loyalty and love for the king remained unshaken. Surely even in his blackest temper Henry must have realized that?

But the sight of the Lady Gwenllian's needlework laid the truth wide open to Gunthar's eyes. *He* may never have written to Laurant with any suggestion of allying their houses, but the king very evidently had.

"If he thinks for one moment that I should allow anyone—*anyone*—to dictate to me—"

Sir John laughed at his friend's fury. "What, Hugh, you can't mean to defy a royal order?"

"Can't I?" Gunthar's glare would have sent any other man backing warily out of the room.

But Sir John had known him far too long to be awed by his withering temper. "Won't do, you know," he said. "The king always has his way."

"Not with this," Gunthar swore. "He can find some other mindless minion to dance his tune. I will choose my own wife, thank you, and it won't be some simpering French widow with more beauty than brains in her head."

"You've scarce exchanged two words with the girl. How can you possibly know what is in her head?"

Gunthar knew, as surely as he knew that her mother was a sweet-faced shrew and her sister an irritatingly spirited minx.

"I cannot believe you stand so blind to all the lady's manifest charms," Sir John said. "There must be something more that puts you off from her. Is it Emmelina?"

Gunthar's attention had wandered, caught up in a memory of brilliantly flashing eyes in a vivid, glowing little countenance. The name drew him back, though for a moment he was not sure why.

"What?"

"Emmelina. Lady Winfield. A bewitching creature, I'll grant, all ivory and ebony and those great, dark, wonderfully soulful eyes . . ."

Sir John seemed to drift off for a moment, then came back to the present with an awkward cough. "Thing is, I was sure she was nothing more to you than a passing fancy. Not that she wouldn't fly at the chance to surrender her widowhood for a countess's title. Are you in love with her? Is that why you stood against the king?"

Gunthar shook his head. He had no illusions about love. Emmelina Winfield was an enchanting beauty, but she was no different from the other women he had known in his thirty-odd years, grasping and ambitious, as hungry for the jewels and gowns he might buy her as for any passion she hoped to arouse.

"No, John, I am not in love with the fair Emmelina. And it is just as well. Her hand is the king's to bestow and Henry means to give it to Lord Ruston. The marriage will help to cement his power in York."

"As he hopes to use you here in Poitou."

Gunthar frowned again. "Perhaps. If I were convinced there were no other way to bind Laurant." He sighed. "I must marry someday, it is true. The duties of my name require an heir, but— No. Laurant has sworn an oath and there is no need for more. Henry can curse me all he likes. I have risked my life for him more than once. I have given him sound counsel and devoted all my energies to see him made secure upon his throne. He cannot doubt my loyalty and good faith, and if it requires my very life's blood to prove it, I should willingly allow it to be spilled. And with that he shall have to be content, for in truth, John, I would rather die than be shackled to some cabbage-headed female for the rest of my days!"

Sir John burst into laughter and after a moment, Gunthar joined in, acknowledging his irrationality in balking at what most men would have viewed but a minor sacrifice to satisfy their king. He dropped back into the chair. Julian, who had withdrawn to a corner of the room at the first signs of his master's ill temper, came forward again and placed a small, round mirror in Gunthar's hand. The Church frowned upon such objects as tools of vanity and pride, but Gunthar did not believe the device itself would set his soul at risk.

"We will not speak of it again," he said to his still chuckling friend. Gunthar watched Julian's reflection as the squire drew out the thick, dark waves of his master's hair with an ivory-toothed comb.

"Perhaps a frigid silence on the subject will be sufficient to dampen the Lady Gwenllian's misplaced hopes. Julian, I will wear my red cap when you are done, the one with the jeweled band, and I think my emerald ring . . ."

Julian paused to bow his understanding and Sir John, taking the hint as well, obligingly remained quiet.

Nevertheless, Sir John had the satisfaction of seeing at least a portion of his prophecy come true. The banner that had greeted them on arriving in the great hall, the black double-headed phoenix rising from flames of gold, had now been twinned with a silver-worked stallion prancing proudly on a field of blue. Gunthar scowled at the sight, then took himself in hand and complimented his hostess upon her skill. The Lady Gwenllian tittered and passed on the compliment to her daughter, Clothilde, whose pleasure it had been to set the stitches for the honor of their noble guest.

Clothilde blushed becomingly. She was ravishingly attired in a pale blue kirtle with long, draping sleeves all trimmed with fur. The round, wide-cut neck displayed a generous view of smooth, alabaster skin and a string of white beads twined gracefully about her throat. Rather to Gunthar's surprise, she no longer wore a veil. Her rich, gold hair trailed over her shoulders as boldly as though she had still been a maid. A gilded chaplet set with several small sapphires encircled her fair brow.

Gunthar saw her long lashes flutter but he waited in vain for her gaze to lift to his. No, she was not going to meet his eyes and her response to his compliment was lost in a blushing whisper.

It was quite otherwise with Heléne, who joined her family some minutes later. Her mother's rebuking glance at her tardiness appeared lost on that damsel. She offered Gunthar a stiff curtsy and returned his regard quite steadily.

"I trust your arm does not pain you too greatly this evening, my lord?" she asked.

Gunthar's lips curved ruefully. "It is a bit sore, my lady. I should have followed your advice and called for more tutsan leaves. The discomfort is a fit rebuke for my manly pride . . ."

He saw the gloating little twinkle in her eyes and bit off the rest. What need was there to own her right about the wine, as well? He felt her shrewd gaze sliding over his slightly flushed cheeks and realized there was no need at all.

Blazes! but she was a presumptuous young thing. She did not even look old enough to be included in this gathering. Her dull, straw-colored gown hung so loose as to conceal any possible maturity of figure and robbed her skin of any color, as well. Her cheeks looked sallow, her eyes, though finely shaped, completely unremarkable in hue. Rather to his disappointment he saw that her hair was still done up in a tiresome braid. It seemed a shameful misuse of what might have been a prime asset to the girl. Though it lacked the burnished sheen of her sister's, her hair was clearly thicker and reached all the way to her hips.

Aye, what changes might not be wrought to her curt little face were one simply to loose the severe confines of that braid and draw it into a veil about her cheeks . . . ?

"My lord . . ." Laurant drew back his attention, indicating that it was time to take their seats.

Gunthar offered a courteous arm to Clothilde and escorted her onto the dais. He took his place directly below the twin banners, between the beautiful widow and her mother, with Laurant to his wife's right and Lord Challons seated beside Heléne on her sister's left. As the highest ranking of Gunthar's vassals, Challons had been chosen to companion their host's younger daughter. But from the frequent admiring glances he cast at Clothilde, Gunthar knew that her sister was destined to suffer a good deal of absent-minded neglect.

The trumpets sounded from the gallery and the remainder of Gunthar's and Laurant's combined courts seated themselves at the side tables that filled the hall. Servants appeared bearing lavers of scented water for the diners to rinse their hands, and then the meal began. Laurant had spared no expense in providing a feast he deemed worthy of his noble guest. The first course alone offered eleven different dishes including venison in frumenty, quince in comfit, cygnets, herring and perch, not to mention a huge roasted boar with an apple stuffed in its mouth.

Gunthar selected a piece of salmon from a passing platter. He dipped it in the sauce a squire spooned onto the trencher he shared with Clothilde and offered it to the lovely widow. She took it from his fingers with a breathless word of thanks, her eyes fluttering to his and away again.

The music drifting down from the hall's high galleries gave Gunthar's mind somewhere to turn when conversation with his companion began to lag, as it did almost at once. Clothilde seemed incapable of speaking above a whisper and then only in monosyllables, which soon set his patience on edge. Her mother's attempts to fill the void with a constant prattle of idle gossip about people he did not know and devoutly hoped it would never be his misfortune to meet, set him to counting the hours until the ordeal would be at an end.

It was almost a relief when Heléne, with a fine disregard for manners, leaned across a startled Lord Challons and inquired as to whether the earl had yet spoken to Etienne.

"Alas, no, my lady. But I assure you it shall be done before this night is out. You shall see to the matter, Lord Challons?"

Heléne looked surprised. "You do not mean to question him yourself?"

"In time. My lord shall feel him out for me. It is one of my lord's great talents that he has a way of getting at the truth."

Challons acknowledged the compliment with a nod of his head.

"And when you learn the truth," Heléne said, "which is that this was all some terribly innocent mistake, you will, of course, release him promptly, will you not?"

Gunthar glanced down at his injured arm. Though the bandages were concealed in the folds of his fashionable sleeve, the steady throbbing kept the image of de Brielle's attack vivid in his mind.

"An innocent mistake, my lady?" The corner of his mouth twitched in irritation at her stubborn defense of a clearly guilty youth. "No doubt the dagger was meant as a gift and merely slipped as de

Brielle attempted to place it in my hands."

She colored at this sardonic response, but said, "If you wish to know the truth then let *me* speak to him. Etienne will not confide in one of your bullies—" her color deepened. "Your pardon, my lord Challons, I do not mean that you— Only it stands to reason that Etienne will be frightened of you. He would be much better approached by someone he knows and trusts."

"That will not be you, my lady," Gunthar informed her in a voice which indicated he expected no further argument.

Challons gave her a kindly smile. "I shall deal gently with him, my lady. My lord earl is not a vindictive man and will not punish a youth's impulsive anger more than its due. Fortunately for your young friend, my lord was but little harmed and my lord is, above all, an honest, fair-minded man."

Gunthar inclined his head, but Challons' flattering smile disturbed him. The baron held two manors from him in England, both of which he had come so near to running into the ground that the source by which he maintained his extravagantly expensive lifestyle remained a mystery. Gunthar never surveyed the jewels Challons wore without a frown. But he had fought in Gunthar's camp on the king's side in the late rebellion and had never given any indication of disloyalty. And the man had talent and cunning, enough that Gunthar was willing to let him deal with de Brielle . . . for now.

"But, sir—"

"That is enough, Heléne," her mother snapped at her. "Attend to your meal and keep your tongue still."

Heléne bit her lip and stared resentfully down at her trencher. Her mother's rebuke seemed unnecessarily crushing. Challons tried quietly to console her, offering her a sip from the silver-plated drinking cup they shared, but Gunthar saw her shake her head. To his regret, the engaging spirit died from her face. Her persistence had annoyed him, but now he sought for a way to restore a flicker of that pleasing glow. He made a sudden decision.

Deliberately raising his voice so that she might overhear his remarks to her father, he said, "I ride to Angoulême tomorrow, where I understand the prince to be residing. I bear messages from his father the king and must make my obeisance before proceeding with my royal commission. Perhaps—" he paused and dipped a slice of soft, brown bread into the stew on his trencher "—you and your daughters might like to accompany me? Prince Richard could not but be charmed by the inclusion of two such comely ladies in my train."

He offered the sop to Clothilde who accepted it with her delicate fingers, but his gaze slid past her to her sister's face. Heléne shot him a furious glance before she returned her contemplation to her trencher.

"My lord, we are honored," Laurant uttered, clearly taken aback by this invitation. "To have our daughters presented to the king's own son—"

The Lady Gwenllian broke in, in her lilting French. "Indeed, my lord, we should be delighted to have you include our lovely Clothilde, but as for Heléne . . . well, you must forgive us, but the truth is, she has nothing to wear for such an occasion."

Gunthar's heavy brows shot up. "Nothing?"

"You must understand, my lord. She has grown by leaps and bounds these last few years. It has been nearly impossible to keep up with her. I do hope she will get no taller, it is quite awkward enough as it is."

"Surely, my dear, we can find her something?" Laurant protested. "Have you not begun her wedding trousseau? There must be something there?"

Gunthar's brows snapped back down at the unexpected word. "Wedding?"

Laurant beamed proudly at the opportunity to boast. "Lord Heywood is eager for her hand. You know the man, my lord? He owns considerable tracts of land, I believe, some of the best in England. Two hundred acres in Northumberland shall be added when once he has wed my daughter."

Gunthar managed to catch Heléne's eye. "Why, I must congratulate you, my lady. Indeed, I am well acquainted with John Heywood and count him as a friend. He is a loyal and honorable man, a faithful supporter to our king. Pray, when are the nuptials to take place?"

Laurant answered, "Before the summer is out, I trust. There are a few details yet to be resolved, but I'm sure my lord will be reasonable." He paused, then gave Gunthar a sly smile. "Perhaps a double wedding should serve us, eh? As you and Heywood are such good friends—?"

"More wine, my lady?" Gunthar tried not to appear rude as he turned back towards Clothilde. This was hardly the time or place to inform Laurant that he was badly mistaken about Gunthar's intentions towards his daughter.

Gunthar motioned to Julian Parr who moved quickly to one of the sideboards and returned with a fresh bottle of wine to refill his master's cup. Gunthar handed the cup to Clothilde, then glanced about the hall, surveying the efficient, well-trained squires of Laurant's house as they waited upon the guests.

"Pray, my lord," he inquired, before Laurant could resume his former course of conversation, "perhaps you can tell me which of these fine young lads in your son?"

Laurant looked rather nonplussed by the query, a reaction Gunthar thought odd.

After a moment, the Lady Gwenllian laughed and replied, "La, sir, but did my lord not tell you? Therri is with his uncle, Sir Rolf, at Castle Gurdon. We have trusted our son to his care these past three years. Tell him, husband, what excellent training for knighthood your brother provides."

In the face of Gunthar's frown, Laurant dared tell him nothing of the kind. Gunthar made no attempt to conceal his displeasure. If he had carefully refrained from including in his prior correspondence any mention of Laurant's daughter, he had certainly been clear about the son. Part of the king's strategy for securing the peace in this corner of Poitou was for Gunthar to take possession of Laurant's heir, a nominal hostage to ensure Laurant's future good-behavior. The boy was to return with Gunthar to England to complete his training in Gunthar's house where, hopefully, he would be thoroughly indoctrinated in loyalty to the English crown.

"I trust," Gunthar said, his voice hardening, "Sir Rolf has already been informed of your son's imminent change of residence? Or did my secretary somehow manage to muddle my instructions?"

Laurant looked panicked. "Aye, my lord— That is— No, no, my lord, of course not. I understood perfectly. It is just that—" He broke off and gave a slight shudder at the gleam in Gunthar's eyes. "I shall send word to my brother first thing in the morning."

"Tonight, my lord."

"Aye, of course, my lord, as you say. Shall I—shall I attend to it now?"

Gunthar could not keep the scathing contempt from his gaze. Such quivering fear disgusted him. He knew it was to his advantage and the advantage of his mission to keep men in awe of him, to flaunt his power from time to time so that no one dared disobey his will. Yet he despised such men as fell into this trap.

"I think," he said, "the letter can wait until our meal is done. Julian, my lady and I will have a bit of that pudding of which the Lady Helen is partaking."

Gunthar observed the way Heléne stiffened when he once more chose to Anglicize her name, but she did not so much as glance at him now. The squire appeared promptly with the requested dish and Gunthar allowed the subject of Therri de Laurant to drop.

The conversation reverted to its earlier pattern, with Clothilde sitting in passive silence while her mother rattled on about a dozen tedious subjects. Thus passed the remainder of the first course and most of the second, though the latter was somewhat enlivened by a pair of troubadours Laurant had engaged for his company's amusement. They began with bright lyrics of knightly lore and romance, but as the hours lengthened and the wine ran free, their verses warmed into a lament for the past.

Gunthar was quick to see the sympathetic chord struck among the Poitevin listeners. The troubadours sang of sultry days of freedom, those wild, lawless days when every man was lord and not even counts or dukes dared say their pleasures nay. Gunthar knew that such music carried the seeds of dissent towards a king who now sought to tame their ways. But he made no move to stop it until the verses turned from regret for freedoms lost to passionate praise for their former countess, the now imprisoned queen.

Eleanor's rich inheritance of Poitou and Aquitaine had helped to establish an Angevin empire that dwarfed the French domains. But Henry, Gunthar had learned, had energy enough to govern twenty kingdoms, and the king made it clear from the start that he had no intention of sharing authority in his newly acquired lands, even with their former duchess. Denied a hand in ruling, Eleanor had sought to assert her political ambitions through her sons. Gunthar had no doubt that it had been her plotting which had set the princes at odds with their father and sent them off to ally themselves with her former husband, the King of France. When Eleanor had been discovered attempting to slip away to join their rebellion, Henry had had no choice but to seize her.

But her confinement to Winchester Castle had caused more problems than it had solved. In these rich lands beyond the Loire, Gunthar knew that Eleanor stood a convenient symbol of the Angevin 'tyranny'. Men like Sir Fulbert de Merval and Count William of Angoulême, whom Prince Richard called friend, used their professed loyalty to the queen to cloak lawlessness beneath a mantle of righteous revolt.

It took no more than a telling glance from Gunthar to Laurant to put an end to the entertainment. Laurant waved the troubadours off the floor and gave a signal that resulted in another blast of trumpets. Six elegantly appointed squires appeared bearing a broad gold platter on which stood a magnificently wrought subtlety: a three-foot-high knight and charger, all spun of pastry and sugar and painted in the blue and silver of the earl's own emblem.

Servants hastened to clear away the dishes as the squires marched in measured paces to a fanfare provided by musicians in the galleries. They circled the hall so that all might see and exclaim over the cunning creation. They came to a halt before the dais and in perfect unison, bent the knee before their master and his guest.

Gunthar rose and began the requisite speech, but in the midst of his eloquence a commotion erupted from the far end of the hall. He could not see its source at once for the press of people there. Someone appeared to be attempting to force his way through the crowd. The voices grew louder and more insistent, until one man broke away from the others and maneuvered his way through the tables cluttering the floor to approach the dais.

"My lord, your pardon," spoke Laurant's seneschal. "I tried to tell them you were not to be disturbed, but they are most insistent. It is Sir Triston de Brielle and the Lady Osanne. They say they have ridden through the night to see the earl, and—"

"And we will not depart until we have been heard!"

A powerfully built man rivaling Gunthar's own height followed the seneschal across the floor. Gunthar remembered him. Triston de Brielle, Sir Damian's elder son, had fought valiantly beside his father to defend their castle from Gunthar's attack. Triston had witnessed the blow and the fall that left his father crippled. And it had been at Triston's command that the bloodshed had ceased with the surrender of the garrison.

Triston confronted the dais now, his serviceable short tunic and mantle laden with dust, his ebony curls romantically tumbled about his passionate face by the night wind. Within moments he was joined by a woman whose smaller steps had failed to keep pace with his. Gunthar watched as she lifted milk-white hands to put back the hood of her mantle, revealing a face of sultry beauty framed by thick, black locks.

"This is outrageous!" Laurant exclaimed. "How dare you come bursting into my hall at this hour? Why, it must be past midnight."

"Outrageous, indeed!" Triston's dark eyes flashed an indignant challenge. "To fling my brother into one of your miserable towers, merely to placate this man's hatred of my father—!" His angry eyes flicked to Gunthar, then back again. "We will not tolerate it, Laurant. We are not dogs, to be treated in this scurrilous way. My father may not have the strength to fight you, but I—"

"Ohhh—"

The moan came from Clothilde. Gunthar turned his head in time to see her sink into a swoon. He reached for her hand, then glanced back round as he caught a blur of movement from the corner of his eye. Triston had taken a sharp step towards the dais, a look of tortuous alarm on his face. Then he mastered himself and swung back to confront the men.

"I am warning you, Laurant. We have been shamed by this man for the last time. Release my brother immediately, or it shall be nothing less than war between us."

Triston pushed back his mantle to grip the hilt of his sword. He turned on Gunthar such a deadly look that Gunthar half-expected his blood to be spilled at once. Enough was enough.

Gunthar moved his hand in a quick signal. Instantly his guards sprang to life. They surrounded Triston before he could react, two of them pinioning his arms behind his back. A third pulled Triston's sword free of its scabbard. Triston struggled and cursed and had nearly wrenched himself free when he froze, white faced, as the guardsman snapped Triston's blade cleanly across his knee.

Heléne placed another blanket around her sister's shoulders. "Are you feeling better, love?"

Clothilde had not stopped shivering since she had recovered from her swoon. She sat huddled now in the center of the bed she and Heléne shared, her golden hair a-tumble, her eyes grown so dark as to appear almost black in the firelight.

Sybil shuffled into the room, carrying a steaming mug in her gnarled hands, cooing with a tenderness she reserved only for Clothilde. "Poor lamb, poor lamb. Drink this, my sweeting, do." Clothilde took the mug and sipped at it, then shivered again. "There now, my lamb, never fear. All will be set right. Sybil will see to it."

Heléne thought Clothilde's trembling deepened as Sybil traced a crooked finger over her sister's whitened cheek.

"Please," Clothilde whispered, "I just want to be alone."

Sybil clucked a little. "That is not wise, milady. Someone should be with you now."

"Then let it be Heléne. Oh, *please* – "

She flinched so openly when Sybil petted her hair that Heléne said sharply, "Go away, Sybil. We don't want you here."

Sybil's tiny eyes narrowed in dislike of her youngest charge, but after a moment she turned and shuffled away without a word.

"She did not mean any harm," Heléne admitted, taking the mug from her sister's shaking hands. "She dotes upon you, Clo. I thought you were fond of her, too."

Clothilde moaned and pulled the blanket tighter. Heléne sighed. She felt sorry for her sister, but these fits were nothing new. Clothilde had always been overly sensitive to the least sort of upset, swooning away at the mildest provocation. Men appeared to find such a disposition admirable, only to be expected of so delicate a flower. Witness Triston de Brielle. He had been visibly struck by the sight of Clothilde tonight, as had every man in the hall.

Well, almost every man. Heléne had never swooned in her life and often felt impatient with her sister's precarious sensibilities. Yet, perversely, when she had seen her own reaction mirrored in Gunthar's face, it had made her mad as fire.

"He is the most cold-hearted, callous, *detestable* man I have ever laid eyes upon!" she exclaimed. "Gunthar must have seen how unsettled you were by the confrontation, but did he care? No! A few soft words might have turned Triston's wrath aside, but instead he humiliated him. Breaking his sword like that—! Triston went livid at the insult, and I do not blame him. It was a despicable thing to have done."

"What—what happened to Triston?" Clothilde asked. She had still been in a faint when the scene in the hall had climaxed, and afterwards had been carried to her room by their father. "He is not—oh, pray do not tell me that he has been thrown in the tower with Etienne!"

"Well . . . no," Heléne said grudgingly. "The earl refused to speak with him about his brother or anything else until morning, but he agreed that Triston and the Lady Osanne might stay the night. But he was quite haughty about it all and looked down his nose at them both in that horridly superior way of his. Triston was still swearing at him when the guards dragged him out of the hall, and I suspect he will not be permitted out of his room until the earl gives leave for it. I hope by then the Lady Osanne has succeeded in calming him. She promised she would try."

Heléne paused, then sat down on the bed. "Why do you suppose Triston brought her along? It seems an odd thing for any lady to be riding about the countryside at such an hour as this. I cannot conceive of Sir Damian allowing it, even with his son. Papa would never have permitted us—"

"Heléne," Clothilde broke in tremblingly, "what do you suppose they will do to Triston?"

Heléne thought it over. "Well, he did not actually draw his sword, although the earl must have feared he might or he would not have called for his guards. But he did not appear inclined to punish Triston for it, beyond breaking his weapon and confining him to a room for the night. And the earl has promised to give ear to him in the morning."

Heléne frowned down into the mug she still held in her hands. She was more worried about Etienne. *He* had actually drawn Gunthar's blood, and had done so with a dangerously incriminating weapon. There was a long silence while Clothilde seemed to join in her sister's brooding spirits.

"Why *do* you suppose he brought her?" Clothilde wondered at length, taking up Heléne's earlier question. "Triston adored his mother. Nothing could dissuade him from carrying out her dying wish that he journey to the Holy Land and there make an offering for her soul. And then to return to find his father married to the Lady Osanne . . ."

"I suppose it must have been a shock to him," Heléne agreed, "to see his mother replaced by a woman no older than himself. But Etienne told me Triston and Sir Damian finally reconciled over it and that Triston made peace with the Lady Osanne, as well."

"What else has Etienne told you?"

"About his family? Why, nothing. We have scarcely seen one another since that last Christmas we all spent together three years ago, just after Triston returned from Jerusalem." Clothilde had been married to Sir Fulbert then. Heléne rotated the mug in her hands. The late-night shadows pressed upon her as she thought again of Etienne. Sir Damian's accident must have been a terrible blow to him, for if Triston had worshipped their mother, it had been Sir Damian whom Etienne idolized. She supposed if anyone were to try to seek revenge for Sir Damian's crippling, it would be his favored younger son.

"Yes," Clothilde said bitterly when Heléne spoke this thought aloud, "and now Triston will be punished, too! Oh, Heléne, it is so unfair! The earl is a *monster*—"

With some reluctance, Heléne once again came to Gunthar's defense. "I do not think he blames Triston for Etienne's rashness. In truth, when he spoke of it to me, he did not seem nearly so angry over the attack itself as he did about the dagger Etienne used. He said—"

She stopped, but Clothilde no longer seemed to be listening. It was just as well. There was no telling what sort of fit she might fall into were the subject of treason to be raised.

Clothilde gave another little moan and Heléne saw the way her delicate fingers clenched at the blanket. "I cannot believe it is all happening again. Oh, Heléne, it is like a nightmare! I thought when Fulbert died that I should be free. I—I even dared to hope—" She covered her face with her hands. "Oh, how shall I bear it? I would rather *die* than become the earl's wife!"

The answer seemed simple to Heléne. "Then don't do it. Tell Mama you do not care for him and—"

Clothilde threw back her head with a hysterical laugh. "Mama does not give one a choice."

"Well, it is what I shall do. I am not going to marry Lord Heywood, and there's an end to it."

Clothilde's beautiful mouth twisted up in a bitter grimace. "Dear little sister, you do not yet know. Do you think I *wanted* to marry that fat old man? I wept and pleaded with Mama, I told her that I could not, *would* not be his wife. I tried so hard to stand firm through all the beatings and her rantings at me and her threats—"

Her sister's passionate words startled Heléne. She had never witnessed any such scenes as Clothilde now described. As far as Heléne recalled, her sister had gone meekly, if not happily, into her first marriage. Of course, there had been those few months before the wedding when Clothilde had fallen ill and Heléne had been banished from their room. Their mother had taken Clothilde to their manor at Beaulac to recover. Clothilde had returned pale but quiet, and she and Sir Fulbert had married within a week.

Clothilde's eyes were huge in her pale face, dark and haunted. Her voice sank to a whisper. "I never believed she would actually do it. She had always said she would, but— How could any woman, any *mother*, be so heartless, so cruel, so—so evil—"

"Clothilde!"

But Clothilde seemed to be in some dark, frightened world of her own. She gave a sob and began rocking back and forth. "She took everything from me, everything I cared for, everything that mattered. She left me empty and barren, and so alone. If only I had died—oh, if only I had died!" She gave a gulping sob and then another, and then the tears burst forth in a torrent.

Heléne set the mug aside and threw her arms around her sister. "Hush, Clo, hush, it will be all right."

"No, no," Clothilde wailed, still rocking in her sister's hold. "She will do it again. She will do it to me *and* to you. You will see—"

*"Shhh."*

Heléne held onto her tightly, whispering, soothing, but it was not until Clothilde had wept herself to exhaustion that the paroxysm of tearful moanings began to subside.

"There, love." Heléne used her sleeve to wipe her sister's face, then pushed her back against the pillows. "A little sleep will make it all seem better in the morning."

"But Mama—"

"We shall talk to her, and the earl too, and if they will not see reason—well, then we shall run away together. You shall play the harp and I shall sing, and we shall give the world as fine a pair of minstrel sisters as ever it has seen."

Clothilde gave a hysterical little giggle, but she clutched at Heléne when she leaned over to kiss her.

"Are you going to leave me?"

"Of course not, love. I am only going to sit by the fire."

Clothilde slowly relaxed her hold so that Heléne could stand up, then closed her eyes and rolled over with a hiccupping sigh.

Heléne remained beside the bed until Clothilde's breaths deepened in sleep. Only then did she walk over to the window and open a shutter to look up into the night sky. Late though it was, the full moon had just risen above the horizon. The stranger had said that she should meet him when the moon was high. She pulled the shutter closed again and moved softly away.

In the bottom of their wardrobe, Heléne kept a box of medicines: washes for tired eyes, comforting syrups, salves for swellings and bruises . . . She slid off her shapeless gown and went to fetch one of the salves. Then she sat amid the rushes and pushed away the sleeve of her chemise so that she could see the ugly, purple mark that had spread over her shoulder. Sybil's work. That nasty rod of hers . . . Heléne rubbed some of the ointment gingerly into her bruised skin. A sweet scent of marjoram escaped as she spread the salve. The throbbing she had endured all evening finally began to ease.

She set down the jar and wrapped her arms around her knees. She could not stop thinking about Etienne. She did not for one moment believe he was involved in anything so sinister as treason. But there was no denying the suspicious dagger he had carried, and reluctantly she recalled the look on his face in that instant before he had leapt upon the earl.

He had meant to kill Gunthar. No matter how badly she wished to deny it, she knew it was true. Gunthar must have thought her a fool for trying to persuade him otherwise. Nothing, she knew, but Etienne's grief for his father could have driven him to such extreme measures. She could not condone Etienne's violence, but neither could she forget that he was a friend. He had taught her how to fish and how to shoot her first bow. How could she simply abandon him now to Gunthar's cold mercy?

Gunthar. Heléne despised him. But she could not deny the disturbing power of his presence, nor the curious, quivery feeling she suffered each time his piercing eyes flicked to sweep the length of her braid. He possessed an unnerving masculinity that must have brought scores of women to his arms, even without the obvious allurements of wealth and title. If she were not careful—

Heléne gasped and scrambled to her feet. Of a sudden, the room seemed inexplicably suffocating. She pulled her gown back on and went to fetch a cloak. She did not care what hour the stranger had named, she would await him in the open air. She paused a moment to listen, then, satisfied that Clothilde still slept, opened the door and went out.

Though a portion of the curtain wall and two of the outer towers still lay in ruins from the siege, the castle grounds were but lightly guarded. Heléne had no trouble slipping unseen through the postern gate in the west wall. She made her way swiftly to the river, but found him there before her, seated on the bank, nursing a pebble between his hands. Moonlight glistened on the gently roiling waters, its tranquil murmur the only sound to be heard but for the *plink-plink-plink* of the stone he tossed across the surface. His blond hair looked white in the moonlight, falling over his shoulders in tightly crimped curls.

Heléne thought about turning back. She did not even know his name and he had given her no proof that what he spoke was the truth. But his manner had been so menacing, so insistent, that she had dared not stay away.

A twig cracked sharply beneath her foot. He sprang up, twisting about with the litheness of a cat. To Heléne's dismay, a dagger flashed in his hand. She fell back with a startled cry, but in an instant the dagger was sheathed.

He greeted her with a sweeping bow. "My dear lady, your pardon. I thought it too early to be you."

She drew herself up and addressed him with a boldness she was far from feeling. "I have come for the letter, sir. You promised to give it to me."

"Aye, certainly, as soon as I have your news. You will find me a man of my word. But come and sit with me here—"

"Thank you, I prefer to stand."

He shrugged at her cold rebuff. "As you will."

He stood with his back to the moon, shadowing his features, but she remembered them in the sunlight. Delicately pretty, his small, full mouth hinting of a sensuous cruelty, an expression in his pale eyes that sent shivers down her spine . . .

"Well?"

She hesitated, then ventured to challenge him. "Before I tell you anything, I think I have the right to know with whom I deal."

He raised a bone-thin finger to her cheek. She saw the gleam of his teeth as she pulled away. "You, my dear lady, have no rights at all, save to know that your father's freedom and quite possibly his life depend upon your cooperation."

"How do I know you're telling me the truth? That such a letter even exists?"

He reached in the front of his tunic and pulled out a folded piece of parchment. It was sealed with a lump of red wax but he waved it under her nose too quickly for her to make out the emblem, other than to see that it was some sort of bird.

"Now then, I'm sure neither of us relishes this game we are forced to play. The letter is yours, as soon as you tell me—"

"The earl has arrived at Pennault," she said, anticipating his question.

"I know that." She flushed at his impatient scorn. "I saw his entourage riding past— What I want to know is, why he has come."

"He comes on the king's commission, to enforce the terms of the Peace of Montlouis."

"And?"

Though she could not see his eyes, she could feel them boring into her. "And—and to marry my sister, Clothilde." It was as though, against her will, he somehow wrenched the words from her.

"Ah, the fair Lady Merval. The king seeks an alliance, then, by means of an incomparable treasure. To secure your father's loyalty, no doubt—as well he might." He tapped the letter with one thin finger. "Yes, yes, this all concurs with what le Reynard told me. But one can never be too careful, particularly when dealing with the slippery English."

"Is that all?" She reached for the letter, but he twitched it away.

"Not so fast, my dear. I'm sure you know more than this."

"I don't—"

"Come, was there not a slight—er, altercation at the castle today?"

"You mean Etienne?"

"Tell me what happened."

She did so reluctantly, never taking her eyes off the letter.

"And where is the youth now?"

"Imprisoned in my father's tower."

"And the source of his fiendish dagger?"

"He will not say."

"You are sure of that? He has confessed to no conspiracy, nor tried to lay the blame elsewhere?"

"No! Etienne is not a conspirator!"

"Gently, my dear. You know the youth well, I presume?"

"Very well."

"Then it may be he will trust you with his secrets."

"I have not been allowed to speak with him. But I know he is not guilty of—"

"Then you do not know what he might have said to the earl." He cut her off curtly.

She glared at him. "The earl has not personally questioned him, to my knowledge. I heard him say he would send Lord Challons to do that task tonight."

"Challons." He repeated the name musingly, but whether he found it familiar or simply curious, she could not say. He lowered the letter towards her outstretched hand, then snatched it away again before her fingers could seize it. "One more thing. What are the earl's intentions over, say, the next day or two?"

She hesitated. She had revealed much of what had already passed, but this question made her uneasy.

"Come," he prompted, "you sat with him at dinner. You must have heard something. Does he plan to amuse himself by hunting in your father's woods? Or pursue more immediate duties by scouting out your neighbors? I suppose the logical starting place would be Vere Castle."

"No," she said. "Sir Damian has sent his son, Triston, from Vere to plead for Etienne, but the earl will not hear him till morning. After that he means to leave for Angoulême, but I do not know for how long."

"Angoulême." He tapped the folded parchment against the palm of his hand. "Well, well. He goes to see the prince. This could prove most propitious."

For the first time, Heléne wished she could read his expression. She did not like the Earl of Gunthar, but if someone were plotting to harm him . . .

"Here." She found the letter suddenly free and in her hand. "There, you see? A man of my word. You have been most helpful to me, my lady. Should I require your assistance again, I trust—"

She did not wait to hear the rest, but turned and ran away. She did not stop until she was safely in her own bedchamber once more.

Clothilde was still asleep. Heléne leaned against the closed door, but even after her breathing steadied, she felt her heart still pounding. How had her father been so foolish? To have penned such treasonous words after his enforced capitulation to the Earl of Gunthar, after swearing on his oath his loyalty to the king—

She hurried across to the fireplace and dropped to her knees. There were little more than embers now, but they would provide a willing blaze for the letter's stiff parchment. She held it out over the smoldering coals, then froze. Something was wrong.

She seized the nearby poker and stabbed at the fire's remains until a tiny flame sprang up. She had to lean closely to study the seal, and felt a jarring lurch in her breast. 'Twas no double-headed phoenix stamped into the wax, but some other bird, so crudely engraved she could not even decipher its kind. She tore the letter open and found it—blank.

He had tricked her. The vile, evil man had tricked her! Heléne crushed the parchment between her hands and hurled it into the flames.

# Six

The screams wrenched Heléne from her sleep. Clothilde was sitting bolt upright in the bed, her face white as chalk, wet with the sweat of terror.

"Clo—" Heléne sat up quickly and embraced her sister as Clothilde burst into tears. "Hush, love, hush. 'Twas but a dream. 'Tis gone now."

Heléne pulled her gently back down to the pillows. Clothilde's whole body shook with her sobs. She clung to Heléne, moaning and weeping, but no amount of coaxing would make her tell her dream.

Clothilde had been troubled with nightmares ever since Sir Fulbert had died. At least, that's when Heléne had become aware of them, after Sir Fulbert's castle had been destroyed by the earl and Clothilde had returned to Pennault. Heléne occasionally suffered frightening dreams herself, but never had she been brought to wakefulness by such stark terror as Clothilde displayed.

She stroked Clothilde's golden hair, wishing she could persuade her sister to speak of it. A burden shared was often more easily borne. But Clothilde would do nothing but cower against her and tremble and cry. Heléne held her a long while, whispering what comforts she could, until the sobs grew thin and the slender body sagged in her arms. Exhausted by her own tempest, Clothilde finally quieted and fell back asleep.

Only then did Heléne ease herself free and sit up. A grey light had stolen around the corners of the room, betokening the arrival of dawn. Assured by experience that Clothilde would not wake again until Sybil came in to rouse them both, Heléne slid from bed and went to stir up the remains of the fire.

As she stared into the newly springing flames, memories of the night just past came tumbling back. Etienne, the earl, Triston, the stranger by the river . . . They were as threads tangled together in her mind. If she were to have any hope of sorting out the skein, it would have to be now, before the rest of the castle awoke and the distracting daily routine began.

What she needed was fresh air to help her think. She pulled on a smock and slipped quietly out of the room. She ran along the passageway and up the flight of stairs that led to her brother's vacant chamber. Separated in age by little more than a year, she had borrowed Therri's clothes many times before and did not hesitate to raid his clothing chest now.

He had left a few of his garments behind when he had gone to their uncle's. She pulled on a pair of linen breeches, then sat on the bed to don some woolen hose. Casting off her smock and chemise, she replaced them with one of her brother's knee-length tunics, blousing it over a leather belt to conceal her womanly form.

She found a mantle in the wardrobe and tossed it about her shoulders. Her braid she stuffed inside the hood, so that anyone seeing her dart across the bailey would think her merely a squire, off to enjoy a little archery before the day's duties began. She fetched the bow leaning in the corner, grabbed the quiver of arrows beside it and set off for the butts in the field that stretched below the castle.

*Thwang.*

The arrow sailed through the air and landed a finger's width to the left of the bull's eye. Heléne lowered the bow with a sigh. Why could she never get it just right? She was an able enough shot with her hunting bow. Of course, it was a good deal shorter and more flexible than this longer cousin that had been sent to her father a year ago by one of her mother's relatives in South Wales. Her father had scorned it as a barbaric weapon, but had passed it on to his son for Therri's amusement. Therri had tried it a half-dozen times, then concurred with his father's opinion and abandoned it for his more familiar crossbow.

He had left it behind when he had been sent away to his uncle's. And his parents would have been furious had they known how frequently over the past few months their younger daughter had borrowed it and carried it down to the field to practice there like a common bowman.

But Heléne was determined to master this weapon rumor had it was sweeping the English countryside. The crossbow was too cumbersome for her, while her shorter hunting bow lacked both power and range. Carved of yew, with its string of long-fibered hemp, the longbow, despite its proportionate height, was much lighter than the crossbow and more flexible in her hand.

Then she should have been able to hit her mark square in the center of its eye. She drew another arrow from her quiver and took careful aim. Her eyes were clear, her hand steady . . . she drew back the string, slowly, slowly ...

The string snapped as she released the shaft—and the arrow landed with a *thwack* a shade to the left of its twin.

"Not bad, my lady. In truth, a most respectable hit."

Heléne whirled at the voice. No one ever ventured down to the butts at this hour—and why on earth did it have to be *him*?

The Earl of Gunthar, casually dressed in a green short-tunic, leaned with one foot propped on a nearby bale of hay, his elbow on his knee and his chin in his hand, watching her with evident amusement. His cool grey eyes swept over her attire before one heavy brow cocked quizzically. To her disgust, she felt a wave of color sweeping into her cheeks.

"I was not expecting an audience, my lord."

"Is that your way of telling me you wish I would go away? But I am a most discreet gentleman. I assure you, no one will learn of your—er—rather novel attire from me." His gaze ran over her again. "Quite convincing, really. I daresay I should not have guessed the truth from a distance—save that this rather gives you away." He left the bale and crossed to playfully tweak her braid.

She had cast off her brother's cloak to permit herself greater freedom of movement, thus freeing her hair, as well. She jerked her braid out of his hand now and turned stiffly back towards the butts.

"I can't seem to get it right," she murmured. "I practice and practice, but . . . Perhaps Papa is right. 'Tis a weapon fit only for barbarians like the Welsh."

She heard Gunthar laugh. "I doubt your mother would agree with that. And I have seen it used to great effectiveness in battle, piercing a mailed knight through both breast and back with a shot loosed more than a furlong away."

She wrinkled her nose in disgust. "That is a wretched commendation."

"Aye, but an accurate one."

"My father and brother both prefer the crossbow."

"A formidable weapon," he agreed, "but slow. A longbow-man can discharge five to six arrows in the time it takes a crossbow-man to release a single bolt. No small advantage when the enemy is thundering down upon one. And if the longbow-man is sufficiently skilled in his aim— But I have already made that point."

"So you have."

She drew a fresh arrow and set it to the bow, wishing fervently that Gunthar would go away. Perhaps if she ignored him, he would take the hint. She drew back the string and looked steadily down the arrow's shaft until the point seemed perfectly aligned to the heart of her target.

"No. Look, if you hold it like this—"

Heléne lowered the bow in annoyance and half-turned to offer him the weapon. To her surprise, he spun her back around. The next instant she found herself locked between his arms, his hands grasping hers on the bow. She gasped a little at the unexpected embrace and stood awkwardly as he guided her in raising the bow again and repositioning the arrow.

"Take your aim thus, and draw back the string all the way to your ear . . . "

The rest of his advice and demonstration was lost upon his pupil, for Heléne's heart beat so loudly that it drowned out the words. She could think of nothing but the unexpected strength of his arms, the deep rumbling of his chest against her back as he spoke, the warmth of his cheek pressed to her hair ...

Somehow he got the bow into position and fired the shaft. It flew straight and true, landing soundly in the very heart of the mark. She should have felt a thrill of satisfaction. Instead, she suffered a bewildering pang of regret when he let her go.

"There, you see? After this— "

"Yes, yes, I see." She cut him off. She dared not look at him, knowing her face to be a flame of color. But he, insufferable man that he was, laid a hand on her shoulder and turned her about.

"Ah, you are angry with me again." One corner of his mouth twisted up in a wry smile. "It seems, Lady Helen, that I cannot do or say anything to please you."

"Don't be ridiculous," she said, more furious with herself than with him. "Of course I appreciate your advice and shall do my best to remember it. Only I have not yet had my breakfast and I daresay it has made me a little cross."

"Then by all means, allow me to escort you."

She eyed his proffered arm askance, then abruptly walked over to the bale of hay and sat down. She dropped her bow in the grass.

"In a moment. Let me cool off a bit. All this exercise— "

"Aye, I can see you are rather flushed."

She shot him a suspicious glance, but there was naught but bland interest in his face.

She fanned herself with one hand. "I thought you and your men were leaving for Angoulême this morning?" Her mother's remarks about her wardrobe, followed by Clothilde's swoon, had effectively squelched her father's hopes of having either of his daughters join the earl's entourage to visit the prince.

"I have promised an audience to young de Brielle's brother first, and to that bewitching step-mother of his," Gunthar said. "Odd, don't you think, that Sir Damian should send his wife along on such an errand? He must believe me peculiarly susceptible to feminine wiles."

"He would be mistaken," Heléne said bitterly, remembering his coldness to her sister.

"Ah, but I am not completely immune to them. If you are thinking, for instance, that I am unable to see the charm of my host's truant daughter decking herself out in some squire's cast-off clothes—"

"They are my brother's— Oh, but you are odious to tease me so!"

Gunthar laughed. "And you, my lady, appear much more than merely charming when your cheeks glow at me like that."

"Oh!" She choked back an impulse to throw something at him and linked her hands tightly in her lap. "It is wretched of you to be offering me flattery, however false it might be, when you are going to marry my sister."

"Am I?"

"You know you are. Why don't you flatter her?"

"I thought I did. I praised her incomparable beauty and grace."

"Then you do think her beautiful?"

"Of course. Do you think me blind?"

"Then why do you look at her like—"

"Like what?"

Heléne bit her lip. By no possible stretch of the imagination had she any right to be questioning him like this. Her mother would have been appalled. "It is none of my business," she muttered.

"No, in point of fact, it is not."

Her chin shot up rebelliously, but the subtle warning in his eyes made her put it down again.

"What are you going to say to Triston?" she ventured, after a few moments of uncomfortable silence.

"I shall listen to what he has to say to me, so long as he speaks with a cooler tongue than he used last night. I have never had much patience with blatant insolence."

She sensed danger ahead for Triston. "I am certain if you will but be fair with him, you will find him quite reasonable."

"He has a good deal of explaining to do if he hopes to find me the same," Gunthar said. "Did he know of his brother's intentions when that youth left home yesterday? And what does he know about the dagger? Did his brother obtain it from the prince himself, or was it put into his hand by a member of his own house? These are the questions I shall lay before Sir Triston."

"You are determined to see them as part of some wicked conspiracy," she accused.

"Where the safety of the king and this realm are concerned, all possibilities must be examined."

"Did not Lord Challons question Etienne last night? What did he say?"

"He completely disavowed the dagger. He swore he'd never seen it before and knew not how it came to be in his hand."

"There, you see?"

"What I see," he said, "is a guilty youth desperately trying to stave off an accusation of treason. Challons made it quite clear to him the cost of such a judgment. Be assured, he will not tell us the truth of his own accord."

"He would tell *me* the truth. Let me speak with him."

"No."

"But—"

"I do not mean to argue this with you again. And I intend to be obeyed. Woe be to you, my lady, if I hear so much as a whisper that you have tried to go to him behind my back."

Heléne felt a chill at the words. How had Gunthar known what was in her mind? His grey eyes held hers with such probing deliberation that for one terrifying instant, she felt as though her whole soul had been laid bare to his comprehension. She shivered and looked away.

To her surprise, when he spoke again there was a rueful warmth in his voice.

"Come, you are thinking me an ogre. Put aside your fears for your friends. If they are innocent in truth, I shall learn it and deal with them as fairly as even you could wish. Come . . ."

She heard him moving, but was not prepared to suddenly find his fingers beneath her chin. He tilted her face back up to his.

"I do not wish to be at odds with you, my lady. In fact—" his fingers formed a cup about her chin, permitting his thumb to lightly brush against her cheek "—I would give much to see you smile, just once."

Heléne sat perfectly still. She was certain that if she moved so much as an inch, the rest of his hand would slide up to her cheek, and— *Oh, please,* she prayed, *don't let him read my heart now.*

The plea was in vain. Suddenly he knelt before her in the grass. She stared into eyes as warm and reassuring as they had been cold a moment before. Could this be the same man who had devastated their castle, who threatened her friends with treason and offered such frigid warnings to herself?

She closed her eyes. The mouth that pressed against hers was not cold. It was warm and strong, and sent through her a violent shiver of delight.

"You found that . . . distasteful?"

She answered before she thought. "No."

She did not open her eyes. She could feel his nearness, a disturbing warmth emanating from his body. Somehow her hands had crept up against his chest and when he kissed her again, her fingers curled into the cloth of his tunic.

Never in her wildest romantic dreams had she imagined a kiss such as this. Her senses whirled and from some astonished corner of her mind, she felt herself leaning into him, her arms slipping beneath his to embrace his body more fully. His hands on her shoulders drew her closer, holding her against him. His kiss deepened . . .

He released her abruptly with a ragged breath. "What do you suppose the guards will think, should they be observing us from the ramparts? I trust they are familiar with your unconventional attire, for I should not like to stand accused of seducing one of my host's young squires." Although the words were light, his voice sounded curiously husky.

Heléne gave an involuntary laugh, and made no attempt to prevent his fingers from caressing the upward curve of her lips. She whispered against them, "You have no objection, however, to seducing your host's daughter?"

She thought a hint of cynicism crept into his smile.

"Ah, that would be quite in keeping with my reputation."

The words shocked her back to reality. This man had been a guest in her father's house for less than a day, and everything she knew of him had only enraged her. His haughty manners, his bullying commands, the mantle of royal authority by which he had swept into Poitou with the intention of subduing her friends and neighbors. And now, to add insult to injury, it had somehow amused him to try to add her to what was undoubtedly a long list of feminine conquests.

He had almost succeeded. For one wildly deceptive moment, she had believed that he actually found her a desirable woman rather than the unremarkable girl she knew herself to be. The kisses, the embrace, it had all been a game to him—a game played too many times before.

She struck his hand away and sprang up.

He rose with her, looking startled. "Helen?" He reached for her arm.

She shook him off and backed away. "It is *Lady Heléne* to you. And don't you dare come near me. I suppose you think because I have never kissed a man before that I should prove an easy mark, but I have no intention of being seduced by you or anyone else!"

He laughed. "Oh, come, you did not think I was serious? Of course I haven't—"

She did not want to hear his lies. She flung her cloak about her shoulders, grabbed the bow and started to walk away. He caught her arm again and swung her back around

"Wait. Lady Helen, you're mistaken if you think—"

"Let me go! How dare you insult me like this!"

"I did not mean it as an insult."

"Trying to seduce the sister of your betrothed? I can find no other word for it."

"I was not seducing you and I am not betrothed to your sister," he snapped. "And what's more—"

"What's more, you never will be if *I* can find a way to prevent it!" She threw the challenge boldly in his face. "You are a base, despicable rogue, hiding behind your lordly title while you abuse our hospitality with your lewd and filthy ways!"

His eyes widened. "Why, you scurrilous, impudent little—"

"You wicked, odious, cold-hearted—"

"You did not find me so cold a few moments ago. And I did not exactly have to force your arms around me. If anyone was doing the seducing—"

Her face flooded with heat at the painful memory. She tried to twist away, but his hand was like a vise on her arm.

"Please . . ." to her chagrin, her voice came out in a shaken whisper. ". . . please let me go."

His lips had formed a hard, thin line and his eyes glinted unpleasantly at her, but after a moment his fingers relaxed and he allowed her to slip away.

She turned and ran away from the field. Tears streamed down her face, as hot as the tumultuous emotions churning in her breast. She did not even care that her braid had tumbled free of its hood so that the servants now stirring about the bailey stared at her as she ran past. Through blurred eyes, she saw Sybil emerging from the stables, dragging a disheveled serving-girl by the hair. Audiart, the pretty stableboy's lover. The girl cried out to Heléne for help, but Heléne was too distraught to stop. She wondered if Gunthar had followed her, then wished him fiercely to blazes and darted on to the safety of the keep.

Gunthar stared after Heléne in a confusion of indignation and regret. Who did she think she was, castigating him, the Earl of Gunthar, counselor to the king, as though he were some uncouth villain? Lewd and filthy, indeed! That was a slur he would not soon forget. And yet . . .

Had the fault not been his? Thanks to the king's meddling, she believed him as good as betrothed to her own sister. Yet there he had been kissing her instead and apparently boasting of the conquest. His reference to his "reputation" had been a major misstep, he owned. She was unlikely to understand the readiness of men jealous of his position so near the king, and women hopeful of winning so wealthy a prize, to spread the kinds of rumors the former hoped might discredit him and the latter trap him into any kind of self-beneficial union, illicit or otherwise.

Heléne had been justly angered by his actions and words. Only a pathetically conceited boor could have held a grudge against so well-deserved a rebuke.

At the very least, he admitted as he turned his steps back towards the castle, he owed her an apology. He should like to have been able to offer an explanation as well, but he found himself completely bereft of that. He could not conceive what had possessed him to kiss her. He hung in mid-step for a moment, remembering the fresh sweetness of her lips, before he proceeded on to the keep. The memory of their encounter lingered, upsetting the familiar order of his mind as he took his place in the hall to give ear to Sir Triston's complaint.

Sir John paced behind Gunthar's chair, while Lord Challons and Gunthar's other men seated themselves with their lord behind the table on the dais. Edmund de Muncey, Gunthar's secretary, sat with a quill poised over a parchment sheet ready to inscribe the proceedings. Laurant, mindful of certain threats made the night before, had strategically positioned several of his guards near the petitioner.

But a good deal of the evening's anger had gone from Triston's face. Clearly, he had not spent an easy night as Laurant's 'guest'. He looked pale and weary and tensely aware that he was surrounded by men who were prepared to seize him again at no more than a lift of Gunthar's finger. Some attempt had been made to smooth out the creases from his dull brown tunic and to brush away the dust, but with little apparent success. The enameled brooch at his throat had previously escaped Gunthar's notice, but he recognized it now as the symbol he had seen painted on Sir Damian's shield when they had fought on the walls of Vere Castle—a five-petaled gilded rose, with a blood-red drop at its center.

Gunthar shifted his gaze to the young man's companion. The Lady Osanne was an indisputable beauty and, unlike her stepson, had had the good sense to borrow a fresh change of clothes. A dark crimson gown clung flatteringly to her voluptuous figure. Lusciously long lashes fluttered over soulful black eyes and it struck Gunthar that her small, moist mouth was the same color as the heart of Triston's brooch.

"Come forward, Sir Triston," Gunthar said abruptly, "and speak your mind."

Triston stepped up to the dais and bowed, but when he came up Gunthar saw that a gleam of heat had stolen back into his eyes.

"My lord, I must again protest this unjust imprisonment of my brother. That in former days you have had cause to quarrel with my father in no way excuses this offensive treatment of his son. I can do no other than to lay this arrant treatment of my brother down to pure and simple spite."

Gunthar raised a skeptical brow. Was it possible Triston did not know of his brother's misdeed? He would test him—but on another matter, first.

"De Muncey, hand me that scroll." The secretary immediately handed his master the desired roll of parchment. Gunthar smoothed it out so that it lay flat on the tabletop. "Come closer, Sir Triston, and have a look at this, if you please."

Triston hesitated before stepping onto the dais.

"Is this an accurate representation of the Castle Vere?"

Triston frowned down at the drawing. "Aye. But I don't see what this has to do with Etienne."

"We shall return to your brother presently. First tell me if you are not familiar with the terms of the Peace of Montlouis? In return for King Henry's pardon, the princes and rebels alike all swore that the fortifications raised against the king during the course of the war would be torn down, returning all castles to the condition they were in before the war began. Do you not recall this?"

"I do, my lord."

The admission caused Gunthar's mouth to tighten. "De Muncey." The secretary placed a second scroll in Gunthar's hand. This one he opened with a snap. It was a nearly identical copy of the former drawing, with the addition of several lines and squares done in red ink. He indicated them with a long, tapered finger. "Here are the additional walls your father built *after* the start of the war. Here he dug a second moat, here extended the barbican . . . Is this, too, accurate?"

Triston did not reply at once. His head remained bent in study of the scroll, averting his expression from Gunthar's gaze. But at last he answered, "Aye, my lord."

Gunthar leaned back in his chair. "You were with your father, were you not, when my men and I breached these fortifications? The southern wall was completely demolished by our siege engines, our mining efforts collapsed another. We filled in your inner *and* outer moats, set fire to the barbican and burned down the towers that guarded the outer bailey. When we were through, your father had little more to do than to sweep away the rubble in order to comply with the king's command. Yet he did not do so—did he?"

Triston did not look up, but his voice hardened. "My father was injured, my lord. We did not know for months whether he would live or die. 'Sweeping away the rubble' was the least of our concerns."

"But your father has lived, and it is a year and a half since the treaty was ratified. Furthermore, I have recently been informed that not only have the foundations of these walls been allowed to stand—" he swept a finger over the red lines "—but they have begun to be rebuilt. Is this true?"

Triston hesitated.

"I can dispatch one of my servants to Vere Castle—"

"There is no need, my lord. Everything you say is true."

Gunthar allowed an ominous silence to stretch for several minutes before he murmured, "So. The pieces begin to fall into place."

Triston looked up, his expression guarded. "My lord?"

"I find it difficult to believe after all the destruction we wrought that your father still possesses the means to undertake so costly a rebuilding effort. Nor that, considering the humbling nature of his injury, he should yet have the audacity to so openly defy the terms of the peace. He cannot be acting alone in this. Someone must be spurring him on, supplying him with money, promising protection."

Triston flushed a little, but insisted, "My lord, you exaggerate the matter. That we have repaired a few walls is true. My father is a deeply embittered man, confined day and night to a chair from which he knows he will never rise again. He dreams grand visions of a glorious revenge, but he has no more strength to carry them out than a child. The walls are a balm to his pride, nothing more. The garrison is now under my command, and I swear on my oath that I mean to uphold the vow of fealty which I have sworn in my father's name."

"Fair words, Sir Triston, but coming from a man whose brother tried to assassinate me less than twenty-four hours ago, I find them difficult to believe."

"Assassinate?" Triston gasped. "That is absurd! Etienne would not—"

"Shall I show you the wound in my arm where your brother's dagger fell? There is a room full of witnesses here." Gunthar made a sweeping gesture that took in Laurant and his guards. "Had there not been a cry of warning, your brother would be facing a murder charge, rather than merely being shut away for questioning."

Triston looked stunned, and for an instant Gunthar was tempted to believe the reaction was genuine.

"But I was told—" Triston broke off and whirled on Osanne. "You told me he had been seized for spite. You said he had ridden over for curiosity's sake, and when the earl learned he was Sir Damian's son, he ordered him flung into the tower. You said—"

Osanne shrank from the fury on her stepson's face. "I was not present, how should I have known? I only repeated what that dim-witted lackey of your father's told me."

"You lying, mischief-making witch," Triston swore. "You expect me to believe you now? What did you hope to gain by this, save to make me look like an utter fool?" He turned stiffly back to Gunthar. "My lord, I knew nothing of this. My brother is an impetuous young hothead, overly zealous to avenge my father's defeat at your hands. He slipped away from Vere without my knowledge yesterday. I deeply regret any injury he has caused you and accept full responsibility for him. If you will only release him to me, I swear I will return him to Vere and on my oath, I guarantee he will cause you no further trouble."

Gunthar shook his head.

"My lord, I beg of you," Triston said. "He is only a boy, he cannot have realized the weightiness of his act. If you cannot find it in you to pardon him, then I implore you to take me in his place. I will stand surety for him."

"No."

The curtness of Gunthar's reply momentarily silenced Triston. Then, with a look of desperate resolve, Triston drew a deep breath and renewed his plea in a slightly throbbing voice.

"My lord, Etienne is my father's life. He dotes upon the boy, he is all my father speaks of day and night. 'I must do this for Etienne, Etienne must see this, I must tell this to Etienne.' He thinks, nay, he lives for nothing else. When he heard that my brother had been imprisoned here, he was worse than angry. He is terrified lest some tragic fate befall his younger son. Should I be forced to return without him— In truth, I fear for my father's health both in body—and in mind." He paused, searching for some sign of yielding in Gunthar's countenance. "My lord, I have sworn an oath—"

"Then I fear you have sworn one oath too many," Gunthar said, "for I will not let your brother go until I have had the truth."

"The truth?"

"John." Gunthar stood up and extended a hand. Immediately, Sir John pulled free the dagger that had been tucked in his belt and placed it in Gunthar's outstretched palm. Gunthar rounded the table slowly. "Do you know this weapon, Sir Triston?"

He extended the hilt for the younger man's inspection and waited for a response.

Triston studied the insignia carved into the pommel before making what Gunthar perceived to be a calculatedly cautious response.

"I have seen such an image worn on the surcotes of men who claim affiliation with Prince Richard."

"Precisely. It is one of Richard's perverted little jokes, one which might have proved deadly to me and which may yet prove to be your brother's undoing."

Triston paled and passed a nervous tongue between his lips. "Are you saying that is the dagger Etienne attacked you with?"

"I am saying exactly that."

"But—but it is impossible! Where would he have gotten it?"

"Where indeed?"

Triston looked truly alarmed now, as if an unexpected trap had just been sprung. "My lord, you must believe me, we have had no commerce with the prince since the end of the war. I do not know how such a weapon can have come into Etienne's hand, but I can assure you it was not put there by the prince." He saw Gunthar's misdoubt, but persisted. "My lord, I pray you. I have owned his foolish impulsiveness. I have lamented the harm he caused you. And I don't doubt but what he has been thoroughly frightened by a night in Laurant's tower. If you will only let me take him home, I swear on my oa— "

Gunthar raised his brows and Triston flushed.

"That is, I am quite certain my brother has learned his lesson and will never try anything so foolhardy as this again."

"Were I to do as you plead," Gunthar said, "*I* would be the fool."

"My lord—"

"No, Sir Triston, I have listened quite patiently to your eloquent pleas in your brother's behalf. Now you will listen to me." He shoved the dagger into the front of his belt, folded his arms across his chest, and leaned back against the table. "Now then, this is the story as I envision it. Prince Richard, like his brothers, is resentful of the terms of the peace that have been imposed upon him by his father. He wishes to rule in Poitou and Aquitaine, but his father does not trust him. 'Prove to me that I am wrong,' invites the king. 'You are lord of Poitou. Bring the rebels, your former allies, to heel. Show yourself responsible and true-hearted, and then shall I grant a ready ear for your grievances.'

"But Richard finds the task difficult. His former friends refuse to tear down their illegal fortifications. By oath, Richard is bound to obey his father, but his sympathies still lie with his friends. He prevaricates. His father grows impatient. The king threatens to do the job himself. Richard views the ultimatum as an insult. Despite his forced capitulation on the battlefield, he has never been fully reconciled to his defeat. He longs to defy the king, but knows that he and his allies cannot sustain another war."

Gunthar unfolded his arms and fingered the hilt of the prince's dagger. "It is here," he said, "that Richard begins to show his cunning, that insidious guile which sets him apart from his blustering brothers. Perhaps he can win in peace what he was unable to gain on a field of blood. Aquitaine has always been a particularly unruly duchy, accustomed to going its own way without regard for royal authority. Poitou has been much the same. It should not take much to raise the suggestion in Henry's mind that his determination to rule in these domains is more trouble than it is worth.

"But Richard requires a pawn." Gunthar kept a careful eye on Triston's face now. "A puppet if you will, to test the waters. Quietly, the prince supplies him with money to clear his moats and rebuild his walls. Others have refused to comply with the treaty's demands to tear down their fortifications, but this knight, this pawn, is the first to openly defy the terms by raising fresh battlements. If he can do it subtly enough to avoid a royal rebuke, then others will surely follow. By the time the king realizes what is happening, he will be placed in an untenable position. Either resume a war which he can ill-afford, either in money or in further disorder to his realm, or look the other way, thus in effect abdicating that very authority for which he originally fought. Richard is gambling that he will do the latter. I, however, assure you unequivocally that he will not."

Gunthar paused. Triston had listened grave-faced to this recital, but still said nothing. Gunthar's voice hardened at the silence. "The king has demonstrated great patience with his son and the rebels who supported him, but his tolerance is nearing an end. When I carry my report back to England, you will find to your grief that there are no more easy pardons to be had. Henry has not suffered a single man to pay the ultimate penalty for his treason. 'Twould be a shame indeed, Sir Triston, were your brother now to be the first."

Triston paled. "But—but it is not what you think. My father is not Prince Richard's pawn, and Etienne—"

Gunthar pushed himself away from the table and whipped out the dagger once more.

"This." He thrust out the hilt towards Triston. "It is this which will condemn you all. Did your father fear I would discover what he was doing and at who's bidding, and tell the king? Richard knows he could never bribe or threaten me to silence. Did he order your father to stop me? And why did Sir Damian send his cherished younger son on so dangerous and risk-filled a mission? Why, Sir Triston, did he not send you?"

Triston stood speechless before this flurry of accusations. Gunthar watched him, weighed him, alert for any flicker of emotion that might reveal the truth.

"Oh, Triston, we are undone!"

Triston's head snapped round at Osanne's wail. Her large, dark eyes glowed mournfully.

"My lord, have mercy on us! I pray you—"

"What are you saying?" Triston demanded.

"It is no use," she moaned. "The earl knows. We will only make things worse by denying it."

With a trembling step, she approached the dais, then sank to her knees and clasped her hands to her breast. "Alas, my lord, it true, everything you have said. The prince seduced my husband into joining his plot, then threatened him with dire consequences if he did not find a way to prevent your discovery, or failing that, stop you from reporting it to the king. My husband would willingly have done the deed himself, but his injuries obliged him to send another. He entrusted the task to his elder son, but—" here she sent a frightened glance at Triston, then seemed to steel herself and finished in contemptuous tones "—but *he*, filled with jealousy for the love his father bears for poor Etienne, persuaded his impulsive young brother that it would somehow be proof of Etienne's devotion to their father if he came in Triston's stead."

Triston's face went as red as it had been white a moment before. "Why, you lying little—" He stepped off the dais, but Sir John sprang after him to block his path towards Osanne.

Tears spilt out of her big dark eyes as Osanne cowered before her stepson's rage. "Oh, stop him, please! He is a veritable devil, without shame, aye, even to the defiling of his father's bed. Aye, it is true!" she screamed when Triston cursed her and tried to push Sir John aside. "He has repeatedly ravished me, forcing me to do his vile will, threatening me with the most hideous punishments if I did not do as he said. He forced me to come here with him in hopes that I might seduce the earl and finish the job that he is too cowardly to do himself. He gave me this dagger—" Gunthar's eyes widened as she pulled a long, sleek blade from the bosom of her gown "—and said that when you lay asleep in my arms, I was to plunge it into your heart."

"Liar!" Triston shouted. He struggled to escape Sir John's hold on him. "My lord, you cannot believe a word of this!"

"I tell you it is true. I swear—"

"You can swear yourself to hell for aught I care. Only let me get my hands on you—"

With a sudden move, Triston rammed the palm of his hand beneath Sir John's chin. The knight's head snapped back. The blow startled him into slackening his grasp.

Triston twisted free with a curse and sprang across the floor to his stepmother.

# Seven

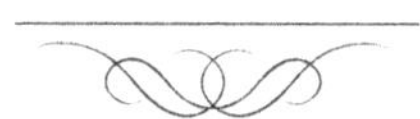

The Lady Osanne screamed as Triston seized her by the shoulders. Triston cursed her again and shook her so hard the pins went flying from her hair. Sir John lunged after him, but he required two of Laurant's guards to come to his aid before they were able to pry Triston's furious grip free of the cringing woman. As Osanne collapsed into Sir John's arms, Triston knocked one of his would-be captors across the floor and threw the other aside so powerfully that the guard stumbled up onto the dais and overturned the table with those who sat behind it.

Gunthar only just missed being bowled over as well. "Stop him!" he shouted. "Laurant—"

The rest of Laurant's guards sprang forward, but two more of them went flying before Triston was finally overpowered.

"Get him out of here," Gunthar ordered above the din of Triston's angry curses. "If he sets foot near Pennault again, throw him into the tower with his brother."

The guards dragged Triston out of the hall, still sputtering with rage.

Gunthar glanced at Sir John and saw that the Lady Osanne had swooned in his arms. "Take her upstairs," Gunthar said. "Request assistance from the Lady Helen. Tell her the Lady Osanne requires accommodations for a day or two." He could not send the poor woman back to Vere Castle to face the violence of Triston's temper.

Sir John bounded up the stairs with his fair burden.

Gunthar brushed aside Laurant's distress at the turn the interview had taken. He told his toppled knights to pick themselves up and make ready for an immediate departure for Angoulême.

But his temper, already sorely tested by the scene with Triston, was further tried when his squire, Julian Parr, claimed an unexpected illness that would prevent him from accompanying his master. And a good hour passed before Sir John could be drawn from the Lady Osanne's bedside. Gunthar had little patience left for Sir John's besotted lingerings. In the end, only the threat that he should be left behind if he did not join Gunthar *at once,* brought Sir John back to a remembrance of his duty, and then it was with considerable grumbling.

His freely voiced resentments stretched into a good half-day's journey along the forest road.

"I cannot believe you simply let that fellow go!" Sir John exclaimed for what seemed to Gunthar the hundredth time. "It was obvious to everyone that he is as guilty as sin!"

Gunthar grunted but said nothing. Twenty years of friendship had inured him to Sir John's rattling tongue and to a familiarity he would have permitted from no other man.

"Sir Triston shames and abuses his step-mother, betrays his own father and brother, conspires with the prince to murder you, and how do you repay him? You let him walk away scot-free!"

"If there is a conspiracy," Gunthar said, "it is between the prince and Sir Damian. Or so confessed the Lady Osanne."

Sir John's face softened at the lady's name. "Poor lass. You should have seen the way she clung to me when I laid her on the bed, calling me her savior, begging me not to leave her. She is terrified of what that man might do to her, now that she has laid bare the treason that lies in his soul."

Gunthar recognized the smitten expression on Sir John's countenance and grunted again. His friend's lingering at the "poor lass's" bedside had set them so far behind that any chance of reaching Angoulême before nightfall had been lost. Gunthar had been forced to send a herald ahead to request hospitality for his company from one of the king's loyal vassals whose castle stood along their way.

"We have no proof that Sir Triston is involved in treason," he said.

"No proof?" Sir John echoed. "Why, the man has no more conscience than an animal. Attacking a woman half his size! And have you thought what risk you are setting yourself at by letting him go? Why, he might even now be skulking somewhere along this road, just waiting for a chance to finish what his brother botched."

"I doubt there is much danger of that, so long as his brother languishes in Laurant's tower. The boy shall serve as hostage to insure both Sir Triston's and Sir Damian's good behavior until this matter can be settled with the prince."

But Sir John scoffed at the response. "I'll wager Sir Triston cares not a fig for his brother. And the Lady Osanne, it's plain as day he means her harm. Now that she has betrayed him, how shall she ever feel herself safe again? It is inconceivable to me what you can have been thinking when you simply turned that blackguard out!"

Gunthar's patience cracked. He was hot and hungry and heartily sick of the sound of Sir John's voice. "I will deal with the matter as I see fit," he snapped, "and I won't be second guessed by a gullible fool with no more sense than an infatuated squire."

Sir John stiffened. Unaccustomed to being on the receiving end of Gunthar's sharp tongue, he apologized sarcastically for forgetting his place and dropped back to join those knights who had taken refuge from their master's temper at the rear of the column.

Gunthar let him go, but glanced over his shoulder as his friend drew away. He caught sight of Lord Challons, riding far enough away to appear inconspicuous, but near enough to have observed their quarrel. Challons was the only gentleman besides Sir John who held sufficient status not to be attired in the earl's colors. His surcote of dark brown was lavishly embroidered with bright threads of red, green and yellow interspersed with a sprinkling of diamonds, making him look, Gunthar thought, something like a spangled peacock. The fact that his eyes were filled with amusement at Sir John's discomfiture struck Gunthar as an arrogant presumption.

He turned his head back round and saw the way his standard's shaft trembled in the bearer's hand. He warned the young man caustically to steady it, then flicked his reins and bounded ahead of the procession.

He slowed a short distance ahead, knowing his men would become alarmed were he to advance completely out of their sight. After Triston's violent display that morning, they were all like to argue that he might be plotting further mischief. And Gunthar had no doubts that Triston's father, at least, was involved in conspiracy. There was, after all, the matter of those rebuilt walls, an express violation of the peace treaty. And the Lady Osanne's accusations had been appalling, none more so than the imputation of her own vile abuse at her stepson's hands. Defiling his father's wife, then forcing her to become an accomplice to his villainy! She was beautiful enough, Gunthar acknowledged, to have been entrusted with his own seduction. And she *had* had that concealed dagger . . .

The trouble was, Gunthar was not quite sure he believed it. Behind the angry challenge in Triston's eyes, he had glimpsed an unhappy, even tormented man, one with dark secrets in his heart. But Gunthar had perceived no evil, such as the Lady Osanne had described. Even Triston's violent temper might have been a result of an unbearable provocation. No, Gunthar was not convinced of the Lady Osanne's probity, and lacking either conviction or proof, he had not been willing to condemn the knight.

Gunthar glanced up at the sky. The sun was mid-way in its descent. A steady continuance of their present course would bring his party to Sir Hervé de Belamé's castle just as the sun was setting. These roads were reputed to have become a favorite haunt of bandits since the war had ended, and Gunthar knew it would not be wise for any company as richly furnished as his to be traveling them after dark. But when a bend in the road brought them into a bustling market town, caution was overwhelmed by a succulent odor that somehow wafted to his nostrils above the otherwise rank odors of market life.

His stomach grumbled, reminding him that he had departed from Pennault without breaking his fast. No wonder his temper was so sharp set. He glanced about in search of the aroma's source and saw a weather-beaten sign swinging on a chain outside a worn looking shop. He could just make out through the badly peeling paint the outline of what undoubtedly had once been the inviting image of a loaf of bread. Before any of his men could protest, he drew up his mount outside the shop, swung out of his saddle and strode through the open door.

Despite the shop's discouraging outward appearance, the inside, though flour-strewn, was surprisingly clean. A fat, red-faced little baker greeted Gunthar, his round eyes nearly popping out of their sockets when he saw the huge sapphire that fastened Gunthar's mantle and the sparkling twin sewn to the glove which held out a silver coin as Gunthar requested a fresh loaf of the baker's best bread. The fat little baker bowed low, but he came up beaming, wiping his hands on his grease-spattered apron, and waddled away through a door at the back of his shop.

He returned with a still steaming loaf. Gunthar swept it out of his hand and tore off a chunk with his teeth, wincing a little as it scorched his tongue, but swallowing the bread with pleasure. From the corner of his eye he could see several curious faces, as round and red as the baker's, peering at him from beyond the kitchen door. Several of Gunthar's men had crowded into the shop behind him, making a room already warm from the nearby ovens, suffocatingly hot and stuffy. Gunthar dropped the coin into the baker's hand, tore off another mouthful of soft, sweet bread, and sent his companions scurrying back out into the street with one of his intimidating stares.

"What do you think you're doing?" Sir John asked as Gunthar strolled out after them. "A few more hours and we'll be feasted to our heart's content at Sir Hervé's table. 'Tis madness to ask us all to risk our necks on these roads after dark, merely for a loaf of miserable bread."

"I doubt Sir Hervé should be able to supply me with anything so delectable as this," Gunthar mumbled, his mouth still full. After all, Sir John had had *his* breakfast, not having been distracted by a perturbing early morning scene with a turbulent sprite masquerading as a lad.

"Then can't you at least eat that on the way?" Sir John asked. "If we resume our journey now, we may yet arrive before—"

"Not until I've washed this down with some good, stout ale," Gunthar replied. "Sir Thomas, perhaps you will oblige me—?"

The request trailed off, but Sir Thomas Enslye needed no more to send him loping across the street to the sign of the alehouse. Sir John sighed in exasperation, but Gunthar ignored him and turned his perambulating steps in the opposite direction. After several hours in the saddle, it was a relief to stretch his legs. While he awaited Sir Thomas's return, he would peruse a few of these good merchants' wares. He strolled past a shoemaker's shop and a draper's, then, having satisfied his hunger, handed the remains of the loaf to Challons while he paused at a bookseller's stall.

Always alert for some new volume to lend interest or prestige to his library, he picked up a likely looking tome bound in relatively fresh leather. Alas, within it contained only a dry Latin treatise on some obscure point of law which he had not the least interest in comprehending. But he did not set it down again at once. Thumbing through its stiff pages, he presented the image of a man deeply immersed in its contents. It provided a useful screen for the true direction of his thoughts, which somewhat to his dismay, insisted on returning to his last encounter with Heléne.

Why should her angry words still cut him so? It was not as though she were some tantalizing beauty whose favors he had been seriously hoping to win. She was not even in his style. She was too tall, too slim, too unremarkable—

No, he caught himself up. That last was not true. He may have viewed her that way at first, but she had since revealed herself to be a most remarkable girl, not perhaps in face or figure, but certainly in spirit. No woman, or man for that matter, had ever faced him down so boldly as she had done. It was her courage that he admired. To suggest the odd attraction he felt towards her was more than that was simply ludicrous. Still, he did not wish to appear a knave or ogre in her eyes, and there was no doubt at all that he owed her an apology for his behavior.

But how to make peace with her? Experience had taught him that a well-chosen gift was the surest way to a woman's heart. He set down the lawyerly tome and found Sir Thomas Enslye at his side. Gunthar spoke a curt word of thanks and took the cup of ale from his hand. The quality of the ale was poor but at least it was wet, a welcome sensation to his mouth, grown dry from the bread. He returned the cup to Sir Thomas and browsed, more attentively now, through a few more books.

He found two dull works on theology, an account of the life of Saint Cecilia, a medical tract reputedly authored by Galen . . . He hesitated over that one, remembering Heléne's demonstrated skills in healing. But the translation was in Latin, not French, and he was ignorant of the extent of her linguistic knowledge. Perhaps she could not read at all. Many, if not most, of his female acquaintances could not. But they professed pleasure in having him read to them, so long as the material he chose was of a romantic or amorous nature.

He continued his search of the bookseller's wares until he found a thin volume bound in faded red leather. Flipping through its vellum pages, he recognized the half-dozen lais transcribed within. Guigemar, Lanval, Eliduc . . . They were the works of Marie de France, half-sister to England's own king, and much in vogue among the ladies of the English court. He possessed an original version himself, a gift from the king last Christmas. This copy was much more worn and lacked the colorful illuminations of his own, but the spritely tales were the same. He slid the book under his arm and doled out the bookseller's price, declining to quibble with what he knew to be an exorbitant sum.

"My lord—" Gunthar caught the nudging movement that urged Challons forward "—I beg you will not take this suggestion amiss, but ought we not to be on our way? It is not that I doubt in the least our ability to guard you on these roads after dark, but Sir Hervé is sure to be alarmed at our lingering."

Gunthar stared over Challons' head to the ring of anxious faces behind him. "Where is Sir John?" he demanded.

His knights exchanged nervous glances before Challons' laughter broke the tension. "Alas, my lord, Sir John grew weary of tarrying for you and cast about his eyes for some affable diversion. A saucy wench came sauntering by and he was off on the instant, with that foolish grin I fancy we all know well."

Too well, Gunthar thought. He did not like it. Too many dangers threatened such loose behavior, violence, theft, disease . . .

"You are right, my lord Challons," he said. "The hour demands that we resume our journey without delay. Sir John shall be obliged to make his way alone to Sir Hervé's when he has done with his pleasure." And it would serve him right, Gunthar thought uncharitably, were his friend to meet with a few brigands along the way and find himself robbed of all he carried. Then again, the saucy wench might do the deed herself. Either way, it would prove a well-earned lesson.

He handed the book he had purchased to Sir Thomas with a strict injunction for its care, then turned away from the bookseller's stall.

*Thwump.*

Something hit Gunthar in the shin. He glanced down to see a small child bouncing off his leg to land with a plop in the dirt.

"What the devil—?"

Still irritable over Sir John, he glared down at the brat, then regretted his ill humor when two vivid blue eyes grew round with terror. To a child reclining in the road, Gunthar realized his towering height and severe expression must make him appear a glowering giant. He made an effort to soften his expression and had gone so far as to reach down a hand to the child, when he found the small one snatched away.

"I am ever so sorry, milord," a breathless voice exclaimed. "I saw him run into you. He was looking back at me, teasing me, not looking where he was running."

Gunthar caught sight of two well-worn shoes beneath a green woolen hem before he straightened to survey the woman before him. The child nestled now in her arms, his face hidden against her neck so that Gunthar could see no more than a head full of wild, dark curls. The woman, clearly a servant, had a cheerful countenance that filled with awe at the sight of Gunthar's magnificent dress. Her eyes took in the elaborate cut of his sleeve, the jeweled pendent on his breast, the slashings up the sides of his dark blue surcote that exposed the scarlet tunic beneath . . .

"Ah, but 'tis wondrous handsome," she exclaimed. "If my master could but see . . . He's a clothier, Master Guillem, and his wife a most expert seamstress."

"Indeed?" The seed of an idea came into Gunthar's mind. "I should like to meet your master, and perhaps have a glimpse of his inventory. We have lingered this long already," he added to Challons' protest, "another few minutes will not make much difference now."

He heard the collective sigh of his men, but none dared offer further objections as he turned to follow the serving wench.

Master Guillem was closing up shop for the day. The salesroom was a bustle with apprentices and assistants sweeping floors, wiping down counters, and stacking bolts of material neatly into chests or onto shelves. The clothier, a stocky, grey-haired man, greeted Gunthar with a bow and a quick, calculating glance. Gunthar suspected the workings of his tailor were being committed to memory so as to be passed on for duplication by the clothier's seamstress-wife.

The serving wench slipped away with the child to a room in the back of the shop as Master Guillem said, "And how may I serve you, milord? Is it wool you desire? I have some fine scarlet imported from Lincoln, or burnets if 'tis hose you have in mind. And my linens, you'll not find a more accommodating range of colors anywhere in France."

With this extravagant claim, he gestured to one of his apprentices, who immediately began flying around the shop gathering up every bolt of brightly hued fabric he could find. But even as the youth staggered towards a table with his arms full of cloth, Gunthar waved him back.

"Nay, nothing so common. 'Tis a gift, you see, for a lady."

The clothier's smile grew wide. "Ah, yes. Well, then!" He snapped his fingers at a second apprentice. "Pierre!" Then to Gunthar, "Have a look at this, milord. 'Tis arrived just this day, from the merchants of Lucca. The queen herself would swoon at the sight and feel of it, all wrought of gold and silk. 'Tis called baudekin, I am told."

Gunthar nodded and reached out a hand to touch the cloth as the apprentice spread it out on the table. He was familiar with the rare, expensive silk from the East. The clothier's obvious pride was well merited. Gunthar noted with pleasure the delicate gold brocade and graceful figures woven airily into a pale background. Aye, 'twas a gift worthy of a queen . . . but . . .

He sighed and his hand fell away. "'Tis all wrong. Gold is not her color."

The clothier stared. What woman would not have given her eyeteeth for such a luscious cloth, color or no? But Gunthar had his mind set on a very specific experiment.

"Something in blue," he said musingly. "Rich and dark—like this—" he fingered the sleeve of his surcote "—but flowing, all in silk—"

"Well . . ." The clothier cast his eyes about his shop, surveying the shelves of material. "I have a bit of samite but a few shades off that color. The silk is very soft and fine, though most ladies prefer a gayer hue . . ."

Gunthar demanded to see it. The apprentice obediently fetched the bolt and draped it out on the table beside the baudekin. Gunthar caught his breath. The deep blue of the silk not only shone with a rich, seductive luster, but cast an enchanting blue glow over the reflective gold cloth by its side.

"Aye," he said softly. The image was suddenly crystal clear in his mind. "The samite for the tunic, with long, narrow sleeves gathered at the wrists, and a round neck, falling thus." He indicated with a finger along the top of his breastbone the desired height of that portion of the garment. "Fashion the surcote out of this baudekin, but it must be cut lower so as to keep the richer color against her face. The surcote's hem should fall short of the floor, perhaps mid-calf, and the cuffs of its sleeves form a pendulum. Keep it a glittering compliment to the blue folds beneath. The girdle should also be made of silk, the same blue as the tunic, but in a broad band trimmed in gold and ending in tassels." He paused, admiring the vision in his mind, then cocked a brow at the elated clothier. "I trust it can be done and in good time? I'll not quibble at your price. I understand your wife to be an accomplished seamstress?"

Master Guillem nodded vigorously, his chest puffing a little with pride. "Aye, milord, as clever a wench as you could wish. She was personal dressmaker for twenty years to Sir Damian de Brielle's first wife. The lady left us a most generous bequest upon her death, which

Sir Damian, poor man, was fair enough to honor. And you need not fear the timely completion of your commission. I guarantee both my wife's swift skills and your lady's satisfaction with the results."

Gunthar had barely begun to digest this intriguing connection to Sir Damian, when an applauding voice spoke up from behind him.

"'Tis brilliant, my lord. The Lady Merval will look enchanting in the ensemble you've described."

Gunthar looked round in annoyance. He supposed he should have realized some of his men would follow him into the shop, but the approving grin on Challons' face immediately set up his hackles. Did his entire household know that he was supposed to be courting Clothilde? Devil take the king's meddling! Or had it been the Lady Gwenllian? Either way, this was not the place to disabuse the notion.

Nevertheless, Challons' remark served a useful purpose, for it reined in Gunthar's fantasy that he could with impunity flatter one sister at the expense of the other—particularly when it was the wrong sister. To shower gifts, no matter how harmless his intentions, upon Heléne would cause more than merely her mother's tongue to wag. It might also suggest a degree of interest to the recipient that he had no wish to convey. He desired to make peace with the minx—and he was deeply curious about the effect a decently cut and colored gown might achieve—but he certainly did not wish to imply anything more than a little sympathy for her.

To guard himself against misinterpretation, he thus, to Master Guillem's delight, laid out a second order. It was an exact duplicate of the first, only replacing the blue samite with one of primrose yellow hue, and fashioned for a lady several inches shorter. Several of his men gasped when the clothier stated the inevitable cost of so much rare and exquisite silk, but Gunthar counted out half the coins without a blink, promising the rest upon completion and delivery. Master Guillem offered to summon his wife to receive a repetition of Gunthar's envisioned design. But before he could do so, the door in the back of the shop flew open, and a dark-haired little urchin tugged a mildly resisting grey-haired woman into the room.

"There he is, Mama!" the child squealed, pointing excitedly at Gunthar. "Just as I told you. A giant!"

The woman was laughing, but her eyes widened with surprise, admiration, and finally ambition as she surveyed Gunthar and his elaborate attire. There could be no question but what this was the seamstress-wife.

The clothier confirmed it, introducing her as Mistress Jeanne, and added as the child ran forth and jumped into his arms, "And this, milord, is my son. You must forgive him. He is but four years old this spring, and I'll warrant your height has dismayed him."

The child no longer looked alarmed, safe as he reckoned himself to be in his father's warm and indulgent grasp. He gazed at Gunthar with so much wide-eyed curiosity that Gunthar's initial irritation dissolved into amusement. He was a beautiful child, his eyes two deep pools of blue, his features delicate and fine, framed by a halo of soft, dark, curly hair. He had been scrubbed clean from his earlier adventure in the streets, and was dressed very neatly in a sensible short woolen tunic and buff colored hose, with a tiny mantle draped over his shoulders clasped at the neck by a brooch—

Gunthar stared in startled recognition at the small piece of jewelry. Enameled in gold, the five-petaled flower held a single blood-red drop at its center. There was no mistaking it. It was the de Brielle rose.

The de Brielle rose. Gunthar thought of it again as he and his men left Sir Hervé's castle in the dim hours before dawn. A full moon had guided them safely to the knight's keep, where Sir John joined them sometime in the middle of the night. But Gunthar, impatient to reach Angoulême, roused his men at the first sign of light and ordered a resumption of their journey.

As grey shadow gave way to a pinkish glow about the hills, and then to a glimmer of sunlight, Sir John resumed his place at Gunthar's side, their quarrel forgotten. He listened with interest as Gunthar repeated his encounter with the clothier's family and nodded his head at Gunthar's conclusions.

"It seems a reasonable assumption," he agreed. "If this Master Guillem and his wife are as old as you say, then the child is unlikely to be theirs. Or hers, anyway. I suppose an indiscretion on the husband's part is not impossible."

"But that would not explain the brooch," Gunthar said. "There can be only one explanation for that child to be wearing that insignia . . ."

He paused, but Sir John finished his thought. "Sir Damian's by-blow."

Gunthar nodded.

"Well," Sir John exclaimed, "I think it a shameful thing to turn one's back on one's own blood." He had fathered a love child of his own. If the Lady Berthe had not accepted with grace her husband's insistence that the child be raised alongside their legitimate offspring, at least, to Gunthar's knowledge, she had refrained from persecuting the product of her husband's infidelity.

"Perhaps the Lady Alyne was not as understanding as your Berthe," Gunthar suggested.

Sir John grinned in rueful response, but said, "Still, even if she had been a regular harridan, that is hardly an excuse for abandoning one's son to a common clothier. I'll wager Sir Damian to this day has not spared the poor brat a second thought."

Gunthar was the last man who wished to defend any of Sir Damian's actions, and yet he heard himself saying, "Master Guillem spoke of a generous bequest left his wife at the Lady Alyne's death. Perhaps it was more than a tribute to the little dressmaker's skills. Perhaps it was, in fact, a settlement on the child."

The sun had now risen above the hills, spreading a warm glow over the countryside. The forests of the early day gave place to an expansive meadow on their left, and a few green and rolling hills on their right, but there were more trees up ahead.

"Aye," Gunthar continued, "the child must be Sir Damian's, born of some illicit union. But why choose the clothier to care for him?"

"Well," Sir John speculated, "you said the clothier's wife made dresses for the Lady Alyne. She must have been frequently about the castle, then. Perhaps she had a daughter who assisted her. A young and pretty daughter—"

"Whom Sir Damian seduced? Then what happened to her? For that child clearly believes Master Guillem and his wife to be his parents."

Sir John disposed of that objection easily. "Died in childbirth. Only parents he's ever known."

"But the brooch—"

"Stolen, perhaps, by the dress-maker. She'd surely have had opportunity, for she must have had access to her lady's chamber and known the insignia of her house. She probably wanted to be able to prove the child's parentage someday."

"That," Gunthar owned, "is possible, though if true, it seems a risky thing to be flaunting the evidence so near to Vere Castle. What if one of Sir Damian's men happened into the town and saw the child wearing the rose? Would he not carry news of it to his master—?"

"What ho! My lord, look out!"

Gunthar's head had been turned in conversation with Sir John, but it snapped round at Sir Thomas's shout. There was a horseman in the road up ahead. He had appeared suddenly from the trees and had a bow in his hands, taking aim—

Gunthar saw the arrow sail from the string and come whirring towards his breast. Instinctively he reared his horse to avoid the lethal confrontation. He heard a snap from somewhere beneath him and the next instant he felt himself flying backwards through the air.

He hit the ground with a thud, flat on his back. The force of the fall drove the air from his lungs. The bright sky above him swirled into darkness as he struggled for what seemed an eternity to regain his breath. But when his sight finally cleared, it was met with a shuddering vision—a pair of wildly flailing hooves thrashed the sky directly over his head.

With horror, he realized he had fallen into the path of one of his own advancing horsemen. He heard the beast scream and knew with a sickening lurch that its rider would not succeed in controlling the startled beast in time. The hooves were already descending. Gunthar closed his eyes and braced for the agonizing crunch that would signal the crushing of his skull.

A hand clamped on his arm and jerked him away, but he felt the rush of wind as one hoof struck the ground inches from his face. The other clipped his shoulder, making him groan in pain. It was a blow he welcomed gladly in exchange for his life. Thanks to—

He opened his eyes, but caught no more than a glimpse of a whitened, boyish face before a crowd of equally white-faced knights pushed his savior aside.

"Great heavens, Hugh, but that was close! Are you hurt?

Gunthar sat up and rubbed his shoulder. Sir John, kneeling at his side, saw the gesture and reached a hand to push away the torn cloth.

"It's nothing," Gunthar said, silently cursing the shaken way his voice came out. "A bruise only. It could have been worse." He glanced down at the purplish welt in his flesh, but a careful probing of the area assured him that his bones remained intact. "To whom do I owe my rescue?"

Sir John repeated the question to the other knights, and after several minutes a fifteen-year-old squire was pushed forward. A handsome youth, with a tousle of red-brown curls, he had a peculiarly gentle pair of clear blue eyes.

"What's your name, boy?" Gunthar asked as the squire dropped to one knee and bowed his head before his master.

"Brandon, sir, Brandon de Vexin."

Gunthar frowned. The name was only vaguely familiar. Not one of his vassals' sons, or men-at-arms'. "You are one of *my* squires?"

"Aye, my lord." Gunthar saw the way the shoulders sank at his failure to recognize the youth. "I am Sir Aumary de Vexin's son. He fought with the king at Le Mans."

Gunthar remembered now the Poitevin knight who had come to the king's aid there and helped turn the tide of battle. He had asked no other reward than that place be found for his younger son in some great nobleman's household. Gunthar had been deeply annoyed when the king had cast the boy upon himself. For the most part, Gunthar had ignored him, turning his welfare and training over to his marshal, Sir Roger Tollerton. He could not recall having even asked about the boy since then.

His indifference now filled him with shame, for it had surely taken a courageous heart to risk his life for a master who had shown him such callous neglect.

"Like a bolt of lightening he was, my lord," Sir Thomas Enslye exclaimed from where he stood behind the boy. "One moment I was reprimanding him for riding ahead of his place, the next he was out of his saddle— Saints! I thought sure he was done for when I saw him diving under those hooves!"

"It was the bird with the yellow crest," the boy whispered, as if it were necessary to explain his wayward actions. "At least, I thought it was yellow. I'd never seen its like before, and I rode ahead to get a better look. That's why I was out of my place—"

Gunthar laughed at the guilty apology. "Then I thank heaven for your curiosity. You saved my life, Brandon de Vexin, and you may be sure I will not forget you again."

The boy reddened with pleasure.

"My lord, perhaps you should have a look at this."

Gunthar's amusement faded at the sound of Challons' voice. The baron was not in the circle of knights who surrounded him, but called the recommendation from someplace nearby. Sir John lent Gunthar a hand to get to his feet, and the circle parted to let them through. Challons knelt over Gunthar's saddle, the defectiveness of which had been the cause of its master's close brush with death.

"The strap is broken," Challons said.

"I'd gathered that." Did the man think he was an idiot? "I am generally accounted a somewhat creditable horseman, my lord, not accustomed to easily surrendering my seat."

Challons flushed at the sarcasm, but said, "Aye, but you had more help than you think. The strap is not only broken—it has been cut."

*"What?"* That came from Sir John, who knelt to examine the saddle for himself. "He's right, Hugh. It was neatly sliced halfway through. The rest is clearly a tear, no doubt aggravated each time you mounted and dismounted your beast. But why did the grooms not catch it?"

"Because," Challons said, "it was dark when we arrived at Sir Hervé's and not yet light when we left today. The glow of their lanterns must not have been sufficient to expose it. The tear undoubtedly grew with each mile of the earl's weight until, at the critical moment of his horse's rearing, it snapped."

Gunthar mulled over all these suppositions, then said abruptly, "It was not dark when we left Pennault."

Sir John gasped, then exclaimed, "Sir Triston! It had to have been him." Gunthar hesitated, but Sir John shot to his feet, leaping eagerly to what seemed, after all, a fair conclusion. "I told you it was dangerous to let that man go. 'You'll rue it,' I said. I'll wager by the time you confronted him in Laurant's hall, he'd already been to the stables and cut the strap."

"He did not know I would be riding for Angoulême the same

day."

"No, he probably hoped you'd go hunting, instead. Had you fallen in the midst of a chase, it is unlikely even the most eagle-eyed squire could have saved you from the thundering hooves of your companions."

Gunthar stood silently chewing his lip, until another distraction arose. A contingent of his knights had gone after the archer, and they now returned with their prize. Sir Roger rode at their head, carrying the villain's bow. The other knights rode with drawn swords leveled at their captive. There was nothing remarkable about the man's countenance that Gunthar could see. He was dressed as an underling in a plain brown tunic, its severity enlivened only by the colorful badge sewn to his shoulder . . .

"Cur!" Sir John strode wrathfully forward. He dragged the man out of his saddle, then slammed him back against his horse. "You blackguardly villain! Tell us who paid you! Who paid you to try to murder the earl?"

The man seemed too stunned by this attack to respond. Sir John, in fury, raised a hand to strike him, but Gunthar caught his wrist.

"Nay, John, we needn't beat the truth out of him, when he wears the answer for all to see."

Sir John followed Gunthar's grim gaze and swore softly. There, sensuously coiled on the badge the man wore, was a mocking serpent-woman. And she seemed to be laughing at them.

Gunthar pushed his way past the guards of Count William of Angoulême. The hall echoed with raucous laughter from drunken, leering men sporting with their harlots and wallowing in a feast, which, from the looks of it, had been going on for hours. The aged count was not a whit behind his younger guests in his debauched enjoyment of the proceedings. A merry, willing wench sprawled across his lap, wantonly returning his lecherous kisses, to the hearty applause of the onlookers.

A fiercely handsome young man with thick waves of reddish-gold hair watched the scene from the center chair behind the table on the dais. The gleeful lasciviousness of his grin spoiled the beauty of his exquisitely molded mouth. His smooth cheeks were unbecomingly flushed with an overindulgence of wine. He possessed a graceful but powerful build, draped in a surcote of crimson layered with gold, and he appeared older than the nineteen years Gunthar knew him to be. He liked to play at being a man, but the way his pretty mouth turned down when his trencher mate pointed out Gunthar's arrival betokened nothing so much as a boy's sulking displeasure.

Gunthar strode up to the dais, dragging the captured archer by the collar, then threw him down so hard that he fell into a humiliating sprawl on the rush-strewn floor.

"I return to you your lackey," Gunthar snapped. "Next time, choose one with better aim."

Prince Richard Plantagenet stared with an admirable semblance of amazement at the fallen man. Then he returned his gaze to Gunthar, taking in his whitened, angry face and the torn sleeve of his surcote. The prince's deep blue eyes took on a derisive glitter, and his frowning lips twisted back up into a sneer. "It appears you have met with some mishap along your way."

The mockery provided the final fuse to Gunthar's sorely tried temper. "You treacherous, murderous whelp!" he exploded. "Were you my son, I should have you flogged within an inch of your life for this vile trick! The king may do it yet. When he learns of the vicious way you have tried to thwart him—and he *will* learn of it, be assured. If you doubt that, you are a fool, which is the one thing I have never suspected you of being—until now."

The prince gasped at this flagrantly insulting attack. "How dare you? How *dare* you speak to me like that?" He pushed himself to his feet, revealing what to most men would have been an intimidating height, but the huge amounts of wine he'd drunk rather spoiled the effect by causing him to sway precariously. He had to prop himself up with his hands flat on the tabletop. His slurring voice shook with a long-standing hatred. "You forget yourself, de Bury." He deliberately used Gunthar's family name as a reminder of the earl's inferior rank. "No matter what misguided value my father places on you, he will not overlook such insolence as this displayed before the royal blood."

Gunthar retorted, "Then start acting like a prince, and stop acting like a spoiled stripling who has been denied his own way. *This*—" he stabbed a toe into the cringing ribs of the prostrate archer "—will not be overlooked, either by me *or* the king, any more than your infernal dealings with de Brielle, and the devil only knows who else."

Here he shot an accusing glare at Count William, but the old man merely glowered back.

"I don't know what you're babbling about," the prince declared. "And who is that swine at your feet?"

Gunthar caught the archer's collar and dragged him up onto his knees. "Take a closer look, my prince. 'Tis your own henchman, the one you sent to murder me."

The prince gasped. "Murder—? I never—"

"Is he not one of yours? Does he not wear the sign of Melusine, the demonic ancestress of whom you boast?"

"Aye. That is, the badge is mine, worn by my retainers, but this man—I have never seen him before in my life. He must have stolen the insignia, or copied it—"

Gunthar snorted.

The prince's already flushed countenance flushed still darker. "Are you calling me a liar?"

"I think you would lie yourself into hell to spite your father. But I did not think you a coward, as well. This man risked his life for you. You might at least have the courage to acknowledge him. To accept responsibility, even for so devilish a plot as you have contrived, would be sign of maturity which might go a long way toward mitigating the king's anger at this new provocation."

"You go too far, de Bury. I will not be accused in this insulting manner of crimes that I did not commit. The king has made me governor of these domains, and I have done nothing to betray that trust."

"I did not conjure this assassin out of thin air, any more than I dreamed that my saddle was tampered with or imagined this stab-wound in my arm. As to the trust which was placed in you, it has been over eighteen months since you were charged with demolishing the rebels' fortifications, yet everywhere I look, I see illegal walls still standing. The king expects enforcement of the treaty which *you* signed, and if you are not man enough to do it yourself, then he has sent me with authority to complete the task in his name."

"Poitou and Aquitaine are *mine*!" the prince shouted. "My mother gave them to me, and I shall rule them as I please!"

He looked, Gunthar thought, suddenly very much like an enraged child, the same malicious little boy who had always been protected from his father's retribution by the arms of his adoring mother. It would not have been extravagant to say that young Richard was his mother's only love and obsession. Denied an active voice in the ruling of her own lands, the most the frustrated Eleanor had been able to do was to persuade the king that Aquitaine and Poitou should stand as inheritance to her favored second son. Henry had acquiesced, declaring young Richard Count of Poitou, even as he had confirmed his third son Duke of Brittany, and crowned his eldest co-regent in his father's lifetime. Henry had hoped thus to dispel all questions of succession which might arise at his death.

But while generous in dealing out titles and honors to his sons, the king retained real authority with himself. Considering the princes' youthful inexperience, Gunthar did not consider it surprising that he should do so. But thanks to their mother's jealous whisperings, the princes' restless resentments had finally erupted into open rebellion. And although ostensibly subdued by the war, it was clear from Prince Richard's outburst that he, at least, was far from reconciled to his defeat.

"Your mother," Gunthar said in response to the prince's complaint, "no longer has any say in this matter. And if you ever hope to rule her duchy free of your father's control, then prove yourself worthy of his faith by enforcing the terms of this treaty. Betray him but one more time, and on the king's own oath, he shall strip away every honor and possession he has granted you and divide them between your brothers."

A vein throbbed in the young prince's temple. "Never! I shall never surrender Aquitaine, and I shall not rest until my mother is free of that monster's tyranny!" His long, be-jeweled fingers clenched around his goblet and he raised the heavy object as though he meant to fling it at Gunthar's head.

Gunthar stood his ground. "Is that a declaration of war?"

Given the prince's impulsive temper and drunken fury, Gunthar was surprised to see him hesitate, then set the goblet back down.

"Nay, you will not back me into that corner. My father is triumphant, and I shall fulfill the treaty—in my own good time."

"In the king's time, rather," Gunthar warned. "And you might do well to start with our noble friend here. These walls of Angoulême should have come down months ago."

It was Count William who now shot to his feet, snarling, "Curse you, Gunthar, and the king as well! We will never bow the knee to one who is not of Aquitanian blood. We have been bullied by the Angevin long enough. We want our duchess freed and our rights acknowledged, and if it takes another war to do it—"

"William—" Prince Richard looked alarmed by Count William's provocative threat, but his protest failed to check his host.

"We do not fear Henry of Anjou and his legions!" Count William shouted. "Let him come to us, let him do his worst. He will find that the prince still stands with us."

"Aye," Gunthar retorted, "I have long suspected who it was who pulled his strings. You are a clever little puppet master, Angoulême, but the play is about to come to an end. By heaven, I shall yet see you humbled in chains before the king!" He swung back to the prince. "As for you, my lord, you had better choose your side and choose it carefully. I give you thirty days. If by then you have made no move to enforce the treaty, I shall take matters into my own hands. And if you think to stop me with such cretins as this—" he threw the archer up onto the dais "—then you have badly underestimated the alertness of my guards and my own determination. You will find me at Pennault Castle when you have made up your mind."

He did not give the prince time to respond, but turned on his heel and strode out of the hall as furiously as he had stormed in.

# Nine

For what seemed like the hundredth time, Heléne rubbed her hand fiercely across her mouth, determined to banish the memory of Gunthar's kiss.

"What is it, sister? Can you not sleep?"

The query checked Heléne's gesture. She rolled onto her side in the bed and gazed at Clothilde where she sat before the hearth in their chamber.

"No more than you, it seems. What troubles you, Clo?"

She thought her sister blushed, but it may have only been the effect of the flames warming her fair cheeks.

"I am not troubled. A little anxious, perhaps. No, no, not that. I mean—" Clothilde sounded distracted. Then she sighed and uttered plaintively, "I wish I could read, like you. It would help the time to pass more quickly."

"Why, Clo, are you waiting for something?"

Clothilde turned her face away from her sister's gaze, back to the hearth. "I mean, perhaps it would make me sleepy. You say it makes you so, sometimes."

"Sometimes." Heléne wished she had such a book now, something to take her mind off— She pushed herself up from the pillows. "Do you wish me to sit with you? If you'd like to talk—"

"No, no, please lay back down." The plea came with a breathless urgency. Clothilde added, "You must be tired. You tossed and turned terribly last night. Please try to sleep. Do not worry for me, I will join you soon."

Heléne sank back onto the pillows, then turned her back to the fire. Sleep. Clothilde was right, it had eluded her entirely the night before. Every time she closed her eyes, she had been haunted by his face, that proud, arrogant countenance with its piercing eyes and haughty mouth . . .

Oh, saints! Her heart leapt into her throat again and she felt her blood begin to pound. It had been well over thirty-six hours since she had found herself clasped in Gunthar's arms and felt his haughty mouth on hers. How could the memory still be so vivid?

She stared at the shadows playing on the wall and tried not to feel the sting of tears in her eyes. She hated him! He had made a fool of her, tricking her into that involuntary response. She had been caught unawares that once, but with every ounce of will she possessed, she vowed it would never happen again. She might be inexperienced, but she was not naive. She was quite certain that if she succumbed to Gunthar's charms, she would soon find herself abandoned and scorned. Her ready imagination conjured up a long train of languishing beauties, weeping pathetically over the inconstant love of their earl.

Love. No, a man like he would not know the meaning of the word. It was an insulting, debasing passion he doled out to women like favors, and if he expected her to surrender like the others—

Her throat tightened painfully. No, that could not have been what he wanted of her. She was not pretty enough, not graceful or shapely or even witty. Awareness of her own inadequacies made the game he'd played with her all the more cruel. She choked back a hiccoughing sob. She would not give him the satisfaction of knowing how deeply he'd hurt her. When next they met, she would show herself cool and composed, and utterly indifferent to his presence. And she would never, never let him come near enough to ever touch her again.

Heléne heard a click and raised her head. "Clo, did you hear—" She sat up and glanced towards the fire. "*Clo?*"

Her sister was gone.

Heléne sprang from the bed and ran to the door, pulling it open just in time to see the swish of a skirt vanish around the corner of the shadowed passageway. Where on earth was Clothilde going at this hour of the night? It was not like her timid sister to go prowling about in the dark. Was she meeting someone?

Heléne closed the door and crossed to the window. She pulled back a shutter. The bailey below was bathed white in the light of a full moon. She waited uneasily, and within minutes her suspicions were confirmed. Two figures appeared in the yard, the smaller wearing a concealing cloak and hood, but with a gliding, feminine gait. The other . . .

Heléne gasped. In the revealing glow of the moonlight there could be no mistaking Gunthar's squire, Julian Parr. The red-gold ringlets draped his shoulders as delicately as a girl's. The youth was supposed to be laid up in his bed, seized with an ailment that had prevented him accompanying his master to Angoulême. But he looked hale enough now as he stood conferring with Clothilde below. They conversed for several minutes, then Clothilde pointed in a westerly direction and Julian gave a curt nod. He drew her hand through his arm and led her off the way she had gestured.

Heléne felt a sickening dread spread through her. Of all the men in the world that Clothilde should choose to spite Gunthar with—! How could she be so mad? Heléne thought again of that moment on the archery field when Gunthar's penetrating gaze had seemed to probe the very recesses of her soul. Whatever the squire's powers of self-possession, Clothilde would never succeed in resisting that discerning gaze. And when Gunthar returned from Angoulême to find himself insulted and betrayed by the woman he had determined to marry, what punishments might his proud, haughty spirit inflict, not only upon her sister, but upon their entire family?

Heléne had to warn them. She had to stop them!

She pulled on the loose woolen gown she had tossed off only a few hours before, slid on her slippers, and ran from the room without bothering to take up her cloak. She hesitated only a moment in the bailey before turning her steps determinedly towards the postern in the west wall. She knew exactly where Clothilde would have led Julian for their rendezvous. She followed their direction into the woods that lay on this side of the castle, marveling at the unexpected courage of her sister. Poor, quivering Clothilde, indulging in secret assignations with the squire of her own betrothed. It almost made Heléne laugh to think how chagrined Gunthar would be. If he learned of it—which, regrettably, she dared not allow.

She pushed aside a low-hanging branch, straining to make out the obscure trail on the forest floor. The trees made the moonlight erratic, but Heléne knew the path by heart. As Clothilde did. There was a clearing up ahead where she and Heléne and Therri their brother, and Etienne de Brielle had played as children. They had called it 'Clothilde's Bower', where Clothilde, beautiful as a faery sprite even then, had sat enthroned on a fallen log, draped in one of their mother's cast off, fur-trimmed cloaks. Therri and Etienne had pretended to be gallant knights come to win the hand of the glorious princess, while Heléne had usually been consigned to the unsatisfying role of Clothilde's lady-in-waiting.

It was years now since she had visited the clearing, but she had no doubt that Clothilde remembered it as well as she—nor that it would make an ideal trysting place for a pair of covert lovers. Heléne shook away the memories and cursed Gunthar again for luring her sister into this dreadful trap. Had he only stayed in England, had he not placed Clothilde in temptation's way by bringing to Pennault his handsome squire—-

She stopped. There was someone up ahead, blocking her path. She took a quick step backwards, then stopped again, realizing the figure, a man, had his back to her and had not heard her approach. The clearing was not far now. She eased her way off the path, thankful that her soft-soled slippers made no sound. She moved several feet to the figure's right, then resumed her advance, darting from tree to tree to block her movements from his view. She rounded the figure and passed him, then, overcome by curiosity, stopped and peeked around a shielding tree. A slim, pale shaft of moonlight fell across his face, but it was enough to catch the fiery gleam of his tresses. Julian Parr—and he was alone!

*Where was Clothilde?* In sudden panic for her sister, Heléne almost screamed the question at him. Then she forced herself to choke back her fear. Surely Julian would not be standing there like a stock if Clothilde were in danger? For some unfathomable reason, she must have gone ahead without him. Heléne started forward again, her heart beating like a drum as, against her own reasoned judgment, she envisioned her sister the victim of a dozen harrowing scenes. Then she heard voices, one of them Clothilde's. She had finally reached the clearing.

She glanced over her shoulder, but she could no longer see Julian. The trees had become thickly interspersed with bushes the height of a man. She had no trouble concealing herself behind them to spy on the couple beyond. The squire had been no more than an escort. This must be the true object of Clothilde's frustrated passions, this tall, slender stranger with pale, tightly crimped curls falling to his shoulders and—

Heléne gasped. *No, it could not be him.* She strained her eyes against the shadows, but she could not make out his features in the uneven light. Clothilde had not put back the hood of her cloak, but her quick, fluttering movements betrayed her agitation. Voices, male and female, whispered elusively in the air, too soft for Heléne to make out the words until Clothilde's voice rose, almost in a shriek.

"You said he would be here! You promised! I would never have come if—"

"Hush." The stranger tried to calm her, but Heléne recognized the nervous hysteria which kept her sister's voice high and shrill.

"You liar! It was all a trick! I suppose you brought me here to try again to seduce me!"

"You were not so averse to my attentions before your husband died."

The stranger's response grew sharp, and Heléne's heart leapt as she recognized his voice. It was he, the same man who had approached her on the river bank and deceived her with that empty letter, using her to gain information about Gunthar, in return, he had made her believe, for her father's safety. And now he was trying to use Clothilde, too! Heléne's indignation nearly carried her into the clearing to her sister's defense, but the stranger's next words froze her in her tracks.

"But for me, my dearest heart, you would not now be a widow

and able to indulge yourself with blissful dreams of being reunited with your erstwhile lover."

"I never asked you to do what you did!" Clothilde cried.

"You asked me to help you. You said you would fly to the ends of the earth with me to escape your miserable life with Sir Fulbert."

"Oh, you fiend! How can you be so cruel? You said you loved me, and I—"

The rest was lost as Clothilde burst into tears. The stranger's voice lowered as he sought to quiet her.

Heléne felt stunned. Had Clothilde truly sought to betray her violent, vengeful husband, Sir Fulbert?

"Hush, my sweet. We will not speak of it again. I suppose it was too much to hope that a poor, persecuted knight such as myself could win the hand of so gentle and fair a lady."

The stranger's lament floated softly on the evening air, but Heléne sensed a subtle edge of mockery in the words. She saw her sister put up a hand to the stranger's face and heard her trembling reply.

"I did not mean to hurt you, Garoux. Only—only I did not think I would ever see *him* again."

"And I do not wish to pain you, but you deserve to know the truth ere you surrender your heart to him again. He has not been true to you. It was I who delivered you from that shameful marriage, while he dallied away his time and passions on a harlot in lady's clothing, unworthy even to kiss the hem of your gown."

Clothilde withdrew her hand, the quaver in her voice deepening. "It—it is true, then?"

"I have seen them together myself. Ask him—"

"Ask me what, Rousillon?"

Heléne jumped at the new, hard-edged voice that broke across the stranger's words. The branches directly across from her were pulled back to allow a third person into the clearing. Again she could not see his face, but this time she did not need to. The voice was enough, being one she had been familiar with all her life.

"Triston! Oh, Triston, I was afraid you would not come!"

From the impassioned way Clothilde threw herself into the

newcomer's arms, Heléne could not doubt that this, at last, was the man her sister had truly come to meet. Triston de Brielle. It made blindingly more sense than had Julian Parr, or even this sinister stranger. Clothilde and Triston had known one another forever. Heléne felt a rush of relief. If it were *he* her sister was in love with—

Her stomach clenched again. No matter how much she knew Triston to be completely honorable and trustworthy, the Earl of Gunthar was convinced he was just the opposite. Heléne had been told of the violent confrontation that had resulted in Triston's eviction from Pennault Castle. Poor Triston was under a dangerous enough cloud without adding the folly of being in love with Gunthar's betrothed. When Gunthar learned of *this*—

"Well, now, my lady." The stranger spoke again. "You see how I keep my word. I assured you he would be here—"

"No thanks to you," Triston cut him off. "Did you think I would not guess who arranged that clever little goose chase to delay my arrival? I'm growing sick and tired of your games, Rousillon."

"I don't know what you are talking about," the stranger said. "Why, it was entirely due to my sympathy for your apparently hopeless plight that I arranged for this rendezvous between you and your adored."

The epithet that Triston flung at him made Heléne blush even in the dark. But the stranger only laughed.

"I will lay down your bad temper to some quarrel with your father, and bid you 'good-night'. I can see my offices here are no longer required."

He bowed and departed the same way that Triston had come. Triston half-turned, as if to assure himself the stranger had truly gone, then turned back at Clothilde's pitiful cry.

"Oh, Triston, I would not have blamed you if you had stayed away. After what I did—"

"It was not your fault," Triston said softly, gathering up her hands. "I expected too much of you."

There was a sob in Clothilde's voice as she answered, "No, no, I swore you an oath and I broke it."

"You swore to love me. Has that changed?"

"Oh, no, no! You must believe—"

"I do. Oh, my heart, I do! And I have never stopped loving you."

He put back the hood of her cloak and kissed her.

Heléne had not felt the least guilt about spying on her sister until now. But there was something so tender, so intimate about the embrace with Triston that she found herself backing away. What would happen when Gunthar returned she shuddered to think, but that trouble would come soon enough. Let them take what happiness they could from one another tonight.

She turned back towards the castle and found a looming shadow in her path. At first she thought it was Julian Parr and cast about in her mind for some way to explain her presence. Then the shadow stepped towards her, solidifying into a man, and she shrank in dread of the truth.

"Do not cry out, my lady. We should not like to disturb the lovers."

"Come one step closer and I shall scream for Triston," Heléne warned.

The man stopped, but said, "He would be of little help to you if I truly wished to harm you—which I do not. Come, my lady—"

"Stay back. You are a liar and a fiend, and I'll have no further dealings with you, Monsieur de Rousillon."

She caught a gleam of white teeth against the darkness. "So, you know my name. Such a clever little eavesdropper had best have a care where she places her ears. I have cut off pretty ones like yours before."

Heléne shivered. There was such a chill in the soft-voiced threat that she was tempted to believe him. But she only repeated, "You lied. There was never any letter from my father."

"I assure you there was, and is. You may have it yet—for a price."

"I have paid your price once and you proved yourself naught but a cheat. I'll not spy for you again."

He waved a hand. "Spies I have aplenty, thanks to le Reynard. He is quite as ruthless as I and resides much closer to your hearth, so I would think twice about repeating anything you may have seen or heard here this night. My confederate's eyes will be upon you—as will mine."

His confederate. A spy in her father's house? Had he bribed one of her father's guards, or—no, of course. It was not her father he wished to spy on, but Gunthar. And who better to serve as informant on Gunthar than the earl's own squire?

"Julian Parr?"

"I will say nothing more. Keep silence, and your father's safety is assured. But speak my name once, and not only will his treason be revealed, but you shall taste my vengeance upon your own body." He paused to allow the menace of this threat to sink in. Then he stepped aside, saying harshly, "Go, begone. Before I decide to drive home the lesson now."

Heléne shivered again. It took no more than a feinting gesture from him to send her flying down the forest path.

# Ten

Sir Stephen Goldingham circled the tall, pale complexioned young lady standing in the center of the hall, eyeing her with a critical gaze. While she appeared quite slender, the subtle color in her cheeks, which he laid down to maidenly embarrassment, was not enough to relieve the disappointing angularity of her features. And he feared that sparkle in her light blue eyes bespoke too lively a spirit for his master's taste. But his master was in little position to quibble.

"I suppose she will do," he pronounced at last. "We had hoped she would possess a least a few of your elder daughter's graces. But she is not repulsive and my master agrees to the marriage, so long as the Northumberland land is included in her dowry."

Laurant bristled at this blunt disparagement of his younger daughter, but his wife caught his eye, so he formed his reply carefully. "Well, now, I presume that is what we are here to discuss. That land is quite valuable to me and is not to be given up without adequate consideration."

"Come, gentlemen, sit," the Lady Gwenllian invited, offering Sir Stephen one of her brilliant smiles. "Eudes here will fetch you some wine while you exchange your terms."

Sir Stephen flicked another disappointed glance at the young lady. "Very well. But on one point my master stands firm. He insists that the marriage take place in England and that your daughter accompany us on our return there, to await her nuptials in my master's house."

"Agreed," the Lady Gwenllian said before her husband could object. "We shall see her made ready in good time. Come, Heléne, let us leave these men to their business."

With a satisfied smile, she swept her daughter out of the hall.

Heléne held her tongue until she and her mother reached the bedchamber. Sybil was there, evidently summoned beforehand in anticipation of this very moment. To the old nurse, her mother imparted a rapid spate of instructions regarding the assembling of a wedding trousseau.

"New cloth must be purchased and seamstresses summoned and set to work around the clock if necessary, to see that all is ready in time for the English delegation's departure. It is not necessary," her mother added, "to hire the best, so long as they are competent enough to achieve an effect of comfortable wealth. It is not, after all, as though Heléne is making a truly exceptional marriage, such as Clothilde is about to do."

"But, Mama," Heléne said, "I do not wish to marry Heywood."

The Lady Gwenllian stared at Heléne as though she had just been treated to a remark of incomprehensible stupidity. "I beg your pardon?"

Heléne thought wistfully of the new gowns. Even had they been of no more than middling quality, they would at least have included the gaiety of a little embroidery and might even have fit. But such a pleasure could not be thought worth the price.

"I do not wish to marry Lord Heywood. And what's more, I *won't* marry him."

"You will do as you are told," her mother informed her, and turned back to resume her commands to the nurse.

Heléne expected her mother to be angry. It had been two weeks since she had learned of the projected betrothal. She should have spoken sooner, before Sir Stephen arrived. To reject Lord Heywood now would be considered nothing short of an insult of the worst sort. But in all the turmoil of Gunthar's arrival, in her worry for Etienne and her fears for Clothilde and Triston, Heléne had forgotten about the threat to her own future.

Until she had been forced to stand in her father's hall and endure the humiliating experience of Sir Stephen's inspection.

"I won't marry him," she said again. "I won't be sold in this degrading way to a man I have never seen, merely to advance your and Papa's ambition."

Her mother swung about and slapped her. "How dare you speak to me like that? You will do as you are told."

Heléne raised a hand to her stinging cheek, but said, "I won't. The Church requires my consent, and nothing you can do will make me give it."

Her mother rewarded her with a contemptuous stare. "Perhaps you are not aware what a singular piece of good fortune Heywood's offer is? I realize you cannot view yourself as the rest of the world may, but let me assure you that you are woefully inadequate for obtaining a husband in any way other than this. No man would give such ungainliness a second glance. That Heywood is willing to take you sight unseen should be accounted a blessing. Reject him and you shall end your days a dismal spinster."

Heléne choked back the hurt of these words, but they were not enough to sway her. "I don't care. Then I shall join a nunnery. But I won't marry—"

"A nunnery?" Her mother cut her off with a trill of laughter. "How absurd. It may, in truth, be where you belong. But Heywood's offer is too good to refuse. You will marry him, and there's an end to it."

"I won't!"

Her mother's delicate mouth tightened as she eyed her rebellious daughter. "Sybil." She spoke the name quietly. The old nurse came forward, her gnarled hand resting on one end of the switch tucked into her girdle. Her mother's eyes never wavered from Heléne. "I will not be withstood in this pert way. Kneel by the bed."

Heléne glared at the cronish figure behind her mother. The

grimace on the wrinkled face almost betokened glee.

"Kneel," her mother repeated, "or I will take up the switch myself."

Heléne hesitated, then swallowed hard and walked over to the bed. She knelt down facing it and tried to suppress a tremor of dread as Sybil pushed her roughly down. There was a moment of silence as Sybil readied her switch. Then Heléne heard and felt the snap as it fell smartly across her back.

She winced, gasping at the stinging line of fire it left in her flesh. She dug her hands into the bedclothes and tried to brace herself better for the second blow. It fell higher across her shoulders, as startling and searing as the first. She pressed her face deeper into the covers. *Three, four* . . . The fifth blow fell with a particularly sharp smack. It nearly made her cry out, but she bit down hard on a thick wad of blanket and tried to squeeze back the tears. *Six, seven, eight* . . . A loud sob welled up in her throat, but her self-imposed gag muffled it into a groan. *Nine, ten* . . .

"Enough," her mother said, "for now."

The hail of blows ceased, but Heléne continued to cling to the bedclothes. Her whole body felt hot and flushed.

"If you think I am not able to bring this marriage about," her mother said, "then you are sadly mistaken. The beating will be repeated every day if need be until you come to your senses."

Heléne turned her head and felt the saliva-soaked bedding beneath her cheek. "I won't marry him."

"So your sister said. She bore the rod as well, with more courage than I would have credited her timorous spirit. It did not break her will, either. Obviously, I cannot lock you away so long as Sir Stephen is here, and as he expects to carry you back with him to England . . ."

There fell a silence, but Heléne hardly cared what might come next. Her back felt as though it had been set afire.

"It may be, milady," came Sybil's cunning voice, "that the Lady Heléne's trousseau would be completed more efficiently at Beaulac Castle."

There was another pause before the Lady Gwenllian said, "That is very clever of you, Sybil. It is, after all, where we finally persuaded

Clothilde, though we have not such ready means at our hands this time. But I shall think of something. Be assured of that, Heléne. If 'twas not the rod that finally broke your sister's spirits, she was broken nonetheless. As you shall be, by whatever means it takes. Until then, see you whip her daily, Sybil. I shall make arrangements for a visit to Beaulac as soon as the marriage contract is signed."

Heléne waited until they were gone, then slid off the bed. She pushed the neck of her gown aside and reached a hand to feel behind her shoulder. She flinched as her fingers found a painful welt. How she hated Sybil and her fiendish switch! But the promise of further beatings did not dismay her as much as her mother's mention of Beaulac. Heléne knew nothing of her father's manor on the border near La Marche, save that her mother and Sybil had taken Clothilde there shortly before her marriage to Sir Fulbert. Clothilde had returned looking like a ghost. Her mother's confidence that Heléne would cease her rebellion once shut away there as well gave her younger daughter pause.

She wondered if the secret of Beaulac was the cause of her sister's nightmares? Whatever the answer, the dreams had ceased in the last two weeks. There were no more terrified awakenings, no troubled moanings in her sleep. In daylight hours, a glow of happiness suffused Clothilde's cheeks. And nearly every night, Heléne felt her sister slip from the bed and knew that she went to meet Triston.

Heléne had not had the heart to spoil Clothilde's joy by reminding her of Gunthar. Rumor had it he was conducting inspections of rebel fortresses throughout the county. But he was likely to return to Pennault any day and he was sure to come demanding a formal betrothal. What might he do to Triston when he learned the truth? The knight was already in disgrace, both for his brother's misdeed and for his father's alleged defiance of the treaty. If Gunthar took it into his mind to crush the hapless knight, Heléne had no doubt that he would do it.

She did not know how she could stop him, but she was determined to try. But she would need a clear mind to do so, and just now her throbbing back made it difficult to concentrate on anything but her own discomfort. She pulled her gown gingerly back up around her shoulders, wincing as the cloth chafed against the welts. A little primrose would help to relieve the soreness. She pulled herself to her feet and went to find a servant to apply the salve.

Pride held Heléne silent through the next two days of Sybil's discipline, but on the third morning she was brought awake by the crack of the rod across her back. Caught at the vulnerable moment between waking and sleeping, she was not prepared for the violent assault. The hail of blows paralyzed her, preventing her from rolling away as pride dissolved into gasping screams. She scarcely noticed when the agonizing volley ceased. She lay trembling and moaning until the anguish in her back subsided enough to allow a shrieking voice to break through.

"Vile, evil woman! Let me have it!"

Heléne turned her head. Clothilde had sprung from the bed and was attempting to wrestle away Sybil's switch. The old woman waved the weapon over her head, trying to keep it out of reach.

"Now, lamb, do not carry on so. 'Twas your mother's orders, and 'tis only to tame your sister's spirits a little."

But Clothilde screamed, "Give it me, give it me!"

Twice she tried to leap high enough to catch the switch and when she failed, Clothilde lashed out with a sharp kick to the old woman's shins. Sybil gasped and doubled at the pain, and Clothilde finally succeeded in tearing the weapon out of her hand.

Sybil's tiny eyes widened. She backed away as Clothilde raised the switch in the air. Heléne pushed herself up and stared. Her sister's delicate features were twisted, distorted into the shrieking image of a half-crazed stranger.

Sybil cowered before the sight and whimpered, "Dearest mistress, I pray ye have mercy."

Clothilde swung the switch dangerously near the old woman's face. "Mercy? *Mercy?* What mercy had you on me when my mother tore my heart away?"

The old woman cringed. "Nay, mistress, I had no choice. But I have begun to make things right—"

"By whipping my sister, as you did me?"

"'Twas your mother's command. To make her consent to the marriage."

"Liar! You only do it for spite!"

"Nay, mistress, I swear—"

*"Get out!"*

The fury on Clothilde's face and another warning swish of the switch finally sent Sybil scurrying through the door as fast as her ancient bones would carry her.

Heléne sat up slowly, holding her breath. She could not believe what she had just witnessed, Clothilde acting like a madwoman, as if some unspeakable demon had seized possession of her sister's gentle body. That terrible, frightening hatred lingered in Clothilde's eyes. Heléne dared not say a word until the switch finally began to lower from its threatening position in the air.

"Cl-Clothilde?" she whispered then.

A convulsive shudder ran through Clothilde's body, then the switch clattered to the floor and she raised shaking hands to her face.

"Clo!"

Heléne forgot her injuries and sprang from the bed. *This* was the Clothilde she knew, trembling and shrinking from the world. She threw her arms around her sister.

"There, Clo, there, she is gone. Come and sit beside me until you feel better."

She led Clothilde to the bed and they sat together. Clothilde's head sank down to Heléne's shoulder as she wept, "Oh, Heléne, what shall I do?"

"About what, dearest?"

"About everything! About the earl and—"

"—Triston?"

Clothilde's head bounced up. "You know? Oh, but you could not!" She looked terrified.

Heléne answered quickly to calm her. "I followed you that first night you met him in the woods. I saw you go off with the earl's squire and I was afraid he had designs on you. But when I saw it was Triston you had gone to meet—"

"Oh! Then that is all you saw?"

Heléne hesitated. Was Clothilde afraid she had observed her encounter with the stranger as well? The delicate face, restored to its familiar if nervous beauty, waited anxiously for Heléne's answer.

"Yes," she lied. "I saw you fall into Triston's arms and I realized you loved him, and I felt ashamed to be spying on you, so I came back home."

Clothilde began to cry again. "Oh, Heléne, I love him so much! But I am afraid of Mama and the earl."

Clothilde had not seemed so fearful a few moments ago. It had clearly been too much to hope that such fortitude could last. "You must be strong, Clo. No one can make you marry Gunthar if you do not wish to."

"Mama will find a way. She did before. Triston says he forgives me, but he does not know all. What if Mama tells him—" Clothilde's voice broke, then rose to a frenzied shrillness. "It was not my fault! I was too weak to stop them. I tried—Heléne, I *tried.* But what if Triston will not believe me? How could he ever forgive me for that? And if he leaves me because of it— Oh, how I wish that I had died too!"

"Hush, Clo." Heléne could not begin to understand the meaning of this incoherent recital, but she tried to stem it before Clothilde's emotions carried her too far. She put her arms around her again and fought the hysteria with soft, soothing words, repeating over and over that Triston loved her, that he would understand, that he would forgive her anything. The moanings quieted until at last Clothilde looked up with a grateful smile.

"Oh, Heléne, what should I do without you? If only I had a tenth of your courage."

Heléne pushed the damp hair away from her sister's tear-stained face. "Then you must borrow a little from me. I will help you, Clo, I promise. We shall find a way for you and Triston to be together."

"But how?"

"You could run away together, before Gunthar returns. If we plan it carefully enough—" Clothilde shook her head. Heléne felt some impatience at her timidity. "It is what I shall do," she declared, "to escape Lord Heywood. I have already decided. When Mama and Sybil take me to Beaulac, I am going to—"

"What?"

"I said I am going to run away, just as soon as—"

"No! Beaulac— Oh, Heléne, you must not let them take you there!"

Clothilde's face went ghastly white, such as it often did before she fell into a swoon. She caught Heléne's hands and gripped them so tightly it hurt clear to the bone.

"Clo—"

"Heléne, it is an evil place. Filled with cruelty and malevolence and—heaven help me—blood! If once they have you there, you will never be able to escape."

Heléne tried to free her hands and failed. "They cannot keep me there forever," she said, hoping her matter-of-factness would preempt the renewed hysteria in her sister's voice. "Even if I am not able to escape, I will never give in to Mama's demands and eventually she will have to admit defeat and bring me home again."

"She won't, she will never do so. Oh, Heléne, you do not know her. You think her hard and pitiless, but she is much worse than that. She is—she is evil!"

"Clothilde!" Even allowing for the overwrought state of her sister's nerves, Heléne was shocked.

"It is true! You must not go to Beaulac. They will destroy you if you do."

"Clo—"

"They will destroy you! They will take everything from you, everything you care about, everything you are, until you are naught but an empty shell. And when you return you will do anything they say, no matter how loathsome or vile . . . simply because it will not matter any more." She let go of Heléne's hands and covered her face on a pathetic sob.

Heléne sighed. She could not take seriously all these ranting accusations, but she was sorry for her sister's distress. Of their mother's cruelty she had no doubt. Her back still ached from its latest evidence. But all this talk of blood and evil? Was it possible the trauma of Clothilde's first marriage had somehow unhinged her mind a little?

Heléne recoiled from the thought and hastily pushed it away.

"Calm yourself, Clo, these tears will avail us nothing. We must both stay calm and think clearly if we are to evade the traps Mama has set for us."

Clothilde gulped back another sob. "But wh-what can we do?"

"I have already said. The easiest thing is to run away."

"Yes, but Triston will not. I have already begged him to, but he says he cannot leave so long as Etienne remains in danger."

Etienne. Heléne had not exactly forgotten about him, but the memory of Gunthar's bleak warning had effectively dissuaded her from trying to interfere. Until now. She had chided Clothilde for her timidity, but Heléne had been no better, abandoning a friend at risk merely because she had been intimidated by Gunthar's arrogant manner. Poor Etienne had been shut away in the tower for more than a fortnight, and heaven only knew what abuses had been heaped upon him there. Heléne was ashamed of herself. How had she stood aside and done nothing for so long?

"Clothilde, are you going to meet Triston again?"

Clothilde hesitated, then nodded. "Tonight. Julian was going to take me to the clearing after you had fallen asleep."

"You need not wait for that. Tell Triston to make arrangements for our escape. We will need horses and money and a place to hide when they come looking for us. You will take me with you, won't you? And Etienne?"

"Oh, Heléne, you have a plan?" Clothilde's eyes glowed with sudden hope.

"I think I know a way to free Etienne," Heléne answered cautiously, "but the rest will be up to Triston. We shall none of us be safe near Pennault or Vere after this. So long as Etienne stands accused of treason, we shall all bear a part of his alleged guilt. Clothilde, we may never see our home again."

Saying it aloud was more difficult than Heléne had anticipated. Pennault was the only home she had ever known. It would not be easy to leave its warm, strong walls, to never see her father's face again or hear the full, hearty sound of his laughter. But then, she reminded herself, she would lose just as much were she to allow herself to be packed off to England.

"Heléne, how soon shall I tell Triston?"

Heléne thought it over. She wished they had more time, but the imminent return of Gunthar would not permit them that luxury. "I will try to see Etienne tomorrow," she said. "And the day after that . . . Tell Triston to meet us in the clearing two nights from now."

Clothilde nodded and hugged her with a tearful exclamation of gratitude and faith.

The biggest hurdle, Heléne knew, would be getting past the guard. Her strategy led her to the kitchens. But when she entered the passageway affixing the cooking area to the hall, she found Audiart there before her. The servant held a tray in her hands and the torches set in the walls threw their light brilliantly on the fiery locks of her companion. Heléne recognized Julian Parr. Audiart looked frightened. She seemed to be pleading for something. Was Julian threatening her in some way?

"Audiart?"

The girl jumped at the sound of Heléne's voice and the tray would have clattered to the floor had Julian not caught it. He turned, looking startled but not particularly embarrassed.

"My lady." He bowed with the tray and came up with an engaging smile. "I woke early this morning and found myself ravenous after so many days of fever. I was on my way to beg some relief from the cook when I encountered this lovely creature on a mission of mercy to some other poor wretch. And she, heartless woman, refuses to allow me even a taste of these simple victuals."

Heléne eyed the tray. An insipid-looking soup had been poured into a thick, wooden bowl alongside a roll of hard bread and a tarnished mug of ale. With the palatable aromas of fresh, early-morning baking floating from the nearby kitchen, she doubtful even a starving man would have spared this dreary collation a second glance. And Julian did not look to be either starving or ill.

"I am happy to see you recovered," Heléne said, "but I am sure you will find something much more appetizing in the kitchen. Audiart will show you the way."

"Oh, but mistress, I must take this to the young master in the tower," Audiart protested, taking the tray back from Julian.

Heléne had hoped for just such an opportunity as this. She said, "I will do it for you. After so lengthy an illness, I don't doubt the earl's squire finds himself weak and in need of a nourishing meal."

She reached for the tray and found, to her surprise, that Audiart would not give it up.

"Nay, mistress, it is my duty."

"No one will know. Let me have it."

"Please, mistress, I daren't. Sybil will beat me if she finds out."

"I am quite sure the earl's squire can protect you."

"But mistress—"

"Audiart, I am not asking you. Give me the tray."

Heléne caught a movement from the corner of her eye that might have signaled a nod of Julian's head, but when she looked, the squire was standing perfectly still, observing the squabble with naught but a mild interest. Audiart let the tray go.

"Very well, mistress."

Heléne sent them both a suspicious glance, but the squire only smiled again and bore Audiart off to the kitchen.

The guard looked none too pleased to be confronted with his master's younger daughter. He demanded to know what had happened to the serving wench. Heléne lied and said she was ill. She was terrified lest Gunthar had left instructions to have her barred from the tower. But apparently he had expected his warning to be sufficient, for although the guard sniffed disapprovingly, he unlocked the door without further question.

Heléne had not realized the chamber was windowless. There was naught but a single candle on a trestle table to relieve the lowering darkness.

She turned angrily on the guard. "Fetch us more lights. It is outrageous to make Etienne suffer in the dark."

"Milady, your father left no orders for—"

"I don't care what your orders were. *Fetch us more lights.*"

The guard hesitated, then bowed and backed out of the room. She heard the lock turn in the door, then went to set the tray on the table.

"Heléne?"

She turned. The only other piece of furniture appeared to be a wooden bench. The shadows were too deep to let her make out the figure reclining there, but she knew his voice at once.

"Yes, Etienne, it is I. I have come to help you." He sat up and she went to sit beside him. Impulsively, she put her arms about his neck and found his whole body cold. "Oh, poor thing! How dreadful it must be for you. I'm so sorry I did not come sooner, but I had no notion they were treating you like *this.*"

"It has not been so bad," he murmured, returning her embrace rather awkwardly. "They've pretty much left me alone to think upon my fate."

She felt him shiver and knew it was not from the cold. She had been half-afraid that he would not want to see her, that he would blame her for the warning that had landed him in this cell. But from the way his arm tightened around her waist, she knew that her fears had been for naught.

"Come over here," she invited, "so we can see one another better."

He stood up and helped her move the bench nearer the table. She observed that he only used his left hand, but it was not until they were seated again in the candle's light that she saw the bandaged splint on his right.

"Your wrist! What happened to it?"

Etienne laid his injured member gingerly along the tabletop. "It's broken. Lord Challons bound it up."

"Broken? How? Have they beaten you?"

He shook his head. "Nay, they've not laid a hand on me. It was the earl—"

"The earl? The earl broke your wrist?"

"Heléne—"

"Oh! I knew he was a bully, but I did not think he was as villainous as this!" Outrage drove her to her feet. "He is worse than a villain. He must be a very devil if he would resort to so vile a tactic to make you say what he wants to hear. It was that, wasn't it? He wants you to confess to treason, and he will use any vicious means to make you do so!"

"Yes—no— Heléne, stop!" Etienne reached for her arm, but she was so angry that she danced away. "Yes, they want me to confess, but I have not even spoken with the earl. It happened in the hall when we struggled and he took the dagger away."

Fresh alarm at this memory brought her back to his side. "Oh, Etienne, where did you get so dreadful a blade? Never say the prince gave it to you and sent you to murder the earl?"

To her horror, Etienne hesitated.

"Etienne?"

"I have never met the prince. I don't know how that blade came to be in my sheath."

"But why did you come here in the first place?"

He started to turn his head away, but she put up a hand to his cheek to stop him. The candle's light flickered across his face, but she saw the truth in his eyes. The chill of it struck her to the bone.

"You *did* come here for Gunthar, didn't you? To kill him—"

"I—" He groaned and pulled his face away, then dropped his head into his one good hand. "I thought it was the only way to protect Father. It is not enough that that monster has crippled him! Gunthar is going to use Father's rebuilding of a few walls as an excuse to throw him into prison. Out of spite, Heléne! Merely in spite for Father's defiance of him during the wars! I couldn't let that happen. It would kill Father to be shut away in some dismal cell like this!"

Heléne's anger surged anew at Gunthar. Threatening Etienne's father for no better reason than that Sir Damian had had the insolence to dare to defy the arrogant earl! But ... "Etienne, if you had succeeded, my father's guards would have cut you down where you stood."

"I know. If you hadn't screamed—" He drew a shuddering breath. "Do you think it makes me a coward that I'm glad you did? I thought it would be a simple task to do for Father's sake. Just strike Gunthar down and the threat would go away. I don't know how I thought I would escape. I suppose I didn't think that far ahead. I just wanted Father to be safe. I thought it would be so simple."

She remembered watching him before his attack on Gunthar. How pale he had looked, the uncertainty she had sensed even through his resentment.

She said, "But it wasn't simple, was it?"

He shook his head, then groaned again. "I must have been mad to agree to try. It has been like a nightmare. I keep telling myself I am going to wake up and find myself safe in my own bed, but every time I open my eyes I am still trapped within these walls."

She could feel his despair. How could Sir Damian have been so selfish as to send his son on such a dangerous errand? Sir Damian must have felt himself desperate! But whatever Sir Damian might have feared from Gunthar, it did not explain why he would command Etienne to do the deed with the prince's dagger.

"The dagger," she said aloud. "Etienne, wherever did you get it?"

"It's not mine," Etienne muttered without raising his head from his hand.

"Did your father give it to you?"

"No! I tell you, I don't know where it came from."

"Then someone must have slipped it into your sheath when you were not looking. Someone who knew when and why you were coming to Pennault. Who could it have been? Think, Etienne."

"I said I don't know!"

The vehemence with which he snapped out the words checked Heléne for a moment. Was he trying to convince *her* of their truth, or himself?

"I think you *do* know," she said. "Or at least that you have a suspicion." When he did not answer, she reached out and shook him. "Etienne, I cannot help you if you do not tell me the truth."

"I don't know," he repeated, more wearily. "And even if I did, it wouldn't matter now. *I'm* the one who attacked the earl with the prince's dagger, and now they are going to cut off my head and carve me up and display me all about the city gates as a warning to others."

She pulled his head away from his hand, so shocked by this horrible prediction that for a moment she could not speak.

"Great heavens, Etienne," she cried when she finally found her voice, "what do you mean?"

His mouth twisted up bitterly. "Lord Challons assured me it is what they do to traitors. First they hang you, but not until you are dead. Then they take you down and cut out your bowels, which they burn before your eyes. *Then* they slice you up into quarters and chop off your head, to be affixed at the king's command where the grisly remains are thought most likely to prove a deterrent for other would-be traitors. Really, Heléne, how can you be so naive about the law? *Ow*!"

She still held his head between her hands and did not realize that her fingers were twisting in his hair until he cried out and tried to pull away.

"We must get you out of here at once," she whispered.

"I should like to know how. *Ouch*! Will you let go?"

Her fingers had gone rigid amid his tangle of curls, but she was too horrified by his words to even hear his complaint.

"Oh, Etienne, I had no idea you were in such danger as this! And all because of that frightful dagger. No, you must not lie to me again! You *do* know where it came from. Tell me!"

He sighed and began with his hale hand to work her fingers free as gently as he could. "I can't. I don't *know*. It is only a guess. But I can think of no one else."

"Who? Tell me who?"

"I can't. I swore an oath. You mustn't ask me."

He winced as she suddenly pulled her hands away, then in a blaze of anger at his absurd response, she slapped him.

"This is not a game, Etienne! We are talking about your life!"

"I know that!" he shouted back. "But I can't tell you! It wouldn't matter anyway. *I* am the one they caught, and *I* am the one they are going to hang."

He was right. But not only hang. "I won't let them," she uttered fiercely. "Etienne, I am going to get you out of here."

"Get me out—? Oh, Heléne, don't tease me."

"I mean it. I know a way. Triston will be waiting for us tomorrow night in the clearing where we used to play."

"Triston? You've spoken to him? Then he knows why I am here?"

"Of course he knows. He stormed my father's hall demanding your release, but Gunthar threw him out. That wretched man has been nothing but trouble since he set foot in our house. It is *his* fault you are here. Oh, I wish we had never set eyes on him!"

"Nevertheless, he is here and he's not going to let me simply walk through that door."

"But he's not here."

Etienne looked surprised.

"He's gone to Angoulême to meet with the prince. So it is now that we must act, before he returns."

"But how?"

His question was more plaintive than hopeful. She took his hand and rubbed it between hers, trying to warm it.

"I have a plan. It's so simple, I wonder I did not think of it sooner. Anyway, now we shall have Triston's help, which is essential for I don't know where I should have hidden you otherwise."

"What are you going to do?"

"I won't tell you," she answered, punishing him a little for his ridiculous loyalty to the dagger's owner. "You shall have to trust me. But I promise we shall all be safely gone from here by tomorrow night."

"Gone? All—?"

"You and me and Clothilde. And Triston, of course. We are going to run away to escape from Gunthar and Heywood and this absurd charge of treason."

"I know I shall have to flee," he said, "but who is Heywood, and what has Clothilde to do with this?"

"She and Triston are in love," she told him, none too sure she ought to be revealing her sister's secrets. "But Gunthar wants to marry her, so what else can she and Triston do but run away? And I am going with them because *I* do not wish to marry Lord Heywood."

Etienne mulled this over, then said, "Even if I believed you about Triston and Clothilde, Triston is never going to leave Vere Castle."

"Yes, he will. As soon as you are safe."

Etienne shook his head. "He won't leave Father. Besides, Vere is his inheritance. He'd never abandon that."

Heléne had not thought of that. "But—but for Clothilde—"

"Heléne, Triston may be smitten with your sister, but he'd not give up his future for her. Women have been throwing themselves at him ever since I can remember. Why, just last year, he and Osanne—" He broke off.

"What about him and the Lady Osanne?"

"Never mind."

"No, tell me!" If Triston were playing fast and loose with her sister, Heléne wanted to know.

Etienne hesitated. "It is not a story for a lady's ears."

"Neither was that grisly scene you described to me awhile ago—cutting off heads and tearing out bowels—! You told me all that readily enough."

He colored. "I know. I should not have— Oh, very well. Triston and Osanne were lovers before Vere fell. He says she seduced him, but that hardly excuses what they did. She was Father's wife! I only found out about it afterwards, when I heard them quarreling one day. Triston swears he's broken it off. And I know they're finished now, because I've seen her with—"

He stopped again, but Heléne did not ask for more. She felt betrayed. She had trusted Triston entirely. This would devastate Clothilde!

"I shouldn't have told you," Etienne mumbled, interpreting her silence for the hurt that it was. "I'm sorry about your sister. But you see how much worse it would have been if I had allowed you to continue to think— She'll get over it, Heléne."

But Heléne shook her head. They both knew Clothilde better than that.

"I won't blame you if you decide to leave me here to rot."

She looked up at him and saw the defeat in his face. She put her arms around him again. "Of course I won't leave you. *We* are still friends, and there is no reason why you should suffer merely because your brother is a knave."

"That's a bit strong."

"What else do you call a man who deceives a woman's innocent heart, merely to amuse his own vanity?"

"We don't know that. Maybe he *is* in love with Clothilde. He may even wish to marry her. I'm only saying he will not abandon Vere Castle to do it."

But Heléne's illusions were shattered. "I shall have to tell Clothilde somehow. But the most urgent thing just now is to get you out of here. I hope your brother does not intend to turn his back on you, as well."

Etienne wisely let that pass. He slipped an arm around her waist and she allowed herself to lean against him for another moment. He felt so cold.

"Heléne, whatever happens, thank you for coming today."

She heard the dejection in his voice and knew he did not believe her. Her throat tightened. "I won't fail you, Etienne. By tomorrow night, I swear you will be free of these hateful walls."

She looked up and saw the sad smile on his lips. Without thinking, she reached up to kiss him.

"Ahem!"

They sprang apart at the harsh sound of a clearing throat. The tower door was open and the guard stood on the threshold. The single candle he carried illuminated the reproof on his face. Heléne felt herself blushing, but before she could speak, he preempted her.

"Your father says one candle is sufficient, my lady, and that you've no business being in the tower. I must ask you to leave."

The guard crossed to the bench and reached out a hand between them to thump the new candle down on the table. He picked up the stubby remains of the other and held its guttering light over her head.

"Please, my lady."

She stood up, then turned to speak one final word of comfort to Etienne. Before she could even open her mouth, the guard took her arm and propelled her out of the room. She cried out an angry protest, but it did no good. He slammed the door behind them and turned to lock it, then handed her the guttering candle and sent her firmly on her way.

# Eleven

The moment he rode into the bailey, Gunthar knew something was wrong. It was after noon, and Laurant appeared to have just returned from a hunt. Two men, balancing on their shoulders a staff to which a slain stag was bound, stood watching the agitated exchange taking place between their master and his captain of the guard. Laurant still sat astride his big bay horse. His face expressed dismay at his captain's news.

"Good heavens, man, how could this happen? Summon your men and begin the search at once. He must be found before the earl—"

Gunthar urged his mount forward at Laurant's exclamation. "Is there a problem, my lord?"

He knew from the way his host blanched that the answer was not going to be to his liking.

"M-my lord," Laurant stammered. "We had no warning that you meant to return today. There has been a slight—er, mishap. But I assure you all is under control. If you would care to retire to your chamber and rest a bit, I will see to this matter, and then I will explain—"

"I will hear the explanation now."

Laurant hesitated. Gunthar knew he was casting about for some way to soften the blow—or perhaps simply evade responsibility for whatever had occurred.

"My lord," Laurant said at last, "as you can see, I went out hunting today, as I do most mornings." He nodded toward the two men bearing up the stag and his frown sent them scurrying off to the kitchens. "As I said, my men and I were off hunting, and ... well, it seems that in our absence my son arrived in answer to my summons to his uncle."

"I am glad that your son has returned," Gunthar said as Laurant paused. "Please continue."

"Aye, well ... He and Etienne de Brielle are of an age, you see. They grew up together, neighbors as we all are, and I suppose they shared a few boyhood larks, and ... Well, apparently some fool—" he glared at his captain, who looked offended and shook his head "—told him that Etienne was shut up in one of my towers, and so he ran right up, demanding to see him. Only when he got there— But perhaps Sir Baudri had better tell you the rest."

The captain seemed dismayed to find the burden abruptly shifted to himself. He took a startled step backwards, as if thrust there by the force of Gunthar's grim gaze.

"My lord," he said, "as you know, de Brielle was injured when he attacked you in my master's hall. You broke his wrist, his right wrist, and it could not have been expected that he should have been able to wield a weapon in his left hand with any skill. I thought one guard sufficient to—"

"Are you telling me," Gunthar cut in, "de Brielle got hold of another weapon and used it to engineer an escape?" He saw both men's surprise and snapped at Laurant, "I'm not deaf, man. I heard you shouting at your captain as I rode through the gate. Who else would you be so urgent to find before my return?" He swung himself from his horse. "Take me to the tower."

On the way, Sir Baudri enlightened Gunthar and Laurant on the details of the escape as he knew them. The captain had witnessed young Therri's arrival, but had not been informed of his attempt to see the prisoner. Apparently Therri had found the cell door open, the prisoner fled, and one of Sir Baudri's men face down on the floor.

Gunthar entered the tower chamber expecting to see the guard lying in a pool of blood. To his surprise, he found the room occupied by three quite vital beings, although the one sitting on the bench looked somewhat the worse for wear. A white linen bandage was being wrapped around his upper arm by a fellow guard, while a dark purple knot swelled his right temple.

A fair, cheery-faced youth stood nearby holding a torch. "What, Papa, are you back? It seems Etienne has flown your coop."

The youth said it with a grin. Gunthar needed no introduction to inform him that this was Laurant's son and heir. He possessed the same breath-taking beauty as Clothilde, though of a more robust nature. His hair was pale like his younger sister's, and his vibrant blue eyes held an appealing twinkle.

"What, in heaven's name, has happened here?" Laurant exclaimed. "Sir Roland, we thought to find you dead."

"But he's not," the youth interposed, "so you can't call it murder."

"'Twasn't for lack of the lad's trying," growled Sir Roland.

"Come now, you owned yourself he only slashed your arm to fend you off. If Etienne had wanted you dead, that wound would be between your ribs. Instead, he felled you with only a blow to the head."

"Be quiet, Therri," Laurant snapped. "You know nothing about this matter. Sir Roland, the earl and I are waiting for an explanation."

Therri, uncowed by his father's rebuke, interrupted with a weighing look at the earl, "What, are you Gunthar? The fellow who's come to marry Clo? Then you're the one they say Etienne attacked."

Gunthar was amused in spite of himself by the youth's irrepressible manner. He gave an ironic little bow.

"Well, I don't believe it," Therri said. "Etienne is not a murderer. There had to have been some mistake."

Gunthar wondered if the youth had been consulting with his sister. Therri, of course, had not been present to witness the actual attack. He had naught but a childhood loyalty and, perhaps, Heléne's stubborn denial to guide him in forming his judgment.

Gunthar therefore forgave the ignorance of the youth's response, but said, "There has been no mistake, save for what has evidently taken place in this cell today. Sir Roland, I am sorry for your injuries, but I must know how the prisoner managed to overpower you."

"He took me by surprise, milord," Sir Roland said. "He was hiding behind the door when I came in to take the breakfast tray away. I heard a noise and turned just in time to see the knife in his hand. I tried to grab it, but he stabbed my arm. Then I felt a blow to my head, and then . . . well, I don't remember anything after that until I heard the young master shouting."

Gunthar frowned. "How the devil did a knife get smuggled in here? Did you take no precautions?"

"Of course we did," Sir Roland said. "No one went in and out of the cell except the kitchen wench twice a day who brought him his food. There were no utensils on the tray and we always searched her. There is no possible way she could have been a carrier for a weapon. And there was no one else spoke to him except Lord Challons the night before you left, and then this morning . . . but—but it could not possibly have been her."

Gunthar observed the guard's distress, as he did the violent flushing of his host's countenance.

"That is preposterous. Are you suggesting that my daughter—"

"No, milord, of course not. I sent her away promptly—that is, as soon as you told me—"

"The Lady Helen was here?" Gunthar said sharply. Not for an instant did the possibility of Laurant's other daughter enter his mind.

"A-aye, milord," Sir Roland stammered. "She brought up the breakfast tray, but was only with him a few minutes."

"Alone?"

"I— Well, she did send me off to fetch some fresh candles. But I found Lord Laurant before he left on the hunt and he told me to order her out, which I did at once."

"And I suppose you searched her, too, before abandoning your post for a candle?"

Sir Roland looked aghast. "Lay hands on my master's daughter? Certainly not!"

"So you let her walk in here scot-free, with heaven knows what concealed about her person, and—"

He paused as Therri gave a crack of laughter. "Saints, but this is rich. I knew Heléne was a sly little thing, but—"

"Shut up, Therri," Laurant snapped at him. "The whole idea is ridiculous. My daughter had nothing to do with Etienne's escape. Heléne is just a girl—"

"She is a brazen, impudent little cat," Gunthar said, "and when I get my hands on her, she will be sorry she so much as blinked behind my back." He turned to the guard. "The rest, Sir Roland. First you will tell me the rest."

"The rest?"

"You must have seen something, sensed something? When you came in or went out?"

"I— W-well I—" The guard sent a hesitant glance at Laurant, but Gunthar would not have him being coached.

"You will look at me, Sir Roland." He caught and held the man's unwilling gaze. Sir Roland looked frightened now. Clearly he knew something he did not wish to reveal. Gunthar could feel him resisting, and allowed a little menace to slip into his gaze.

Sir Roland obligingly crumbled before it. "Milord, I am sure it meant nothing. The Lady Heléne and Master Etienne have been friends almost since birth. I am sure it was completely innocent."

"What was innocent?"

"Their—their embrace—and her kiss—"

"Her *what?*"

Sir Roland jumped at Gunthar's bark. Then the guard saw Laurant's face and cringed.

"Why, you scurrilous—"

"No." Gunthar put out a hand to stop Laurant's outraged advance on the guard. He felt a curious sympathy with his host's evident desire to choke the man, but he had to know the rest. "No more prevarication, sir. You will tell me everything you heard and saw pass between the Lady Helen and young de Brielle."

Sir Roland sagged in defeat. "Aye, milord. Milady was angry about the darkness of the chamber and sent me off for candles. When I returned, they were sitting on this bench in one another's arms, and I heard her saying that she would not fail him and that by tomorrow night he would be free, and—and then she kissed him."

Gunthar found himself caught up in a searing vision that left him trembling with revulsion and rage. He uttered an explosive curse and strode out of the tower chamber.

The women screamed when Gunthar burst into the bedchamber. He was dimly aware of their cries and scurryings, but he had eyes only for her. She stood on a chair in the middle of the room, dressed in a sleeveless chemise. A woman who was evidently a seamstress was holding up a length of cloth to her. The woman turned at Gunthar's entrance, bringing the cloth with her and permitting him a glimpse of smooth white arms before the lady on the chair gasped and twitched the cloth away to draw it hastily up to her bosom.

"Get out!" Gunthar shouted at the women. "All of you get out!"

Most obeyed instantly, but when the seamstress hesitated he seized her arm and propelled her over to the door.

"How dare you! Let her go at once!"

He ignored the indignant cry from the lady on the chair and flung the seamstress across the threshold, slamming the door in her face. He turned back to find the lady's cheeks a glowing blaze of color.

"How dare you!"

"We've some reckoning to do, my lady Helen. Unless you wish your servants to witness your being turned across my knee—"

"If you lay a hand on me, I shall scream!"

"A hand? Saints, but you will be fortunate if that is all I lay on you! How *dared* you disobey me? I expressly forbade you to step foot in that tower, and the minute my back is turned where do you go trotting? Did you honestly think I would not discover what you had done?"

She lifted her chin. "Of course I went to see Etienne. He is my friend and I would not leave him to endure your tortures alone."

"Torture?"

"You broke his wrist!"

"The boy attacked me. I was defending myself."

"As he was defending his father from your spiteful threats!"

"What threats?"

"To throw Sir Damian into prison, merely because he had the temerity to defy you! No doubt it is that same spite which makes you refuse to believe Etienne's word about the dagger. It is not his, but you are going to use it as an excuse to draw out his bowels and cut off his head and cut him up into quarters and—" She broke off with a shudder.

"Great heavens!" Gunthar said. "Who threatened him with all of that?"

"You did! You said it is what happens to traitors!"

"It is, sometimes. But I never—"

"You are a brute and a monster," she cried before he could finish. "You have brought nothing but misery to us since the day you set foot in our house. You have bullied my father and terrified my sister, and now you threaten Etienne with a hideous punishment for a crime he has not committed. Were you the king himself I should not stand by and allow that to happen."

"So you smuggled him a knife and told him to kill a guard. That is murder, my lady, and is also a capital offense. You did the boy no favors, and are like to find yourself charged as an accomplice to his deed."

"Murder?" she gasped. "What are you talking about? I gave Etienne no dagger—"

"Oh, please, spare me the innocent air. Fortunately for you, your 'friend' struck with something less than expert skill. *Un*fortunately, the guard not only lives, but saw and heard enough to condemn you both."

He took her deepening color as an admission of guilt and advanced angrily towards the chair.

"Stay away from me!" She jerked the length of cloth closer to her chin. It was a dull, apple green color, particularly unflattering to her complexion, even when flushed with the slight confusion which now suffused her cheeks.

He stopped, but said, "Did you not tell de Brielle that you would help him escape? Think twice before you answer. The guard—"

"Oh, very well, yes, but not with a knife. I was going to—"

"What?"

Her chin shot up again. "I don't see what it matters now. If Etienne was clever enough to escape on his own, all the better. You said the guard is not dead, so he hasn't murdered anyone. And if you were not so obsessed with conspiracies, you would know that he has not committed treason, either."

Gunthar felt an almost irresistible urge to shake her. Her blind loyalty to the guilty youth infuriated him. Or was it more than mere loyalty? He swung away from her, locking his hands behind his back as he paced the length of the room. Scattered across the bed were several bolts of material, all of similarly drab hues to the cloth she was holding against her face. He wondered briefly what she was being fitted out for. Then the anger flowed back, surging with another emotion that he refused to name.

"De Brielle did not escape on his own," he said, pausing to glare at her over his shoulder. "That knife could have been smuggled to him by only one person. You brought him the breakfast tray and sent the guard away on a mindless errand. But he returned and caught the pair of you entwined like a pair of—"

He broke off, choking at the word, the image . . . He looked away and took a deep breath, steadying himself for the question he did not want to ask.

"Tell me the truth. Are you and he lovers?"

"Etienne and I? Oh, no!"

She sounded shocked, but how could he be sure it was not another pretense? "Then I suppose it was mere 'friendship' that locked you in his arms?"

"We were not—"

"Not what? Not embracing? Not kissing? Was the guard hallucinating then?"

"No—but it was not what he and you think."

He forced himself to turn around and search her face. Was she lying? Her actions, her heated defense, worst of all, the look in her eyes when she spoke of Etienne . . . all betrayed a depth of emotion for the youth which roused a queer resentment in his breast. If not love, what was it he saw there? And why did it leave him with an irrational desire to grind the unfortunate youth beneath his heel?

"What are you going to do about Etienne now?"

"We are going to find him and lock him back up." He paused, then added provokingly, "And this time he may well find himself in chains."

He expected to receive a hot rejoinder to that, but she answered him with silence. He watched as she took her lower lip between her teeth and saw the way her gaze seemed to drift away, as though she were imagining something far removed from this room.

"Plotting yet another way to thwart me, are you?"

She started. "How did you—"

"I can read you like a book, Lady Helen . . . much to my grief." He took another step towards the chair and caught again the defensive fluttering of the cloth. "What the devil is that vile thing you are clutching at?"

She glanced down at the cloth. Her fingers rubbed it a little wistfully. "It is to be one of the gowns for my wedding trousseau."

"Wedding?"

"To Lord Heywood. Mama will be very angry that you turned out the seamstress in the midst of her labors, besides the fact that it is quite indecent for you to be here at all."

"Indecent, is it?" His eye kindled a little at that. "Are you afraid of me, then?"

That won him an unexpected grin. "Afraid you might ravish me, you mean? We both know how absurd that is. After all, you have no need for my dowry and I have no charms to entice a man otherwise."

"It seems you had no trouble at all enticing young de Brielle." The caustic remark slipped out before he could stop it.

It wiped the merriment from her face. "I was only comforting him."

"Do you always comfort men by kissing them? Saints! I could use a little comfort like that of my own."

"Stop," she said, as he took another step towards the chair. "You are quite close enough. I-I know you are only teasing me—p-punishing me because I defied you—b-but—"

"But what?" he prompted, intrigued by the little stammer in her voice. He was near enough to touch her now, and she was looking adorably confused.

"P-Please—do not look at me like that."

"How am I looking at you?"

She hesitated, then said tentatively, as though afraid he might laugh, "Like—like men sometimes look at Clothilde. Only I know that cannot be what you mean, for I am not at all pretty, but—but it bothers me just the same, so I wish you would stop."

He surveyed her critically for a moment, then said abruptly, "You know, you could be quite taking if you only knew how to dress. These dull, pale colors are all wrong for you. Haven't you anything in a deep forest green or a royal blue?"

"But this is silk," she said of her apple green cloth, as though that were all the recommendation it required.

"It is twaddle," he said, "and I have stared at its offensive hue quite long enough."

He tried to twitch it out of her hands, but she anticipated his move and held on to it. Irritated by her resistance, he gave a quick tug and was startled when she tumbled off the chair into his arms.

His surprise lasted only an instant. Then he bent his head to her gasping lips. She dropped the apple green silk to push against his chest, once, twice . . . the third time her fingers curled into the breast of his tunic. Suddenly he felt as though he had never kissed a woman before in his life. As her lips warmed to his, he drank her in like a man parched by a desert sun.

"Helen."

He whispered it against her brow, enjoying the feel of her name on his tongue, then lifted her arms to his neck before he kissed her again. His fingers traced the back of her neck, playing with the little wisps of hair escaped from her braid. She shivered, her arms tightening. Some voice far to the back of his mind warned him that he should stop. He had no right to be doing any of this. Heywood would not thank him for these stolen kisses with his future wife.

Stolen kisses. It was not Heywood who flashed into his mind, but a handsome, dusky-haired youth. Gunthar's guilt flared into some primitive emotion, so foreign to his nature that he could not have begun to identify it, even had he been inclined at the moment to try. But its unfamiliarity made it no less real.

He kissed her again, a little more fiercely. "Is this what you gave de Brielle?" he murmured. "And this . . . and this . . . ?"

He tried to block the images out, along with the renewed shove against his chest. Desperate to make her want him as much as she wanted Etienne, he clung to her arms and pressed fervent, coaxing kisses to her lips, her cheeks, her eyes . . . Another, less urgent shove, and then she melted against him once more. Encouraged, he slid one hand over her shoulder and swept it down her back.

She twisted her head aside on a gasp. He caught a spasm of pain on her face. Startled, he released her, but not before his grip on her shoulder inadvertently pulled the sleeve of her chemise partway down her arm.

The spasm of pain vanished, replaced with renewed indignation. "Get out! How dare you kiss me like that! How dare you make me wa—"

She slapped a hand to her mouth.

Want you? Those could not be the words she had been about to blurt out. Not when her hand suddenly scrubbed across her lips as though to banish the very taste of him. To his surprise—and horror—a tear splashed out of her eyes to wet her knuckles, before she abruptly turned and fled across the room to the window.

In the muted light of the late afternoon sun, he could see her trembling. In fear? Revulsion? But she had embraced him, too, and he could have sworn . . .

His thoughts broke off. Still bright against the silvery whiteness of her partially bared back stood two red welts. The sight stunned him. He started after her, then stopped as she covered her face with her hands.

"Helen—" he heard his own voice hoarse with horror "—who did this to you?"

"Go away."

He stared at her, cringing beside the window, and nearly choked at the loathing that flooded through him. He had been wrong. The only reaction he had managed to stir in her was disgust. What madness had possessed him to behave as he had? In answer, he saw again the vision of her clasped in Etienne's arms, and felt anew the stirring of that bitter, almost violent response. Determinedly he fought it back. If she and Etienne were in love, it was no business of his. Her folly would be ended soon enough once they recaptured the youth and forced him to stand trial for his crimes.

And she would hate *him* for it. That would be bad enough. But Gunthar did not want her to hate him for this day, as well.

He moved to her side, keenly aware of the way she shrank at his approach. Nevertheless, he took her and turned her firmly towards the window, then slowly lowered her chemise a few inches more. Her back was covered with welts and bruises. Only two people could have authorized such mistreatment—Lord Laurant or the Lady Gwenllian. He had taken both their measures, and had little doubt at whose hand lay this crime.

He felt Heléne shiver again and forced the blaze of his anger down. Gently, he rearranged the chemise modestly about her shoulders. Then he bent to brush a feather-soft kiss to the nape of her neck.

"Lass, forgive me."

He touched the wisps of her hair regretfully, then turned and left the room.

# Twelve

By heaven," Sir John exclaimed, "that's a callous thing to say!"

Gunthar did not apologize for his flash of ill temper. He had not come ten minutes from Heléne and he was not in the mood for this. But he made an attempt to modify his language.

"I shall be happy to address the Lady Osanne's concerns," he said to Sir John, "but this is hardly the place."

He cast a significant glance towards the bed hangings, hoping she, at least, might take the hint.

A blush stole up into the Lady Osanne's cheeks. Gunthar was not surprised that she had elected to remain at Pennault rather than return to Vere and face Triston's wrath. But it did not please Gunthar to see how quickly his friend had fallen under her spell.

She reached out a hand now to Sir John's arm. "Please, sir, my little fears are not sufficient cause to intrude upon my lord's privacy."

Her lip quivered piteously. Gunthar's sympathies remained unmoved, but his friend's response was immediate and fervent.

"Your fears are perfectly valid. Hugh is only being difficult. I assure you his bite is not nearly so frightful as his bark would lead you to believe."

Gunthar lifted a brow as though to dispute this judgment, then satisfied himself with saying, "Everything possible is being done to find de Brielle. If that is not sufficient for you, then by all means, do not leave my lady's side. Comfort her to your heart's content—but don't do it here."

He turned away from them and walked over to the bed, stripping off the dusty mantle still clasped about his neck and flinging it down onto the blankets.

"It is not sufficient, devil take it," Sir John swore behind him. "My lady's life may be in danger, and all you can do is stand there like an unfeeling brute. Fiend seize it, Hugh—"

"Go to blazes!" Gunthar swung about. "That boy is in no condition to be a threat to anyone, and I hardly think he will put his freedom at risk by trying to murder his step-mother."

"It was not a tendency for prudence that prompted him to brave a roomful of guards to try and murder you. And when he hears how she has betrayed the truth to us— What can it hurt to set a few men about her, just in case?"

"Oh, by all means, then. Rally the entire garrison about her if you wish. After all, a nineteen-year-old youth with a broken wrist may well slaughter us all in our beds."

Sir John colored angrily.

The Lady Osanne hastened to intervene. "My lord, pray forgive Sir John his earnestness for my safety. I have told myself my fears are foolish, that Etienne will not think to do me harm. But when I recall his brother and the way he attacked me—"

Sir John put his arm around her. "How can you expect her not to be afraid after that? Both those iniquitous pups have displayed their murderous blood, and if you are not going to do something to stop them—"

"What do you want me to do?" Gunthar said. "The guards are searching the castle and grounds, the exits have all been sealed off. I tell you, the boy will be found."

"And what about Sir Triston? He is the one who sent his brother here to assassinate you, who cut your saddle strap before you left for Angoulême. I'll wager it was he, as well, who paid that archer to appear along the road. I tell you, it is he who is plotting with the prince to undo the king's peace, and if you do not stop him soon, they may well succeed at the cost of your own life."

"We have no proof of any of this."

"We all witnessed his attack upon Osanne. What further proof do you need?"

"I need proof to call him traitor. I acknowledge your fears, my lady, and deeply regret the incident that caused them, but I cannot ignore the fact that in regard to conspiracy, it is your word against Sir Triston's. I cannot arrest a man on suspicion alone."

"Rubbish," Sir John said. "You're a deal too scrupulous, Hugh. I say lock the man up now, let him languish a few days in Laurant's dungeon, wave a hot iron or two before his face. I'll warrant we'll have the truth out of him soon enough."

"My lord," the Lady Osanne interposed, seeing the angry tightening of Gunthar's lips, "there is another way to gain the evidence you require."

"My lady?"

"There is a place in the woods nearby to Pennault Castle, a clearing where Triston sometimes meets with an agent of the prince. I could take you there and you could hear for yourself that what I have told you is the truth."

Gunthar weighed that beautiful, guileless face. That it had thoroughly smitten his friend was evident, but dared he trust it? "I will assign a few of my men to watch this place you speak of. If Sir Triston appears—"

"No. My lord, you must go yourself." Even Sir John looked surprised and she added, "Triston is no fool. He will bring guards of his own and they will find and engage your men while Triston simply flees. Nothing will have been gained, and he will not give you a second chance to trap him."

"It makes sense, Hugh," Sir John said. "One man is more easily concealed than a band. Now, if I went alone—"

"You? Oh, no!"

Sir John smiled at the Lady Osanne's quick protest. "There now, don't be afraid. I should be silent as a cat. I need only hear enough to corroborate your testimony. I presume—" he shot a glance at Gunthar "—you will not doubt the integrity of *my* word?"

"No," Gunthar said.

"Well, then—"

"But it shan't be you, John. If anyone is to go, it shall be myself."

Gunthar saw the faint line of displeasure vanish from the Lady Osanne's forehead. Aye, that had been what she wanted to hear.

But Sir John exclaimed, "Don't be ridiculous. Think of the chance you would be taking, the danger were you to be discovered."

"I do not ask others to hazard what I am afraid to risk."

"If this is a matter of pride—"

"It is not. Nevertheless, we shall delay that decision for a day or two. My lady, I thank you for your counsel, but before I avail myself of it, I've a mind to broach this subject directly to its source." Her ivory forehead creased again, dissolving into alarm when he added, "I think it is time Sir Damian and I met face to face once more."

Sir John said, "You mean, ride over to Vere? I say, do you think that wise? Bearding the lion in his own den?"

"Given the nature of his injury, I can hardly expect him to come here."

"Aye, but—"

"My lord, you must not! Sir Damian—"

"Will not dare do me harm," Gunthar said in answer to the Lady Osanne's cry. "Not so long as his son is still in our power. John, see to it that pup is in hand and back in the tower by the time I return."

Sir John looked surprised. "You're not leaving now?"

Gunthar could think of no better way to distract himself from his latest disastrous exchange with Heléne. "'Tis no more than an hour's ride to Vere. I will say what needs to be said to Sir Damian and be back before nightfall." He opened the door and called for a squire. A boy with a tousle of red-brown curls appeared. "Brandon, find Julian Parr and see if he is well enough to ride. Tell him to prepare me a fresh horse and one for himself. If he is still ill, you shall ride with me in his place."

The boy bowed and hurried off.

"That's it?" Sir John said. "You plan to invade Vere Castle with a single squire at your side?"

"Don't worry for me, John. I know what I'm doing. Now take the Lady Osanne away and comfort her. She is looking most distressed at my decision."

Gunthar's mind was made up and Sir John saw it. He shook his head, then pulled a reluctant Lady Osanne out of the room.

Some twenty minutes later, Gunthar strode into the bailey expecting to find his horse ready and waiting. If it was, he could not see it for the crowd of people gathered there. A burst of applause suggested that they were witnessing some delightful spectacle. Even with his superior height, Gunthar was not able to see immediately the source of their pleasure. He tapped the shoulder of a rough-looking servant standing on the fringes and inquired as to what was so riveting.

"The stableboy's gone mad," the man muttered, glowering at the backs of those who blocked his view. "A rare sight it was before they shoved me to the rear." Only after grinding out this complaint did he look up at his inquisitor. His small eyes widened and he snatched the tattered cap from his head as he dropped into a servile bow. "My lord."

Gunthar ignored him and maneuvered himself into the crowd. Slurs of resentment were hastily swallowed and a path cleared for his advance. Within moments he stood at the fore, observing a rare spectacle indeed.

The pretty stableboy laughed and swung his pitchfork menacingly at the fiery-tressed squire. Julian sprang lithely out of reach. The stableboy's laughter turned to anger and a curse.

"English swine! I shall spit your black heart!"

The inciting shout of the crowd swallowed the rest of his words as his lunge towards the squire grew wilder.

Julian Parr, looking perfectly hale if a little flushed, parried as best he could with his long-bladed dagger. The yard-long shaft on his opponent's lethally pronged implement left him at a sore disadvantage. Gunthar could see the frustration on the squire's face as he feinted towards the stableboy but was forced back by a warning swipe of spiked iron.

"Not so bold now, eh?" the stableboy jeered. "When 'tis not a woman you're debauching with your knavish lust. Aye, I call you knave. Rascal, villain, dog—"

"Your wench came to me freely, churl," Julian retorted. "Do not blame me if you were too loutish to keep her."

The stableboy howled, but once again Julian nimbly evaded his lunge. Then the stableboy caught sight of Gunthar. The dirt-smudged chin came up as a smirking smile danced over his pretty, pinched lips.

"Your master's come to rein in your leash," he sneered. "He may shrug off your wanton seductions, but what about your perfidy to himself? When I tell him what I have seen, and where and with whom—"

"You know nothing, fool. And if you do not lay that weapon down now, my lord shall have you flogged for this insolence to his servant."

"Servant? Shall I tell him what service you render him in the woods, when you escort his own sweet lady—"

"My lord will not believe your slanders."

"'Tis not slander, but the truth. I have followed you each night when the moon is high. I have seen you leave the lady at her tryst, then withdraw to speak to the pale knight—"

"Be silent!" Julian sprang recklessly at the stableboy and nearly impaled himself on the thrusting spikes.

"Ha!" the stableboy mocked as Julian twisted backwards. "*'Tis* that you fear. Being called not lecher, but traitor."

"Lies, slanders and lies! Your jealousy has unhinged your mind. Put down your mad weapon and I will give you back your wench, aye, and pay you, too, for her time."

The stableboy's pretty features contorted with rage. "Pig!" he screamed. "English pig!"

He leapt at Julian, thrusting the prongs straight at the squire's chest. Julian sprang back, but this time he stumbled, hitting the ground on one knee. Gunthar saw his panic as he threw himself into the dirt. The prongs pierced his cape, ripping it from his shoulders as he rolled. The stableboy freed his weapon from where it had sunk into the earth and came at the squire again with a murderous shout.

Gunthar flinched as the prongs flashed downward, aiming for the squire's throat. The crowd roared with horror, then cheered when the stableboy went flying backwards through the air.

"Well done, lad!"

"A well-laid kick!"

Julian rolled to his knees, his face white and shaken.

Gunthar moved at last to end the folly. "You there, seize that fellow. This madness has gone far enough."

Two men jumped forward at Gunthar's command and tried to take hold of the stableboy. But the stableboy swung his implement about like a staff, cracking one on the head with it and driving the wooded end into the second's stomach. Then he went bounding towards Julian again. Julian dodged, then whipped out a foot to his opponent's ankle and tripped him neatly off the ground. Caught in a forward advance, the stableboy flew through the air and landed face down in the dirt.

Gunthar approved the judgment that sent Julian after him to kick the pitchfork out of his hand. But when the squire fell on his opponent's back and raised his dagger—

"Julian, no!"

The dagger fell before he finished the shout and came up again stained red.

Gunthar strode forward to pull Julian up, then rolled the stableboy over. Blood gushed from a wound in the base of his neck. Gunthar knelt and lifted his head, but it was too late. A gasp rattled in the stableboy's throat. Gunthar felt the life flow from the body as the eyes glazed over like glass.

He rose slowly to face his squire.

"My lord, he attacked me. You saw the way he attacked me. I was only—"

Julian's defense withered in the face of his master's glare.

"Go back to the castle. Confine yourself to my room until I return."

Gunthar voice was soft as a winter's snow, but its authority was implacable. Julian backed away, nearly as white as his fallen opponent. He turned and ran across the yard as the crowd began sidling forward to surround Gunthar and what remained of the pretty stableboy.

Gunthar summoned Brandon de Vexin and began his journey to Vere. The squire, three years younger than Julian Parr, held himself several paces to the rear as they rode. Gunthar was content to have it so. He had not thought anything could drive his encounter with Heléne from his mind, but Julian's scrimmage with the stableboy had done it.

Gunthar had witnessed the stableboy's murderous attack and had no doubt at all but what he had meant to kill Julian. No law would condemn his squire for ending the quarrel in blood. And yet it had been singularly unnecessary. The menacing pitchfork had been removed and its wielder no further threat, had Gunthar been allowed to order him taken into custody. But Julian had acted too quickly. In revenge for the attack? Out of lust for some wench from whom he wished to eliminate a rival? Or had it been something darker, something touching Gunthar himself and the squire's own faith?

What exactly had the stableboy said that had caused that subtle change in Julian's manner? Gunthar thought back to the moment when he had seen Julian's disdain and bravado slip. There had been something about the woods and the moon, a pale knight and a lady . . .

"Yes, de Vexin, what is it?" Gunthar tried to impart with a look the knowledge that he did not wish to be disturbed.

Brandon hesitated. Anyone with half a grain of sense would have known to fall back again. But Brandon took a deep breath and made a visible effort to master his fear of Gunthar's scowl.

"Well?"

"My lord, forgive me, I do not mean to intrude upon your thoughts, but—but there are some things I think you should know."

"Indeed?"

"Aye, my lord." Brandon held his ground. "I followed you into the tower today and while you were berating the guard for de Brielle's escape, I made so bold as to look around."

"Did you?" That had been presumptuous of the whelp. "And what did you find?"

"I think I know how the knife was smuggled in."

"That has already been established. The Lady Helen had it concealed about her person when she visited de Brielle."

"Well, that might have been it, only then it makes what I found very strange."

Gunthar did not appreciate having his judgment challenged. "And just what is it you found?"

"When I picked up the wooden bowl from the breakfast tray ... Did you know it had a kind of notch carved out from the bottom? About this long and this wide—" Brandon demonstrated with his fingers "—and deep enough to sit flat had it been set over a small knife. I'm sure of that, because after you left I took the bowl back to the kitchens and tried it. They have many such knives there that would have fit."

Gunthar was impressed in spite of himself. The boy had been busy, and to good effect, it seemed. "You make from this, then, that Sir Roland was stabbed with a kitchen knife?"

"Well, I have not seen many daggers that small. And I do not believe the Lady Heléne knew it was there, either."

"She carried the tray."

"Aye, but she took it away from the serving girl whose usual chore it was to carry it up to the tower."

"How do you know that?"

"I asked in the kitchens. The cook said the tray left with the girl named Audiart. *She* was in the kitchens all the time and could easily have smuggled a knife under the bowl."

Gunthar marveled at the intrepidness of the boy's investigation. "Did she act on her own or with an accomplice?" he asked.

"There was an accomplice, of course. Someone else carved out that notch, though she must have given him the bowl. But I do not think she told him to do it. It was someone else's idea."

"The Lady Helen's?"

"I don't think so. I sought out the girl and questioned her. She looked terrified when I told her I was your squire and burst into tears, wailing that she hadn't wanted to do it, but that he had made her—"

"He?"

"Aye, my lord. It was a man she meant, though even when I threatened her, she would not name me his name."

Gunthar's brows rose in amusement as he tried to picture the mild youth at his side attempting to bully a woman. "I suppose," he said, though by now he never doubted the answer, "you thought to ask around the castle as to what sort of men she might have been seen with?"

"Aye, my lord. They said in the kitchens that there had been a quarrel between her and one of Laurant's stableboys. He was jealous of some rival for her affections, though none could tell me who the rival was."

Gunthar's amusement faded. "A stableboy?"

"Aye, my lord."

"Do you know which one?"

"'Twas the same who attacked Julian Parr in the yard today."

And ended his life at Julian's hands. The pieces began to fall into place. Julian must have stolen the stableboy's lover and seduced her into smuggling a knife to de Brielle. But who had seduced *him* into such a deed? Julian's father was one of Gunthar's vassals. The futures of Julian's entire family rested in Gunthar's hands. To set at risk his mother and sisters for some trivial passion or greed . . . No, Julian had served Gunthar for over ten years. He did not believe the youth would have cast aside his loyalty for lust or gold.

The stableboy might have known the answer. Certainly he knew the face behind Julian's duplicity. It must have been that knowledge that had driven Julian to the desperate act of silencing him at the point of a dagger.

"Is there anything else, Brandon?" To Gunthar's regret, the squire shook his head. "Very well. Then I would be left to myself. And well done, lad."

Brandon blushed at his master's commendation and fell back again.

An upcoming wind tossed darkling clouds about the horizon. Gunthar glanced at the woods to his left, remembering the near-calamitous appearance of the prince's archer on the road to Angoulême. He had dispatched no herald to announce his coming. How had the prince known where he would be and when? He had announced his destination only the night before his departure, and had subsequently suspected Laurant of leaking, perhaps inadvertently, the information. But now he acknowledged the possibility that it had been, not his careless host, but his own trusted, personal squire who had deliberately betrayed him. No wonder the youth had pled illness to avoid the journey.

Perhaps Sir John was right. Perhaps he was tempting fate by guarding himself only with a fifteen-year-old squire and a sword. He fingered the jeweled hilt at his side, ruefully aware that the weapon would be of precious little use against another bowman. He glanced over his shoulder at Brandon. The boy's ingenuous eyes darted sharply back and forth across the road. He, too, must be remembering the prince's archer. Gunthar signaled to him to draw closer once more. Other than Brandon and Sir John, only Julian knew that he was at this moment traversing the road to Vere Castle. He did not believe that there could have been time for Julian to impart that information to another confederate. But it was only prudent not to allow young Brandon's respect for his master to cause him to stray too far behind.

Brandon's tension grew visibly the further they traveled from Pennault. Gunthar heard the boy's breath of relief when the square stone keep of Sir Damian's fortress loomed into view. The curtain wall, which eighteen months ago had been reduced to rubble by Gunthar's siege engines, had been rebuilt and one of the crumbled towers was in the process of being reassembled by what looked to be a team of laborers drawn from Sir Damian's fields.

"Hold!" a voice called out. "Proceed no further. State your name and your business at Vere Castle."

Gunthar drew his mount to a standstill and looked up at the gatehouse from whence the challenge came. He could not see its author, but the archers on the flanking towers stood with bows readied and arrows trained on the intruders.

"I am Hugh de Bury, Earl of Gunthar, and I come in the name of the king."

The archers kept the bows steady and awaited their orders. They were some time coming. Gunthar imagined a messenger was being sent to the keep to receive instructions. He bided the waiting patiently, using the time to study the moat, which had been cleared of the rubble of war and its sides reinforced, but had not yet been refilled with water.

At length, he heard the grinding of machinery that raised the portcullis and lowered the drawbridge. A voice called out, "Enter, my lord Gunthar. Sir Damian awaits you within."

Gunthar rode across the drawbridge and into the bailey. He was greeted by a knight whom he recognized as the mercenary captain who had served as Sir Damian's lieutenant during the war.

"We meet again, Sir Oliver."

"My lord, your arrival is unexpected—but most welcome." A sneer twisted up the captain's thin lips as he glanced at the boyish squire. "You travel lightly, I see."

"I come in peace, sir. I trust your master is prepared to meet me in the same." Gunthar threw a significant look at the half-dozen men-at-arms who accompanied Sir Oliver.

But the captain only rubbed his hands together and answered, "Well, now, that's as may be. If you will be so good as to dismount?"

Gunthar hesitated. There was a gleam in Sir Oliver's eye that he did not trust, and accordingly he kept to his saddle. "Perhaps you would be so good as to request Sir Triston to step into the bailey? We might all be the better served—"

He broke off as a scraping of metal signaled the appearance of Sir Oliver's sword. Instantly, six more were drawn, all with their glistening blades pointed directly at Gunthar.

"Alas, my lord, Sir Triston is not available. But his father is most anxious that you attend him without delay. So I fear, my lord Gunthar, that I must ask you one more time to dismount."

Gunthar's lips tightened, but he rose up in the stirrups, preparing to obey.

"Insolent dogs! How dare you draw steel on the Earl of Gunthar?"

Gunthar looked round to see his outraged squire maneuver his horse towards the nearest of Sir Oliver's companions.

"Brandon, stay back!"

The order came too late. Brandon kicked out at the sword that swung round to meet him and sent the blade spinning through the air. With a howl of fury, the disarmed man pulled the squire from the saddle and hurled him to the ground. One of his fellows tossed the man another blade.

Gunthar sprang from his horse as the man raised his arm to strike the youth. "No!"

He caught the man's wrist, but knew he would not be able to stop the thrust's momentum. With a lightening maneuver, he shot out a foot to Brandon's ribs and flipped him out of the way. The man cursed in surprise when his blade struck the dirt. Before he could recover, Gunthar dealt him a blow to the mouth that sent him to the ground with several loosened teeth.

"Dastard, to attack an impulsive boy. Come, now, if 'tis blood you want, you may try to take it from me." Gunthar drew his own sword and swung it round in so threatening an arc that the remaining men-at-arms sprang back in alarm.

"Cowards!" Sir Oliver shouted. "You are four to one. Stand like men and seize him for your lord!"

One man lunged forward at his captain's command. Gunthar caught the man's steel on his. He forced both blades down, then swept them up again with such abrupt force that his opponent's sword sailed from his hand. The man stared after it. Gunthar stepped forward and snapped a fist into his face. The fellow toppled backwards, but at Sir Oliver's frantic urging, three more surged to take his place.

Gunthar held them off with a dogged determination, but as quickly as he fended off one attacker, the others recovered and renewed their assaults. He could hear Sir Oliver shouting and the pounding of feet that signaled the arrival of reinforcements. He would soon be overwhelmed. Brandon appeared at his side with one of the disarmed attacker's swords. He wielded it with commendable skill, but Gunthar could see the squire's strength was not equal to his more mature oppressors. Still, his efforts created sufficient distraction for Gunthar to press the advantage of his own arm. He sent two more blades flying before he was driven to his knees by a barrage of blows that seemed to burst from every direction.

"Sir Oliver, call off your dogs!"

At the barking command, their attackers drew back. A horseman had ridden into their midst.

"My lord Gunthar! Great heavens!"

Gunthar looked up. From the coldness in his cheeks, he knew the blood had drained from his face. He stumbled to his feet, shaking with fury and reaction. He spared only a glance to assure himself of Brandon's safety before rounding on the horseman.

"This is unpardonable, Sir Triston. An attack not only on myself, but on the king in whose authority I came—"

"What the blazes is going on here? Sir Oliver, have you lost your mind?" Triston turned from glaring at the captain to plead with Gunthar. "My lord, I do not know what madness has seized this man. I assure you it was not on my orders and on my oath, I shall see him rightly rebuked."

"And *I* shall see him strung up from the highest tower of Vere, along with his master and his villainous son," Gunthar swore. "I gave you the benefit of the doubt when you proclaimed your innocence before, but this—*this*—"

He was so angry he could not even finish, but stood trembling, clenching and unclenching his fist on the hilt of the sword that remained in his hand.

Triston swung himself off his horse and hissed to Sir Oliver, "Get out of his sight. Take your dogs with you." Then to Gunthar, "My lord, Sir Oliver is overzealous in my father's cause. I will not try to excuse him and whatever judgment you deem worthy of this offense shall not be withstood. But my father and I knew nothing of his intent. We had no word of your coming. I was not even here when you arrived, and my father is too broken to—"

"I suspect he is not too broken to issue orders," Gunthar snapped. "He knew I waited without the gate, for I spoke my name clearly to your gatekeeper. I came in peace, in the name of the king, and Sir Oliver knew it and your father knew it. This treason is going to end *now*—unless you intend to cut me down where I stand?"

Triston blanched. "My lord, this is all some dreadful mistake. I beg of you—"

"Enough. Take me to your father. I will hear what *he* has to say."

Triston hesitated, then as Gunthar slammed his sword into its scabbard, turned and led the way into the keep.

The great hall of Vere Castle was smaller than that of Pennault, but it possessed a smooth elegance of line. The windows, slitted narrower than a man's shoulders, were laced with iron bars that cast a latticed pattern of shadow and light across the rush-strewn floor. Four shields framed the wall behind the party on the dais. Between the shields hung a long silk banner, the five-petaled de Brielle rose brilliantly woven in gold against a dark green background.

"So, my lord Gunthar, we meet again—at last."

Gunthar frowned to see that Sir Oliver and his men had retreated to the castle and stood with arrogant swaggers around the man who issued this subtle-edged greeting. Sir Damian de Brielle. For a moment, Gunthar thought he must be mistaken. This could not be the same insolent, strong-framed knight who had spat curses from the battlements and fought Gunthar nearly to a standstill. This man with sunken cheeks and a dismal shawl over drooping shoulders . . . Only the eyes, burning like coals from the cadaverous face, hinted at a life still clung to and the smoldering passion that animated it.

"Father, I have tried to explain to my lord that Sir Oliver must have mistook—"

"Silence," Sir Damian snapped at his son. "We will not insult my lord's intelligence. He knows the truth."

"But Father—"

"I said silence!" Sir Damian gripped the arms of his chair with skeletal-like fingers, as though he would push himself to his feet. Then Gunthar saw the blanket in his lap, draped over his knees and legs. "Get out and leave me to my business. Sir Oliver and his men shall stay."

Sir Oliver smirked.

Triston said, "Then I shall stay as well."

His father glared. "You're not needed here, Triston."

"Sir, Lord Gunthar is an emissary of King Henry. He must be treated with the same respect and honor we would impart to the royal blood."

"Honor? Fah! The Angevin is not my king and I have never, and shall never, bow the knee to him." A grotesque grimace twisted up the sallow face. "Thanks to my good lord here, I shall never bow the knee to anyone. Even Henry cannot require it of me now."

"I have bowed the knee for you, Father," Triston said, "and have sworn an oath in your name. The war is over. There has been enough anger, enough grief, enough blood—"

"Nay," his father said, his burning eyes fixed on Gunthar, "there has not been enough of that yet."

He gestured, and Sir Oliver moved to a position behind him. It was then Gunthar saw the wheels attached to the chair, one to each corner. There were two pegs on the back where Sir Oliver could lay his hands and wheel his master where he willed. He pushed the chair to the edge of the dais, then stepped back when Sir Damian waved a hand again.

"What is it you want of me, Gunthar? I am no threat to you or anyone now. Will you persecute me to the end?"

The pity Gunthar had felt evaporated as he remembered the altercation in the bailey.

"You are treading a dangerous line, de Brielle," he said. "This dissembling impotence of yours is a sham. Out of your hatred for me, you allow yourself to be used like a pawn. But Henry will not be driven from what is his. Richard will learn that yet, and when he does you will find he has forgotten such minions as you as he scrambles to salvage what he can from this miscalculation."

"I am not the fool you think me, Gunthar. I have friends, men who will protect me, men who do not fear you or your king."

"Friends like Angoulême? His days too, are numbered. Henry has been merciful until now, but he intends to enforce this peace and any who stand against him will be swept aside. You have had but a taste of his punitive temper, the madness he is capable of when his passion is aroused. You have not seen the razed fortresses in Brittany, the wasted countryside, the smoldering villages on the Norman border—"

"We do not fear the Angevin lion. We are not Norman nor Breton, but free men of Poitou and Aquitaine. Our allegiance has ever been to his queen alone and we will swear no fealty but unto her. If Henry thinks to win our love by terror, he will find he has seized a bear by the tail."

"You cannot win this fight, de Brielle," Gunthar warned. "Think long and hard before you continue this course. Henry has pardoned you once, he will not do so again. You are leading your whole house headlong into disaster."

"Perhaps," Sir Damian sneered, "but you will not live to see it."

"Father—"

"Stay out of this, Triston. This is between Gunthar and me. If you have not the stomach for the game, then skulk off where you can do no harm."

"No, the earl is right. You risk us all with this reckless revenge. But think what it will cost to *us*, to Etienne, to Osanne, to myself—"

"Aye." Sir Damian's bitter gaze engulfed his son. "I think often of you and Osanne." Triston flushed, and Sir Damian added brutally, "Go away. It sickens me to look upon you. Your penances and tears might have won you my forgiveness with Osanne, but your surrender of Vere? I would see you in hell for that."

"Sir, we thought you dead—"

"You thought yourself lord, you mean. You thought me gone, you thought Vere yours, and waited not to know the truth before yielding like a coward to my enemies."

"The battle had already been lost," Triston said, "long before you tumbled from the wall. My submission saved lives, lives that you would have tossed away like pebbles at a stream."

Sir Damian muttered a curse at him.

Triston's handsome face tightened. "It is time you faced truth, Father. The days of our arrogance are gone, the days when we mouthed fealty to our dukes and dealt insolently behind their backs. They were too weak to bridle us. Each man ruled at the point of his sword, seizing land where he willed, spilling blood with impunity because it pleased him to do so and there was none to say him 'nay'. But we have a new master now. Henry is our king, and like it or not, no amount of intriguing is going to change that. He brings us law . . . and if we let him, he will finally bring us peace."

"Angevin peace," Sir Damian hissed. "Better that I had died than lived to see the day my own blood forsook our ancient liberties. 'Tis a coward's voice I hear from you, Triston."

"Nay, Sir Damian," Gunthar said, "'tis the voice of wisdom. Listen to your son—"

"My son, my heir—a coward, like his mother. You have corrupted him, you and your 'law-loving' lord. Well, when I die he may lie down with you both, but while there is breath left in my body, he has sworn to adhere to my word. Have you not, my son?"

Triston's face creased unhappily, but he did not deny the rebuke.

"Then I am sorry," Gunthar said, genuinely saddened by the young man's silence. He had glimpsed in Triston a man of reason, a man of vision, who longed for the order and security that Henry's reforms had already imposed upon the English isle and now sought to extend to the far-flung corners of his realm. It was men such as Triston on whom the future would be built. But the quiescent defeat in the young man's face, the sour satisfaction in Sir Damian's, made clear to Gunthar that, whatever Triston's sympathies, he would not stand against his father's hatred.

Gunthar looked back at Sir Damian. "Henry will know of the part you both have played. He will not regard your injury in his judgment. At the least, you shall suffer imprisonment and your lands be confiscated. At the worst—"

"Worst?" Sir Damian's voice went shrill. "Look at me, Gunthar. What could be worse than this?"

Without warning, he tore the veiling blanket from his lap. Legs that had once been strong and powerful now lolled aimlessly from the chair, shrunken into useless spindles, hose bagging over withered calves.

"This is what you have made me! Never again shall I walk the length of my own demesne, or ride a charger into battle, or know the joy of my wife's charms. I am no more a man, but a wasted, miserable shadow—albeit one with bite!"

He gave a signal and Sir Oliver rounded the chair, a hand upon his sword.

Sir Damian's eyes were a veritable blaze of bitter spite "Henry may do as he will to us all, but first I will have my revenge. It will be a pleasure to kill you, Gunthar. My only regret is that I am unable to cut you down myself."

Gunthar had no doubt but what the knight was about to carry out his threat.

"Father—" Triston stepped forward.

But Gunthar waved him back. "Are you sure this is the way the prince wants it done?" he said to Sir Damian. "A personal reprisal to avenge your own wrongs? What purpose will that serve in the grander scheme to cast off his father's shackles?"

Again Sir Damian sneered. "Ah, yes, Triston told me how you have reasoned it. You think yourself very clever, do you not? You think you know what lies within my heart. Well let me tell you this—*you know nothing!"*

He leaned forward and screamed the words at Gunthar's face.

Gunthar held his ground against the glitter in those dark, consuming eyes. "I know that my life has been threatened four times, most recently by your lawless henchman there. Twice more was the prince's hand clearly revealed, once by your son Etienne—"

"Etienne." Sir Damian groaned out the name as though the very forming of it were an agony of pain. " You will free Etienne!"

Gunthar perceived a chink in his opponent's presumptive armor of advantage. "The boy is a traitor," he said, "and attempted assassin. He will answer for his crimes."

"No!"

"You should have thought more clearly before you sent the boy to kill me. Did you honestly think he could do the deed in the sight of my own guards and escape?"

"I did not send him. I did not even know he had left the grounds. Etienne did not attack you at my command."

"At whose, then? He carried the dagger of Melusine, the prince's device. Do you expect me to believe he won the blade and the commission from the prince himself?"

"He has never met the prince. 'Twas some madness of his own, to avenge me, perhaps, but—"

"That won't serve, Sir Damian. It does not explain the dagger. Where else could he have gotten it, if not from the prince or from you?"

Sir Damian hesitated, his pale lips trembling.

"Tell him, Father." Triston moved forward suddenly, his voice urgent as he positioned himself between Sir Damian and Gunthar. "Tell him!"

"I . . . don't know." The answer came hoarsely. Sir Damian's face was as grey as the dust.

Triston looked incredulous. "Father—"

"Be silent, Triston."

"But Father, it is Etienne. Will you sacrifice his life to protect that devil—"

"I said be silent!"

"But—"

"Triston, you have sworn. We all have sworn!" Sir Damian looked sick, but there was no doubting the message of warning he sent to his son.

It was Triston who went white now. Gunthar saw a flash in his eyes as bitter as anything he had witnessed in Sir Damian.

"Aye, I recall the oath, imposed over my mother's grave, the one oath you knew I would not break. Very well, let it be as you will—and may Etienne's blood haunt you into hell."

Triston swung on his heel and strode from the hall, leaving a shivering silence in his wake. Sir Damian stared after him. The fire in his eyes ebbed until they appeared two hollow pools in a face of death. Sir Oliver and his men shifted about uneasily while their master sat unmoving in his chair.

Gunthar finally broke the tomb-like silence, speaking with a gentleness that surprised even himself.

"Damian, if there is someone else behind this, you must tell me."

Sir Damian brought his empty stare back to Gunthar's face. "There is no one else."

"But Triston said—"

"Triston is a coward and a fool. I need no encouragement in my hate for you."

"A hate that is going to destroy you and both your sons. Damian, I could help you if you would only tell me the truth."

"The truth?" The glitter returned to Sir Damian's eyes and his fingers curled grotesquely about the arms of the chair. "The truth is this. Do I want you dead? Yes. Do I know men who would pay fortunes to set the kingdom in upheaval? Yes. Would I consent to be their agent if one goal could be accomplished by the other? Yes, yes, yes! But I did not send Etienne to kill you and he is innocent of the part you charge. You must not judge him for my crimes."

"Damian—"

"Look at me! Look at what I am! A cripple, condemned for the rest of my days to this miserable chair. What light shall remain in my life if you take away my son? I would never have set him at risk of your vengeance by sending him to Pennault, not even to feed my own hatred. My lord, you must release him. I beg you—I implore you—send my son home."

Tears welled up in the burning eyes and fell over the sunken cheeks. Gunthar could only guess what it had cost Sir Damian to make that plea. He wished he could have answered it mercifully. But he could not forget the prince's dagger, or his own duty to the crown.

"I cannot, Sir Damian. Too much here smells of treason. If Etienne is innocent, I shall learn it and return him safely to your care. But if not—"

The reply enraged Sir Damian. He gave a choking sob, though whether of anger or grief, Gunthar could not tell. "Treason? If you want treason, I shall give it you. Sir Oliver." At his signal, the captain and his men drew their swords and leveled them at Gunthar. "Free my son now, or look upon your last light of day."

"Your son's, as well," Gunthar said. "What will my death prove but that Etienne, like his father, was an assassin all along? My men are already chafing to punish him in their own way. I have protected him thus far, reserving him for the king's judgment. Kill me now and I assure you, he will never live to see the king's face—or yours again, either."

Their eyes locked in blunt challenge, but in the end it was Sir Damian who broke. He sank into his chair in such a way that he seemed somehow to sink into himself.

"The devil wins, as always. Put down your swords."

"But sir—"

"Put them down!"

One final flash of spirit from the defeated depths, quickly gone. Sir Oliver and his men obeyed.

Gunthar turned to leave, but was halted by a parting shot.

"There are others who want you dead, Gunthar. Some who hate you as much as I. Look to yourself, my lord. The king's face may yet elude your gaze, as well."

Gunthar hung in mid-step for a moment, then made his way unhindered out of the hall.

# Thirteen

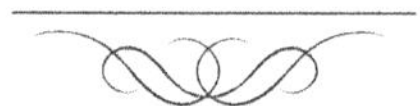

Twenty-four hours later, Sir Damian was dead.

The news spread first among the peasants, from the fields of Vere to the fields of Pennault. The bailiff informed the seneschal, who brought word up to the castle. Sir Damian had been found that morning dead in his bed, a victim apparently of his own declining health, for there were no indications that he had gone other than in his sleep.

Knowing the unreliability of churlish gossip, Gunthar dispatched an agent of his own to Vere Castle. He sent Lord Challons, for Gunthar desired not only the details of Sir Damian's death, but someone who might be able to ferret out the dark machinations he was convinced were going on there. Challons was a clever, subtle man with clever, subtle ways. If there were someone other than Sir Damian behind this web of intrigue, Challons would learn of it and bring back the truth to his lord.

But Challons discerned no sinister forces poised in the castle's shadows. Triston, he said, had been tight-lipped and uncooperative, but appeared to have taken command of the garrison. Only grudgingly had he permitted Challons to view his father's body, but there had been nothing there to contradict the word of Laurant's seneschal. There had been no marks upon the body, no signs of a struggle, nothing but the appearance of a quick, quiet death such as all men might pray to receive in the end.

Gunthar listened to the report in silence, then dismissed Challons with a curt word of thanks and ordered his secretary to arrange a mass for Sir Damian's soul.

The diners laughed heartily at the jesters' peppery riddles and jokes, applauding their grace and energy as they tossed their glittering balls into the air and tumbled comically after them. Gunthar tried to look amused as well, for the jugglers were skillful and worthy of commendation. But his thoughts kept drifting away. Not to the unexpected death of Sir Damian. Not to the still missing Etienne, nor the subsequent disappearance of the serving girl who had smuggled him the knife. Not even to Julian Parr, who had so inadequately answered all his probing questions regarding that same girl and his quarrel with her stableboy-lover. Gunthar had intended to keep an eye on Julian by allowing him to serve him tonight at the table. But from the moment she had stepped into the hall, Gunthar had been able to think of nothing but her.

He allowed Julian to place a currant tart on his trencher, welcoming the excuse it gave him to try yet again to engage her attention.

"A bite, my lady? The pastry is most marvelously light, and the custard . . ."

He trailed off at Heléne's withering stare and sighed as she turned her silvery gaze back to the frolicking jugglers. She had not spoken one word to him throughout the meal, despite the fact that they shared trencher and cup. He was not sure he blamed her. He had behaved like an utter churl in her chamber.

She had entered the hall with a militant gleam in her eye, glaring at him as though he were somehow responsible for the indisposition that had claimed her sister and would force her for the evening to take Clothilde's place at his side. But her hostility had bounced off him, overwhelmed by a vision that snatched his breath away and left his brain spinning with admiration at his own genius.

He had not been the only one to stare. The gown he had so impulsively designed with the clothier and his seamstress-wife had arrived with its twin for her sister that afternoon. How her mother had persuaded Heléne to wear it in her present mood, he could not guess. But it had completely transformed her.

The rich blue silk brightened her pale eyes to silver and turned sallow skin into shining translucence. There were roses in her cheeks he'd never seen before, not the fiery glow of indignation, but a tender, natural bloom. The surcote glistened softly, its pale gold the same shade as her shimmering hair, still twined in a thick, sweeping braid and tied with an embroidered blue ribbon. The blue-tasseled girdle finished off the enchanting ensemble. He marveled at his own flawless judgment in choosing a cut that so splendidly enhanced the quiet, graceful curves of her figure.

Though tall and elegantly regal in her new gown, he was obliged to own it was not precisely beauty she possessed, but something more elusive. Her nose was still imperious, her chin still pointed and decisive. Still, he had thanked every star in the heavens for Clothilde's unreliable health and moved to take possession of his creation, only to find his path blocked by a swarm of squires and courtiers who, in the absence of the lovely Clothilde, seemed suddenly eager to console themselves with the sister they had hitherto ignored.

She received their attentions with a charming confusion at first, but he watched as her shyness turned slowly to confidence and her blushes to laughter. The last vestiges of the impudent minx who had so maddened him and the awkward child who had so amused him alike vanished before his eyes. He felt an odd twinge at the loss, but nevertheless moved to shoulder aside his unexpected rivals. They dispersed reluctantly, only Sir Stephen Goldingham hesitating as if to challenge his claim, but even he finally slunk away at Gunthar's uncompromising stare.

It had been almost a relief to feel her fingers stiffen in his as he drew her hand though his arm and escorted her onto the dais. This mutinous wench he knew, and he would sooner have her frowning at his side than glowing under the pretentious flattery of one of those vainglorious young pups. Still, she might have shared just one glimmer of that new-found charm with him. Instead she sat in chilly silence, refusing to touch any of the food he offered her, only with reluctance and of necessity drinking from the cup they shared.

He had tried a dozen ways to revive her spirits, and finally murmured innocuously, "You will waste away to nothing if you continue to pick at your food like that."

To his surprise, her chin shot up and she signaled to the squire cutting meat before her father. She requested him to place a slice of venison on their trencher. Gunthar took the opportunity to study anew his host's young heir. Therri executed the carving with squirely skill. In feature he was remarkably like Clothilde, eclipsing even Julian Parr with his beauty. But that he shared his spirit with Heléne could be seen from the mischievous twinkle in his eye and the rueful grin she gave in response. She sobered almost instantly, as though determined to show no pleasure so long as she sat at Gunthar's side.

He watched as she broke off a morsel of meat, holding it neatly between her thumb and second finger, then saw the way she hesitated at dipping it into a nearby bowl of sauce. He recognized her difficulty at once, and reached out a hand to push back the pendulous cuff of her glittering surcote. The movement caused the tight blue sleeve of the under-gown to slip a little away from her wrist. Without thinking, he ran a finger over the smooth white skin thus exposed. She jumped and pulled away so abruptly that she nearly dropped her morsel. His hand closed quickly over hers, trapping the meat against her palm.

Her act of involuntary revulsion, if that's what it had been, suddenly enraged him. He was not some grotesque lout, that she should flinch from his touch. He tore the morsel out of her hand and flung it to one her father's hounds scavenging among the rushes. He scrubbed her palm clean with the edge of the tablecloth, then broke off another piece of meat and held it to her lips.

"Eat."

It was not a request, and he caught her hand as she tried to snatch the bit from his fingers. An angry blush stole up into her cheeks.

"I don't want—"

"I did not ask you if you wanted it. I told you to eat it."

She closed her lips and glared at him.

"There has been enough of this nonsense, my lady. Everyone is staring and above all things I abominate a scene. The meat is your own selection. Now open your mouth and eat."

Perhaps it was his commanding stare. Perhaps it was her mother's warning gaze, brimming with a promise of punishment for her daughter's intractable attitude all evening. Or perhaps it was merely embarrassment at all the shocked eyes viewing her defiance of Gunthar. In any event, she opened her mouth and he popped the morsel inside. Glorying in his first victory of the night, he followed it with another and another, until the slice of venison was gone, and so was his currant tart. Her silvery eyes glared daggers at him, but she obediently swallowed each mouthful and he finally judged her ready for some wine to wash it down.

He placed the cup between her hands, locking them between his on either side. She looked outraged at this further coercion, but he forced it up to her mouth and she drank. The cup was almost empty. He signaled Julian to refill it. This time he succeeded in doing no more than pressing it under her nose, for she refused to obey him further and obstinately kept her mouth shut.

Gunthar let her go and sat back in his chair, satisfied just the same. She would not dare to ignore him again. He would allow her to sulk a little, and when the meal was ended he would have the tables cleared away for dancing. Laurant, he knew, would oblige him, and she would be required to accept his hand. He would request something quick and complicated, involving leaps, that she might see his grace and skill, and lifts that he might have license to span her waist with his hands. And perhaps while he held her in the air, he would grow clumsy and allow his grasp on her to slip. She would then slide down into his arms, and he would feel her slender body close to his again ...

His blood coursed at the thought and he reached again for the cup, this time to slake his own thirst.

A sharp slap dashed it out of his hand. The wine splashed across the table, staining the tablecloth and drenching a platter of food. Gunthar turned his startled gaze in the direction of the blow and saw Heléne on her feet, staring after the tumbled cup with wide, frightened eyes. Her hand still hovered in the air and she was shaking like a leaf.

"My lady—?"

"Cowbane," she whispered. "Poison."

A shaft of sunshine broke through the hovering clouds and the roses danced their tangled heads against the breeze in what remained of the Lady Gwenllian's pleasure garden. Though spared devastation from the siege by its remoteness from the curtain walls, it had nevertheless been much neglected these eighteen months while rebuilding had gone forward in the outer bailey. The stables, the barracks, the forge, all had had to be raised again almost from scratch, so thorough a job had Gunthar's fiery missiles done. The orchard and herb garden had been maintained for their usefulness to the castle's occupants, but save for mending the dovecot, damaged by a winter storm, Laurant had insisted the roses would have to wait.

The bushes had grown shaggy and tall, climbing over the low, enclosing walls, and would have choked off the gate had Heléne not kept a path well pruned. She loved it here in the wild bower it had become, where no one ever seemed to venture but she. She did not mind that the benches were peeling, that the flowery mead had become a confusion of disordered weeds, or that the fountain had gone dry. The trill of the nearby doves usually soothed her nerves while she plied her needlework or immersed herself in one of the rare books she cajoled her father into buying. But on this grey, dismal morning both lay neglected, the former on the dusty plank beside her, the latter in her lap.

She did not hear the footsteps in the tangled grass. Her thoughts were a thousand miles away. But when Gunthar spoke her name and she looked up into his face, she realized perhaps they had not been so distant after all.

"My lord, I am glad to see you well this morning."

"Thanks to you. I am again in your debt, my lady Helen." The sun threw its shaft from behind him, casting a softening aura about his formidable build, but also shading his expression from her. She could not tell whether he was teasing her or not when he added, "I had not realized you were so adept in your knowledge of poisons. Healing, yes . . ."

"Well for you that one is required to recognize the noxious so as not to mistake it for the benevolent." She spoke coldly, in case he was mocking her. The shocking way the evening had ended had shaken her somewhat from her anger, but she had not forgiven his humiliating treatment of her at the table, still less his unpardonable behavior in her chamber.

"No doubt," was all he said. "What was it then, this 'cowbane' from which you saved me?"

"'Tis a wild herb that grows near streams and in the swales of pastures. It looks very much like angelica, a harmless medicinal herb, but the rootstock of cowbane is deadly. The juice of a young plant's root such as might be found in the spring can kill a man in less than thirty minutes . . ."

She trailed off and caught the tilt of Gunthar's head, which threw his gaze briefly upon the roses. Knotted and wild they might be, but they were also large and brilliant, their glory testifying of the vernal season.

"I see." His voice hardened. "Then I am in your debt, indeed."

She felt a tug of sympathy for his grimness. The escape from death had been frighteningly narrow. She unbent enough to admit, though not without a dig at his atrocious behavior, "'Twas a rare piece of luck. Had you not been playing the bully and forced that cup beneath my nose, I would never have caught the scent. As it was, I very nearly missed it, masked as it was in the wine."

He picked up her abandoned embroidery and sat down on the bench beside her. The last of her coolness vanished as her pulses leapt. She inched away from the disturbing warmth of his nearness.

"Relax, my lady, I am not going to attack you again. You have made it abundantly clear that my advances are repugnant to you, but I had supposed we could conduct a simple conversation without you suspecting me of intending rape."

Her cheeks flamed. "I never— Oh! You are the most abominable man I have ever met!"

"And you are a most aggravating woman. But that doesn't alter the fact that you are quite right. I allowed you to provoke me into 'playing the bully', and as a consequence it was you who nearly drank that wine. Had you not chosen to turn stubborn at just that moment . . ." He looked down at the embroidery in his hands and rubbed a thumb across the stitches. His voice lowered, deepening to a note she had never heard there before. "That thought haunted me all night. You might have died, and all because of my stupid, arrogant, injured pride."

"You could not have known," she said, disquieted by the droop of the powerful shoulders beneath his light spring mantle. "Whoever laced that wine felt no compunction whatsoever about risking innocent lives to murder you."

"You do not suppose it was an accident, then? That someone merely confused angelica with cowbane?"

"Of course not. There was no reason for anyone to put angelica into your wine."

He sighed. "Then that makes four."

"Four what?"

"Attempts on my life. Unless you count the assault at Vere, but I do not think that was the same."

"Vere? Is that where you went after—"

She stopped, hesitating to revive further memories of their encounter in her chamber.

But he completed her thought. "After I left you? Aye. I needed to confront Sir Damian about Etienne, about Triston and the prince. There was an incident on the road to Angoulême, you see. Someone cut my saddle strap, and just for good measure there was an archer waiting in the woods to ambush me. The man was one of Richard's minions and wore the prince's badge, but the strap—that was tampered with before we left Pennault."

Both these revelations alarmed her. "Are you saying you think one of my father's men—?"

"No. My men suspect Sir Triston. He spent the night here, you'll recall, and may have taken the opportunity to tamper with my strap before he returned to Vere. But he did not know that I was traveling to Angoulême. How that archer knew where I would be and when—"

"It was not common knowledge? That you would pay your respects to the prince?"

"Aye, but the timing. After the rough crossing from England, I might have been expected to rest a day or two. Some of my men were still rather green from the sea. I debated waiting and only made up my mind during that interminable banquet your father treated me to my first night here. My own men were not informed until the meal was over, but even if someone overheard me it seems incredibly unlikely that the information should have reached the prince in time to set an assassin on the road. And yet . . ."

"Perhaps—perhaps the information did not need to reach the prince. Perhaps he had an agent near to Pennault ready to act in his name."

"Such as some mysterious 'pale knight'?" Gunthar turned his head, and she felt the probing force of his eyes. "Is there something you wish to tell me, Lady Helen?"

She looked away quickly before he could fix her gaze, before, she prayed, he could read the guilt in her face. She had no doubt that word of his whereabouts had come from her. She had heard him discussing the journey to Angoulême with her father and had told Rousillon. And Rousillon had used that knowledge, *her* knowledge, to try to murder Gunthar. She felt sick at the thought, but she could not tell him the truth, not so long as Rousillon still threatened her father. If her father were plotting to betray the crown— She remembered the hideous punishment described by Etienne, shivered, and held her peace.

"Well," Gunthar said, when it became clear that she was not going to answer, "you will at least be relieved to know that I have acquitted your young swain in this matter of poison. It is doubtful he would have risked being seen in your kitchen, where he would have to have gone to tamper with the wine. He would have been recognized and seized."

She *was* relieved, but said, " Etienne is not my swain. How many times must I tell you—"

" —you are just friends."

She glanced at him, then looked away again, her heart fluttering. He was staring, not at her face, but at the crimson surcote she wore. She twitched at one of the elbow-length sleeves, then linked her hands together over the book in her lap and tried to appear indifferent to his study. The truth was, she felt like a fool and was certain that he would burst into laughter any moment.

But of course, the Earl of Gunthar was far too well bred to do anything so discourteous, no matter how outrageous the temptation. Perhaps to distract himself, he solicited her opinion.

"Tell me, Lady Helen, how do you think that cowbane got into my wine?"

She had been pondering that question herself all morning and gladly turned her thoughts away from her own embarrassment. "It was served by your squire— "

"Whom, of course, I have questioned. He claims he was an unwitting carrier, says he was handed the bottle by some servant whose face he could not recall. I admit, recent events have caused me to reassess Julian's loyalty somewhat, but I think in this he was telling the truth."

"Then you have questioned the servants as well?" She thought of Sybil, remembering the surly way the old nurse had responded to *her* inquiries. Pray heaven she had not been so rude to Gunthar.

"Aye, my men have interrogated them all, to little effect. No one saw anything, no one knows anything, and of course someone is lying. How to prove it is the problem. And then there is that missing serving wench. What was her name? The one whose place you took in the tower with young de Brielle."

Audiart, she thought, but did not say it. She felt her cheeks warming again and hoped her silence would persuade him to drop that subject.

"I suppose I should apologize for accusing you of smuggling him that knife. My young squire Brandon assures me it was not done by you. He suspects the missing wench and some male accomplice, though their motives remain a mystery. Of the deed, therefore, I must acquit you, but of the intent . . . Tell me, my lady, for curiosity's sake, how was it you meant to free him?"

She hesitated. She vaguely remembered blurting out her guilty intention when he had confronted her in her chamber. She did not know why she should condemn herself further in his eyes, yet she heard herself replying, "I was going to drug the guard."

From the corner of her eye, she saw his brows shoot up. "Drug? I suppose I should have expected that from you. What kind? Something less lethal than cowbane, I trust?"

She permitted herself a scathing glance at him. "Of course. I did not want to kill him, just put him to sleep. Then I was going to take the keys from his belt and unlock the door and set Etienne free."

He gave a low whistle. "Simple, clean, no one hurt. But there was still the escape from the castle."

"That would not have been difficult. The exits were not uniformly blocked until after Etienne's escape was discovered."

"Ah. So you hoped to smuggle him off the grounds before we learned he was gone? Unfortunately your brother came home and precipitously overturned your cart."

"It was not my cart. I didn't do anything."

"But you meant to. And you will not deny that if the boy came to you, you would try to hide him from my guards?"

She met his gaze squarely now, for she was not ashamed of her loyalty. "Yes, I would. But he has not come to me and I do not know where he is, though every day I pray he may safely escape your malice."

"My malice?" His lips twitched and she saw a flash of anger. "Is that what you believe? That I would punish the boy to satisfy some sort of private vengeance?"

She caught her breath, unable to tear her eyes away from the springing fire in his. No, it was more than anger, more than indignation at her charge. It was something deeper, hotter, something much more personal.

"Well?"

Private vengeance was exactly what Etienne had accused him of. But Sir Damian *had* violated the peace treaty. Whatever threats Gunthar might have made against Sir Damian had no doubt been justly made in the name of the king. Suddenly the foundation on which she had built all her suspicions and distrust seemed to crumble away.

"No," she murmured. "Forgive me, that was unjust."

The fire ebbed only a little. "Then do both yourself and the boy a favor, my lady, and help me find him."

She shook her head. Gunthar's relentless devotion to the crown would prove just as dangerous to Etienne as any self-serving revenge. "You will only call him traitor and lock him up again."

"I must know the truth of that dagger he carried."

"It was not his. Someone put it into his sheath when he was not looking."

"Put it into his sheath—? That is absurd. Even if I believed such a ludicrous story—"

"It is not ludicrous, it is the truth!"

For a moment, she thought he looked frustrated enough to shake her. Then he stood up and took several pacing steps away. She saw the tight control on his face when he turned back around.

"You must forgive me if I am disposed towards some skepticism in this matter. I find it somewhat unnerving to know there is someone walking about who wants me dead."

She watched with some chagrin the way he was crumpling her embroidery between his hands. The repetitive tensing and easing of his fingers betrayed the stress which he otherwise concealed so masterfully.

She said, "There may very well be a conspiracy against you and the king after all, but Etienne is not a part of it. At least," she added, remembering the dagger, "not a witting part."

"He did attack me."

"I know. But he thought he was protecting his father. Sir Damian told him that you were going to imprison him for rebuilding Vere's walls in defiance of the peace treaty. I don't know why Sir Damian chose to defy the treaty that way, but if he knew about a conspiracy he did not tell Etienne."

Poor Etienne. What would he do when he learned of Sir Damian's death?

Gunthar murmured, "I wonder if de Brielle realizes what a fortunate youth he is. Would I could count among my men one heart so loyal as beats within your breast, Lady Helen."

She blushed. There was no mockery now, but rather a look that made her heart skip. She reached out a hand and asked breathlessly, "My embroidery, please?"

He seemed startled, as if he had not realized he was holding it. He looked guilty as a pageboy when he saw the havoc his restless hands had wrought upon the delicate fabric. "I hope I've not ruined it beyond repair?"

She sighed as she took it from him and studied the creases. At least it was not torn. "It was stained anyway from the dust. I should not have laid it on the bench. Mama says I am far too careless." She dropped it sadly into the workbasket near her feet.

"A pity," he said, "for the pattern was skillfully stitched. My own seamstresses could not have done half so cleverly."

The compliment pleased her, for she held some pride in her needlework. It was one of the few talents at which even her mother agreed she excelled.

"What is it you are reading?"

She had nearly forgotten the book in her lap. Her motion towards the basket must have drawn his attention to it.

"Something Father Dominic gave me. A dreary tale for a dreary day." The sun had flitted back behind the clouds and the breeze was picking up, swirling Gunthar's mantle about his broad shoulders. Before she anticipated his move, he plucked the book out of her lap.

The volume was small, designed for a woman's hands, and there was a scroll in gold leaf around the edges of the green leather binding. It was one of her treasures and she regretted her impulsive characterization of its contents, for no matter how dry the text, the essence of the story was compelling.

"Ah." She saw the lift of his heavy eyebrows as he scanned the delicate vellum pages. "I had not realized the fame of our local saints had spread so far. Translated into French, no less."

"It was all Papa would allow me to learn to read," she said, though she added with no small pride, "and that is my very own book. Father Dominic most kindly and generously commissioned it for me last Christmas. Is it not beautifully bound?"

"Aye," he agreed. "No doubt he hoped to inspire you to follow its heroine's course straight into a nunnery."

His tone offended her. "Christina of Markyate was a renowned holy woman and her courage and determination in the face of her parents' opposition to her calling can only be admired."

"I suppose she was sincere enough in her desire for a religious life, and they say she did much good for her abbey and the poor. But the miracles ascribed to her since she died fifteen years ago grow more outlandish every day. I trust you are not gullible enough to believe everything written of her here?"

"You do not believe in miracles, sir?"

"That the sick or the blind might be healed through the prayer of faith is a principle taught clearly by Our Lord when he walked upon the earth. And I will not dispute the efficacy of the Saints to intercede on our behalf. But that a man should pray to Saint Swithin when he is lost in the woods and hear his horse speak to tell him the way, or that a fish should crawl out upon dry ground to feed a starving woman—well, I must admit, such tales sorely stretch the limits of my credulity." She giggled at the exasperation in his voice, and he responded with a rueful grin. "My own chaplain would be appalled at my blunt disbelief. He is very young and passionate in his faith. I'm sure he longs frequently to chastise me, but is still too new in his place and remains somewhat awed by my title."

"It is not your title that intimidates men," she said. "It is everything about you. Your height, your bearing, the way you look at men, as though you could pierce their very souls . . ."

She stopped. The way he was looking at her now. She saw his eyes flicker, felt his gaze moving over her face, lowering to her neck and the plait spilling over her shoulder, its feathery end tumbled in her lap.

"I see you have taken my advice and found something more flattering to wear."

The mild comment made her squirm. He *was* laughing at her. She had borrowed the crimson surcote from her sister and of course it didn't fit. It fell too short of the white tunic beneath, though many such garments these days were cut higher in the front. The wide cuffs of Clothilde's full-length sleeves trailed, albeit gracefully, at Heléne's elbows, but she had consoled herself with rumors that such a style was popular among women of the prince's court. But the bodice was embarrassingly tight. Her shoulders were wider than Clothilde's and drew the soft woolen cloth snugly across her bosom. From the way he was staring at her, she knew he found such boldness shocking.

"It was a mistake," she said miserably. "I should not have worn it."

His gaze lingered as if fascinated on the curves exposed by the clinging wool. "The color is charming on you," he said softly. "You are as beguiling in crimson as you were in blue."

So that was it. He was teasing her because she had not yet thanked him for his gift. The gown had taken her by surprise, but she had told herself that it signified nothing more than pity for her pathetic wardrobe. Had he not sent an equally grand gown to Clothilde, though she had been too ill to wear it?

"It was most kind of you, my lord. My sister and I were overwhelmed by your beneficence, and we—"

"You were a vision, you know," he interrupted, his gaze sweeping back to her face. "You shook your father's entire court. Even Sir Stephen was impressed, and is bound to send a glowing report of you back to his master. Heywood will be pleased."

His words confused her. They might have been mocking again, but the look in his eyes . . . It was the way he had looked at her in her chamber, just before he had—

"A pity," he added, "now that we have finally got you dressed to advantage, that you shall have to give it all up again."

"What do you mean?"

"The Church frowns on such vanity. If you intend to become a novice, you shall have to accustom yourself to the dreariest of browns and blacks."

"A novice?"

He tapped the book with one finger. "I presume you study the life of Christina of Markyate because—"

"Oh, no, I have no wish to be a nun. It is only her courage that I admire, for she stood firm against railings and threats and beatings and would not marry against her conscience the man her parents had chosen for her."

Too late did she see the twinkle in his eye, and it was only for a moment, for it vanished on her word.

"Is that why your mother beat you? Because you will not marry Heywood?"

She looked away, ashamed that he had seen the marks on her back. The boards creaked as he resumed his place at her side. He pressed the book back into her hands. His strong, brown fingers lingered over hers.

"She will have to find some other way to persuade you, now. You will not taste her rod again."

"You—you spoke to my mother?"

"This morning. She did not much like me telling her how to rear her daughter, but she smiled at me through her teeth and agreed."

"Thank you." She hoped the agreement extended to Sybil, as well.

He gently stroked the back of her hand. "Is it so bad?" he asked. "My touch?"

She dared not answer. The warmth spreading through her body was frighteningly familiar. It had flooded through her veins last night when he'd brushed her wrist, startling her, confusing her, as had his kisses in her chamber. This time, she did not pull away when he pushed back the cuff of her tunic and lightly caressed her wrist. Tiny, fiery tingles danced all up and down her spine, a dismayingly pleasurable sensation. It was that which terrified her. Not the feel of his hand, not the warm desire in his eyes, but the intensity of her own reaction.

"What are you doing?"

He had released her wrist and taken up the end of her braid. "Something I have been wanting to do ever since I saw your inquisitive face at the window, staring down on me in the bailey."

He loosed the ribbon and began slowly to unplait her hair. He took his time, fingering and caressing each strand he loosed, as though he would savor every inch of the long, silken tresses. She watched the movement of his hands, marveling at their fluid grace as they worked their way higher and higher . . . Her breathing quickened the closer they came to her face. And then the last strand was free. He spread her hair like a veil about her shoulders, drew it in a web about her cheeks . . .

"Please . . ." She could feel the heat of his palms framing her face through her hair. His mouth was so close to hers she could feel his breath on her lips.

"Helen."

She tried to hold him off and felt his hands tighten about her face.

"Don't— " he pled. "Please don't push me away. I swear I will not frighten you again. It will be like the first time, when I kissed you on your father's archery field. You liked it then."

Oh, saints, she *was* afraid, but not of him. She *wanted* him to kiss her, wanted it desperately, so desperately that the pounding force of it made her shiver.

"Shhh, I won't hurt you." His hands moved reassuringly over her cheeks. He brushed his lips against her brow, then closed her eyes with his mouth against her lids. Then he lifted her face and kissed her.

The pleasure that washed through her was almost more than she could bear. The book slid out of her hands and she felt herself drifting away, floating in a warm, golden glow.

His mouth lifted. "Helen . . . ?"

His voice was hoarse and for a moment she was terrified that he was going to leave her. She felt his hands sliding through her hair to close about her shoulders, pushing her hesitantly away. It was then, as she gazed into his eyes, that she realized he, too, was afraid. Afraid that she might not want him, that any moment he would overstep the bounds as he had in her chamber, and that she would . . .

He must have thought she was trying to break away when she shifted her body. His grasp on her instantly slackened, but she had no intention of escaping this time. She only wanted to rearrange herself, to wrap her arms around his neck and give him a kiss that would send the last of his foolish doubts from his mind.

It took several such kisses to convince him. Then he dragged her into his arms, his hands sliding down her back to press her closer—

Heléne tried not to cry out. She knew what would happen if she did, but the sound burst from her lips as pain exploded through her back. She glimpsed the bewilderment in his face as he freed her, just before her eyes blurred over with tears. The agony of her beatings paled beside the despairing fear that she had driven him away again.

Then his arms wound around her once more, cradling her, not with passion, but gently, comfortingly against his breast.

"Sweetheart, sweetheart, forgive me."

The words were a caress, as tender as the mouth he pressed against her hair. She gave a little sighing sob. She curled one hand into the front of his surcote, as if by dint of sheer physical force she would prevent him from ever letting her go again.

"I should have remembered."

"It is all right," she whispered, adding, though a lie, "the hurt is already gone."

She looked up, anxious that he should believe her, then closed her eyes when he kissed her again. A curious contentment spread through her. The soft, gentle movement of his mouth wrapped her in a sweetness as potent as anything that had come before.

She sighed again, this time without tears, when he drew her head down to his shoulder. One of his hands played with a flowing strand of her hair.

"Promise me you will never bind it again."

A smile danced over her lips. "What, not even when I am old?"

"No," he said, "not even when we are old."

It took a moment for the subtle change in pronoun to sink in. Heléne's heart stopped. Had it been a slip—or was he making some sort of declaration? She lifted her head to look into his face, then gasped as he shoved her away.

"My lord—?" She reached out a frantic hand as he rose and took a pace away from her, then shrank as a gentleman's voice floated across the air.

"My lord, I beg you will forgive this intrusion, but Jean aux Bellesmains has arrived and is requesting an interview."

"Bellesmains?" She heard the surprise in Gunthar's voice. "What is the Bishop of Poitiers doing here?"

Heléne leaned sideways a little to catch a glimpse of the man whom Gunthar was blocking from her view. She saw Lord Challons, looking very resplendent in a yellow and green surcote trimmed with a diamond and ruby studded chain. There was a red cap on his head, with a yellow feather curling cockily over the brim. She saw his quick eyes dart from Gunthar to her peering face and drew hastily back out of sight.

Challons gave an awkward little cough before answering Gunthar's question. "The bishop did not confide in me, other than to say he is sent to fulfill a commission from the king. But from his demeanor and the questions he put to Laurant—well, I suspect, my lord, it has something to do with the betrothal."

The betrothal. Heléne felt herself go white. How had she been so mad as to forget? Gunthar was promised to her sister and the bishop would only formalize what was already understood. But surely everything had changed? Surely now he would send the bishop away or—

Gunthar turned back round, but she could not read the expression in his eyes. It was as though a veil had dropped over them. "My lady—"

She held her breath, certain he would speak some word of reassurance, however subtle.

He bent to pick up something off the ground.

"—your book."

She took it mechanically from his hand.

"You will excuse us? The bishop is waiting. Come along, Challons."

She stared after him, stunned, as he strode out of the garden.

# Fourteen

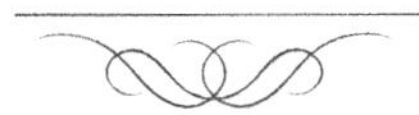

"Heléne. *Heléne.*"

Heléne did not know when the persistent hissing evolved into a voice. In the back of her disordered mind, she had thought it the rustling of the breeze in the grass. But the urgency finally penetrated her haze and she turned about to look for its direction.

*"Etienne?"*

He was crouched beside one of the tall, unruly rose bushes. Her joy at seeing him did not succeed in wiping away her confusion over Gunthar's departure, but she ran to him and fell to her knees to embrace him.

"Oh Etienne, how glad I am to see you!"

He slid one arm around her waist. "Heléne, are you all right?"

"Me? Of course I am. Why shouldn't I be?"

"I saw that devil taking advantage of you, knowing you would not dare to resist an officer of the king. I wanted to stop him, but this kitchen knife's no match for that dagger he always wears, and with my injured wrist— Still, if that lackey of his hadn't come when he did, I would have—"

She put up a hand to his mouth. This bush stood opposite the garden gate. Etienne must have been concealed behind the bush all morning and witnessed her interlude with Gunthar.

"Stop. Etienne, Gunthar was not assaulting me."

Etienne pulled her hand away. "You can't mean—" His eyes

widened. "Heléne, have you lost your mind?"

She said nothing, for at the moment she was none too sure of the answer.

"He is going to marry Clothilde," he reminded her. "You said so yourself. It is all over the county that is why he has come to Pennault."

"They are not betrothed yet," she said.

"They will be. Father said it's a direct order of the king, and Father's source is never wrong. Heléne, think. It is *Gunthar*. You know he would never defy the king."

Her confidence wobbled. "But he does not love Clothilde."

"A cold fish like that would not love anyone," Etienne scoffed. "That has nothing to do with marriage." He paused, then added with a sudden incisiveness, "But you're in love with him, aren't you?"

She bit her lip. When had it happened? How *could* it have happened? Yet she knew with unwavering certitude that Etienne had discerned the truth she had not, until this moment, dared to admit to herself.

Etienne found her hand and squeezed it.

"I'm sorry, Heléne, but you know it's true. He will only use you and cast you aside. He is not flesh and blood like other men, but a stonehearted monster. Look what he has done to Father, what he has done to me—" he waved his bandaged wrist "—and think what he yet will do if he catches me again."

She did not want to believe, after the tenderness they'd shared, that Gunthar could still be a threat to anyone she loved. But Etienne was right. A few kisses, even had they been sincere, would not change the man. His implacable devotion to the crown would see Etienne imprisoned or worse, as surely as it would drive Gunthar undeterred to the altar with Clothilde.

She blinked back the sudden sting in her eyes and stood up, drawing Etienne with her. "Is this where you've been all the time?"

He nodded. "I ducked in here in a panic when I saw your father's guards. I don't think they saw me enter for no one searched it at once, and when they did come I dodged behind that bush." He pointed to a big, shaggy specimen against the east wall. "Saints, Heléne, how I was shaking. I knelt there on the ground and listened to their footsteps and thought of the noose and the knife—" He shuddered. "I didn't know what to do, so I prayed. I've never prayed so hard for anything in my life, and then—it was like a miracle. Someone gave a shout that I had been found and they all ran off after him."

"There have been several false sightings since you escaped," she said. "My father is afraid of the earl, and the guards are afraid of my father. They jump every time they see a shadow and claim that it's you."

"A miracle is a miracle," he insisted. "I'm not going to question why."

She smiled. The talk of miracles reminded her of Gunthar and his mocking skepticism. Would he have laughed at Etienne's account? Her smile faded. Nay, he would be too busy clapping Etienne into irons.

"I have got to get you out of here," she said, "in case the guards decide to finish the search your miracle interrupted." Her brow creased as she tried to think of a safe place to hide him.

"Heléne," Etienne asked when the silence stretched on, "is it true someone tried to murder Gunthar last night?"

"How did you know that?"

"I heard you and Gunthar talking. I couldn't catch everything you said, but I'm certain I heard the word 'poison'." She told him about the tainted wine. "Does he suspect me?"

"No, he does not think you'd have been foolish enough to risk being seen. But that does not lessen your danger. There have now been four attempts on his life, and at least two of those seem to have been directly linked to the prince. Etienne, unless you can explain that dagger—"

He gave a resolute shake of his head.

She eyed him worriedly for a moment. Her next words were going to hurt, but the urgency of the situation precluded taking time to soften the blow.

"Etienne, if you are thinking to protect your father with this stubborn silence, there is no longer any need. Sir Damian died yesterday night."

She watched as the blood drained from his face. She reached out a hand to his arm, but he jerked away.

"No. He can't be—"

"I'm sorry, Etienne. He went in his sleep. It is said to have been a quiet death."

That appeared to be little comfort to him. She knew this was not the time to press him further about the dagger. Later they would deal with that and other things, but what he needed now was to be left alone to absorb her painful revelation.

"I have an idea," she said, "of where to hide you, but it will take some time. Wait here for me and keep yourself low to the bushes."

He did not seem to hear her, but he did not resist when she pushed him back behind the branches. He sank onto the ground and dropped his head into his sound hand. Her heart ached for him. She could not ease the anguish of his spirit, but his threatened body she was determined to save. She ran off to set her plan into motion.

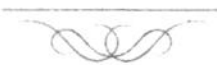

Her brother jumped at Heléne's request, as much for the lark it would be as out of friendship for Etienne. Therri, wearing Etienne's clothes, would dart off in the opposite direction making sure he was seen and followed, while Heléne led Etienne on an unobstructed course to the ruins of the South Tower. Under no circumstances, she warned, was Therri to allow himself to be caught. If it were discovered that it was *he* wearing Etienne's clothes, the fat would truly be in the fire for all of them.

Therri went gamely off to the garden to begin the exchange of dress, while Heléne made her way to the kitchen to gather a few helpful supplies. The cook looked surprised at her request for a picnic basket, but Heléne reminded her that it seldom rained this time of year before sundown and assured her that she and Therri would be back long before then.

Cook smiled indulgently. While she was busy stuffing the basket full of meat pies and apple tarts, Heléne went to the cupboard and surreptitiously removed two candles. She hid one each inside two wooden goblets, then placed them in the basket, with a request for a bottle of wine. One of the lower servants was sent to the cellars. Heléne occupied the waiting with a study of the kitchen's looming stone oven and the ash pile that was raked to one side. Cook made no rebuke when Heléne accidentally dropped a clay jar into the cinders, but handed her young mistress a cloth to wipe her hands.

Heléne passed three guards on the way back to the garden. The first two made no comment as to her direction or the basket she carried. She expected the third to be equally disinterested, especially when she saw the Lady Osanne hanging familiarly on his arm. Heléne frowned. Osanne had made no attempt to conceal her scandalous interest in Gunthar's friend, Sir John, during her stay at Pennault Castle. Heléne wondered what Sir John would say now, had he seen the sultry smiles Osanne was bestowing on her father's guard.

Heléne hoped to pass them with no more than a nod, but Osanne, perhaps in annoyance at being caught flirting with the guard, stopped her, the sultry smile cooling into a challenge.

"Good day to you, my lady. If you are looking for your brother, he passed by here a few minutes ago, as though headed for your mother's flower garden."

Heléne's heart gave a skip at Osanne's mention of the garden. Thankfully, the guard and his companion were not within sight of the garden's gate and so would not see Therri bolting out of it in a few minutes wearing Etienne's clothes. Still, she would have to warn her brother not to begin his false-flight along this path, lest this guard grow suspicious at the direction from which the "fugitive" hailed.

"My brother and I are off to a picnic," Heléne said, when Osanne lifted her brows at the basket on her arm. "He promised first to pick a few of my mother's roses for me to twine into my hair."

Osanne's sly eyes flicked to Helene's trailing tresses. Undoubtedly she wondered at their unusual loosing from the customary braid, but she only said with a skeptical glance at the darkening sky, "A picnic?"

"It is to celebrate my brother's homecoming. We have scarcely had two moments alone together since he came back from my uncle's. Yes, I know it looks as if a storm is brewing, but I do not think it will rain so early in the day as this. Forgive me, my lady, but my brother is waiting for me."

Heléne hurried on before Osanne could say anything more.

Therri and Etienne were waiting for her in the garden, Etienne still pale and distraught, Therri somewhat sobered by his friend's grief. They each wore the other's clothes, but Heléne saw that the right sleeve of both tunics had been slashed, a necessary accommodation for the splint on Etienne's wrist.

"Sir Geraud and the Lady Osanne know we're in the garden," Heléne warned her brother. "You'd better choose a different path for your flight."

"I know," Therri said. "I passed them too. I'll slip around the other way and let the guards on the west wall catch a glimpse of me. They'll sound the alarm and once the uproar starts, you can steal away with Etienne."

He started towards the gate, but she touched his arm.

"Wait."

She set the basket down on the peeling bench and took out the clay jar she had dropped in the kitchen and slipped in with the food when Cook had turned her back. Heléne unstopped the jar, poured out a handful of ashes and reached them up to her brother's pale gold hair.

"Ho, there!" Therri caught her wrist. "What do you think you're doing?"

"I'm trying to make you look like Etienne. No one will believe you are he with your hair shining about your face like a halo."

But Therri was vain about his hair. "You're not going to do it like that. Let me wear a cloak and hood."

"That would cover Etienne's tunic and ruin the whole disguise."

"A hat, then."

"We haven't got one. And anyway, the guards know Etienne was not wearing a hat when he escaped."

Therri's mouth went mulish. "I am not going to let you—"

His protest had grown blusteringly loud. She sought to quiet him with a warning kick to the ankle.

*"Ow!"*

"Hush *up*," she said.

He glowered at her and bent over to rub at his injury. Seeing him in such an accommodating position, she poured the contents of the jar over his head.

"Hey!"

"Be quiet. Do you want to bring the guards down upon us? You can wash it out later."

He glared, then sighed and gave it up. The damage was done. In resentful silence, he allowed her to work the ashes briskly through his hair until his locks were as black as Etienne's airy curls.

"Now then." She wiped her hands on the linen cloth Cook had used to cover the basket. "Remember what I told you. Lead them away from the South Tower, towards the postern gate if you can, or—"

"I know what to do. Just be sure you don't bolt before I've made the coast clear."

He glanced at Etienne and the ill humor died from his face. His friend looked numb, too distracted even to care about all their plotting on his behalf.

"He will be all right," Heléne said softly.

Therri gave a curt nod and went through the gate to do his part.

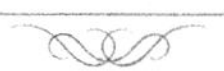

Heléne held Etienne's hand tight, appreciative of its support as they picked their way cautiously through the rubble. The devastation of the South Tower and its adjoining wall had been thorough. Both had been shattered by a volley of stones, some as large as fifty pounds, hurled with remarkable accuracy by Gunthar's mangons during the siege. Through this breach had surged a swarm of shouting, battle-ready knights. Seeing his defenses overrun, her father had thrown down his arms and surrendered.

In the early days following Gunthar's triumph, she had come here often to gaze on the ruins, fanning her anger against the man who had wrought such terror and humiliation upon her house. She had hated him then, hated the man she did not know, the man she had believed him to be. It had all been so easy in her bitter imaginings, before she had learned the reality of the man he was.

Arrogant, yes. Bullying when it suited him. But Gunthar was not cruel. He might have used the darkest, most insidious means to force Etienne to speak. But save for Etienne's broken wrist—which, in all honesty, had been a matter of defense—Gunthar had shown nothing but patience with his would-be assassin. As for herself, his behavior had certainly been mystifying. But even during those few baffling moments in her chamber, when his gentle, seductive kisses had briefly roughened with his taunts about Etienne, it had never entered her thoughts that her virtue might be in danger at his hands. In the back of her whirling mind, she had sensed too much subtle discipline in his passion. Nay, when she had finally escaped his embrace, it had not been fear of his intentions that had set her shrinking from him. Her only fear had been that if she let him kiss her again, she would never want him to stop.

Just as she had not wanted him to stop in the garden today.

She stumbled over a shard of broken stone and felt the quick strength of Etienne's hand as it steadied her. Rubble lay everywhere, an unwelcome reminder of that aspect of Gunthar's character she least wanted to face: his passionate, impelling allegiance to the king and the uncompromising lengths he would go to, to establish Henry's cause. Etienne was right. If an eight-foot thick, twenty-foot high stone wall had been unable to stop him, he surely would not let himself be swayed from a royally dictated marriage by some inconvenient affection for another woman.

She let go of Etienne and stepped onto the threshold of what had once been the doorway to the South Tower. The highest fragment of the remaining walls stood no higher than a man and the fallen debris had caved in the wooden floor, leaving a large, gaping hole to the basement. Built deep into the earth, only it and a connecting portion of winding stone steps had escaped the obliteration of Gunthar's destructive missiles. She nudged aside a pile of pebbles with her slippered foot and carefully began the descent.

The provisions that had once been stored here had been cleared away. Except for a ladder with two broken rungs leaning in the corner, the room held nothing but a litter of rocks. A rough pathway had been cleared through the debris by the servants who had emptied the stock, but a slab of broken wall still blocked Heléne's goal. She had to enlist Etienne's help in shifting the slab, and with the limited strength of his one good arm it took them more time than she liked to succeed. Had Therri managed to elude the guards? If not, it would not be long before they, and quite possibly Gunthar, came looking for the truth.

She fell to her knees and grabbed the iron ring that lay flat against the floor, almost obscured by gravel and dust. To her relief, the trap door attached to it swung open at her pull. A blast of damp and mildewed air made her choke and sneeze. Her heart sank as she stared into the ominous darkness of the tower's oubliette.

"Oh, Etienne, I thought we could hide you here, but it would be too dreadful."

"Better that black hole than what Gunthar has planned for me," Etienne said. "Have you got any candles?" She nodded. "Then light one and we'll check it out. I'll get the ladder."

Ordinarily, prisoners were lowered into the oubliette by means of a rope and permanently forgotten. To Heléne's knowledge, no one had suffered this fate at Pennault for over a generation. But then her father did not tell her everything and as she followed Etienne down the broken ladder, balancing a candle in one hand with the basket on her arm, and feeling cautiously for the next step past the missing rungs, she could not help but wonder what she might find at the bottom. But her fears were nothing more than that. The little chamber was empty, though cold and dank. It was no more than six or seven paces square, carved into the natural rock that formed the foundation of her father's castle. The sweep of her candle revealed smooth walls, without so much as a rude straw pallet on the floor to ease a prisoner's misery.

"Well," Etienne muttered, as he dropped down onto the cold, stone floor, "I guess this is where I wait." He sent her a dismal glance. "Just what am I waiting for?"

She sighed and sat beside him. She set the candle down and slid the basket off her arm. "It won't be much longer," she said. "Therri and I will find a way to get you back to Vere."

He shrugged. "It doesn't matter now. With Father gone—" His voice broke and he turned his head away.

She touched his arm and felt the gentle shaking of his tears. She wished now that she had not told him about Sir Damian. It could have waited until he was free, until he was safe—

"Saints, Heléne, how it hurts. I never thought— This must have been what *he* felt, why he went even when Father cursed him for going."

"Who? What are you talking about?"

"Triston. Father told him it was foolish, that he needed him at Vere, but Triston would not listen. And I thought Father was right. We grieved for Mother too, but why should a pilgrimage to the Holy Land serve her soul any better than the prayers we offered for her here?"

Etienne's voice lowered, thickening with guilt. "I was so awful to him, Heléne. I shouted terrible, hurtful things at Triston as he rode away. I thought he was abandoning Father, and I hated him for it. But now I know why he had to go. He did it for *her*, because she believed that it would somehow bring her peace, and he loved her so much—" his voice cracked on a sob— "he loved her so much that even in death he would have gone to the ends of the earth for her. Just as I was willing to do anything for Father. *Anything*, Heléne, even murder Gunthar. And *he* knew that. He used me. He told me it was the only way to protect him, and then he slipped that wretched dagger into my sheath and sent me off to Pennault—"

"Etienne, I can't understand how your father can have done it. I thought he loved you! To have sent you to kill Gunthar to defend his own dishonor in breaking the treaty—and then to give you the prince's dagger to do it with!"

Etienne turned his head and stared at her through the flickering candlelight. "Father didn't send me to kill Gunthar."

"But you just said—"

"Not *Father*. He would have locked me in my room if he had known what I intended to do."

Heléne drew so deep a breath that she choked on the sour, mildewed air. "Etienne," she croaked, "if your father didn't send you, then who did? Not Triston—?"

Etienne shuddered. "*Nay*. And I cringe to think what Triston will do to me when he sees me again. He warned me a dozen times not to listen to that miscreant, said he would bring nothing but grief to us all. But Father seemed to trust him, so I—" He stopped, then groaned and twisted the fingers of his hale hand into his mop of curls.

"Etienne, who are you talking about? Who did Triston warn you against?"

"Rousillon." He did not seem to hear her gasp. "He told me that Gunthar meant to use his 'royal commission' to enforce the peace treaty as an excuse to crush Father once and for all. He said Father would not be given a chance to explain why he was rebuilding our walls, but that Gunthar was going to order him seized and imprisoned. By calling Father traitor, he would be able to confiscate our lands as well. But I didn't agree to do it for the lands. I did it for Father. Imprisonment would have killed him, Heléne. Rousillon said that's what Gunthar wanted."

"But why would Gunthar want to kill your father? Sir Damian was in no condition to be any kind of threat to him now."

"Rousillon said Gunthar held some kind of grudge against him that went back before the wars began. He wouldn't tell me what it was and when I tried to ask Father, all he did was rant and fume about the 'Angevin usurper's hellhound'. I know how Father hates King Henry, so I thought the grudge must have something to do with that. When the wars began and Father heard that Gunthar was fighting for the king in Poitou, he sent Osanne and me away from Vere. Rousillon told me that when Gunthar besieged our castle Father tried to surrender, but Gunthar forced him to fight instead. He chased Father up onto the walls and when Father pled for mercy and tried to lay down his sword, Gunthar dealt him that cursed blow which sent him to the ground and crippled him. Rousillon said that villainous act proved that Gunthar had wanted Father dead. He said if Gunthar now succeeded in sending Father to prison, he would see to it Father never came out alive."

"Etienne, Gunthar told me that during his battle with your father he thrice gave Sir Damian an opportunity to lay down his sword, but that Sir Damian refused each time. Either Gunthar or Rousillon is lying—and I do not think it is Gunthar."

"I know that *now*. Triston only said that Father was crippled when he fell from the wall during his battle with Gunthar. Rousillon was not at Vere then, but I thought Father must have afterwards described the battle to him. Rousillon came to Vere eighteen months ago. He spoke to Father in private. Then Father summoned Triston and me and all the servants and men-at-arms into the hall and made us all swear that we would not reveal Rousillon's presence at our castle nor ever speak his name outside our walls. But ever since you told me Father was dead, I've been thinking of the way that Rousillon sent me off to Pennault, and about the prince's dagger and about all of Triston's warnings ... Heléne, Father is dead and I know, somehow I *just know* that Rousillon is to blame."

"Etienne, are you telling me that all this stubborn silence about that dagger has been to protect a villain like *Rousillon*?"

"Father made me swear! They were plotting something together. Father would not tell me what, but I know it was something dangerous, something ... something ..."

"Treasonous?"

His fingers in his hair writhed more tightly. "Ah, saints, Heléne, what else could Father's rebuilding of our fortifications mean?"

Yet even in the painful admission, she sensed something in him akin to relief. At least Sir Damian would now be spared the ghastly fate that might have been his had he and Rousillon been apprehended in their conspiracy. It was a fear that must have been haunting Etienne ever since he had been threatened with the grisly punishment himself.

As appalled as Heléne was by Etienne's attack on Gunthar, a stinging guilt of her own prevented her from rebuking him. Where was the difference between what Etienne had done and her own actions? Etienne had sought to protect his father with the blade, but her revelation to Rousillon about Gunthar's journey to Angoulême had proven nearly as deadly to the earl. Both had been desperate attempts to protect a parent whom they loved against the consequences of that parent's rash attempts to betray the crown.

"Etienne," she said, "is Rousillon still at Vere?"

Etienne hesitated, but apparently with Sir Damian dead he no longer felt himself bound to his oath of secrecy. "Aye."

"And you know nothing of what he might have said to your father? What sort of conspiracy they might have been involved in?"

Etienne shook his head. "I know only that he told Father Gunthar had wronged him too, and that together he and Father might achieve what neither of them could accomplish alone. He said he came with a great man's warrant and that their vengeance could be made to serve a higher cause. Father agreed to listen, but he sent Triston and me away. When he called us back, he made us both swear not to speak Rousillon's name. Triston was furious and at first he refused. I don't know how Father finally made him agree. Triston loathes Rousillon. And Osanne does not help. She and Rousillon are lovers now. Father knew it. But he hates Gunthar for his crippling and would have closed his eyes to anything to avenge himself for that."

Heléne thought of the sultry beauty. So she was Rousillon's spy. Gunthar should be warned. Might he not pardon Etienne in return for the information Etienne had just revealed to her? That was what Gunthar had wanted all along, the name of the man behind the conspiracy against him and the crown.

But if Etienne had been freed by Sir Damian's death, Heléne felt as trapped as ever. So long as Rousillon held her father's letter, she could say nothing to Gunthar. She assuaged her conscience with the thought that it would only be for a little while. *Somehow* she would get that letter back, and then she and Etienne would confront Gunthar together with the truth. Surely he would forgive them, forgive her, for her silence?

A silence that each moment might bring him nearer the hour of his own death. It required but one skillfully aimed arrow, one sip from a tainted cup . . . Her stomach twisted. If this conspiracy succeeded, what would the king lose but a little land, a little power? But Gunthar would lose his life, and she—

"Are you going to tell Gunthar?" Etienne asked, startling her with his perception of her thoughts. "About Rousillon?"

She did not know what to do. "Do you want me to tell him?"

"It will mean trouble for Triston. I think he found out what

Rousillon was plotting. I overheard Triston quarreling with Father about it. But he has kept his oath not to betray Rousillon. By his silence, he is as guilty as Father. *I* can only guess, but he *knew* what Rousillon was planning and has done nothing to stop him. How do you think Gunthar will judge him for that?"

*Harshly*, she thought. She loved Gunthar desperately, but her aching heart told her she still could not trust him.

"You were right about Triston," she murmured after a moment of dull, throbbing silence. "He told Clothilde he would not run away, even for her. She is in despair. All she does now is lie abed and weep. Mama has threatened to flog her, but it does no good. She no longer seems to care for anything."

"I knew he wouldn't," Etienne said. "Now that Father is gone, Vere will be his. Though if Rousillon's plot goes awry we shall none of us live long enough to enjoy it."

"Do you think," she asked, torn between hope and dread of his answer, "that Triston might feel himself released from his vow by your father's death and turn his back on Rousillon? If he confessed everything to Gunthar—"

"—the earl might condescend to be lenient? I don't know. I do know that he hates Rousillon, but—there was something else between them, something Rousillon seemed to be holding over his head. No, I do not think he will speak. Not yet, anyway. I suppose that leaves me here in this pit for the unforeseeable future."

Her sorrow for Triston vied with relief for her father, but she reached out a hand to Etienne's arm and said stoutly, "Your brother has not forgotten you, Etienne. He told Clo that he has a friend in the East with whom you will be safe until this matter with Gunthar is settled. He is confident he can smuggle you out of Poitou if we can only get you away from Pennault."

That was the difficulty, getting him past her father's guards. Since Etienne's escape, no one had been able to leave the grounds unnoticed, a circumstance which had only heightened her sister's hysteria, preempting as it had any further meetings with Triston.

She studied Etienne's haggard profile and asked abruptly, "How long has it been since you've eaten anything?"

He shrugged. "Two days ago, I think. I drank that soup you brought up to me in the tower. That's how I found your knife. It was hidden beneath the bowl."

She frowned over that. "Etienne, I knew nothing about that knife. That was not how I meant to free you."

He seemed surprised, though he said, "Well, I thought it a harsh method for you to choose. And I didn't want to use it. I'd like to think I learned *something* from my insane attack on Gunthar. But I didn't want to stay where I was, either, knowing what they meant to do to me. When I heard the guard unlocking the door, I hid behind it, trying to decide what to do. I must have made a sound because he turned and saw me before I could make up my mind. He lunged to grab me and I felt the knife cut him, but it was too dark to see where. But he was still standing, and I knew if I gave him a chance to call for more guards— So I cracked him on the head with the hilt." He paused. "Heléne, if you didn't put that knife on the tray, who did?"

"I don't know," she said. "The knife must have already been on the tray when I took it from Audiart. And now she is missing, so perhaps she knew who placed it there and was afraid to speak."

"Or someone wanted to keep her from doing so," Etienne said. "If she was sent by Rousillon, perhaps through Osanne—"

"Or le Reynard," she murmured.

"Who?"

"Le Reynard. It is a name Rousillon spoke, a spy, I think, but not your stepmother. I'm afraid it may be someone in Gunthar's own household."

"Heléne, what do *you* know of Rousillon?"

"I—" Her carelessness took her by surprise, and for a moment she was at a loss.

"You've spoken with him, haven't you? You've known all along—"

"Not that he was residing at Vere, or that he had anything to do with Sir Damian. I met him down by the river one day. I did not even know who he was."

"But you knew when I spoke his name. And I'll wager it was no accident you met. He wanted something from you, didn't he? Perhaps still does?"

She shook her head. She was not prepared to tell Etienne or anyone about Rousillon's blackmail. She started to dismiss his concern, then found his hand on her arm, gripping it hard.

"Heléne, you mustn't go near him again. Triston says he is a viper, and he's right. It's Rousillon's fault I am here, he planted that devilish dagger upon me. And I just *know* he had something to do with Father's death."

"Etienne, that is ridiculous. Gunthar sent Lord Challons to Vere and he confirmed that your father died in his sleep."

"He couldn't have. Heléne, he was crippled, he was not ill. They are not the same."

"Etienne—" she put up a hand to his face "—you are tired and hungry and are not thinking clearly. I know your father's death was a shock. You want to blame someone else for the hurt, but it was no one's fault. Here." She pushed the basket towards him. "Eat something. It will help more than you think."

He shook his head, so she put a meat pie in his hand.

"I'll eat it," he said, "but it won't change anything. Promise me you'll stay away from Rousillon."

"Don't worry."

"Heléne—"

She stood up. "I have to be going. I'm sorry to leave you here in the dark, but there's another candle in the basket and plenty of food and a bottle of wine. You must be patient if I do not return for a day or two. We have to be careful if we do not want you thrown back in the tower. No, don't get up—" She pressed his shoulders when he tried to push himself up with his one good hand still filled with the pie.

"How are you going to get back up the ladder?" he asked.

It would not be easy with the broken rungs. "I shall have to tie up my skirts. So be a gentleman and close your eyes."

"You're going now?"

"I'd better. I need to find out what happened to Therri." She glanced again about the cell. She did not like leaving him here in the darkness that would descend when the trap door was closed. "It will not be much longer," she promised. "I'll send Therri with a pallet and blankets. And he and I will put our heads together and have you out of here before you know it." She could no longer see his expression. He had turned his face away from the light. "I will call out to you before I close the door."

He nodded, but said nothing.

She knotted up her skirts. Then, with a final glance at his dispirited frame, she began the ascent that would lead her back into daylight and leave him to battle the shadows of doubt alone.

# Fifteen

Gunthar tried to discipline his thoughts for the confrontation he knew was coming. The distress on the Bishop of Poitiers' countenance was foreboding. His thin, patrician features bespoke a dignified, middle-aged man, but his vitality was reflected in the animated fluttering of his hands and the soft flapping of the episcopal robes against his agitated pacing. They met in Laurant's council chamber, which Gunthar had appropriated days ago for conducting the business of the king. The desk against the wall, beneath the banner of the phoenix, had been brought in from the antechamber and its litter of parchment and pens, together with the uncapped inkwell, attested to the haste with which his secretary had been turned out for this interview.

The bishop looked as disturbed as Gunthar felt, though Gunthar took care to conceal his own emotions. Jean aux Bellesmains had never learned the art of such dissemblance. Though not without diplomacy, he was, Gunthar knew, at heart a forthright man. His incorruptible character commanded the respect of the Poitevin barons and his royal master alike, even when he often disagreed with both on questions of ecclesiastical authority. But there was no doubting that he supported the crown in all matters secular or that he should execute a royal charge without delay.

He exclaimed without a pause in his fretful strides, "I could not believe it, when he wrote. I thought there must be some mistake. To be sent to rebuke you, of all men—"

"So," Gunthar said with a cheerless twitch of his lips, "Henry is still angry."

"Angry? I have not seen such a string of curses committed to parchment since that appalling letter he penned to the Pope deriding Becket's behavior at the Conference of Montmirail."

Gunthar laughed at the memory. "Which, on your very good advice, he tore up before sending."

"This is serious, Gunthar," the bishop said sharply. "The king is enraged. He says you have defied him. *You*, who stood unflinching by his side, scorning the wrath of the Church in those dark days after Becket's murder. It was that loyalty and courage more than any feat of arms that won you to his heart, a heart you know, as well as I, he has opened to very few men. He has trusted you, Gunthar, the way he trusts William Marshall—the way he trusted Thomas Becket—and now—"

"I have done nothing to betray his faith," Gunthar said. "I would lay down my life for Henry. I have proven it more than once."

Bellesmains stopped with a troubled nod. "The wounds you suffered ten years ago at the siege of Fougères, the ones that won you your spurs at the king's own hand."

"And the assassin's arrow I took for him two years later when he sought to discipline the rebels of Brittany." Gunthar forbore to mention the much more recent threats he had suffered in the name of the king.

"Henry has a long memory," Bellesmains said, "but it has been forever stained by the archbishop's death. No more than Becket did I agree with the king's offensive policy towards the Church, but Becket's methods of defiance were untenable. It was pride that led to his downfall. In the end, his sin was as great as the intemperate passion of the king, whose immoderate words sent those blustering knights across the channel to strike the archbishop down in his own cathedral."

Gunthar knew how that admission pained Bellesmains. The bishop had loved Thomas Becket, and no one had grieved more deeply for the archbishop's schism with the king.

Still, Gunthar sprang to the king's defense. "Henry has long since been absolved by the Pope himself of either intent or complicity in—"

But Bellesmains held up a forestalling hand. "I am not his judge, Gunthar. I love Henry as well as you, and serve him in my own way. Because I will not be his puppet in no way lessens my devotion to the man or his interests. Henry respects men with minds of their own, men who will not abandon conviction for the sake of some fleeting favor, even though that favor be proffered by a royal hand. It was not because Becket stood by his conscience, but because he was arrogantly provocative in doing so, that he won the king's enmity. Henry thought he knew Becket through and through, only to find too late that he had never known his 'friend' at all. That betrayal has left him wary of even his most intimate counselors. And I suspect it is why he has flown into such a blasphemous passion over what, I am convinced, is but a minor misunderstanding between you."

Gunthar knew too well where this was leading. He thought of the conspiracy that seemed all but assured against the crown. The threats to his life he bore, not happily, but willingly for the king's sake. Where was the royal gratitude? Of course, the king knew nothing of how matters stood in Poitou. Gunthar had procrastinated informing him in the hopes that he might yet be able to bring the prince to the error of his ways and return him to his father's favor. Still, after so long a record of unwavering service, it seemed bitterly unfair that the king should insist on harping over the one subject Gunthar had ever challenged him on.

"It's the betrothal, isn't it?"

Bellesmains nodded. "Apparently Henry expected the matter to have been concluded by now. That it has not been, and Laurant assures me it has not, he has taken as a flagrant act of disobedience on your part."

Gunthar walked across the room, then stopped at the wide oak desk. He swept his fingers over the polished wood on top. "There are complications."

"Complications? Has Laurant proved unreasonable?"

"No, it is not that. It is—" Gunthar paused, unsure for a moment of his own defense. In a burst of irritation at himself and the king, he exclaimed, "Why the devil can Henry not be patient? It has been little more than a fortnight."

"Time enough, in the king's mind. From what I could decipher between his shocking streams of invective, he had specifically commanded you to—"

"I know what he commanded me to do. I suppose he has been haunting Southampton, waiting for my future bride to materialize on the shore?"

"No, he has sent Richard of Ilchester to do that, though he is to conduct her to the king's court as soon as she arrives."

"Then Richard shall have to cool his heels there awhile longer. These things cannot be rushed. The lady is in a delicate frame of health, and . . .

"And?"

Gunthar hesitated, then turned to face the bishop. "I find myself reluctant for the match."

Bellesmains' thin brows twitched down over the bridge of his aristocratic nose. "Reluctant? For what cause? I myself conducted the marriage that joined the Lady Clothilde with Sir Fulbert de Merval. There is not a fairer, gentler woman in all of Henry's realm."

"I have no quarrel with her looks," Gunthar said.

"Then perhaps you are concerned about her failure to provide Merval with an heir? I would remind you that Sir Fulbert was an old man and—"

"It is not that, either. I am sure she is quite capable of doing her duty by me."

"Then—?"

Bellesmains waited with that steady patience for which he was renowned. Somehow it provoked Gunthar into an unexpected admission.

"But I am not in love with her."

Bellesmains' jaw dropped. "Not—in—love?"

Gunthar felt his cheeks redden in a way they had not done in years. He could not believe he had blurted out such a ridiculous statement and for one horrible instant, he thought the bishop was going to burst out laughing.

"Forgive me," Bellesmains pled, attempting to conceal his amusement with a sudden coughing fit. "I thought—That is— Ahem! What I'm sure you meant to say is that you are not yet sufficiently acquainted with the lady to share with her those feelings of common purpose upon which every sound Christian marriage should be built. I assure you, such union of mind and spirit almost always follows the union of bodies sanctified by the Holy Church."

Gunthar snorted at the hollow promise, thinking of the endless quarrels he had witnessed between Sir John and the Lady Berthe. They had bred four children together, and their marriage was still as empty as the day they had wed. Like his parents' marriage, though his parents had never spent enough time together to quarrel. Theirs had been a cool, political match, their sole "common purpose" being the rearing of their only child and heir.

He had never really imagined his marriage would be any different, though he had certainly hoped for more compatibility than he envisioned ever finding with Clothilde. He had thought he would be content to enjoy a dutiful, if detached, sort of affection for his 'wife', that hazy, nebulous creature always floating at some comfortable distance in his future.

Until he had met Heléne. With her, he had experienced sensations he had not even known existed in the world of men and women. Passion he was familiar with, lust he had occasionally battled, but love—? That was a device of minstrels' lays, a poet's fiction, the reality of which, despite his protest to Bellesmains, he still was not convinced. And yet, when he had held Heléne in his arms, it had been more than passion thundering through his veins, more than lust for her sweet, fresh charms. Somehow he had felt . . . complete.

Bellesmains coughed again, more discreetly this time. "I'm afraid the king is adamant in this. The alliance with Laurant is crucial. We both know the man has the steadiness of a willow tree, and without this marriage to cement his loyalty he is likely to bend in an undesirable way when the winds of rebellion sweep through the land again. As we both know they will."

He was right, of course. No one was truly satisfied with the terms set forth at Montlouis. Sooner or later, with or without the prince at their head, men like Angoulême would try to reassert their 'ancient rights' and throw off the Angevin yoke.

"Suppose," Gunthar said, "just suppose I were to agree to an alliance with the younger daughter, instead. Would that content the king?"

The question clearly took Bellesmains by surprise, but he was quick to dash the elusive hope. "That would be an unforgivable slight to the Lady Clothilde, one I cannot imagine her father would consent to. And Laurant tells me he has arranged a betrothal for the Lady Heléne to Lord Heywood. Were you suddenly to deprive Heywood of his anticipated bride and her dowry, claiming 'twas done in the name of the king— Well, the last thing Henry needs just now is another irate baron breathing down his neck." Bellesmains stopped, then asked, "Why? Are you 'in love' with the Lady Heléne?"

The last of Gunthar's self-delusions slipped away, and the warm, bright spot she had touched in his soul grew cold.

"No," he said. "That was a poor choice of words. I merely thought she and I might be better suited, but if there is no other way— Well, I am Henry's man to the death. I will do my duty as he requires it."

Bellesmains looked relieved. "Then I shall write to the king and tell him—"

"Tell him," Gunthar said, "to warn Richard of Ilchester to expect, not my betrothed, but my wife." He had made his decision, and he would now have it over and done. "I see no reason to delay this matter any longer. As soon as the Lady Clothilde is recovered of her illness, I will marry her." He strode to the door, then paused with his hand on the latch and shot Bellesmains a look that made him jump. "I trust you will do us the honor of officiating?"

Bellesmains stammered something that Gunthar took as an assent. It was all he required. He pulled open the door and shut it hard behind him..

Heléne stared down at the handsome, slightly worn book bound in red leather that Brandon de Vexin had just placed in her hands. "He said it was for me?"

"Aye, my lady."

"To keep?"

Brandon smiled. "Aye, my lady. He said he hopes you will find it cheerful reading, even on a dreary day."

She flushed with pleasure and flipped through the pages, noting the curious names within: Guigemar, Lanval, Eliduc. A wide, crimson ribbon dangled from between two pages. When she opened to the place it marked, she found the band not sewn to the binding, but sliding loose into her hand. It was a very fine silk, with a pretty diamond pattern woven in gold down the center. And it was long—long enough to be threaded through a woman's hair.

She glanced at Brandon, suddenly self-conscious about the heavy tresses flowing over her shoulders. But if he thought anything odd about either the gift or her altered appearance, he was too well trained to show it.

"Thank you," she said, and the squire bowed and went away.

From the other side of the room, a trembling voice asked, "Heléne? Who was it?"

Heléne slid the ribbon back into its place in the book, then turned to her sister. "It was no one, love, just a servant. Are you hungry? Would you like me to send to the kitchens—?"

Clothilde shook her head and huddled back into the window frame. It was all she seemed to do these days, cower in her bed or, when Heléne could coax her, sit a few minutes near the light. A grey, dismal light of late, with clouds that threatened but did not deliver their promise of rain. None of their mother's rebukes had succeeded in prying her elder daughter out of her chamber and into Gunthar's company. Clothilde did not quarrel, she no longer even wept. She simply sat with that empty, tragic look on her face and mutely refused to budge.

Triston had refused to run away with her. Heléne remembered the wrenching, pathetic sobs with which her sister had poured out the tale of his rejection. But she had not shed another tear since. Her weary sigh drew Heléne to her side. Heléne sat down, placing the book on the seat between them, but Clothilde did not seem to notice. She stared with vacant eyes across the room. Heléne had seen her sister strike many tearful poses through the years, but she had never seen her like this, so quiet, so pale, so lost, as though she were trying to withdraw completely and finally from the world and all its pain.

"Clo, if you would only eat something you would feel so much better. Only let me—"

Clothilde did not flinch from her touch so much as she simply slipped away from it. Heléne watched as her sister drifted to her feet and floated across to the bed, looking more like a frail, ethereal wraith than a living, breathing woman.

After a few moments, Heléne turned her attention back to the book. She picked it up, guiltily aware of the way her concerns for her sister vanished into a little thrill of happiness for herself. Surely Etienne was wrong? She was more than just a passing fancy to Gunthar. These gifts proved it. She removed the silken band, leaving the book open in her lap. She had promised not to bind her hair. How, then, to wear the ribbon? There must be some fashion she was not familiar with, some merry style he had seen, perhaps, at court. She would ask him to show her, she thought, quivering at the memory of his strong fingers working amidst her hair. She closed her eyes and saw his face, felt again the warmth of his mouth ...

No, she must not allow herself to be swept away. She set the ribbon aside and opened her eyes to study the book. The letters, though somewhat faded, had once been starkly drawn, and seemed somehow too brusque for the pretty, elegant words inscribed on the page.

*Love's arrow sent its shaft over the parapets of his heart. His heart shook with the thunder of a castle besieged. The fiery missiles of the lady's beauteous eyes set his body so afire that memories of his homeland melted away. Love maddened him. The pain of his wound dissolved, replaced by a scorching anguish in his breast. He pled the lady to leave him alone to sleep. She went away, consumed by the same fire that blazed in Guigemar's heart.*

Heléne hugged the book against her breast. Surely Gunthar meant these words for her? Madness, anguish, fire. He must have hoped that she would read them, that she would realize he loved her, that he was in pain for her, that he wanted her for his—

The door flew open. She scrambled up, hiding the book behind her back as her mother came in with Sybil. The Lady Gwenllian's mouth thinned ominously when she saw Clothilde in the bed. She marched across the room and flung off the covers.

"Get up. There has been enough of this nonsense. You are wanted by your father and the earl."

Clothilde moaned and shrank against the pillows. The Lady Gwenllian muttered an oath that would have made her husband blush. She seized the cowering girl and dragged her out of the bed.

"Mama, what has happened?" Heléne asked in alarm.

"Gunthar has made up his mind and I am not about to give him time to change it again." Her mother pushed Clothilde towards Sybil. "Wash her face, comb her hair, do your best to make her presentable. Bring her to the hall as soon as—"

"Mama," Heléne broke across these commands, "what do you mean, 'Gunthar has made up his mind'?"

"I mean he is going to marry your sister."

"Marry—*Clothilde*?"

"If we can get her to stand up without swooning long enough." The Lady Gwenllian waved a warning finger at her elder daughter. "I will not endure any more of these foolish fits. The earl has decided to dispense with the betrothal and take advantage of the bishop's presence to proceed directly with the marriage. And you are going to stand meekly by his side and repeat the words that are put to you. If you threaten by so much as a sigh to fall into another one of your spells—"

Heléne barely reached the window seat before her knees buckled. She sank down upon the cushion, her ears ringing, the room swirling before her eyes. She had a panicky feeling of falling and tried to catch herself, leaning hurriedly into the embrasure of the window.

"And you—" her mother's sharp voice swung round to Heléne "—don't think to mimic your sister's tricks. You have never fainted in your life. I suppose you are afraid Gunthar's sudden resolve will encourage Goldingham, and you are right. He warns against his master's impatience and has even offered to escort Gunthar's bride to

England for him when he carries you to Heywood. So there will be no more dawdling on your trousseau. There is no time to take you to Beaulac. You must be readied within the week, in time for your sister's wedding."

Heléne gasped. "A week? But you said they were waiting for her now—"

"To sign the contract. Gunthar agrees to a wedding on Friday, but only if he is convinced your sister's health will allow it. He will not accept your father's assurances, but insists on seeing her for himself." Her mother turned back to Sybil and the shuddering Clothilde. "Get her dressed," she told the nurse, "and bring her downstairs as quickly as you can. Gunthar refuses to sign until she joins us."

The Lady Gwenllian turned to leave, then whirled back round as Clothilde gave a shriek.

"No! Murderous, filthy witch, let me go!"

Sybil had Clothilde by the arm and was endeavoring to lead her over to the water basin, but Clothilde erupted into a frenzy, kicking and clawing at the old woman.

"Hush, lamb, hush. Sybil will not harm you. You must trust her, my sweet, my angel—"

The nurse's cooing words failed to soothe the fury. Clothilde caught a shock of the old woman's hair, then raked her nails over the withered face. Sybil staggered back, and Heléne saw the bright red stains on her sister's fingers.

"Blood!" Clothilde wailed. "Blood for blood! Blood for my innocent! Your sin will cry against you from the grave!"

The old nurse howled and clutched at the five scarlet stripes springing down her nose and cheek. The Lady Gwenllian stepped between her daughter and Sybil, then shrank when Clothilde's hands came flailing at her.

"Heléne!" Lady Gwenllian screamed.

Heléne ran forward and caught her sister's hands before they could descend like talons on their mother. "Clothilde, stop! You must stop!"

Clothilde nearly swept Heléne off her feet with her wild strength.

Then, as suddenly as the scene had erupted, Clothilde collapsed into her sister's arms.

"Send them away," she whispered. "Oh, Heléne, send them away."

Heléne stared desperately at her mother. "Mama, please—"

The Lady Gwenllian moved towards the door, then stopped. "I want you both below stairs within the hour, calmed and presentable. If there is another outburst like this one—" she looked straight at her elder daughter "—your chastisement will make the last seem but a frightful dream."

She swept Sybil out on the chilling words, leaving Heléne too numb to comfort her trembling sister.

# Sixteen

"Ahem. My lord, perhaps these matters would be better dealt with in a day or two? When you are not so preoccupied with tomorrow's events?"

Gunthar looked round at the discreet voice of his secretary, then glanced at the pile of documents awaiting his attention. His mind had indeed been elsewhere. He picked up a handful of the parchment sheets and sifted through them. There were reports from the knights he had dispatched to the rebel barons detailing their compliance with the treaty; petitions from Poitevin landholders seeking his mediation in their petty disputes; a request from the burghers of Poitiers that he visit the city as soon as was convenient and lend his ear to some quarrel between the wool-mongers and the weavers' guild . . .

Worst of all were the seemingly endless appeals from noble and ambitious fathers, imploring him to consider their sons and daughters for inclusion in his household. The pleas consisted of page after page of paeans to their children's talents and grandiloquent flattery directed towards himself. His first year as earl, such inflated bombast had been amusing. By the second, it had begun to pall. Now he pushed the letters away with disgust.

"See to this, will you?" he said, and watched as de Muncey promptly gathered the letters up and carried them to the far end of the desk. Gunthar said nothing for several minutes as the secretary stood sorting the correspondence into neatly stacked piles, but when de Muncey returned to his seat, Gunthar asked, "I take it everything is in readiness for the ceremony tomorrow?"

"I believe so, sir," the secretary answered. "Julian assures me the alterations to your surcote will be completed by this evening, and your jeweled collar—an excellent choice, if I may say so, for the wedding gift—has been shortened and adjusted as you ordered."

"You think the Lady Clothilde will be well enough to receive it, then?"

"Indeed, sir. I thought she appeared just a bit less pale at dinner yesterday."

*Hogwash*, Gunthar thought, *she had been as white as a ghost.* He pushed back his chair and stood up. De Muncey was right, he could not work. He walked across to the table by the window and poured out a cup of wine, but the burning liquid did nothing to ease the tightness in his belly.

"Sir John and Lord Laurant snared a splendid stag this morning," De Muncey remarked. "I understand it is to be the centerpiece of tonight's feast. A pity you had not time to join them on the hunt."

He should have gone, Gunthar told himself. He had accomplished nothing here. But there, in the thunder of hooves and the rush of the kill, he might have found some relief from the memory of her stricken face.

He drank again, then cursed the Lady Gwenllian to perdition. He had demanded that her daughter be present for the signing of the marriage contract—*her daughter*, he had said, and since it concerned no one else he had expected only Clothilde to be summoned. He had been stunned to see Heléne descending the stairs at her sister's side. Their eyes had met only for an instant, but he had seen her shock, and not an hour had gone by since that look had not haunted him.

He had hurt her. He had known he must. He had not known how to warn her, how to soften the pain of the blow. Perhaps there had been no way. For now, he knew her youthful heart would hate him. But some day, when she had children of her own and sought to explain to them the unalterable demands of duty, perhaps she would gaze upon the ribbon and the book and her memories would be—forgiving?

"Hugh?"

Gunthar turned and saw that Sir John had entered the council chamber. He nodded to de Muncey. "Thank you, we will finish this later."

The secretary bowed, gathered up the documents, and quietly went out.

"What's the matter?" Sir John asked, closing the door behind the clerk.

"What do you mean?"

"I mean—" he joined Gunthar by the table "—you look like a man who has just lost his last friend." He refilled Gunthar's cup with wine. "Nervous about tomorrow?"

Gunthar drank, but said, "It's too soon. Anyone with half a brain can see the Lady Clothilde is not up to it."

"Then why did you agree to the wedding? A betrothal would have given you both more time."

"Time is one thing the king does not have. If war flares up again, we will need Laurant firmly on our side."

"You think Richard's plot may succeed, then?"

"Only if he succeeds in killing me. Henry would not be able to ignore the provocation of a royal officer murdered by his own son." He shrugged and added, "On the other hand, it should no longer be my concern. And I would not have to face the prospect of being locked into marriage with a woman who is fast coming to resemble a corpse."

"Oh, come now," Sir John said, "it is not that bad. The Lady Clothilde has lost a little weight in the last few weeks, but it has only made her more enchantingly frail than ever. You must be the luckiest, most ungrateful dog in all the realm."

Gunthar grunted. To lull his concerns over her daughter's health, Clothilde had been repeatedly dragged from her room by her mother and forced to sit by his side each day at dinner. It had been a sadly inadequate ploy. None of her mother's gently menacing rebukes over the last week had resulted in bringing any life to the once lustrous eyes. Had it not been for Gunthar's persistence in pressing an occasional morsel to her pale lips, she would have sat through entire meals without ever consuming a bite.

She was still lovely, as Sir John had said, thin as a reed, white as a lily. But it was an empty loveliness. Whatever spark had animated her when Gunthar had first come to Pennault was gone. He had suggested postponing the ceremony until the ailment that so obviously beset her could he healed, but her mother would allow no delay. Clothilde was not ill, she laughed, merely overcome at the prospect of becoming a countess.

But Gunthar was not misled. Clothilde was clearly in a precarious state. He might have insisted, might have faced down his hostess and forced her to consider her daughter's welfare before her own ambition. But he had not. He had been too afraid that he would lose his resolve, that if one more day beyond the necessary passed, he might throw caution and duty to the winds and abscond with the maddeningly alive Heléne in her woeful sister's place.

Heléne. Her vivid little countenance had been filled with fire last night. He had watched her from beneath his lashes as she sat with her sister by the hearth, listening to his conversation with her parents. Goldingham had joined them to discuss arrangements for transferring her to England along with Gunthar's bride. Gunthar had seen the way her eyes narrowed each time Heywood's name was spoken. From the mutinous tilt of her chin, he knew she was plotting an escape. He feared she was intrepid enough to try something truly rash—like running away in her brother's clothes and trying to pass herself off to some dim-sighted knight as a squire. That thought, and the vision of what might ensue when such a disguise were inevitably penetrated, had drenched him in a cold sweat and solidified his determination to see her safely delivered into Heywood's hands.

"She says he will be there tonight waiting for his brother. I tell you, Hugh, if we wait any longer, we are likely to lose them both."

Gunthar looked up from his empty cup. His thoughts had been miles away from what Sir John was saying. His friend sighed with exasperation, but at Gunthar's request, he patiently reiterated his story.

Gunthar listened with brows drawn low, then uttered at Sir John's conclusion, "Planned escapes, rendezvous—? I don't see how the Lady Osanne can know any of this."

"She has followed them."

"Them?"

"Lord Therri and the Lady Heléne."

*Heléne?*

"Why would she be following the Lady Helen?"

"Do you remember that uproar a week ago, when the guards thought they finally had young de Brielle cornered? Osanne said only moments before de Brielle unexpectedly appeared to the guards on the west wall, she saw Lord Therri and the Lady Heléne headed in the direction of their mother's garden. The Lady Heléne carried a basket and spoke some folderol about gathering roses for a picnic she and her brother were on their way to enjoy. Not long after that, someone who appeared to be de Brielle led your and Laurant's guards on that rousing, but ultimately unprofitable chase all over these castle grounds. Yet no sooner had our fugitive mysteriously disappeared again, than Lord Therri appears in a hat and cloak and strolls out the front gate declaring, not that he's off to a picnic with his sister, but that he is off to the river to fish—alone. Osanne became suspicious when she heard of it. She started watching the Lady Heléne and noticed that she often slipped out of the castle with that same basket on her arm."

"So she followed her. And found—?"

"She and her brother have hidden de Brielle in the ruins of the South Tower. Osanne is certain they mean to try to smuggle him out tonight."

Gunthar did not want to believe it. "You are sure of that? She has seen the Lady Helen with young de Brielle?"

"Not seen, but heard. Osanne hid herself nearby when the Lady Heléne took him a basket of food yesterday and listened to their conversation. She and her brother mean to take advantage of tonight's banquet, hoping you and the rest of the company will be so distracted by thoughts of tomorrow's wedding that they can escape unnoticed."

The revelation hit Gunthar like a blow to the face. The little cat had lied to him. She had sworn that she knew nothing of Etienne's whereabouts and he had been so foolish, so smitten, that he had believed her.

He sent a darkling look at the opposite wall. "And this

'rendezvous'?"

"Osanne says Lord Therri is supposed to divert the guards again tonight while his sister and de Brielle slip through a postern gate in the west wall. Sir Triston will be waiting in the woods to spirit them away."

So that was how she planned to escape her unwanted marriage. Running away, not by herself, but with Etienne de Brielle. The thought set Gunthar's blood boiling.

"Find Tollerton and Enslye. Tell them to meet us at the South Tower immediately."

"Osanne thinks we should wait until tonight. She has shown me the clearing where Sir Triston is to meet his brother and the Lady Heléne. Were you and I to watch nearby, we could apprehend the three of them together."

"I've no intention of giving that pup another chance to slip through my fingers," Gunthar said. "We know where he is and we are going to take him now."

"But Osanne thinks you should—"

"I don't give a snap for what the Lady Osanne thinks."

Sir John flushed, but said, "What about Sir Triston?"

"There is no reason for him to guess that his brother has been recaptured. If we keep the matter quiet, he will still be waiting in the clearing. We will deal with Sir Triston tonight." *And the Lady Heléne, as well.*

Sir John nodded and went out, leaving Gunthar simmering in her betrayal.

Gunthar and his three knights traversed the stairway to the South Tower's cellar and found all they needed to confirm the Lady Osanne's story. The trap door was open and as soft as the voices were from the yawning oubliette, Gunthar knew Heléne's feminine tones. He motioned his men back against the wall and took up a position near the opening in the floor, stopping just short of where he might have been visible from the depths. And then he waited.

It was not long before he heard a rustling and a creaking of wood. From the huffing and puffing that accompanied it, it was apparent that someone was having difficulty climbing up the ladder. Gunthar waited until a slender hand emerged from the darkness, then stepped forward and offered his assistance.

Her cry of surprise echoed to the crumbling walls above them. His hand locked over hers and he drug her straight up. He caught her about the waist and swung her out of the hole. Then he pulled her against him and stepped back.

"Take him," he snapped.

Sir John signaled the others and the three armed knights vanished down the ladder into the oubliette.

"No!" Heléne twisted, but Gunthar held her fast.

They both heard the shouts from below, the sound of scuffling feet and Sir John's angry oath. Heléne tried to break away. Her slippered toes kicked Gunthar's shins with commendable force. He bore the attack for several bruising minutes, then caught one of her flying ankles with his, pulled her off balance, and dropped her onto the floor.

"Cat," he whispered, pinning her against a fallen slab of stone. "You lying, conniving, two-faced little cat."

Her hair spread behind her like a fan. His scathing gaze identified as straw the small brown strands clinging there. At first, he thought the fact that her hem was above her knees merely an unfortunate consequence of his rough handling of her. A pair of white stockings, gartered at the knees exposed the pretty curve of her calves. Then he saw the knot that caught the corner of her hem up along her thigh and his mind spun into a dizzying rage.

Her fiery eyes glared back at him, but before either of them could speak another voice rang out.

"Cur! Get your filthy hands off of her!"

Gunthar looked up in time to see Etienne break free of the captors who had pushed him up the ladder. The youth barreled into Gunthar's back, sending them both into a sprawl across the rubble-strewn floor. Before Gunthar could recover, Etienne's fingers were in his hair, snapping back his head. A string of savage oaths assaulted him as an arm passed round his neck and bore with crushing strength against his windpipe. Gunthar groped at the hold without effect, then remembered the broken wrist. He felt for the bandages and splint, found them to the left of his chin, and yanked unmercifully.

Etienne screamed and tumbled off. Gunthar struggled to his knees.

"Get him out of here," he said to his guards.

"No!" Heléne scrambled to the youth's side and threw her arms around him.

Gunthar got to his feet, his voice shaking. "Come, my lady." He took her arm and pulled her up, then caught her wrist as her fist came swinging towards his head. "Put him back in the tower," he told Sir Roger. "Shackle him if you must, but this time keep him there."

Etienne, his face crumpled with pain, sought in vain to resist as the guards dragged him off.

"You villain! You devil!" Heléne struggled like a hornet in Gunthar's grasp, until Sir John emerged from the oubliette.

He had a kitchen knife stuck in his belt and a red-bound object in his hand. "The boy's been living in the lap of comfort down there. A pallet and blankets, rushes on the floor—with a sprinkling of violets, if my nose does not deceive me—a basket of food and wine, and lest the hours pass too slowly, this to read by candlelight."

Heléne stilled abruptly and Gunthar's arms fell from about her. He said nothing for a moment. Then he took the book from Sir John's hand.

"Go back to the castle," he said to his friend. "See that the prisoner has been safely bestowed. I have yet a word to speak to the Lady Helen."

Sir John mounted the stairs that took him out of the cellar.

Heléne lifted her chin when Gunthar turned to confront her.

"How dared you?" The book trembled in his hand as he held it up. "How dared you give him this?"

Her eyes flashed back at him. "And how dared *you* insult me with such an obscene gift?"

"Obscene?"

"Did you think I would be so taken with the romance of those tales that I would not notice they are filled with wantonness and adultery?"

"Oh, for heaven's sake!" he exclaimed. "They are not to be taken seriously. That is a poet's convention, no worse than the lays the troubadours sing in your father's hall."

"They *were* worse, they were shameful! Guigemar and Lanval sinned happily with women who were not their wives, and Eliduc—" Her face flamed. "If you think I intend to play Guilliadun for you—"

*"What?"*

"You sent that book hoping to seduce me! I saw it at once. *You* are Eliduc, and Gualadun is Clothilde, your wife. And like the false knight in that story, you think to win me away from my father's house with pretty words and empty promises, all the while knowing you can never love me with honor because you are already married to someone else."

Gunthar was flabbergasted at a comparison it had never entered his mind that she might make. "Great heavens, girl, have you lost your mind?"

"It is true!" she cried. "You are going to marry Clothilde tomorrow. You *always* intended to marry her. You never wanted me for anything but your mistress."

"No— Helen—"

"Stay away from me. I'll not sell myself to be your harlot, any more than I shall sell myself to be Heywood's bride."

The defense was perhaps unwise, for it caused him to rake her tumbling hair and heightened skirts. "You are not so nice in your notions, I see, where de Brielle is concerned. You have no compunction at all in displaying for him what simple modesty demands a *lady* should keep hid from the lustful eyes of men."

He allowed his own gaze to linger on her slender legs, and despite his voiced rebuke, felt some regret when she undid the knot in her skirt and whipped the hem back around her ankles.

"I tied it up so I could climb the ladder," she said, "and you are an idiot if you think to make anything more of it than that."

"I'd be an idiot were I not to believe the evidence of my own sight." He reached out a hand and plucked a strand of straw from her hair. "What else did you give him besides my book?"

"What do you mean?"

"Such 'obscene' tales must have lent him a bold idea or two. The pair of you have been hidden away, if Sir John is to be believed, in a veritable lovers' bower. How was it you passed your time? Tumbled on a bed of rushes and violets, with wine to heat your passions?"

"How dare you!"

"I am sick to death of your lies, Lady Helen. Let us visit your fair bower together and see if it is true."

He caught her wrist and pulled her towards the oubliette.

"Let me go!" She pried desperately at the fingers locked on her arm. "You are mad!"

"Mad, aye," he uttered hoarsely. Images of her and Etienne danced wildly through his mind. He jerked her abruptly against him and kissed her, not once, not twice, but over and over. The blood throbbed in his veins, pounding in his head as he sought to drive away the image . . . her and Etienne among the rushes . . .

She shoved sharply against his chest but he held her fast until, in her struggles to break free, her foot slipped into the empty darkness of the oubliette's shaft. He felt her sliding out of his arms and clutched at her, his heart in his throat. A fall from this height would be fatal. He stumbled back, pulling her with him, then fell with her to his knees.

Her arms were around his neck, her face pressed into his shoulder. Suddenly there was no one in his mind but her.

He pressed her back against the stones of the floor.

"Helen, Helen—"

He murmured the name against her lips. She answered with a gasp, but her struggles ceased. Her body went limp, her hands falling to either side of her head.

It was all he wanted at first, that she should not resist. Not by so much as a quiver did she try to deny his kisses now.

In fact—

It took him several minutes to realize that she was not reacting to him at all. This was not what he wanted, to kiss a rag doll. *Confound the little minx*. Her eyes were closed, but the rosy blush of her cheeks assured him that she had not fainted. If she hoped to put him off with this charade, then she had badly underestimated his tenacity—and the power of her own charms. She had wanted him before, on the archery field, in her mother's flower garden . . . He wound his hands into the thick mane of her hair and drew her head up to meet his kiss, determined to rouse that flicker again.

Her mouth was slack beneath his, offering no response. He cursed her silently, but frustration only egged him on. He shifted his head to nuzzle her ear, then found the back of her neck with his fingers. From the silky wisps at her nape, he slid his touch around to lightly trace the warm vein of her throat, stopping to linger at the throbbing pulse at its base. The veriest hint of a shiver wove through her. Ah, this was better. Encouraged, he kissed her again. He thought her lips warmed for the barest instant before he felt the swing of her arm.

Pain exploded through his head, blotting out both passion and triumph. He rolled away with a groan, blinded but for the myriad of stars swimming before his eyes.

How long he lay stunned he did not know, but when his ears stopped ringing and he found the strength to sit up, she was still there.

"Are you all right?"

The stars faded and he blinked his eyes until her double image melded into a single blur. She sounded half-guilty, standing now safely out of reach, still clutching a shard of broken stone in her hand.

"Was it necessary to try to brain me?" He winced at the pangs that shot like lightning through his skull.

"You did not seem inclined to stop on your own."

"You didn't ask me to."

"I thought if I— I thought you'd—" She sounded flustered and confused, then added more stoutly, "I shouldn't have had to."

He grunted, too sick from the agony in his head to reply.

"You're bleeding," she murmured, after he had sat for several minutes with a droning buzz in his ears.

"I don't suppose you mean to do anything about it?" He might have been drunk, for the way his voice slurred.

"You don't deserve that I should. After your despicable behavior—"

"You have made your point." He dropped his head into his hands and groaned again. He felt like an utter fool. "Just go away."

He was too ill to care whether she heeded him or not. Then through the fog in his brain, he heard the shrill ripping of cloth and squinted open one eye to see her tearing a length from the hem of her chemise.

He winced away from the pain as she daubed at his wound.

"Sit still," she chided.

He did his best to oblige, but he could not help but flinch from the searing sparks her cleaning caused. Once or twice they threatened to swirl away into a merciful darkness, but he fought the weakness. When she tore off a second strip and started to wrap it around his head, his obstinate pride reasserted itself and he caught her wrist.

"Please, allow me to return to the keep with at least one shred of dignity."

"You ought to have a bandage."

"Have you wiped away the blood?"

"As much as I could."

"Then just brush my hair down over it. The fewer questions asked, the better—don't you think?"

She hesitated, then combed her fingers through his hair with a feather-soft touch.

"I did not mean to hit you so hard," she said, again sounding guilty. "I just wanted you to stop."

Her image danced in a mist. "The fault was mine," he muttered. "Where you are concerned, I do not seem to recognize myself anymore. But I meant you no harm—or dishonor."

To his surprise, he felt her hand on his, squeezing it gently. Then she released him and rocked back on her heels.

"What are you going to do to Etienne?"

He sighed. "You know what I must do."

"He does not deserve a traitor's death."

"He may or may not receive one. But I have a duty to do, which is to learn the truth—"

"No matter what it takes, no matter who it hurts?"

He had no response to her bitter accusation.

"And is it your duty to marry Clothilde, as well?"

He was grateful, now, that his vision was still unsteady. He preferred not to witness again the hurt upon her face. "Aye."

She stood up and started to move away.

"Helen, wait." She turned. Even through the haze, she was lovely. "Helen—"

"No, you have said enough. You have done enough. Just marry my sister and sail back to England and *leave me alone*."

He thought the words ended on a sob, but she fled up the steps so quickly that he would never be sure.

# Seventeen

Heléne stifled a frustrated sigh. It was impossible to assess her situation while Sir Stephen Goldingham droned on in her ear. His whining voice had her nerves so set on edge that she wanted to scream. She glanced at Lord Challons who was seated on her left and envied the bright laughter on his partner's face. The Lady Osanne sparkled beneath Challons' good-natured flattery. Heléne bemoaned the fates that had condemned her to exchange so witty a trenchermate for the dull, toplofty Sir Stephen.

Heywood's deputy had ousted Challons as her companion at dinner days ago and Heléne had not enjoyed a meal since. Sir Stephen's long-winded discourses on how she would be expected to conduct herself as Heywood's wife were nothing short of insulting. She longed to tell him to his face that she had no intention of marrying his pompous-sounding master, but the truth was there was little time left to plot an escape. Thanks to Gunthar, Etienne was again under lock and key, and any hope of winning him free by drugging the guards had been spoiled by her confession in the gardens. Gunthar had left a strict injunction that no wine or other delights of the evening's feast should be served to the men standing watch outside the tower door.

Still, there must be a way. If only Sir Stephen would stop talking long enough to let her think. Her sister's wedding was tomorrow, and the next morning she and Clothilde would be packed off for England.

Heléne slid a glance past Sir Stephen to her sister, seated between him and Gunthar. Clothilde now seemed resigned to the marriage. Or perhaps indifferent would have been a better word. Since Triston had rejected her, she no longer seemed to care for anything.

Gunthar reached for the cup he shared with Clothilde and Heléne saw the tremor in his hand. From the pallor of his cheeks, she guessed him to be suffering a thunderous headache. He ought to be in bed with a comfrey poultice and a bandage and— No. She pushed her concern away. It served him right. He'd had no business kissing her like that on the eve of his marriage to her sister.

The pulsing ache in her breast finally drowned out Sir Stephen's sonorous voice. She took up her knife and traced in the thick sauce on their trencher an outline of a heart, then flexed her fingers into a fist and plunged the blade's tip straight through the center.

The voice stopped. Sir Stephen stared askance at her deed, but a blast of trumpets forestalled her having to fabricate an explanation. Thrice before the banqueters had "oo"-ed and "ah"-ed over the pastry-maker's subtleties: a sea horse, all spun of painted sugar; a ship of marzipan; a pastry dragon that spouted real flames. But even Heléne, who had grown up in wide-eyed admiration of his art, had never seen anything like the magnificent soaring castle now being borne into the hall by six of her father's squires. Sculptured from pastry and sugar, it stood well over five feet high, surrounded by miniature animals of prey—deer, rabbits, partridges and pheasants, all so realistically fashioned that it seemed as if they might leap off the tray. But what delighted the audience the most was the fountain of wine spraying in a sparkling arc from the castle's highest tower.

The squires, of whom her brother Therri was one, paraded their wondrous burden up and down the crowded aisles, garnering much praise and applause from the diners before they carried it to the dais and presented it to the guests-of-honor.

Gunthar rose with a rather strained smile and extended his goblet into the jetting stream of wine. He made a prettily worded speech on his joyful anticipations for the morrow, then turned and, with a courtly bow, offered the cup to Clothilde.

Clothilde did not look up. Her silence caused an uncomfortable murmur to spread through the hall. Heléne saw the gathering storm on her mother's face, the growing irritation on Gunthar's. After several awkward moments, he made an attempt to place the cup into one of Clothilde's listless hands.

Clothilde sprang to life. She bounced to her feet so fast she nearly toppled over her chair. She whispered something no one could hear, then turned and ran out of the hall before anyone could stop her.

Heléne rose to follow.

"Sit down," her mother said. "This is none of your affair. I will go—"

But Gunthar caught the Lady Gwenllian's arm. "I pray you will not distress yourself, my lady. Your daughter informs me that she is a bit overwhelmed by the company. She needs but a few moments to compose herself and will, I am sure, rejoin us directly. In the meantime, perhaps you will do me the honor—?"

The Lady Gwenllian had no choice but to accept Gunthar's goblet and sink back into her chair, gritting her teeth on a smile.

Heléne knew that he was lying. Clothilde had not told him anything of the sort, and it was highly unlikely that he would lay eyes on her again till morning. Drat the man! Just when she had convinced herself that he was the most unfeeling brute to ever walk the earth, he did something kind and protective like this.

"Such precipitous behavior would never be tolerated at Winbourne Castle," Sir Stephen murmured. "Remember it, my lady. As Lady Heywood, you will be expected to—"

"Ease off, Goldingham. The Lady Heléne has endured enough of your ridiculous lectures for the night. Her patience with your patronizing discourse has been remarkable, but I am heartily sick of the sound of your voice, and I am telling you now to *stow it*."

Heléne cast a startled look at Lord Challons, who had leaned across her more imperatively than politely to address the pompous knight. Sir Stephen seemed so taken aback that he actually fell silent.

"Bombastic windbag," Challons muttered. The jewels encrusting the breast of his surcote winked like a constellation of stars.

"Thank you," she whispered. "I don't know how much longer I could have borne it without saying something rude to him."

Challons laughed. "Then I am glad I was able to say it for you. He would have been sure to complain to your mother, and I fancy she has been embarrassed enough for one night."

Clothilde's departure *had* been embarrassing, and Heléne knew that her mother would punish Clothilde for it. She peeked around Sir Stephen's stiff body and saw that Gunthar had engaged the Lady Gwenllian with some sort of clever story. For the moment at least, the anger had gone from her mother's face.

Heléne could not but appreciate his efforts to distract her mother. For the remainder of the banquet, Gunthar lavished attention upon the Lady Gwenllian, treating her to story after story of titillating gossip from the English court, the sort of scandalous tales her mother delighted in hearing and repeating. Had the Lady Gwenllian had the least perception, she must have seen beyond the courteous smile pinned to his lips and realized that his sagging shoulders and whitened face bespoke a battle with discomfiting pain.

But Heléne recognized it. In spite of her earlier anger, she felt her heart flowing out with worry for him. An injury to the head was nothing to scoff at. He ought to be in bed.

"My lord," she turned impulsively to Lord Challons, who had resumed his conversation with the Lady Osanne, "can you not do something? The earl looks unwell."

Challons glanced down the table at Gunthar, then signaled to Julian Parr. "What's the matter with you, boy? Have you no eyes in your head? Your master looks as though he is ready to drop and you stand there like a block."

Julian blanched. "My lord, I daren't interrupt—"

"Nonsense. Would you rather have a taste of his temper now or have all hell break loose on you tomorrow when he finds himself too ill to stand for his own wedding?"

Julian hesitated, then moved to whisper something in Gunthar's ear. To the squire's evident relief, Gunthar drew back from the Lady Gwenllian with a polite but firmly worded apology. The hour was indeed late, he said, and the morrow would require the best from them all. Laurant overheard Gunthar's remark and intercepted his wife's protests to bring the banquet to an end.

Unlike the Lady Gwenllian, Gunthar's pallid countenance had not gone unnoticed by the rest of the company. Sir John Lee materialized almost instantly at his shoulder, followed by several other knights of his household. Heléne took advantage of the subsequent confusion to slip away from the hall.

At last, the roar of the throng faded and Heléne's mind began to function once more. Even so, it was an effort to force her thoughts round to Etienne. Gunthar kept getting in the way. Fear that she had caused him some terrible injury with her blow competed with the dull, sickish sensation she felt every time she thought of tomorrow's wedding. If only he had not interfered, she and Etienne might have been miles away by morning. Now, unless she could devise another plan quickly, she would have to stand by her mother's side in the morning and listen as Gunthar spoke the vows that would bind him irrevocably to another woman. And then she would have to watch him kiss Clothilde and, come nightfall, it would be her sister, not she, who would lie in his arms and know the fulfillment of his love . . .

For a moment, she was so engrossed in the pain of her vision that she did not hear the voices emanating from the bedchamber she shared with Clothilde.

"I don't want you with me. Why can't I go alone?"

"'Tisn't safe, my lamb. Who knows what sort o' brigands roam about this time o' night? I'll stay near enough to guard ye only. Trust me, my sweeting—"

Heléne was across the threshold before it registered that she was intruding. Sybil turned to glare at her, then slunk silently out of the room.

"I'm sorry. Did I—?" Heléne's apology trailed off. To her surprise, Clothilde was wreathed in smiles. She danced across the room to take Heléne's hands and pull her the rest of the way inside.

"Heléne, oh Heléne, the most wonderful thing!"

"What is it, Clo?" Heléne pushed the door closed with her foot. Whatever had brought this glow to her sister's face was not likely to be something the Lady Gwenllian would be pleased to hear.

"Triston! Sybil has spoken with him and he wishes to see me again. He still loves me, Heléne, and he promises there shall be no wedding tomorrow."

Heléne's heart leapt. "No wedding? But you have already given your consent, and the earl—"

"It doesn't matter. Triston is going to stop it."

"How? You said he would not run away with you."

"We are not going to run away. He—" Clothilde's mouth drew into a pout. "Oh, I don't know how he is going to do it. But when I meet him tonight—"

"Tonight? Clothilde, you can't mean to try to steal away tonight?"

"But Triston will be waiting."

"Yes, but Mama— What if she comes looking for you? She was terribly angry at the way you cut Gunthar in the hall."

Clothilde sank down on the bed, her skirts billowing out around her. "I could not help it, Heléne. I knew then that I could never bear to be his wife. I was lying here weeping, not knowing what I should do, when Sybil came in and told me—"

"Clo—" Heléne knelt beside the bed and took her sister's hands "—are you sure you ought to trust Sybil? I thought—I thought you hated her." There was no other word for the violent scenes she had witnessed between Clothilde and the old nurse.

Clothilde shook her head, though somehow Heléne sensed that it was not meant as a denial. "I know what sort of witch I deal with, sister. No, I do not trust her, but she will take me to Triston, and that is all that matters."

Heléne did not challenge her story further. She could see it would be no use. Clothilde clearly believed that Triston was going to save her from marrying Gunthar, a possibility Heléne greeted with strange ambivalence. Until now she had been able to indulge the dream that, had it not been for the inexorable duty the king had laid upon him, Gunthar would have chosen *her* to be his wife. But what if, even with Clothilde removed, he still only wanted Heléne for his mistress? She was not sure she wished to live with a shattered illusion.

It was after midnight, and it would be still later before the castle was sufficiently quiet to permit Clothilde to escape to her assignation. Though none too sure that Triston truly possessed the ability to avert the morrow's events, Heléne thought it at least prudent to encourage her sister to remind him of Etienne's situation and press him to seek out some solution to that, as well. Clothilde promised, rather absently, to do so, but Heléne's confidence was not high. If Etienne were to be saved an ugly fate, she had better come up with a plan of her own.

Perhaps Therri could help. Heléne did not know what she would have done without her brother. She could never have gotten Etienne safely to the South Tower by herself, far less have furnished the oubliette with any degree of comfort. Therri had smuggled the pallet and blankets out of the castle, though he had balked at her suggestion that they cut some rushes for the oubliette's floor. That was servants' work and beneath his dignity, he'd said, and besides, what did Etienne need rushes for? But Heléne was insistent. They would warm the floor. How would *he* like to be shut up for days on end in a cold, dark prison that resembled a tomb? So Therri had swallowed his pride and accompanied her out to the meadow. The violets had been her idea too, to combat the dank, mildewy smells of the pit.

But worse, she knew, than the physical unpleasantness of Etienne's surroundings must be the mind-numbing boredom he suffered. That was why she had lent him Gunthar's book. And this morning when she had visited him, they had lain together in the rushes with a candle at their head, taking turns reading the verses of Eliduc and the story of his adulterous love for the fair Guilliadun.

It was the one tale she had not yet read. The others, though admittedly immoral in their themes, she had been able to dismiss as poetic contrivances, while still allowing their magic and romance to entrance her. But Eliduc had cut too near to home. By the time Gunthar had jerked her off the ladder, she had understood all too well why he had sent her such a gift the same day he had committed himself to marry her sister. He had thought he could have it both ways, like the duplicitous Eliduc, but even Guilliadun had shrank from so wicked an intent. So she had played Guilliadun in her faint. Eliduc, on seeing his love swoon, had had the nobility to weep and repent. Gunthar, shameless man that he was, had tried to seduce her anyway.

But Heléne was not going to be seduced. And perhaps, if

Triston's plan succeeded, she would learn at last exactly where she stood in Gunthar's heart.

By the time Sybil came to fetch Clothilde to her tryst, Heléne was eager to see them gone. She knew she would not be able to sleep until Clothilde returned happy or devastated again, so she curled up on the window seat and cracked open the shutters to watch the yard below. She saw her sister and the nurse flitting like shadows against the darkness. Sybil carried a lantern with the shade pushed down to permit only the barest gleam of light. They darted towards the postern gate and vanished from her view.

Heléne drew a deep breath and leaned against the ensconcing wall to wait. Then she scrambled up again. A second figure had entered the yard, and even without a light, she knew him. He was too tall to be anyone else, though she wondered how he had recovered of his injury enough to regain that quick, confident stride. But there was no time to question what was clear to her eyes. Gunthar was following Clothilde, and if he caught her with Triston—

Heléne did not stop to think. She grabbed her cloak off the peg near the door and flung it round her shoulders on her way out of the room. She did not know what she could do to avert the disaster, but she knew she must do something.

Minutes later she scurried through the postern gate, heading for the woods and the clearing where Clothilde had kept her tryst before. There was no reason to think she would be elsewhere tonight, and as Heléne caught sight of Gunthar's billowing cape, she knew she had guessed aright. She stayed as near to him as she dared, wondering how to stop him. Should she call out his name? How was she to explain her presence on his heels if she did?

It did not take him long to near the clearing. He seemed familiar with the way, even though Clothilde and Sybil had had a sufficient head start to escape his direct observation. But he would be upon them any moment if she did not act quickly. She stooped and picked up a rock. If she threw it in the opposite direction, perhaps the sound would divert him just long enough for her to slip around him and run to the clearing with a warning.

She flung back her hand, and found her wrist caught in a vise-like hold.

"Drop it, my lady," a voice hissed into her ear.

Heléne dropped the rock and twisted about to find herself face to face with Rousillon.

"Wha—"

He pressed the palm of his hand against her mouth. "Hush now, there's a good girl. It will all be over in a moment."

Heléne's eyes widened. It was a trap, but not for Clothilde.

She lashed out with a wild kick and heard the crack as her toe connected with Rousillon's shin. He gave a muffled yelp and his hold on her slackened. She tore herself free, evaded the hand that flashed out to catch her, and ran for the clearing.

She was almost there when her foot caught in a tangle of undergrowth. She landed hard on her hands and knees, then felt herself pulled up by Rousillon. Frantically her fingers undid the ties at her throat. Before he realized the inadequacy of his grasp, she slipped away, leaving him holding her empty cloak.

She heard his curse in the darkness. He pounded after her once more, and above the sound of their thudding feet came a shout, a cry of surprise and pain. At last she stumbled into the clearing, but someone threw her back so that she fell into Rousillon's arms. And then she saw him, on his knees, at the center of a bloody circle.

There were too many for him to escape. She saw his sword fall from his hand as a blow of steel caught him in the back and another in the chest. Rousillon made no attempt now to smother her screams. He held on to her with a wiry strength, enduring the lash of her heels as she writhed in his arms. Swords swooped into the air and flashed down again and again . . .

And then they stopped and drew back from the dark, silent stain on the forest floor.

# Eighteen

Heléne had no memory of how she made her way back to the castle. It was as though everything simply stopped, then started up again when she found herself weeping in her father's embrace.

"We can't make heads or tails of it," someone complained. "She came stumbling up to the gate all frenzied like, weeping and moaning and calling out his name."

Her father carried her into the hall and set her down beside the hearth. He rubbed her hands and tried to quiet her.

Then she heard a voice . . .

"What has happened here? My lady—?"

Helène sprang up with a shuddering sob and flung her arms about the speaker.

"I thought it was you. *I thought it was you.*" She clutched at him fiercely, her fingers curling into the warmth of his back, her ear nestled against the reassuring thud of his heart.

"Helen."

Gunthar breathed her name softly, then lifted her chin and smoothed the tears from her cheeks. She could not stop crying and shaking, but she made an effort to answer the urgency in his eyes.

"Sir John," she gasped. "In the woods. I saw them— There were too many— I could not—"

"Easy, love. There's my girl. Just tell me."

Another aching sob burst from her throat. "He's dead. They k-killed him. And I thought it was you."

He caught her as her knees gave way and lifted her into his arms. For a moment, there was no sound in the hall but her own shattered weeping. He carried her back to the fire and tried to place her on the bench, but she clung to him, so he sat down beside her.

"Helen, get hold of yourself. Are you sure—?"

"I saw them! They had swords and they kept striking him—over—and over—" Oh, heavens, she was going to be sick.

"Laurant," Gunthar snapped, "get your wife. I will take the Lady Helen to her room."

"No, please, I want to stay with you."

"Helen, you're ill—"

"I'm not ill! I know what I saw!"

"Then we must go and see too, mustn't we? Tollerton, get some torches and round up some men."

"You're not going into the woods?"

"Is that not where you saw Sir John fall?"

"But what if they are still there? Sir John was a mistake. They were waiting for you."

Gunthar did not ask her how she knew that, perhaps because he was not yet convinced of her veracity in the face of her evident shock. He allowed her to lean against him, but said nothing more until the Lady Gwenllian appeared, looking cross at having been roused from her sleep. Then he pulled Heléne's hands away from his tunic and stood up.

"Attend to her," he said to her mother.

The Lady Gwenllian took his place on the bench. "Honestly, Heléne, you will be the death of me. Where, in heaven's name, have you been this time of night? And just look at you! Were Goldingham to see you like this—"

"I'm s-sorry, Mama," Heléne stammered.

"Hmph. Flora," the Lady Gwenllian called to the freckle-faced serving girl who had accompanied her, "fetch the Lady Heléne some wine, and then we will put her to bed." To her daughter, she added, "I will expect an explanation in the morning. And don't you dare wake Clothilde tonight. I will not have her all unsettled again before the ceremony tomorrow."

Clothilde. Oh, heavens! What if she were still with Triston?

"I want to wait here," Heléne insisted, "until the men return."

"Nonsense. How can you be so foolish?"

"Leave her be," Gunthar said. "Let her sit by the fire and sip some wine. I fancy she'll not sleep until we bring her the truth."

The Lady Gwenllian waited until Gunthar and her husband were gone, then muttered, "Arrogant man. Telling me how to rear my daughters. Were he not counselor to the king, I should wish him to the very devil." She rose and said to Heléne, "Stay there," then signaled to Flora and led the servant out of the hall.

Heléne had no intention of moving, but she wished her mother had not left her alone. The leaping shadows on the wall reminded her of flashing arms, the red in the fire of blood. She dared not close her eyes for fear of the visions she might see. What if Gunthar wandered away from the other men? What if *they* were still waiting? She stared down at her trembling hands and breathed prayer after prayer for his safety.

By the time her mother returned, Heléne had begun to cry again. The Lady Gwenllian handed her a cup. Heléne drank from it gratefully. The wine burned as it ran down her throat, making her choke a little, but it spread a welcome comfort through her body. At last, the paroxysms of horror and fear subsided and the vivid memories dulled.

"The very idea," she heard her mother say. "Expecting you to sit up all night and not look frightful for your sister's wedding. Eudes!"

Heléne glanced up as a thickset servant came forward. She had known him all her life and felt no alarm when he pulled her to her feet. The comfort became a heaviness, as though great weights were attached to her limbs. She sank into the servant's arms and swirled away into a soothing mist of darkness.

Heléne awoke with a start. She was alone in the bed, and after a moment she pushed herself up in a panic. Where was Clothilde? What had happened to Gunthar? Had it all been a dream?

The door opened and Flora came in with a tray.

"Your mother sent me up with your breakfast, milady, in case you were still feeling ill."

Heléne scrambled out of the bed, then dropped dizzily back.

"The sleeping draught," Flora explained. "The effects linger sometimes."

Heléne shook her head. How had she not recognized a draught in the wine?

"Flora, where is Clothilde?"

"With your mother, milady."

"With Mama?" Had her sister been found out, or— "Are they preparing for the wedding?"

"'Tis to be no wedding today, not after what's happened to poor Sir John. Terrible upset, the earl is. He's not left the chapel all morning. Here now, milady, you're not thinking to go out like that?"

Heléne stopped halfway across the room. No one had even bothered to remove her torn clothes. She pulled off her gown, told Flora to fetch her another, then ran over to the wash basin to scrub her face and arms. The cool water helped to clear her head. She dressed hurriedly in the fresh chemise and tunic the servant brought her, then stood impatiently as Flora did her best to comb the tangles from her hair. At last Heléne flung her locks over one shoulder, exclaiming it good enough, and flew out of the room, ignoring Flora's cry that she had forgotten her breakfast.

She found Gunthar in the chapel, as Flora had said. Sir John's body had been laid out near the altar, with candles lit all around his head. Heléne approached reluctantly, shivering in dread of what she might see. But there were no signs of violence now. The murderous wounds were concealed beneath a red cap and a handsome green surcote, with a ruby-studded collar laid across the unmoving chest. The hands, folded as if in prayer just below the jewels, held a small, gold-leafed cross. All evidence of pain or terror had been smoothed from the pleasant, homely features.

Gunthar stood as unmoving as the corpse of his friend and almost as white, his fists clenched, his back a rigid line. He gave no hint that he was aware of Heléne's presence, even when she came to stand beside him. He stared down at the knight, his face an emotionless mask.

"There were seven."

The silence was so intense that Heléne jumped when he finally spoke.

"Seven blows to kill a man who never had a chance to defend himself."

His expression did not change, but Heléne could feel it now, his pain, and more acutely still, his loss.

"He was important to you, wasn't he?" she asked softly.

He hesitated, then answered, his voice low and even. "John Lee was the first friend I ever had. He was reared in my father's house alongside dozens of other boys, all scions of noble families hoping to advance through the old earl's favor. All were warned that they must defer to the earl's son, for my father had very strict notions of dignity and rank. I was expected to stand apart from others, to hold myself aloof from their common sentiments and games. But John would have none of it. He was as tall and gangly as I, and stubborn even then. He plagued me until I joined him in one of his larks, and when my father beat me for it, John only laughed. He said I had been too top-lofty to begin with and could only be improved by being taken down a peg or two."

He paused, never taking his eyes off that silent, sober countenance. "He was right, of course. I'm afraid I am more like my father than I care to admit, even now. But John bore with it all, my sharp tongue, my haughty temper . . . He never complained. And he never turned away."

But now he was gone. Heléne ached to comfort Gunthar, but she did not know how. Impulsively, she touched his hand and was surprised when the stiff fingers opened to receive hers. She slid her palm into his and gave it a gentle squeeze. After a moment, he turned his head and looked at her. And then the veil slipped.

"It should have been me," he said in a hoarse whisper. "It was supposed to be me in that clearing, but my head— John saw that I was sick and said he would go in my place. So I went to bed, and he—"

She stopped the rest with her free hand against his mouth. "Oh, don't," she said, her throat numb with tears. "I am sorry for Sir John, but if it had been you—" She swept her fingers against the swelling on the side of his head. She had not, she acknowledged now, struck him so much in defense of his advances, as in defense of her own weak longing to yield to his passion. But regardless of where the fault lay, she thanked every star in the heavens for the impulse that had prompted her to wield that broken shard of stone.

"You saw it all, didn't you?" he asked.

She shivered and nodded.

"Even this?"

He opened his fist. She looked down at the shred of cloth he held out. It had been carefully torn to preserve the image on the badge: Melusine, the serpent-woman.

"Yes," she whispered. She knew exactly where it had been found, clutched in Sir John's hand. "Please," she said, as she saw the anger surge into Gunthar's face, "there are things I must tell you, but—must I say them here?"

No matter how peacefully laid out the body was, standing in its presence revived the terrors of the night. Gunthar caught her nervous glance and understood. He gave a curt nod and led her out of the chapel.

"Well?"

Alone with him in her father's council chamber, Heléne's courage ebbed. The gaze with which he weighed her had grown implacably cold. Sir John was dead, and there would be no mercy in Gunthar's heart for anyone remotely implicated in the killing.

"Let me make this easier for you," he said, when she hesitated. "I know all about your rendezvous with Triston de Brielle."

She blinked. "My what?"

"Please—" he walked over to the desk "—my head aches bad enough without indulging in any more of these games. You were to take your young swain, Etienne, to that clearing in the woods, where Sir Triston had agreed to meet you and spirit you both away. But my men and I upset those plans yesterday when we recaptured Etienne. Still, you knew Sir Triston would be waiting, so you went to the woods alone."

Tossing aside any pretense of good manners, he sank into a chair while she continued to stand by the door.

"Did you not even think to ask for a salve to ease your head?" she said, observing the lines of strain at the corners of his eyes.

"I saw no point," he said. "I knew you would not attend me, and to explain a lump of this sort to anyone else, I should either have had to appear unbelievably clumsy or told the truth."

She crossed the room to examine him more closely. She realized now that his pallor was not completely due to the loss of his friend. His thick hair concealed the swelling, but her keen eyes detected its effect in the tightened muscles of his face.

"It was foolish to be so prideful. It is a wonder you are able to think straight. Let me run to the kitchens and I will—"

"No." He caught her wrist as she turned away. "Forget my head. Helen, I need to know what you saw last night. I need to know the truth." He pulled out the secretary's chair and waited for her to sit. "I know you would prefer to forget. I regret that you were forced to witness what you did, but—"

"It was not Triston," she said quickly, anticipating from his former words where his suspicions were going to lead him.

"But you went there to meet him. That much I know. I do not blame you for what must have happened next. Sir Triston must have seen that you were followed and attacked John before he scarcely had time to draw his sword. There was no blood on his blade, that is how I know John could not have struck a blow himself. Loyalty is an admirable thing, but when a man proves himself so base that mere killing is not enough—" Gunthar pulled her down to the chair. "He was butchered, Helen. There can be no other word for what John suffered. Seven thrusts, any one of which would have proved mortal of itself. You are protecting a savage murderer."

"I'm not! Triston wasn't even there. And Sir John wasn't following me, I was following him."

Gunthar frowned. "That is absurd. You went to that clearing to meet Sir Triston, to tell him about his brother. He was expecting you to bring him Etienne."

Heléne shook her head.

"Do you deny that you and your brother planned to smuggle him away from the castle last night? That your brother was to divert the guards while you slipped Etienne through the postern gate and escaped with him into the woods?"

"Not to the clearing. Triston didn't know about our plan. How could he? Since Etienne's escape from the tower, you have had the exits so well guarded there has been no way to send him a message. I have not left the grounds and Therri has gone no further than the river. And he would have told me if he had seen Triston there."

That checked Gunthar. His frown deepened. "Then where did you intend to take Etienne?"

Heléne hesitated. The answer would probably have been obvious to him had someone not fixed his thoughts so firmly on a false target.

"Who told you about the clearing?" she asked.

"Does it matter? You were overheard plotting with your brother and Etienne."

"But we never mentioned the clearing. Etienne and I were going to strike a path through the woods straight for Vere Castle. Triston would not have been expecting us, but he would not have turned us away. He has friends—no, I will not say where—to whom he might have sent us for safety. And you would have been so preoccupied with my sister and the banquet that you would not have realized we were missing until it was too late."

He looked skeptical of this strategy. "It would have taken you all night to reach Vere on foot. And it would have been the first place I should have sent my men to search."

"That's just the point," she said. "You did *not* think of Vere because someone misdirected you to the clearing. Whoever overheard our plan must have known the truth, but he told you otherwise.

Etienne and Triston and I were never meant to be in the clearing. But you were. And that's why they were waiting."

"They?"

"It was dark, and I was too upset to count them, but there must have been at least five or six men, all armed with swords and—" She faltered at the memory and felt his hand brush her face.

"Take a deep breath and tell me."

She nodded. Sir John's murder had brought home to her just how real the threat to Gunthar was. Even had her heart not been involved, her conscience would not allow her to keep silent any longer.

"Last night I saw from my window a figure I took to be you, crossing the courtyard. I—I was curious as to where you were going that time of night, and—and I could not sleep, so I followed you." She knew the explanation was inadequate, but she was not going to incriminate Clothilde and Triston when they had clearly had no part in what had occurred.

She saw the doubtful tightening of Gunthar's lips, but he only said, "Go on."

"Well," she said, "I followed you—I thought it was you—into the woods and saw that you were headed for the clearing. But they had set someone to watch and when he saw me trailing you, he grabbed me from behind. That was when I realized you were walking into a trap and I tried to scream to you, but he covered my mouth so I could not. So I kicked him until he let me go, and then I ran to the clearing, only it was too late. I saw them—with their swords—hitting you—and hitting you—"

Their chairs were near enough that he could pass his arms around her, and he did so, drawing her head against his shoulder. He stroked her hair, but said, "There is more, is there not?"

"Yes," she whispered, swallowing back the horror. She steadied herself for the rest. "The man who had grabbed me caught me again and held me while the—butchers—did their work. When they finally drew back, their victim was crumpled on the ground. The man who held me professed satisfaction and let me go, and I saw him tear something from the shoulder of his tunic. He approached the body and flipped it over with his foot. And then he swore."

"When he saw they had the wrong man."

She moved her head against his shoulder in another nod. "At first he was enraged. Then he said they could still make some use of the mistake, and he pressed his scrap of tunic into Sir John's hand. Only somehow—somehow Sir John was not yet dead. So he took his sword, and vowing next time it should be you—he—he c-cast it through Sir John's h-heart."

She felt all cold and shivery, like one sometimes did just before being struck down by a fever. She looked up as Gunthar groaned and saw his hard-held mastery washed away. His eyes were closed, but in the raw anguish on his face she knew that he was reliving that final, bloody scene for himself.

It was several minutes before he gave a shuddering sigh and locked the pain back up. Abruptly, he pushed her back in her chair.

"The man who held you. Can you describe him?"

Her heart was pounding doubly now. She knew she had to tell him the truth. Pray heaven it would not destroy her father!

"I saw his face," she said, "and I know him by name. It was Garoux de Rousillon."

Gunthar stared as though the name were the last in the world he had expected to hear. "*Rousillon?* Are you sure?"

She nodded.

He stood up, his expression flowing from surprise to anger. He strode across the room and back several times before muttering, "I had not believed even Richard could be so insane as to ally himself with that devil."

"My lord, who is he?" she asked, disturbed by his reaction.

Gunthar's perturbed strides did not slow as he said, "The blackest, most execrable villain I ever let slip through my fingers. He poisoned his own father and cast the blame on his brother, who stood between him and the inheritance. He used his lackeys to torture a confession of shared guilt from his father's mistress, and when she sought to recant, he had the poor wench strangled. His brother was judged guilty and hanged by a royal court before the truth became known. And it might never have done so, had he not developed an insatiable lust for the sister of his squire, the accomplice in his deed."

"What happened?" she asked as Gunthar stopped. He turned to face her and seemed to be weighing whether the rest of his tale might not be too unsavory for her ears. The answer, when it came, was brutal.

"He raped her and got her with child. To soothe his squire's anger, Rousillon agreed to help her conceal her shame. He knew an old woman who claimed she possessed a potion that was capable of ridding a lass of such 'inconveniences' as unwanted babes. At Rousillon's insistence, the squire administered the drink to his sister. It was that little touch of irony that sent the squire over the edge to betray his master. The potion sent his sister into convulsions and finally death. Rousillon claimed it was a tragic mistake, but the squire did not believe him. During the campaigns against the princes, while I was encamped near Parthenay some twenty miles from Rousillon's castle, the squire came to me and accused his master, so grief-stricken that he freely admitted his own crimes, as well."

Gunthar's gaze drifted from her face to her father's banner, draped against the wall. "I sent the boy back, thinking to keep Rousillon off his guard while I took a contingent of men to investigate the charges. When inquiries of his neighbors and serfs confirmed a cruel and treacherous nature, I dispatched a herald through the gate, demanding that Rousillon meet me on the plain before his fortress to answer the accusations leveled against him. At the appointed hour, my herald returned alone, tied into his saddle, with a knife in his back. The next day, my men found the squire's body floating in the moat. His throat had been savagely cut."

His gaze swept back to her and he paused to allow this awful recital of violence to sink in. "Helen," he said then, "I tell you this to warn you. If you know Rousillon's face and name, it can only be because he has revealed himself to you. The man is half-mad, a scorner of both heaven and hell. What hold does he have over you that he allowed you to witness his murder of John Lee and let you live to tell the tale?"

From the coldness in her cheeks, Heléne knew there was no blood left in her face. "He—he did not think I would speak," she said, "but you must not ask me why."

"Helen—"

"Please, I will tell you anything else, but I cannot tell you that."

He crossed the room and pulled her to her feet. "Can you not trust me, even now?"

She tried to speak and failed. He read the answer in her eyes and let her go.

She caught his gleam of disappointment as he turned away and resumed his pacing, but his voice was crisp as he said, "Very well, then, tell me the rest, as much as you can. This—" he waved the torn badge of Melusine "—proves that Rousillon is in league with the prince. I gather you have knowledge of an alliance with the de Brielles, as well? Sir Damian hinted to me of another's hand in the plot, so if that is your secret—"

"No," she said, "Etienne has already admitted as much. He suspects it was Rousillon who put the prince's dagger in his sheath."

"Without his knowledge? That seems unlikely. Why?"

Heléne had been brooding over that question ever since Etienne had voiced his suspicion. "My lord," she asked, "why would the prince wish to kill you?"

"I cannot read Richard's mind," Gunthar said, "but the most probable answer would be to prevent me from reporting something back to his father which he did not wish the king to know."

"Like what?"

"That he is not, and has no intention of ever, enforcing the terms of the Peace. That he is allowing men like de Brielle and Angoulême to rebuild their fortifications in defiance of the royal command and in anticipation of renewed rebellion against the crown."

"They are not strong enough to challenge the king directly now?"

"No, not after Henry's decisive defeat of the French forces at Rouen. It was French encouragement and money that kept the princes' cause afloat, and once that was withdrawn the rebellion crumbled. To provoke another war now on his own would prove disastrous for Richard. However, given time to regroup and refortify, a day may come in the future when he will feel confident enough to challenge the king again."

"But would not the murder of his father's counselor force the king to investigate? Then he might learn what the prince is about and the prince would be punished, would he not?"

"Aye, but if Richard were desperate enough to want to keep me quiet—"

"But if he made your death appear to be an accident, then there might not be any questions asked at all. Would that not be the better scheme?"

Gunthar stopped and looked at her. "What are you suggesting?"

Heléne lifted her shoulders, but said, "Does it not seem strange that there should always be such obvious evidence of the prince's hand whenever someone has tried to kill you?"

Gunthar thought it over. "Not every time. The poison in my cup was anonymous enough. And though I suspect Sir Triston of cutting my saddle strap, I have no proof that he did so and certainly no clear evidence that it was done at the prince's command."

Heléne wrinkled her brow at that. "No, and that is odd, too, isn't it? Both of those incidents were different."

"Not so different," Gunthar said. "I should have been just as dead had either of them succeeded. But I see what you mean." He held out the badge again. "This was not torn as John struggled with his attackers, as I had first supposed. You saw Rousillon place it in his hand after the murder was done. A deliberate act to implicate the prince."

"Like Etienne's dagger," she pointed out.

"Very well, I will give you that for the moment. Then the question becomes, why? Sir Damian said there were others who hated me and wanted me dead. He meant Rousillon, of course. But what is his purpose in trying to blame the prince?"

Heléne drew nearer to him. The brutality of Sir John's murder took on a new light as she asked, "Why *does* Rousillon hate you so?"

"Because I was the instrument of his downfall," Gunthar said. "When he refused to surrender himself for the murders of my herald and the squire, I stormed his castle and set it ablaze. So miserable a miscreant was he that his own men refused to defend him, but he nevertheless managed to slip away in the smoke and confusion. He has lived as an outlaw since then with a royal price on his head, seeking shelter, it appears, among such hardened rebels as Sir Damian and his sons."

"Etienne thinks he is blackmailing Triston."

"Like he is blackmailing you?"

She looked away, her heart in her throat. "I told him the day you would be on the road to Angoulême."

There was a moment of silence before he said, "I see. Then that explains the archer." He sounded maddeningly calm. "Did you know about Osanne, as well?"

"Osanne?" she repeated breathlessly. She did not dare look at him.

"That she is his spy? She must be, for it was she who overheard your plan to free Etienne and told John that you would take him to the clearing."

Heléne gasped a little at this revelation. She remembered her encounter with Osanne on her way to the garden, just before she and Therri had set in motion their plan to smuggle Etienne to the South Tower. She had tried so hard not to rouse any suspicions in the woman. Clearly, she had failed. Osanne must have followed her. Heléne supposed it served her right for concealing from Gunthar the knowledge she now felt compelled to admit.

"Yes, I knew she was a spy. Etienne says that she and Rousillon are lovers. And I did not tell you, and because of that you believed her report and Sir John went to the clearing, and now he is dead."

She felt his hand on her shoulder and tried to twist away, but he pulled her firmly into his arms.

"Helen, don't. It is not your fault."

"It is! If I had only told you then—"

"I don't know that it would have changed anything. John was so smitten with the wench that he might well have refused to believe it. He was stubborn enough to have gone to the clearing, just to prove me wrong." He lifted her face and rubbed his thumb against her cheek. "At least I know now who my enemy is. I shall know better how to guard myself."

She caught his fingers and held them against her face. "Osanne is not the only spy. There is someone else, one of your own men, I think. Rousillon calls him 'le Reynard.'"

"The Fox," Gunthar murmured. "It is probably Julian Parr. I suspect it was he who smuggled the knife to Etienne, no doubt on Rousillon's orders. Rousillon must have been afraid Etienne would reveal his presence at Vere. No doubt he hoped the boy would either make good his escape or be killed in the attempt."

"It was Rousillon who persuaded Etienne to come here and try to kill you," she said. "He told Etienne that if he didn't, you would throw Sir Damien into prison. Etienne feared his father was no longer strong enough to survive such a punishment. For him, it was a matter of life or death for his father." She gazed pleadingly up at Gunthar. "My lord, can you not have mercy on him? Now that he realizes how Rousillon used him, he will not threaten you again. Can you not release him from my father's tower?"

Gunthar's arms dropped from around her and he stepped back. His eyes narrowed, but he only said, "For the moment, I think he is safer where he is. Unless you wish him to return to Vere and risk the fate of Rousillon's squire?"

She shivered and shook her head. "Then what will you do now?"

"Find a way to smoke the devil out. And *you* must have nothing more to do with him, blackmail or no. Rousillon would not be averse to slitting *your* throat if he thinks you have betrayed him." He saw her hesitance, and in his urgency he caught her arm and held it over-roughly. "Helen, you must promise me, you must *swear* to me that you will not. I don't care what he holds over your head—pray heaven I may never know, if it is as bad as you think! But were anything to happen to you, were you to fall into that fiend's hands—"

She winced at the crushing strength of his fingers, but her blood soared at the emotion on his face. He loved her! Nothing else could account for what she saw in his eyes. But that same passion, colored now by fear, could well prove his undoing. The fact that it could, even for a moment, cause his mask of impregnable self-possession to slip bespoke a dangerous intensity. Were Rousillon to somehow learn of it and try to use her against him—

"I will not go near him again," she promised with such fervor that he accepted it as a vow and let her go.

For a moment, she thought he still looked shaken. Then his features settled back into their usual impassive lines. He walked over to the desk and stood stiffly for several minutes, then leaned into it with both hands braced against the top.

"Please," she said, "will you not go lie down now? I will send Flora up with a salve for your head. She is a good, obedient girl and will not speak of it to anyone, if I warn her not to."

"I cannot. Not until I have dictated a letter to John's widow. If you would be so kind as to find my secretary and ask him to attend me, I would much appreciate it."

"Very well. But only if you will promise *then* to—"

"Then I will lie down." He sounded too weary to do anything else. "And you may send up your trustworthy maid. In fact—I would welcome it."

Heléne smiled at this small victory, and went away to do as he asked.

# Nineteen

No sooner had Heléne finished preparing the salve and instructing Flora in its intended use, than she was summoned to her mother's chamber. Clothilde was there as well. Their mother looked cross, but the lingering glow on Clothilde's cheeks suggested that her lovers' tryst remained a secret.

The Lady Gwenllian demanded to know what her younger daughter had been doing wandering about the woods in the middle of the night. Heléne repeated the half-truths she had earlier told Gunthar. Her mother did not challenge her story, other than to decry as shameless and forward the curiosity that had led her to involve herself in movements which had been none of her affair. Her mother's only reaction to Sir John's murder and her daughter's trauma was to exclaim that she hoped the unpleasantness would teach Heléne not to stick her nose where it didn't belong.

"Goldingham is much put out by it all," the Lady Gwenllian said. "He had hoped to be on his way to England tomorrow, and now the earl is demanding a delay. Temporary, of course, as I have explained to your sister, and understandable in view of the circumstances surrounding Sir John's death. But when Goldingham spoke of his master's impatience and remarked that he saw no reason not to depart with you in the morning as planned, Gunthar gave him such a frown that the poor man actually trembled and begged his pardon. Goldingham is now unhappily resigned to waiting until your sister can accompany you. And heaven only knows when that will be! The earl refuses even to discuss a new date for the wedding."

Heléne was amazed that her mother had had the temerity to broach such a subject with Gunthar while his closest friend lay freshly dead in the chapel. Whatever his response had been, and Heléne guessed that it must have been blighting, it had clearly had no other effect on her mother than to put her out of temper.

"Until he *can* be brought to discuss it," the Lady Gwenllian continued, "I do not intend to be further embarrassed by either one of you. I have already warned Clothilde against any more odd starts such as she displayed at the table last night. The earl's forbearance was remarkable, but cannot be expected to be repeated."

Heléne stole a glance at her sister, but Clothilde appeared unfazed by their mother's rebuke. In truth, she looked as though she were in some other world.

"Goldingham, on the other hand," the Lady Gwenllian said with an icy stare at her younger daughter, "was less than amused to learn of your midnight wanderings. Had the choice been his own, I believe he would have abrogated the contract then and there. But he admits the Northumberland land is more important to Heywood than a quiet wife. Nevertheless, if you engage in one more escapade like last night, I shall have Sybil beat you until you are as meek as even Goldingham could wish. And don't expect the earl to come to your rescue again. How I choose to discipline my daughters is none of his affair."

The Lady Gwenllian paused until she was sure that Heléne had understood her threat, then dismissed both her daughters with a terse nod.

Clothilde caught Heléne's hand as they sailed through the doorway, but she waited until they were alone in their own chamber before saying, "You needn't be afraid of Sybil anymore."

Heléne plopped down on the bed and gazed at her sister in surprise. "What do you mean?"

"She's gone," Clothilde said.

"Gone? Gone where?"

Clothilde shrugged and her pretty lips turned down. "Away. Does it matter? She'll not hurt either of us again.

She took the hairbrush from the table and swept it through her glowing locks. Their mother's early morning summons had come before Clothilde had had time to bind or veil her hair, and though it was not as long and thick as Heléne's, Heléne still envied its brightness. She glanced down at her own pale tresses and sighed.

The rhythmic motion of the brush soon banished the tiny frown from Clothilde's face and a dreamy smile danced its way back over her charming mouth.

"Clo," Heléne asked, recognizing the happy blush on her sister's cheeks, "what happened between you and Triston last night?"

Clothilde threw back her head with a merry laugh and spun about on her toes. "He loves me, Heléne. We are going to be together forever. Triston swears it!"

Her simple faith touched Heléne, but it worried her, too. How could Triston be so sure that Gunthar would not succeed in marrying her sister? With that question came a tumble of others that Heléne had been too shaken or confused to consider in the immediate aftermath of Sir John's murder.

"Clo, where were you both last night? You were not in the clearing."

"Triston met me down by the river."

"Why there? Why not in the clearing where you always met before?"

"I don't know. It is where Sybil took me and where Triston was waiting." She whirled around again, as lightly as a fairy sprite. "Oh, Heléne, it is going to be so *wonderful!* I have waited so long!"

"What about Gunthar?" It did not matter that Heléne knew Gunthar to be in love with herself. Triston and Clothilde could not know it, and he must surely remain an impediment in their view.

"He does not matter. Triston has promised. He said I should not have to marry Gunthar today and it was true. Triston is going to protect me from everything until we are together again."

Heléne felt a little shock run through her. How could Triston have known there would be no wedding unless he had been privy to the trap that had been set for Gunthar? The murder had been orchestrated by Rousillon, but was not that villainous knight residing at Vere Castle? Triston *must* have known. And his confidence that Clothilde would eventually be his suggested not only that Rousillon intended to try again, but that Triston would be informed of it, as well.

"Clothilde, how does Triston mean to save you from Gunthar?" If he had let something slip to her sister, Heléne could pass on a warning. She held her breath for Clothilde's reply.

"He did not say how, only that he would. Sybil promised it, too, but we did not need her help. She was a wicked, evil old bawd and I am glad she is gone."

The hostility that flitted over her sister's radiant features was now familiar to Heléne. She echoed her sister's sentiments, but felt compelled to ask again, "How can you be sure she won't come back? I did not think she would ever leave us till the day she died."

Clothilde looked confused for a moment, then said, "Do you remember when we burned her switch? I thought I saw demons in the flames, chattering as they devoured her soul."

It was no doubt the fate that Sybil deserved, Heléne thought. "Yes, but where would she have gone, and why? Surely she must have said something?"

Clothilde shook her head. Heléne sighed. Perhaps she could learn something more about Triston then, some word, the significance of which her sister might not have understood.

"Come sit beside me, Clo, and tell me everything that passed between you and Triston last night."

The joyful smile returned to her sister's face and she skipped across the room to join Heléne on the bed.

"Is that your determination, then?"

Gunthar did not immediately reply to his secretary's question. Two days had passed since John Lee's death, and in that time Heléne's salve, discreetly administered by the freckle-faced maid, had eased his headache to nonexistence. Until he could assess the situation undistracted by pain, he had refused to discuss the implications of the murder with his council. But it was dangerous to procrastinate a decision any longer. He had assembled his men to weigh their advice. Challons, Tollerton and Enslye held his greatest respect, if not all his trust. As something of a gamble, he had included Laurant in the gathering. The man was shifty and ambitious, but pathetically susceptible to Gunthar's flattery. Standing with the earl's council had puffed him up nearly to insufferability. Still, Gunthar fancied it was better to keep him under his eye than to have him working mischief behind his back.

"Are you agreed in your opinion?" he asked, his gaze sweeping the circle from Sir Thomas's stolid face to Challons' smooth, cunning one.

It was Challons' preeminence to answer. "It seems to us the wisest course. The evidences of the prince's hand cannot be ignored. He must be confronted and made to confess his part."

"And Rousillon?"

"Undoubtedly the prince's agent. Bring the prince around, and Rousillon will be made to follow."

Gunthar was not so sure, but he did not voice his doubts aloud. Or rather, Heléne's doubts. It was quite possible, after all, that she was wrong and that the prince was behind the conspiracy exactly as he appeared to be. Challons was right to press a meeting. At the very least, the prince had sought to thwart the king's intent by inaction. At worst, he was guilty of issuing the orders that had resulted in John Lee's death.

"Will the king pardon the prince, do you think?" Laurant asked, as though the question of the king's benevolence were of particular interest to himself.

"Probably," Gunthar said. "Henry can deny his sons very little when they weep and abase themselves before him. He will not see that no sooner does he forgive with one hand, than the whelps are off plotting how they can bite the other."

"Then," his secretary interposed, "how would you have me write? Will you travel again to Angoulême?"

"Ah, now," Challons said before Gunthar could reply, "that I would not advise. Ride into Count William's lair? The puppet-master,

I have heard you call him. I think I should find a way of severing the strings before you meet the prince again."

Sir Thomas offered, "Some neutral territory, then. Laurant must know some knight who did not take sides during the war."

"Everyone took sides," Gunthar said. "One was either for the king or against him. Henry allowed no one to sit on the fence."

There was a momentary silence while his counselors appeared to find themselves at a loss.

Then Challons remarked, "Perhaps what we need, then, is not a man of war, but of peace."

Gunthar lifted a brow.

"There is much bad blood between you and the prince, my lord, especially now that matters have become—shall we say, personal?"

Challons spoke the word tentatively, with a wary eye for Gunthar's reaction. Everyone knew how close John Lee had been to him. But Gunthar only gave a curt nod and bade the baron, "Go on."

"Aye, well," Challons said, "the prince, like his father, is renowned for his infamous temper and may take ill your accusations, be they true or no. It seems to me—" this with a self-deprecating little bow "—in my most humble opinion, my lord, that a mediator might be useful in bringing about an accord."

Gunthar struggled briefly with his bitter loss. Accord was the last thing he wished to find with John's murderers. But Challons was right. He had not been sent to indulge in private vengeance. Whatever Henry's blusterings and threats to the contrary, Gunthar knew that what his royal master desired most was reconciliation with his son. Nothing short of a reckless, blatant act of treason would alter that resolve. If, to retrieve his son's errant loyalty, the king were required to blink an eye at the violent death of some unfortunate but insignificant knight, Henry would blink—and expect Gunthar to do the same.

"A mediator," Gunthar repeated. One might well be needed to keep him from Richard's throat. "Who did you have in mind?"

"Why, my lord, the name should be obvious to us all. He resides between these walls at this very moment, waiting to assist you with yet another royal commission. I speak, of course, of Jean aux

Bellesmains, Bishop of Poitiers."

Gunthar's council greeted the name with a unanimous murmur of approval. Gunthar agreed the choice was brilliant. Bellesmains was a man who served his conscience as zealously as he served his king. His quarrels with the king over royal prerogatives in Church matters were legendary, but the humility with which he colored his immutable integrity had prevented him from walking Thomas Becket's road. His courage and independence were so well known that the prince would not be able to reject his arbitration without appearing willfully intransigent.

Gunthar nodded. "Very well. Laurant, if you would be so good as to seek out the bishop and ask him to attend us—"

He stopped as the door opened and Julian Parr came into the room.

"My lord." The squire bowed. "I pray you will forgive this intrusion, but the Lady Heléne is requesting an audience with you."

Gunthar frowned. "This is not a good time, Julian. Tell her—"

"I have done so, my lord, but she is most insistent. The word she used was 'urgent'."

Heléne was not a woman given to irresponsible flights of panic. Gunthar moved towards the door, calling over his shoulder, "Challons, find Bellesmains and make the arrangements. And if the pair of you can think of a way to prevent Count William from attending whatever conference you design, I shall be much in your debt."

He followed the squire into the antechamber just beyond the council room and was surprised to find it empty.

"She is in the passageway, my lord," Julian said, then checked Gunthar's departure with a hand to his sleeve.

Gunthar glanced down, startled at the squire's boldness. "What is it, Julian?"

The youth looked pale and agitated. "My lord—" His hand fluttered away, as though he were aware that he had acted presumptuously. "About Sir John. I—"

Gunthar waited, but he felt the grimness hardening his face. Julian and Rousillon. Was the squire about to confess?

Julian stared at the floor. "It was a shame," he said, his voice so low as to approach a whisper. "That he died that way, I mean."

"It was supposed to be me, you know," Gunthar said. "I was the one they wanted to kill. Sir John was just a tragic mistake."

Almost he thought he discerned a barely perceptible nod of the red-ringleted head. Julian's eyes remained fixed on his embroidered blue shoes.

"My lord, when you have done with the Lady Heléne, might I have a word with you? There is something that I must—"

The clicking of the door behind them caused the squire to jump nearly a foot off the floor. Challons stepped across the threshold from the council room. Julian went so white, Gunthar thought he was about to be physically ill.

Challons could not have failed to observe the squire's reaction.

"Am I intruding? I did not realize you were engaged in here, my lord. There is no other exit from the council chamber, and you did request me to find—"

"It is quite all right," Gunthar said. He gathered Julian did not wish to speak in Challons' presence. Given the incriminating nature of the information he expected to receive, Gunthar did not blame the youth. "Come to my room before dinner," he said to Julian, hoping he did not sound as cold as he felt. "We will talk then." He nodded to Challons and left the antechamber.

Heléne was waiting for him in the corridor, but he shushed her, mindful that Challons would be on his heels. She obediently fell silent and let him take her arm, not uttering a word until he had steered her out of the castle and into her mother's ruined garden.

"Now then," he said, when he fancied they were alone and safe from prying eyes, "what was so 'urgent' that you felt it necessary to disturb me in my council?"

"Look!" she said, so excited that she could hardly stand still.

Gunthar looked at the small wooden box she held out. Inside was a thick, grey, shriveled mass of such repugnant aspect that he felt himself recoiling.

"What the devil is that?"

"Cowbane root!" she exclaimed. "And still deadly, even old and dried as it is."

"Where did you find it?"

"I didn't, Flora did. I told her to search Sybil's things, thinking they might give us a clue as to where she has gone, but all Flora found was this. She recognized at once that it was cowbane, and it so frightened her that she brought it straight to me."

"Sybil? You mean the old crone? Why would she wish to harm me with that? Unless Rousillon paid her—"

"Sybil does not care for money. She would not have done it for that."

"Then why?"

"It must have been for Clothilde," Heléne said, too exhilarated with her discovery, he guessed, to show caution in her reply. "Clo does not wish to marry you, and she has done nothing but weep and be sick since Mama said that she must. And I thought Sybil was only trying to comfort her, for she has always doted on Clo. But since Flora brought me this, I have been thinking and thinking, and I have remembered how Sybil kept saying things to Clo like 'trust me' and 'I will make everything right'. Only Clo was always shrieking at her like a banshee, so it never occurred to me what she meant until I realized that she knew about Triston and was resolved to help them. And I knew she was a wicked old woman, and I suppose I should have suspected her at once when I smelled the poison in your cup, for there was cowbane in one of the ointments she sent up from the kitchens that very first day when Mama made me attend to your arm— Yes, and I'll wager she cut your saddle strap, too, because I saw her coming from the stables that morning you kissed me on the archery field just before you left for Angoulême. She was dragging poor Audiart out by the hair, but that doesn't mean she could not have—"

"Helen, stop," he said, his patience exhausted with these convoluted ramblings. "I haven't a clue what you are talking about."

"I'm talking about *this*—" she thrust the box with its disgusting contents towards him "—and why Sybil should wish to put it in your wine! Don't you see? We do not know where she has gone, but as long as she fears you might marry Clo she will be meaning to try this or something like it again."

Gunthar closed the lid and pushed the box away. The evidence of the old woman's malice seemed irrefutable. "How long has she been missing?"

"I saw her last the night of Sir John's death. She escorted Clothilde to a rendezvous with Triston. That was why I followed Sir John. I thought it was you, and I was afraid you might catch them together and be angry, and—" Her lashes fluttered in uncharacteristic shyness. "That was before I knew the truth."

Gunthar was puzzled, but her revelation took precedence over the curious blush in her cheeks.

"Your sister was with Sir Triston the night John died?"

"They met by the river, so Triston could not possibly have had anything to do with what happened in the clearing. I thought at first that he might have known, for Clo seemed to think he was somehow going to stop the wedding, but now I think she must have had it muddled. It was probably Sybil who told them both *she* had a plan, though what it was Clo did not seem to know. And neither of us can guess why she has gone away, but I know it cannot be for good and I am terribly afraid of what mischief she might have in mind for you, so you must not be silent any longer. You must tell everyone . . ."

"Tell them what?" he asked as she hesitated. Her bright color had faded, but coupled with the anxiety in her eyes was a disarming glow of trust.

"I realize you must have your reasons for not wishing to speak of it openly," she said, "and I do not mean to press you before you are ready, but it has become *vital* that you say something. You needn't say why. Only tell them that you do not wish to marry Clo after all. That will put you safe from Sybil, and perhaps Triston would not feel so threatened and he might even help us catch Rousillon, and then I—I should not have to be so terrified for you."

Her lip quivered as she broke off, though she stilled it almost instantly between her teeth. Gunthar stared in dismay as her meaning became clear. Standing there in her loose yellow tunic with her pale hair all a-tumble about her shoulders, she looked so much like a tremulous child that he wanted nothing more than to snatch her up in his arms and kiss away her fears.

The fact that they were all for him both touched and shamed him.

He had no right to that sweet regard in her face, especially now when his answer to her had to be—

"Helen, I cannot do as you ask because it wouldn't be true. I am sorry for your sister's distress, but I must marry her just the same."

"Must—? But I thought—" The apprehension in her eyes turned into bewilderment. "But you do not love Clothilde. I know you do not."

"Love has nothing to do with it. The king requires me to take your sister for my wife, and that is exactly what I intend to do."

"But—" she backed away as though afraid his next words might wound her like a blow "—what about me?"

He had to curl his fingers into the palms of his hands to stop himself from reaching for her. "My heart is at your feet," he said roughly, "but there is nothing more I can give you."

She ducked her head so that her hair fell forward over her face. A long, aching silence stretched between them before she whispered, "Then at least—you do love me?"

It would have been kinder to lie. But if the truth held pain for them both, it was to him a sweet, triumphant anguish. That elusive emotion that he had first scorned, and then for so long denied, now seemed as easy to confess as his own name.

"Yes," he said without further doubt or fear, "I love you, Helen de Laurant. I will never be complete without you. But I cannot have you for my wife, and I will not ask you to surrender to me in any other way. So all that is left to us is friendship, and I hope—I pray—you will not refuse me that."

To his surprise, his voice quavered a little. How was it this slip of a girl unnerved him so? He waited, half expecting her to run away and not knowing how he would bear it if she did. When she did not move, he put out his hand, and felt a warm wash of relief when she met it with her own.

She said nothing and would not look at him, but she let him lead her over to the peeling bench. Her free hand still clutched the battered box. He took it from her and set it on the ground as they sat down. Despite his best intentions, he could not bring himself to give up the comfort of her fingers, however transitory such pleasure must be. A bittersweet silence stretched between them. But there were things he still needed to know, so at last he broke it with a brisk, bracing question.

"Tell me about the woman Sybil. Do you honestly believe she would try to murder me, just to prevent me from wedding your sister?"

Heléne kept her face turned away. "She would do anything for Clo, though Clo hates her now. I do not know why. She has lived here forever and was nurse to my father before my sister and me."

She stopped and bit her lip again. Gunthar knew she was still struggling with her hurt, but she was too proud to let him see her tears. He caught the rapid blinking of her lashes and the straightening of her back before she continued, more steadily.

"Sybil taught me most of what I know of herbs and healing, but she clings to what she calls the 'old ways'. I have seen her jabbering over objects and plants in a jumbled sort of chant. The other servants call it witchcraft, but Father Dominic says they are just silly phrases of corrupted French and Latin. He has tried to chastise her, but she only curses him, and when he complains to Papa, Papa only laughs. I think Papa pities her because she is so old."

"But not too old for mischief of this sort." Gunthar nudged the box with a booted toe.

"Sybil has an ugly temper that is feared throughout the castle, and she is dreaded for her vicious rod."

"Was it she who laid those welts to your back?"

Heléne's voice became more subdued. "Yes, though it was at Mama's command. Mama is the only one in the castle whom Sybil will obey."

Gunthar did not doubt that the icy Lady Gwenllian would be able to stare down the most rebellious servant, and probably would not hesitate to have the flogger flogged were she to prove impertinent enough.

"So Sybil turned her malignance on me to save your sister from a loveless match?"

"Yes, and I know she will try again." Heléne's fingers tightened on his. "And now she has disappeared, like Audiart, so we shan't even be able to watch her, and that puts you in danger from *two* directions."

Gunthar said, "I am not entirely convinced that she is not somehow linked to Rousillon. That traitor has lodged himself at Vere Castle, and did you not say the old crone was resolved to help your sister fulfill her love for Sir Triston?" He smiled, albeit rather crookedly, when she glanced up in swift alarm. "Yes, I know you told me that before you realized she was not yet safe from my advances, but you needn't be afraid. It is not something I shall hold against her in our marriage. It is not required for one's heart to be engaged to do one's duty, and duty is all I intend to bestow on her, and all that I will demand in return." He raised a finger to her cheek. "It is a lesson you must learn as well. When you are Heywood's wife—"

She tossed her face away from his touch, her eyes flashing with a familiar spirit. "I am *not* going to marry Lord Heywood. I don't care what Mama says—"

"It is what *I* say," he told her. "If I cannot have you for myself, I will at least have you safe with a man whom I know and respect."

She snatched her hand away and bounced to her feet. "*You* say? What right have you to say anything? How can you be so—so arrogant as to think you can reject me for *duty's* sake and still try to control my life?"

"Helen—" Drat the girl, could she not understand that he meant it for her good? That it was only *because* he loved her that he could with any degree of equanimity, contemplate giving her up to another man? Anything to save her from the reckless consequences of her own impulsive nature.

She stood all a-quiver with indignation. "I shan't do it. I would rather marry Etienne, if he would have me, than be sold to your respectable friend."

That brought him up with snapping brows. "Don't be absurd. If you think I am going to stand by while you throw yourself away on that worthless whelp, you are much mistaken. I will drag you back to England myself, before I'll—"

"It is none of your business what I do. You've no right to be jealous now."

"Jealous? *Jealous?* I am not—"

The word caught in his throat. He gazed within himself in horror, confronting for the first time the nature of the rage in his breast. Great heavens, that's exactly what he was! He *was* jealous, he was wild at the thought of her and Etienne. He knew she did not love Heywood, and could at least indulge the hope that she never would. But her fierce affection for Etienne she had demonstrated again and again. The thought that she might yield her heart to someone other than himself was enough to drive him mad. He wanted to curse them both to blazes, this winsomely provoking young lady and her hot-blooded swain in the tower.

"Your accusation in ludicrous," he said, refusing to admit the humiliating weakness she had discerned. "As ridiculous as the idea of you setting up house with a nineteen-year-old boy for a husband. Even were he otherwise acceptable—which I tell you frankly, he is not—I would feel obliged to stop such insanity as that."

"At least Etienne is not ashamed of me," she cried. "He does not claim to love me in one breath and cast me off in the other."

"I have not cast you off. Were the choice mine, there is no woman on earth I would sooner have for my wife than you. But the king—"

"Yes, I know. I could not possibly compete with your love for the king. Marry my sister, then, if you think Triston and Sybil will let you. But if you find yourself laid out cold, do not expect me to weep for you."

She spun on her heel, but had not run two paces before he croaked out, "Helen, don't go. Don't leave me like this again."

She whirled about as his voice broke. He did not care what she saw now in his face, if only she would not leave him in bitterness and hate.

Whose movement it was that brought her into his arms, he did not know, but he wound them about her so tightly it was a wonder she could breathe.

"I'm sorry," she panted as he crushed her to his chest. "I did not mean it. Were anything to happen to you, I should want to die, too!"

He lowered his head with a groan, but found his mouth blocked by her hand.

"No, you must not. I cannot betray my own sister like this. She will be your wife."

"And you are my love," he said savagely. "Helen, I cannot endure it any longer."

"Let me go."

"Helen—"

"Let me go."

Her voice was quiet but firm. There was no mistaking her resolve. He gave a despairing shudder and released her.

When she walked from the garden, she took his heart with her, leaving him more devastated and alone than he had ever felt in his life.

# Twenty

"My lord, please, you must come inside." The boy sounded anxious.

Gunthar was not so engrossed in the dismal turn of his thoughts that he had not noticed the thickening of clouds over his head or the cool mist stirred up by the breeze. "My constitution is exceptionally hardy, Brandon. A little rain is not going to hurt me."

"It is not that, my lord. It is Julian. He . . ." The boy trailed off.

"Has he come to dress me for dinner? They must be serving early today."

Gunthar removed his contemplation from the roses and glanced up at the darkening sky. The overcast made it impossible to tell the time. How long had he been sitting here, how long had it been since she had gone?

He looked back at the flowers, noting how cheerfully they bobbed in the face of the coming storm. It seemed a curious piece of defiance when one recalled how gardens far more tenderly nourished than this had been humbled in a single blast.

"My lord—"

Gunthar sighed and stood up. "Very well." He turned to follow the boy. Then he saw Brandon's face and stiffened. "What's happened? What's wrong?"

"Come inside," Brandon said, his lips as pale as his cheeks, "and you will see."

Gunthar strode ahead of the boy into the keep, only pausing long enough inside for Brandon to catch up and indicate the direction.

There were a handful of servants gathered outside Gunthar's chamber door, apparently drawn there by the high-pitched wail issuing from inside. The servants parted with deferring curtsies and bows when Brandon called out the earl's name, and Gunthar advanced to his threshold unhindered.

He stopped there, not believing his eyes at first. *She* was there, hovering over a weeping maid who stood with a broken jar of salve at her feet.

"Helen?"

Heléne looked up, her face brightening with relief. "Thank heaven you have come! Brandon, take Flora away and stay with her until she calms down. And shoo the other servants away as you go. The earl will deal with the matter now."

Gunthar followed her hesitant glance across the room and uttered an oath beneath his breath. "The matter" appeared to be Julian Parr, sprawled on his back across Gunthar's bed.

Gunthar stepped aside to allow Brandon to escort the hysterical maid out of the room, then shut the door behind them.

"I heard her scream," Heléne said. "She said she came to tend to your head and found him—like that."

Gunthar crossed to the bed. One would have thought the youth merely slept, so peaceful was the cast of his countenance. The reddish lashes brushed his cheeks like two fine, tiny webs of silk and the luxurious ringlets, arranged over his shoulders with haunting care, reflected their fire off his ivory skin. The illusive blush tricked Gunthar into thinking that it might not be too late. He reached for the youth's hand, held it a moment, then dropped it again. Despite a lingering warmth in the flesh, the fingers were already stiff. One had not to look far for the cause: a bloody gash across either wrist and the dark, wet stains on the bedclothes.

"Is he dead?"

Gunthar gave a curt nod. A dagger, the squire's own, lay on the floor near the bed, together with a letter. Gunthar bent to pick the folded parchment up. He opened it and read it through, then swore.

"What is it? What does he say?" Heléne asked.

"*He* does not say anything. This, however, says a great deal." He handed the letter to her and watched her puckered brow as she scanned the signature.

"Who is Sir Adam Parr?"

"Julian's father, one of my vassals. I left him in England during the wars with the princes, assuming he would guard my interests there, and the king's. But it appears—" Gunthar indicated the letter she was holding "— he chose to take advantage of my absence with a little double dealing."

The shock of their discovery of Julian swept away any awkwardness they might otherwise have felt at being thrust together again so soon after their painful parting in the garden.

Heléne read the contents through more carefully, then asked, "What is Norwich Castle and why is it important?"

"It is important," Gunthar said, "because it might have cost the king the war."

She waited for an explanation.

"While Henry was pinned down defending this part of his empire from the princes and their French allies, Count Philip of Flanders, egged on by France, threatened to invade the isle of England. He sent an advance party that, with the help of the king's rebellious northern barons, took bloody possession of the royal stronghold of Norwich Castle. It was a challenge the king could not ignore. He was forced to abandon his defense of Normandy and sail for England. But no sooner had Henry set foot in Southampton than Count Philip abandoned the invasion and joined King Louis in an attack on Normandy. France has coveted the duchy ever since the Conqueror's days. And they might have obtained the prize, had Henry not been the military genius that he is. In less than a month, he subdued the English rebels and was back at Barfleur. His return took King Louis by surprise, and when a last-ditch effort to conquer Rouen failed, France sued for peace, forcing the princes to do the same."

Heléne studied the letter anew. "Then Sir Adam was aiding the rebels."

"So it would seem," Gunthar said. "Sir Adam was probably no

more than a single link in an insidious chain of spies and traitors, but without the information penned there, Norwich Castle might never have fallen."

Thunder sounded in the distance, followed by a soft flash of light through the partially opened shutters.

"But I thought the king had pardoned all the rebels," she said. "Why would Julian kill himself for this?"

"For shame, perhaps. Those who fought the king openly, whether for conscience or simple hatred, Henry was charitable enough to forgive. But those who betrayed in the shadows while professing loyalty in the sun—well, it is doubtful Henry's mercy would extend to such. Most assuredly, mine would not."

He retrieved the letter from her. This must have been what Julian had meant to confess. There was no doubt in Gunthar's mind that his angelic-faced squire had been the "le Reynard" of Heléne's conversations with Rousillon. Rousillon had probably been blackmailing Julian with knowledge of his father's crime. Moved by regret or horror at the results of his treason, Julian must have waited for Gunthar, and when Gunthar tarried in the garden, must have lost his resolve and, like a coward, chose to end his life rather than face Gunthar with the truth.

Heléne sounded troubled. "You think Julian knew what his father was doing, then?"

"Most likely not," Gunthar said. "The boy was with me the entire course of the war, and my campaigns centered almost entirely in Poitou and Aquitaine. No, he could not have known. But once he learned of it, he would have understood what the consequences would be."

"You mean for Sir Adam? What will you do to him?"

"He will stand trial in a royal court. If convicted, he will be imprisoned and his lands confiscated by the crown."

"What will happen to his family? Or is Julian all?"

"Sir Adam has a wife and four daughters, two of whom currently reside at my seat in Kent."

"Then they will be safe." She sounded relieved.

"Not in my household," he said. "I hold no traffic with traitors, nor with their families."

Thunder cracked closer now, and a burst of lightening illuminated her shock at his response. "You mean you would turn them out? But *they* are not guilty."

"In the eyes of the law they are. And we see that blood will out. Julian's alliance with Rousillon proves him his father's son." Gunthar picked up the dagger and threw it on the bed beside the squire's body, then turned and started towards the door.

Heléne cried out after him, "I do not blame Julian for going to extremes to conceal that letter if that is your view! What other choice did he have?"

Gunthar whirled back round. "He could have come to me! He could have told me the truth! His silence cost John Lee his life, and if I cannot have justice from the prince or Rousillon, then I will have it from the youth who could have stopped it!"

Her silvery eyes blazed into his. "Justice—or revenge?"

"Either will do." Gunthar flicked a scornful glance at his squire's remains. "He should have faced me like a man. Instead he died a coward and suicide. He cannot even be buried in consecrated ground. Think what comfort that will be to his mother."

He watched as Heléne bent over the body and saw the pity in her face. Poor Julian, she was thinking. Gunthar knew that she found him hard, but hard was what he felt. And pity would not bring Julian back, any more than grief could restore John Lee.

"I must find someone to clean up this mess. Are you coming?" He did not want to leave her there alone, but neither was he going to stay and indulge her sorrow for Julian's corrupted youth. When she neither moved nor replied, he shrugged and pulled open the door.

"My lord, wait. I know this scent."

He paused, glancing at her over his shoulder. She had leaned so far down that her face was mere inches from the squire's.

"What the devil are you doing?"

"Poppy mixed with wine." She straightened. "He must have been drugged."

"What?" Gunthar left the door ajar and returned to the bed. "Are you sure of what you smell?"

"Of course I am. But don't you see what this means? Julian—"

"—undoubtedly needed help in steeling his nerves," Gunthar said. "Don't make more of it than it probably was."

"But—"

"Suicide is an ugly business, Helen. It destroys not only the body, but the soul. Trepidation might cause one's hand to falter at the last moment, to neglect the necessary depth of cut. And then there is the fear of pain and death—"

"Then where is the cup?"

"What?"

"The cup. I don't suppose Julian could have conjured such a drink out of midair?"

Gunthar surveyed the room. "He must have drunk it before he came."

"Or someone else tricked him into drinking it, and he did not kill himself at all!"

Gunthar sighed and rubbed his brow. "Helen, that is ridiculous."

"Why? Perhaps—" he could see the speculations flashing through her mind "—Rousillon did not want him to reveal their alliance, so he—"

"—smuggled himself into Pennault, poisoned my squire, then slashed his wrists for good measure?"

"No, of course not. He would not have done it himself. But if Julian had threatened to betray him to you, he might have paid someone else to do it."

"One of your father's men, or one of mine? It could not have been a woman. Even your wicked nurse would not have been able to move his drugged body to my bed from another room."

She hesitated, obviously reluctant to accuse any of her father's house, and not quite daring to accuse his.

"Leave it alone," he said. "There is no mystery here. Julian betrayed me, and shame drove him to this." He moved to close the shutters against the rain that was gusting in. "Come, I need you to find your chaplain and tell him what has occurred. I will inform your father myself."

He did not give her the chance to argue, but took her arm and propelled her out the door.

*Guilty by association. Guilty by blood.* The words ran with chilling frequency through Heléne's mind in the days that followed Julian's death. Though Gunthar had not actually spoken them, he had left her no doubt that they reflected his philosophy. Julian had been a traitor's son who had proven the axioms by betraying Gunthar. Sir Damian had plotted against the crown, and all evidence indicated that his son, Triston, was involved in the same. Both stood inexorably condemned in Gunthar's eyes. Would he look any more favorably upon a traitor's daughter?

All her bittersweet joy in his admissions of love were swallowed up in the dread of her father's discovery. Gunthar would learn of it somehow. Rousillon would tell him, if only for spite. Heléne found herself in an anguishing quandary. If she told Gunthar herself, he would at least be forced to admit her courage and honesty, though it would be sure to extinguish whatever tenderness he felt for her. But how could she serve her own family so? Her father would be imprisoned, their lands confiscated. Yet if she kept silent, would she not be just as guilty as Julian or Triston? And should Gunthar somehow die as a result of her silence, how would she ever live with that?

Every night she wore out her knees in prayers for his safety. And every morning she pled that he might never learn the truth.

Then the morning came for his departure for Poitiers. Jean aux Bellesmains had returned there to lay the foundation of a parley between Prince Richard and Gunthar. Both sides had agreed to meet in the capital city to discuss their grievances and, with the bishop's mediation, hopefully be brought to some accord. Heléne had studiously avoided Gunthar since the day they had found Julian's body, but now she sped out to the bailey, alarmed by the news that had reached her ears.

"What is this? You are not taking a body guard?"

Gunthar had been in the act of mounting his horse, but he left the reins with young Brandon and drew her aside. "Of course I am, but a small one. It is a pledge of good faith, negotiated by the bishop, that the prince and I are each to be accompanied by no more than a dozen men, only half of whom are to be trained knights. But the six I have chosen are six of my best. They will defend me with their lives should the need arise. And you see we ride in full armor. You must not be afraid for me."

"How can I be anything else?" She looked scornfully at his mail hauberk overlaid with a surcote bearing his crest. "You announce yourself to all the world with that silver stallion blazoned across your breast. And *twenty* swordsmen will not protect you from another archer, any more than that chain mail will if he aims at your head. How can you call this armor 'full' when you aren't even wearing a helmet?"

He laughed, and she stamped her foot at his twinkling eyes.

"You scold like a wife, my lady. Be at peace, I pray you. Brandon is carrying my helm, and there are two roads to Poitiers. None but I and my marshal, Sir Roger, knows which one I mean to take. You distress yourself unduly for my sake."

"Something is going to happen." She whispered it with such vehemence that it took him aback. "I know it, I can feel it. Somehow he is going to be waiting for you."

Gunthar hesitated, then said, "Then I must be on my guard, and the rest we must leave to God."

His hands found her elbows as she smoothed the emblem against his chest.

"Saints," he muttered, "if I could only kiss you one more time."

"Come back to me," she said, her fingers tightening into fists on his garment. "Only promise me you will come back."

"I will come back," he said, "if God be willing."

But they both knew it would not be to her.

She watched him ride away, then hurried inside before anyone in the yard could see her crying. She swept up the stairs to the council room and let herself into the antechamber, knowing it would be empty now that Gunthar was gone. If her mother should want her, it would be hours before she thought of looking for her here. There was a small scribe's desk in the corner. Heléne sank into its chair. She leaned her arms against the desk and laid down her head with a sob.

She would willingly surrender him to Clothilde, if only he would not come back like Julian or Sir John. She would let Sir Stephen take her to England, would marry Heywood and never see Gunthar's face again, if only he would come back safe. She made vow after vow in tearful prayers for his protection. She wept until her eyes were sore and her head ached, and still the dread voice whispered: *they will be waiting.*

At last she pushed herself up, spurred by a frustrated sense that she should be doing something. She rubbed her cheeks to wipe them dry, then stood and paced across the floor and back. Should she ask her father to send men after Gunthar? What if Laurant would not believe her? It was only a feeling she had, a terrible, frightening intuition that threatened to suffocate her with its force. Gunthar was riding into danger, and she did not know how to stop him.

Tears had flooded into her eyes again when the latch lifted on the antechamber door. Heléne fled into the council room, desperate to evade whoever it might be. It took her only a moment to realize the futility of her retreat. It was undoubtedly the Lady Gwenllian come looking for her, and when she saw her daughter's blotched face she would demand to know why she had been crying. Heléne could not bear to lay her fears open to her mother's scorn. Perhaps she could fabricate an excuse to divert the Lady Gwenllian's attention.

Impulsively, she pulled down her father's banner that draped the wall by the window, and tore out a portion of the hem with her teeth. She would say that she had come to mend it. Hoping to forestall her mother's questions with the evidence in her hands, she hurried to reopen the door before her mother could enter.

But it was not the Lady Gwenllian who stood partnered by one of Gunthar's clerks in the center of the antechamber. This woman had sweeping black curls and seemed to be thoroughly enjoying the clerk's groping embrace. They were exchanging the lewdest kisses Heléne had ever witnessed. Although the scene made her blush to the ears, it also held her riveted in a kind of repelled fascination.

She shook herself out of the spell and was about to close the door when the clerk slurred in a thick, heavy voice, "Torturess, enchantress! You have teased me long enough."

He swung the woman about and thrust her back against the desk. The woman's startled cry sent Heléne over the threshold, her tongue quivering with denunciation for the clerk's lustful assault. But before she could speak, the woman drove him off herself, boxing his ears so briskly that he staggered back to the center of the room. It was in that instant, while the woman stood coolly rearranging the disheveled neck of her gown, that Heléne recognized the Lady Osanne.

Heléne flew back to the council room. She closed the door as quickly and quietly as she could before either of the occupants of the antechamber could see her. She waited a few minutes, then cracked it open again, certain that she had stumbled upon no common lovers' tryst.

Osanne had her arms around the clerk's neck and was trying to urge him back into good humor.

"Come, sir, my little hands have done you no great injury. You shall have all that you desire, by and by. But first tell me what you have heard."

"Nothing," the clerk muttered, nursing his offense. "They've been mum as mice about the earl's direction."

"But you must know something." Osanne shifted herself to stroke his shoulders and arms. "Did not the earl alert the bishop to which road he meant to take?"

"When he sent his acceptance of the terms of the meeting. But only Sir Roger was privy to the contents of that letter."

"Are you sure? I have heard it said the earl's writing is so bad, he rarely employs the pen himself."

"He wrote this time," the clerk said, then added as his partner stretched up to nuzzle his ear, "but he had his secretary copy it over."

"Ah. Then you saw something, did you not?"

"A mere glimpse before de Muncey saw me and covered it up."

"But it was enough. Tell me."

"My lady, I dare not." The clerk's back was to Heléne, but she could hear the trepidation in his voice. "I am in trouble enough with the earl for my gambling debts. He has warned me that one more misstep and I shall be turned off."

Over the clerk's shoulder, she could see Osanne's sultry smile. "Then we must find you a new master, one powerful enough to protect you even from the earl's wrath."

"You have connections to the prince?"

"Perhaps. You can be assured of my aid—so long as I am assured of yours."

It took but another moment—and a hot breath blown from the lady's ripe lips—for the clerk to make up his mind.

"I saw only the word 'northeast'. If it denoted his direction of travel, then he has chosen the longer of the two roads to Poitiers."

She saw Osanne nod. "The country spanning that road is mostly flat, fields and meadows lending little cover for attack. It will be difficult—"

"Attack?" the clerk gasped. "But—"

"Hush, it is useless to consult your conscience now. You must carry this news for me to Vere. And you must be quick. The earl has more than an hour's lead on us."

"My lady—" the clerk sounded panicked "—I cannot be party to—"

"You are already party to it. If you do not do it, I will send somebody else and you will lose your position anyway when the earl is murdered on the road. Go now and my friends at Vere will show you proof of the master whose service you enter. And if that is not enough to content you, then hurry back and I will give you an equally ...satisfying ...reward." She leaned into the clerk by tantalizing inches as she offered this last encouragement, and settled on his mouth a deeply sensuous kiss.

The clerk was persuaded and hurried off to do her bidding.

No sooner had he gone than Heléne burst into the antechamber, unable to contain her indignant outrage any longer.

Osanne turned, startled at her seeming appearance out of thin air. "Where—?" Her sloe-like eyes slid to the open council room door and her sultry voice hardened. "You heard it all, I suppose. What do you mean to do, my lady?"

"What do you think? I am going to call my father's guards to stop him."

Osanne shook her head, setting her black curls swaying. "Ah, no, we can't have that. Gilles!"

A man appeared in the doorway from the corridor, short but thickset with a heavy, scowling brow and muscles that were clearly discernable beneath his servant's tunic.

"The Lady Heléne is unwell," Osanne said. "See that she rests here an hour or two—or better yet, in that room beyond. Yes, they would not hear her cries from there should she choose to be difficult."

The man nodded and moved towards Heléne. She backed away, but stopped on the threshold of the council room. If once she stepped across it, she would be trapped. She feinted to one side and then the other, but the man spread his brawny arms to prevent her from darting around him. Heléne knew that she would be no match for his strength. But she was taller than he and she reacted with the only defense she had. Her father's banner was still in her hands. She flung it over his head, danced away from his blindly groping hands and made a desperate lunge for the antechamber door.

# Twenty-One

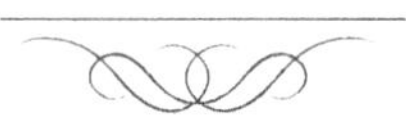

No you *don't!*"

Heléne felt the ripping of her skirt as Osanne grabbed it, but she jerked herself free and fled through the door.

"After her, you fool! If she gets away, your master will beat you into oblivion."

Heléne flew down the corridor and up the steps. The thudding footsteps behind her so frightened her that she did not look where she was going and collided headlong with the figure at the top.

"Heléne!" Her brother's strong arms caught her as they both went staggering. "What the devil are you—"

"Hurry, Therri," she gasped, trying to tug him after her. "He will be upon us any moment."

But Therri refused to budge. "Who? That fellow? Is he threatening you in some way?"

Her brother released her and made as if to descend on the man who had stopped uncertainly at the foot of the steps. The man fell back a pace, then bared his teeth and laid a hand to his dagger.

"Therri, don't," she cried. Her brother was unarmed. "Come *on*."

Therri hesitated, not liking to run from a fight, but he finally let her pull him away from the steps and through the first door they came to.

They landed in Therri's bedchamber. Her brother wasted no time in snatching up the dagger he had left on the table near the bed. "Now we will see—"

"No." She flung herself in front of the door. "Stop it. You don't even know what this is about."

"I know I don't like the look of that fellow's face. Assault my sister, will he?"

"He wasn't going to hurt me," she said. "At least, I don't think he would have dared, under our own roof."

"Then how did your gown get torn and why was he chasing you?"

"To stop me from telling Papa. Oh, Therri, we must do something. They are going to murder Gunthar!"

That checked him in his attempt to force her out of his way. "Who is going to—?"

"Rousillon. The Lady Osanne is his spy and she has sent Gunthar's clerk to Vere to tell Rousillon which road Gunthar rides to Poitiers."

"Rousillon?" her brother repeated. "Isn't he wanted by the crown for murdering his father?"

"Yes, and he killed Sir John, thinking it was Gunthar, and now he is going to try again. Oh, there isn't time to explain it all. It is too late to stop the clerk, and now Rousillon will be able to ride ahead and ambush Gunthar, and he has only six men to defend him. Therri, we have got to tell Papa and make him send Gunthar some help."

Therri thought it over before he replied. He had heard about the archer on the road to Angoulême and had seen his sister dash a cup full of poison from Gunthar's hand. It was enough to persuade him there might be some merit to her fears.

"Which road is he traveling?" he asked.

"The clerk said it was the northeast way. And Osanne said it would be difficult because of all the open space, but—"

"It would be," Therri said. "I don't see how . . . unless . . ." He frowned.

"What is it?"

"There is one portion of the road that leaves the fields and winds around the base of the motte where Michelet's castle used to stand. The keep was destroyed during the war, but the ruins are still there. I suppose if I wished to conceal an ambush party, that's where I would do it. But they would have to ride like fiends to reach it before Gunthar, with his headstart."

"But could they?"

"I suppose they could. Where are you going?"

"To tell Papa. *We* shall have to ride like fiends as well."

Therri caught her arm and pulled her away from the door. "Are you daft? If that fellow out there is in league with Rousillon, he isn't going to let you run down the steps and spoil all his plans by telling Papa."

"Then what do you suggest we do?"

He walked over to the window and leaned out.

"What are you looking at?"

"That old vine crawling up the wall. They haven't cut it down, I see. I wonder if it's still strong enough to support my weight?"

She joined him and looked dubiously at the meandering green maze that scaled the stones in which the window was set. Therri's chamber stood at the back of the keep, out of the way of the everyday eye, and had consequently escaped the careful tending devoted to the forepart of the castle.

"I don't see how you are going to climb down that," she said.

"It was sturdy enough when I was a boy. I would slip out at night and run down to the river to meet Etienne. Sometimes we would fish, if the moon was bright, or we would lie on the bank and stare at the stars . . ." Therri's sunny face grew dark. "Are you sure you want to help Gunthar? After the miserable way he's treated Etienne?"

Remembering their exchange over Julian's corpse and Gunthar's bitterness for Sir John's death, Heléne had little hope that either of the de Brielle brothers would be permitted to escape Gunthar's 'justice'. Her heart ached for Etienne, but just now it pounded in panic for Gunthar.

"We shall have to worry about Etienne later," she said. "There is more to this than you know, Therri. If Gunthar is killed, it could mean another war. We *must* tell Papa."

Therri nodded. Even his antipathy for Gunthar would not condone another murder. He heaved himself into the window frame.

"Are you sure it's safe?" she asked. "You are much heavier now than you were as a boy."

"Even then it wasn't always easy," he said. "That's why I used my dagger one night to chip some hand-holds into the stones on my way down. I've scaled this wall so many times, I could do it with my eyes closed."

"Well, I have not your practice," she said, "so wait for me at the bottom to catch me if I slip."

That brought Therri's head sharp around. "*You're* not coming with me."

"The devil I'm not. I can ride as well as you."

"You can't climb down in those skirts. You'd be bound to trip and break your neck."

"Then I'll borrow one of your tunics. I've done it before and I can change in a trice."

"No." She blinked at the unwonted authority in her brother's voice. "This is not a game, Heléne. You stay here. I will do what needs to be done."

"But Therri—"

"Stay—here." He leveled a warning finger at her, then turned and vanished out the window.

Heléne did not wait to see him reach the ground. She ran to his clothing chest and began pulling out tunic and hose. It would take time for her father to gather sufficient men to ride to Gunthar's aid, and even then they might arrive too late. But one horseman riding swiftly might be able to reach Gunthar with a warning before he arrived at the ambush point and turn him safely away.

She tugged on the change of clothes, then braided her hair with flying fingers and stuffed it inside the neck of the tunic. She crammed a hat on her head to complete her disguise and was at the window ready to descend when it occurred to her that she ought to have a weapon. She glanced back around the room, but Therri had taken the dagger and all that was left was the Welsh longbow leaning in the corner. A moment later, she had slung both it and the quiver of arrows beside it over her shoulder.

She held her breath as she scuttled down the vine. Urgency left her no time for hesitation but once she located the first of the notches Therri had chipped into the wall, she was able to guess at the proximity of the others and felt them out to speed her way down. She dropped to the ground without mishap, but landed in a puddle left by the storm several days before. The muddy water soaked through her soft-soled shoes. She shook her feet free and ran around to the front of the bailey where the stables stood.

Therri and her father were nowhere in sight, but the seneschal had just returned from a survey of the fields and was calling for a groom to tend his horse. She pulled her hat down over her eyes and trotted forward to take the reins.

"Let me do it for you, sir," she said gruffly.

He nodded to her with scarcely a glance and surrendered his beast. Heléne counted to ten as he walked away. Then she sprang into the saddle and flicked the reins. The startled horse gave a shrill whinny and the seneschal turned round. He dashed towards her with an angry shout, but she galloped through the gate before anyone could respond to his alarm.

She flew down the road on the seneschal's steed, following the bend that led northeast. It wove past her father's fields and the fields of Vere, and entered upon wild meadowland. She understood at once the Lady Osanne's complaint. The grasses, though tangled, were low, allowing no cover for men who plotted harm. If all the country-side were like this, Michelet's motte would be Rousillon's only hope.

But she had no idea how far ahead that mound of earth might lie. She had never ridden the road to Poitiers and unfamiliarity with the way precluded her hazarding a shortcut. She could do naught but pound straight on. Her eyes streamed in the wind and mud spattered up from the road to stain her hose. From the distance came a roll of thunder.

She could not begin to guess the hour through the heavy clouds obscuring the sky, but her body ached from what seemed an eternity of jostling before a crack of thunder startled her horse into rearing. She almost lost her seat. For several minutes, she struggled to control the frightened beast. Then she saw it, bathed in the lightning. The mound rose off to her left, surrounded by land that bore an aspect of abandoned cultivation. *Michelet's deserted fields.* The road ahead wove around the mound's base. If Gunthar were on the other side, if Rousillon were waiting— She pounded her heels into the horse's flanks and it flew into motion once more. She cut a straight line across the dilapidated fields. The outline of the former fortress's remains soon came into view, but she did not slow down until she reached the base.

Rocks and low vegetation covered the sides of the motte. There was nothing to conceal her approach as she urged her mount to begin the ascent. She could only pray that Rousillon's attention would be focused elsewhere.

She saw nothing at first when she reached the top but a crumbled wall and tower. Michelet's fortress must have been little more than a single stone keep. She maneuvered forward slowly, straining her eyes and ears for a movement, a sound among the ruins. All was still. Perhaps her fears had been for nothing. Perhaps Rousillon had never been here at all.

She threaded her mount through the fallen debris and approached the only remnant of wall that stood high enough to obstruct her view. If she rose up in the stirrups, she could reach her hands along the top. She found a crack in the stones and slid her toe in, then boosted herself up.

The sight from the other side so dismayed her that she nearly lost her balance. Drawn up mere yards away, over two dozen armed horsemen waited while a row of archers trained their crossbows on the small traveling party in the road below. One of the mounted men held his hand high in the air. Rousillon. She knew him from his long, crimped curls. Frantically, she counted the riders on the road. There were only thirteen. The one at the forefront had to be Gunthar. Twelve men to protect him, and only six trained at arms . . .

She scrambled to her feet atop the wall and whipped the longbow from her shoulder. At any moment Rousillon's hand would fall and his band would go swooping down the hill . . . She fitted an arrow to her string and listened again to the memory of Gunthar's voice: *Take your aim thus and draw back the string all the way to your ear.*

Her shaft struck an archer square between the shoulders. The archer pitched to the earth and the other bowmen wavered in their formation.

"Hold your line! Fire! Fire!" Rousillon shouted.

They resumed their aim at his cry. Heléne loosed two more arrows. Two more bowmen fell.

Rousillon's furious orders were not enough now to stop the others from whirling about to seek the source of the attack. Several of the horsemen also turned her way. A few made as if to bolt after her, but Rousillon shouted, "No, to the road! He must not escape again! I will deal with the whelp!"

Heléne knew she would never have a better opportunity to rid the world of Rousillon's black existence. He was riding straight at her. His mailed shirt would offer no resistance to her shaft's power, were she to loose it at his heart. But the surviving archers were readying their bows again and Gunthar, though alerted now by the commotion taking place above him, was as defenseless to their arrows as Rousillon was to hers. She had no choice but to try to pick more archers off. But it required only one more man to fall for the remaining few to throw down their bows in surrender.

She got off three more shafts, these into the band of horsemen galloping towards the road, but she had not time to see if any of them struck home. Rousillon had reached the wall and to her consternation, her horse had wandered away to graze outside the rubble.

"Now then, my lad—"

Heléne swung her bow at his head, forcing him to shy away, then lowered herself over the other side of the wall. She dropped to the ground, only to suffer so sharp a twinge in her ankle that she collapsed with a plop in the muddy earth. Gritting her teeth on the pain, she struggled up again. She limped towards her horse, but Rousillon vaulted his mount over a lower segment of the adjoining wall and raced to cut her off. The clattering hooves came so near that she actually feared he meant to trample her down. At the last moment he drew up and halted her advance with the edge of a sword leveled across her throat.

"Easy, lad. I suggest you drop that pretty bow of yours if you hope to live out this day."

Her hesitation brought the chill touch of steel against her skin. She threw down the bow and, at his command, dropped the quiver, too.

"There's a good lad. Now turn about slowly and step back."

She obeyed. She watched in silence as he trotted his horse back and forth across the quiver and longbow until they were naught but a pile of shredded leather and shattered wood.

"Now then," he said when he had done, "who are you? You wear not the badge of the earl's house. How come you to be here, meddling in what is no concern of yours?"

Heléne tried to tilt her face away, but he slid the tip of his sword beneath her chin and forced it up.

Recognition dawned slowly. Heléne saw the incredulous widening of his eyes. She winced as the blade swooped up and snatched the hat off her head. Still, it was not until he had rounded her once, and again employed his blade, this time to lift her braid from where she had tucked it down the back of her tunic, that he let out an amazed whistle, followed by a hearty laugh.

"The lad is a lady, it seems, and one of consequence at that. And yet, I fear—" he touched his point to the hollow of her throat "—a traitor, like her father. You have thought to do me an ill turn, my lady. I have cut men's throats for that, though I usually reserve women for a slightly different fate. And you, standing here neither woman nor man—how shall I deal with you, eh?"

She scorned to answer him, just as she refused to flinch any more from his threatening steel. She guessed herself in little imminent danger. It was not his way to kill quickly or cleanly. He would make his victim suffer first, and he had not time for that just now. A battle raged in the road below, one Rousillon intended as a massacre for a man he hated. Until that was finished, he would not trouble himself to conclude her punishment.

But neither would he permit her to escape a reckoning for her interference. He leaned down, seized her about the waist, and scooped her up before his saddle.

"Come," he snarled, "we will see what damage your little attempt at diversion has wrought. If Gunthar is not lying in his blood in the road, I will strangle you before his eyes."

The horse bounded forward, carrying them both back over the wall and down the mound towards the road. They thundered past the fallen and scattered archers and three wounded horsemen. Rousillon swept past them all, his arm locked around her waist, his mouth uttering hot threats in her ear.

A veritable mêlée had engaged in the road below. Heléne sought desperately for some sign of Gunthar amid the press of thrashing, armored men. The very continuance of the fray gave her hope. Had Gunthar been killed, Rousillon's assassins would not still be fighting, though how long he could continue to hold at bay a force more than double the size of his own—

Only as Rousillon drew up and let burst a string of curses did her heart leap at her mistake. Gunthar was *not* outnumbered. There were twice as many men as there had been before, and the mêlée was fast becoming a rout. Gunthar continued to elude her sight, but she caught a glimpse of her father. With a surer knowledge of the way, Laurant must have been able to lead his guards to Gunthar's rescue by pursuing the shortcut she had not dared to try, probably the same course Rousillon had followed to arrive at the ruins before the earl.

But her joy at the sight of Rousillon's men falling back was checked when he spurred his horse forward again. He carried her to the edge of the battle, then stopped and commenced shouting for the earl to come forth from the ranks.

Heléne met her father's eyes. He stared as though he misbelieved his own sight, then turned and vanished into the heart of the clash. Within moments, the flashing battle slowed, then ceased. Gunthar pushed his way through the guards, flanked by Laurant and Therri. He flicked one glance at Heléne, then fixed his steady gaze on her captor's face.

"So, the jackal shows himself at last," Gunthar said. "You surprise me, Rousillon. I should have thought you would want to be in at what you supposed would be the kill."

Rousillon answered savagely, "And it would have been just that, were it not for this meddlesome wench. But the game is not over yet. I made her a vow should I find you still alive, and honorable men keep their vows, do they not?" He slammed his sword away, then clamped his hand about her throat.

"What do you want from me, Rousillon?" The intensity of the question was the only sign that the move had alarmed Gunthar. His face remained an impassive mask.

"I want you dead," Rousillon spat, "but as you and Laurant have me outnumbered, I must content myself for now with another revenge."

He jerked Heléne's head back to his shoulder and closed his hand crushingly against her windpipe. She clawed frantically at the cruel fingers, but they were like bands of steel about her throat. The clouds overhead spun in a dizzying dance.

"Stop!"

"Stay back, Gunthar, unless you'd rather I broke her neck."

"Let her go. She has done nothing—"

"She has cheated me of your death, and for that she will pay—But I am not as mad as you think me." His hand dropped away. She slumped forward, gasping, against the horse's neck. "If I kill her now, there will be nothing to prevent you from cutting me down where I sit. No, her punishment shall await another day. In the meantime, she shall serve as hostage to ensure my unimpeded return to Vere."

"Surrender her to her father," she heard Gunthar say, "and I give you my word you may ride where you please."

"Your word," Rousillon sneered. "'Tis a regrettable weakness of yours, Gunthar, that you would allow yourself to be bound by that. Nay, if le Reynard is correct, she means a great deal too much to you. I prefer to keep her in my own hands for now. She will guard me far better than any honest oath of yours." He pulled her back up between his arms. "I trust I'll not be followed? Should so much as a rabbit startle me along the way, you can look for her body in a roadside ditch."

He took Gunthar's silence as the assurance he sought, and

galloped off with her down the road to Vere.

# Twenty-Two

The sky had exploded in a torrent of rain, but Triston nevertheless strode out of the castle to meet them.

"Now what are you about, you scoundrel?" Triston demanded. "Who is this—?"

Rousillon pushed Heléne off his horse so violently that she might have been seriously injured had Triston not leapt to catch her. He saw the tumbling braid that framed her streaming face and uttered a startled oath.

"Get her out of my sight," Rousillon spat. "I have resisted the impulse to fling caution aside and choke the life out of her these many miles, but if I am compelled to look at her one more moment, remembering what she has cost me—" He swung himself off the horse and seized Heléne by her braid.

"Let her go," Triston said.

Rousillon responded by giving the braid a vicious twist, and found a fist in his face that laid him flat.

"Keep your filthy hands to yourself. I've had it with you, Rousillon."

Rousillon sat up, livid in the mud, a splash of blood on his lips. "You are going to regret that, de Brielle."

"I doubt you'll have time to keep that threat. Abducting the Lady Heléne is the most insane thing you've done yet. Her father will be laying siege to our walls before nightfall."

"Not if he wants to see his daughter alive again. She is going to prove a very pretty bargaining piece to get me my revenge on Gunthar."

Heléne cried, "You were stupid to tell him you were bringing me to Vere. And you are mad if you think he is going to sit helplessly waiting for you to name your terms. He will assemble an army, if need be, to free me and send you to the gallows where you belong."

Rousillon got up with a snarl. "Get her out of here, de Brielle, before I shut that pert mouth the way you've tried to shut mine."

He raised a fist and Triston, apparently disinclined to challenge him further, pulled Heléne across the bailey and into the keep.

On seeing her limp, Triston passed a supporting arm around her waist, then swept her off her feet and carried her up the stairs. He called to a servant to hurry ahead and light some candles in his father's bedchamber. The room was smaller than her parents', as everything about Vere was smaller, but there was a pleasant elegance to the smooth lines of the whitewashed walls. Heléne saw a curious, four-wheeled chair pushed into one corner. Against it leaned a large, painted shield displaying the gilded rose. The same device was woven, not once, but dozens of times across the crimson bed curtains that the servant drew back.

Triston deposited Heléne on the bed, then went into the small, connecting room that had served as his father's wardrobe. He returned with a blanket which he wrapped around her shivering shoulders. She used the cloth's edge to dry her face, but neither of them spoke until the servant had lit a fire in the fireplace and been dismissed. Triston leaned down, then, to touch her ankle.

"How did this happen?"

"I was trying to escape from Rousillon." She sat forward and rubbed her hand over it. The ankle felt hot and puffy beneath her wet hose. "I don't suppose you have any thyme? It would help to relieve the swelling."

"There's bound to be some in the kitchen garden. I'll send someone to look." He straightened, then frowned. "Heléne, what are you doing with Rousillon and why is he so angry?"

She stared uncertainly into Triston's face. She was reluctant to believe that this man, whom she had known all her life to be gentle and honorable, could have become so corrupt as to have known of Rousillon's wicked plan against Gunthar and done nothing to stop it. She clutched the blanket closer.

"Did Rousillon tell you what he meant to do today?" she asked him.

"No," he said. Then seeing her doubt, he added, "Some clerkish-looking man came this morning and spoke in private with Rousillon. When they were done, Rousillon came out saying he required some men from the garrison and that they would be back before nightfall. I did not ask him why or where he went, and he did not offer to tell me."

"But you suspected something, didn't you?"

His mouth tightened, but he shook his head.

"Triston, he tried to murder the earl again today. If I hadn't learned of it and ridden to warn him, Gunthar would be dead. And Rousillon is going to punish me for that, as soon as he has used me to bait Gunthar into yet another trap. If he succeeds, you know as well as I do that it will mean another war. If he fails, you will go to the gallows with him, adjudged a traitor by complicity through your silence."

She held out her hands to him. He sank down onto the bed with a stifled groan. Her slender fingers gripped his broad shoulders.

"I do not believe your heart is in this evil. Etienne says you are being blackmailed, and I know it is true, because Rousillon has blackmailed me, too. So you must not be afraid to tell me the truth. I will understand, and I will help, if I can."

Triston's fingers had twisted into his wet dark curls, but now his tortured eyes glanced up. "He has blackmailed you? Then you know about Clothilde?"

"Clothilde?"

He checked. "You do *not* know. But you said—"

"What about Clothilde? How could Rousillon possibly be blackmailing you over her?" He hesitated, and she shook him. "Triston—"

"Oh, Heléne—" he dropped his head into his hands again "—it

has been a nightmare. I warned Father not to let that man through our gates, but he was so bitter, so consumed with hate for Gunthar that he would not listen to me. And now Father is dead, murdered by that monster, and he killed Sir John Lee and he is going to kill Gunthar, and whether I go to the gallows for my part in it or not, I still cannot speak."

The warmth of the fire had begun to spread through the room, but Heléne felt more chilled than ever at these words. "What do you mean, he murdered your father?"

"I cannot prove it, but I'm certain that he did. I heard them quarreling after Gunthar challenged Father and left. Father was in an agony over Etienne being in Gunthar's power. He threatened to expose Rousillon in exchange for my brother's freedom, and I heard Rousillon saying he would never allow it. And the next morning we found Father dead where he slept. I do not know how Rousillon did it. A pillow, perhaps. Father was not strong enough to have fought him."

"Triston, if you believe that, how can you continue to protect Rousillon?"

"I swore an oath."

"Etienne told me. But surely Sir Damian would not still wish you bound by that?"

"Not Father," Triston muttered, "Rousillon. It was he who forced the words upon me, and I keep it not for the sake of my soul, but for she who means more to me than life itself."

She had no doubt whom he meant. "Triston, tell me what it is. Clothilde is my sister. I love her as well as you and will protect her just as earnestly. Tell me how Rousillon threatens her."

He groaned again, then lifted his head, his face pale and haggard. She guessed it was exhaustion at carrying the burden so long alone that finally made him answer.

"If I do so, you must swear to tell no one, not your parents, not Therri, and especially not the earl." He saw her hesitation as he spoke Gunthar's name. "Heléne, you must promise. It would mean Clothilde's life."

"Gunthar would not let anyone harm my sister," she cried,

outraged that so dire a threat should be lodged against Clothilde.

"He would have no choice," Triston said. "Gunthar is King Henry's officer, and as such he is sworn to uphold the king's laws. For the most part those laws are just and good, but a man like Rousillon knows how to manipulate them to his own advantage and another's grief. If Gunthar learned of this, even from you, he would have no choice but to deliver Clothilde to the courts. And if once she comes there—Heléne, you must swear, or I can say no more."

"I—swear," she said, stiff with fear of what he was going to tell her.

He nodded, put up a hand to his head, then dropped it again. He seemed to be trying to gather his thoughts.

"I have loved her since we were children," he said at last. "She was so beautiful and merry, and courted by so many men richer and more powerful than I. I dared not tell her, I dared not even dream that she might love me too ... until I found her the morning of her sixteenth birthday, weeping in the woods. Her parents had just informed her of her betrothal to Merval, and she had fled to the clearing, the one where you all used to play. I don't know how I happened there, but when I saw her tears, I sought their cause and before I knew it, she was in my arms. She said she loved me, Heléne. She said she always had."

His hands abruptly fisted. "It was my intention to fight for her! I did not fear your father or Merval, or my own father, either. I would have defied the world for Clothilde! Mother would have understood. If only she had not been so sick, if she had not died—" His voice cracked and his eyes went moist. "I could not refuse her dying wish that I pray for her soul in Jerusalem. But I knew that in my absence, they would try to force Clothilde into marriage with Merval. And I knew that a mere pledge of love would not be sufficient to sustain her fragile will against your parents' threats and recriminations after I was gone. I begged her to come with me, but she was afraid to leave the only home she had ever known. So I sought a bond I thought would be of such strength as to give her the courage she would need to resist all persecution until my return. I thought that if she were my wife, no power on earth would be able to compel her to sin against her conscience and God."

Heléne gasped. "Triston, are you saying that you and Clothilde are married?"

"These five years. I bribed Father's chaplain to do it."

"But that is not possible! Clothilde was Lady Merval, and the earl—"

"She is my wife," Triston said, with a flash in his stormy eyes, "and if Gunthar lays one hand on her, I'll—"

"He does not know. If he did, he would never— But why have you not told this before? Clothilde has been in despair, thinking you would abandon her to Gunthar."

The flash died and he plunged one hand back into his curls. "It has all become so muddled, Heléne. Though we wed in secret, I never intended to keep it so. I meant to take her to Vere and leave her with Father until I returned. But again your sister's fears thwarted us. She was afraid of my father and said she would not live at Vere without me. Nor would she allow me to tell your parents what we had done. She insisted that nothing could compel her to break her vows to me, that she would wait for me at Pennault, that if your parents' threats became too great, she would appeal to my father's chaplain to prove our marriage and they would be forced to cease their attempts to wed her to Merval. She left me no choice but to trust in her love."

It had not been enough. Heléne pressed his arm. "Triston, I am sorry. I think she did try to wait for you. But Mama—"

Triston dropped his hand and stood up, his face cold. "I know what your mother did. Clothilde has told me everything. But then, all I knew was the unutterable horror of returning home to find *my wife* wed to another man."

"It must have been horrible for you," she whispered, "but it has been far worse for Clothilde. Merval was a wretched, loathsome man. I do not know how Clothilde bore it." She paused, then asked, "But why did you not speak? Merval delayed the marriage for nearly the full year of your pilgrimage. He and Clothilde had been wed for little more than a month when you returned. If you had spoken then, their marriage would have been declared invalid."

"It was not that simple. Before I left, I paid my father's chaplain to keep an eye on Clothilde, promising him more if I returned to find her safe. He was a greedy old man. He promised to keep our confidence as long as he could, but agreed to reveal our marriage if it were necessary to protect her from Merval. But if he ever did speak, someone, either your mother or Merval himself, must have paid him more than I to spread the truth no further. And then the chaplain caught fever and died. Without him, when I returned there was no way to prove that Clothilde was my wife, no witnesses, no record—or so I thought."

Triston crossed the room and back, then stopped beside the bed again. "Oh, I tried. I confronted Merval, but he laughed at me. I demanded to speak with Clothilde. At first he refused. So I slammed him into a wall and laid my sword across his throat. He might have had his guards strike me down, but he did not. Nay, he had a better way to disarm me. He summoned Clothilde, and the moment he laid his hand to her shoulder, I knew we were lost. Clothilde refused even to look at me. I begged her to confess our marriage, but she would neither confess nor deny. She only whispered to me to go away. I knew she would not dare to speak with Merval at her back. And I knew that if I pressed her, if once she spoke, before witnesses, a denial of our marriage, all hope of winning her back as my wife would be lost."

"What did you do?" The throbbing of her ankle seemed to echo the anguish she felt emanating from Triston's soul.

"Before I could do anything, Merval had his guards throw me out and told them to cut me down if I approached his walls again. I did not know what to do. I returned to Vere. At first I was bitter, bewildered that Clothilde had not spoken in time to stop the marriage to Merval. Then the images began. Merval holding Clothilde, kissing her, loving her . . ." Triston broke off with a choking sound. "I could not make them stop. Until I downed a cup of wine—and then another and another. Like I had done too many times on my pilgrimage when my loneliness and fears for Clothilde threatened to overwhelm me."

His eyes flicked briefly to Heléne's, and she saw the shame in them.

"It seemed the only way to stave off the visions. So I drank myself blind, and I stayed that way for months. I must have truly been out of my senses, for when I finally came out of my haze I found myself accused of having seduced my father's new wife. I do not remember much about that period, but certain impressions and Osanne's behavior towards me led me to fear it must be true. Only later, when I saw the wanton way she strewed her favors on every man who pleased her eye, did I suspect the seduction had lain more in her hands than in mine. But it made me no less guilty of the sin. I felt—*dirty*, Heléne. How could I condemn Clothilde, how could I even face her, with that profanity on my conscience?"

He crossed the room again with an agitated stride. "I wept bitter tears for my father's forgiveness. I sought out our village priest and pled with him to assign me some penance worthy of my crime. But he did little more than shrug my offense away by prescribing a few fasts and paternosters. They proved woefully ineffectual in healing my soul. So I turned my tears to God. I have made Him many promises, Heléne, and have touched neither wine nor woman since, nor will I save for she who is in His sight my wife. But it took me many months to work out my pardon. By then, the wars had begun. When Merval died suddenly in the midst of the earl's siege, it seemed that my prayers had finally been answered."

Triston stopped by the window and stared broodingly out.

"Why did you not come for Clothilde then, after Gunthar returned her to Pennault?" Heléne asked.

"Rousillon." Triston nearly spat the name out. "After his exposure for murder by the earl, Rousillon sought refuge with Merval, a villain whose blackguardly heart rivaled his own. Too late did I remember seeing his face in Merval's hall when I went there to confront Clothilde. How he mocked me later! All the while I railed at Merval and stood helpless before Clo's silence, Rousillon watched me, smirking, knowing he held the fate of our marriage in his own dastardly hands."

"*Rousillon* knew about your marriage?"

"He had met my father's chaplain drinking in the village tavern one night while I was on pilgrimage. Rousillon, always looking for some whiff of scandal to facilitate a little blackmail, kept the chaplain drinking until he let slip that Merval's 'wife' was no wife at all, but secretly wed to his own master's son. Rousillon asked what proof the chaplain had beyond his own word, and the chaplain admitted that he had recorded our marriage without my knowledge. I suppose one never knows what scrap of parchment may one day prove useful for tormenting some innocent soul. Rousillon bought the document off our greedy chaplain's hands."

Heléne caught the bitter snap in Triston's voice.

"When Merval was defeated and his fortress leveled, Rousillon fled to my father, bringing with him both proof of my marriage and a devilish scheme for revenge on Gunthar."

"And your father listened," she said. "I can understand Sir Damien, why he would hate Gunthar so. But was it the marriage proof that held you silent? Did Rousillon threaten to destroy it if you exposed him?"

"Nay. Oh, aye, that too. But it is not my marriage alone I am trying to save."

Heléne shivered again. "You spoke of a threat to Clo's life."

Triston closed his eyes, and she saw the tight-drawn planes of his face. "Clothilde has not told me everything of her life with Merval, but she has said enough to convince me that he used her vilely. I have tried to understand the despair she must have felt. Once Merval threw me out of his keep, she did not believe she would ever be allowed to see me again. I suppose Rousillon can be seductive enough when he wishes. He courted her behind her husband's back. Clothilde swears it never went beyond a few indiscreet kisses, but he won her trust and confidence. At last, in her distress as Merval's wife, Clothilde was so incautious as to express her hatred for her husband and her desperation to be free of him. Rousillon took it as a commission, and at the height of the earl's siege, Rousillon poisoned Merval."

Heléne gasped and Triston turned, his face a study of grim despair.

"The penalty for a woman who murders her husband is death by fire. It would not matter that it was Rousillon who did the actual deed. He would be certain to twist Clothilde's words to make her appear his accomplice. The court's horror of murderous wives is such that they would be bound to show her no mercy."

"But Rousillon would have to incriminate himself."

"He is already a condemned man. What would one more charge be to him? Besides, he would not have to publicly accuse her. He could do it with a whisper. Once the rumor spread, questions would be asked and eventually Clothilde would be obliged to answer them."

Recalling the snippets of conversation she had overheard between Clothilde and Rousillon, Heléne knew that the threat to her sister was real.

Triston took an urgent step towards her. "Heléne, you understand, don't you? If I do not do everything he says, Rousillon will destroy Clothilde. I would pay any price to protect her. I would give my own life—"

"But it is Gunthar's life he is asking," Heléne said. "Triston, there must be some way to save them both."

"I have not been able to think of one." He sank back down on the bed.

"I won't let him murder Gunthar!"

Triston turned his head. "It is true, then? You're in love with him, and he with you?"

Heléne betrayed herself with a blush.

"Rousillon has a contact at Pennault," Triston said, "a spy whom he calls 'le Reynard.' He saw Gunthar embracing you, and apparently is familiar enough with the earl to have discerned other signs of his regard, as well."

Her eyes filled with tears. "I do love him, Triston, as much as you could ever love Clothilde. I cannot let Rousillon harm him."

"Do you want to see Clothilde burn?"

"Of course not! But there must be something we can do to stop him without risking Clothilde."

Triston shook his head, but said, "I won't let him harm you. That much I *can* promise." He pressed her hand, then stood up. "Get out of those wet clothes and go sit by the fire. I'll send someone to tend to your ankle. And I suggest you keep to this room as much as you can. Try to stay out of Rousillon's eye. I'd prefer to avoid a confrontation, if I can."

Heléne did not need the warning. She watched Triston go out, then sank into the pillows and gave vent to her tears of frustration and fear.

Even the surprise of seeing Audiart on the threshold bearing a basin of water to bathe her foot, failed to revive Heléne's spirits for more than a few hours. The fugitive servant confessed that she had been sent here by Julian Parr after he had persuaded her to smuggle the kitchen knife to Etienne, and bitterly sorry she was that she had ever listened to that faithless squire. He had murdered her stableboy-lover, she said, because he had followed Julian to a tryst with Rousillon, and now Julian had delivered her into the devil's own power. She blinked not an eyelash of regret when Heléne told her that Julian was dead. Little good that did her, she protested. Naught but *Rousillon's* death would free her from the vile indignities that she had suffered here.

Heléne did not inquire what form these indignities had taken. Her curiosity was but marginally piqued, she was in such despondent humor. But since Audiart seemed inclined to linger while she soaked her foot in the hot, thyme-treated water, she roused herself to ask whether Sybil were at Vere, as well. No, Audiart replied, pursing her lips, and milady must not ask her more for she had been warned not to speak, nor would she, save to say that the old witch had finally got what she deserved. This intrigued Heléne more than Audiart's tale of woe had done. But the servant remained mum to all her questions, and finally departed with the basin, insisting the water had cooled too much to be useful.

Thrice a day, Audiart returned with a fresh basin, until the swelling in Heléne's ankle had completely healed. After that, she appeared only briefly each morning when she carried in the breakfast tray. Triston brought up the evening tray and always sat with Heléne while she ate. It was from him that she learned how events were transpiring outside Sir Damian's chamber. Triston told her that

Rousillon was recruiting mercenaries to replace the men he had lost to her father's guard and had completed the fortifications that Gunthar's forces had torn down during the war. The storms had passed, and any day now, they expected to find Gunthar at the gates, demanding Rousillon's blood.

But Gunthar did not come. His delay heartened Heléne at first. He was too clever, she told herself, to fall so easily into Rousillon's trap. But a week turned into a fortnight. Rousillon's temper shortened as it began to appear that Gunthar had no intention of taking his bait. Rousillon had virtually ignored Heléne since bringing her to Vere, but on the fifteenth day, he burst into Sir Damian's chamber.

Heléne, who had begun to suffer a few doubts of her own as to whether anyone ever meant to come to her rescue, whirled about from her study of Sir Damian's shield and his curious wheeled chair. She screamed when she saw the twisted rage in Rousillon's face and the vicious-looking dagger in his hand.

He snarled, "Either you were never anything more than a toy to the earl, or he has not been sufficiently convinced of your danger. He will come to me on my terms, not his. Take her."

Heléne tried to dodge the two henchmen that lunged after her, but they were faster than she and caught her by the arms.

"Let me go!"

She pulled in vain against their hold, then stilled when Rousillon held up the blade before her face. There was a smile of almost fiendish anticipation on his lips, and his eyes blazed with a dark malignance.

"Wh-what are you going to do?" she stammered.

"What I should have done in the beginning. If Gunthar requires inducement to bring him to our walls, then I will send him a message he cannot ignore. On the bed with her."

They dragged her, struggling, across the room and flung her on her back on the bed. Heléne screamed again and struck out wildly with her feet, but Rousillon overcame the thrashing danger by straddling her legs. He pinioned them with his weight while one of his henchmen caught her shoulders and forced them down into the blankets. The other drew out her right arm.

Heléne did not comprehend Rousillon's intent until he stretched out his blade towards her hand.

"When Gunthar sees your pretty fingers, he will know that I am not to be trifled with. Hold her arm still. I should not want to botch the job."

The henchman locked his palm with hers and bore down with a crushing strength. Rousillon touched the point of his blade to her wrist.

*He was going to take off her hand.*

Her body convulsed in terror, but Rousillon only laughed. The blade swooped up. Heléne shrieked and tried to writhe away, but a cruel grasp held her shoulders against the bed and her arm remained locked in a vise. The steel sliced down in a flash of light.

*"No!"*

The man's shout was lost in Heléne's screams. For a long while, she could hear nothing but her own piercing sobs. It was minutes before she realized she was free and her aching voice surrendered to the curses thundering in the air. She sat up, gasping as she saw her hand safe, then stared at the scuffle taking place beside the bed. Triston was trying to wrestle the dagger away from Rousillon and, had he succeeded, looked furious enough to have thrust it through the villain's heart.

"I won't let you do it, Rousillon! Take what vengeance you will on Gunthar, but leave the Lady Heléne alone!"

Rousillon swore at him. His wiry strength maintained the hold on his dagger, but Triston was the larger man. He shoved Rousillon up against the wall and locked one hand around the villain's throat.

"Nothing would give me greater pleasure than to choke the life out of you."

"Try it and your lady will go to the flames," Rousillon croaked. Triston's hand did not move, but his grip must have eased, for Rousillon's voice continued more strongly, "Must I remind you that I have written out my confession in the matter of Merval's poisoning, with the name of the woman who conspired with me to do the deed? It is sealed and in the hands of my confederate, le Reynard. Should anything untoward befall me, he has orders to make known its contents to the world."

Heléne saw the blazing hatred in Triston's eyes, but the angry flush on his cheeks paled at the threat to Clothilde. He dropped his hand from Rousillon's throat and allowed the man to slide away from the wall.

"That is better. Now stand back and let me finish my errand. I can destroy the Lady Clothilde with a word, and I will do it if you interfere again."

To Heléne's horror, Triston stood frozen as Rousillon strode towards the bed.

"Now then, my lady—"

Heléne flung her hands behind her back and shrank away with a sob. "Triston, please!"

"Come," Rousillon said, "it will be over in a trice. The blade is sharp and my wrist is quick." He grabbed her arm and pulled it forth. "Sit perfectly still, now, and I will be done before you know it."

*"No!"* she screamed.

He jerked her hand towards him and lifted the dagger.

"Wait!" Triston moved suddenly and caught Rousillon's wrist. He cast a desperate look at Heléne, then his dark eyes lit as the stratagem came to him. "Let her hand alone and take her hair instead."

"Her hair?" Rousillon was startled out of his glare by the absurdity of the suggestion.

But Triston made haste to point out its sense. "What is there to prove to Gunthar that the hand is not merely that of some luckless servant? But I've seen no other woman with hair as long as hers in the entire county. And she always wears it in that distinctive braid. If you were to cut *that* off and send it to Gunthar, there would be no mistaking it."

Rousillon eyed her heavy plait, then glanced again at her hand. "'Twould not be as satisfying," he said, "but—" He released her fingers. "You may be right."

He ran the flat of his blade along her jaw. Heléne shuddered, but she did not flinch when he drew her braid level with her chin and neatly sliced off her twined tresses.

Rousillon's laughter rang in her ears long after he was gone.

Triston lingered to comfort her, but she pressed her burning face into the pillows and told him bitterly to go away. In the silence that followed, she hugged her hand to her breast and rebuked herself for ingratitude. Triston had saved her from a hideous fate, but all she could think of were her shorn locks and Gunthar's dismay when he saw her again.

# Twenty-Three

No one spoke for several minutes after Gunthar unwrapped the package. There was not a man in the room who was not chillingly familiar with the sight of the Lady Heléne's luxurious braid slung carelessly over her shoulder. Now the pale plait lay severed on the table before them, looped in the middle and tied together at the ends with a ribbon the color of blood.

"Heléne," her father whispered. "What has that devil done to her?"

"Steady yourself, Laurant," Gunthar said. "He has merely cut off her hair."

*"Merely?"* In his alarm, Laurant pushed Gunthar aside and grabbed up the braid. He turned in a fury, shaking it in Gunthar's face. "I warned you, I *begged* you not to turn your back on my daughter. You said she would be safe—"

Gunthar sought to stem Laurant's panic even as he fought off his own sickening wave of shock. "There is no evidence that Rousillon has harmed her—"

"Not harmed her? How do we know this is all? When last I saw her, Rousillon had his fingers locked about her throat!"

Gunthar was horribly aware that he might have miscalculated the situation. He had assumed that Heléne would be in little danger once Rousillon had used her to secure his escape. Unlike Clothilde, whom all the county knew Gunthar intended to marry, Heléne was an insignificant younger daughter, of no particular importance that Gunthar should risk his life for her in confrontation before Vere Castle. Or so he had expected Rousillon to reason. Not wishing to give the villain cause to suspect that she was anything more, Gunthar had deliberately resisted Laurant's pleas to launch an immediate assault on Vere. Instead, he had proceeded to Poitiers and his parley with the prince.

Standing now in the hall of the house he had rented for his sojourn in the city, he realized that he should have given more credence to Rousillon's remark on the road about 'le Reynard.' But it had seemed inconceivable to him that he should have let slip some hint of his feelings for Heléne in front of Julian Parr. And he had taken such care to avoid displaying any public affection for her, that no one else could have—

No, there had been one misstep. That instance in the South Tower when anger and jealousy had provoked him into losing his head and two of his knights, together with the captured Etienne, had surprised him and Heléne in the midst of a wrestling match. Was it possible that Julian had not been alone? That there had been another watching him as closely as the squire? Gunthar turned his gaze upon Sir Thomas Enslye, who stood whispering with the marshal, Sir Roger Tollerton.

"We must delay no longer," Laurant's voice broke across Gunthar's suspicions. "I risked my own men's blood to defend you on the road to Poitiers. If you will not come with me now, then my men and I shall go alone."

"You'll go nowhere until I give you leave to do so."

Gunthar signaled to Sir Roger to block Laurant's exit. He abhorred himself for the words he was now compelled to speak. Only the most rigid training enabled him to voice the pitiless truth that his office laid upon him and from which, even now, he could not allow himself to retreat.

"There is more at stake here than your daughter's life. In all our debates of the last two weeks, the prince has consistently denied any alliance with Rousillon, yet every attack on me has been deliberately designed to point back at the prince. Either the prince is lying, or this conspiracy is more devious than I had supposed. Someone is using

Rousillon to try to sow the seeds of violent discord between Prince Richard and his father. Rousillon holds the answer and my obligation to the king requires me to see the villain apprehended and exposed before it becomes too late." With a callousness that shamed him, Gunthar added, "I will do what I can to save your daughter, but if it comes to a choice—Rousillon must not be allowed to escape again."

Therri took his father's arm as Laurant staggered at these words. To Gunthar's surprise, tears sprang into Laurant's eyes and rolled down his florid cheeks.

"But my Heléne—Rousillon will—"

Gunthar cut him off, resentful that he should be denied a share of that frank emotion. "Take your father to his room," he told Therri, "and stay with him until he composes himself. I have a siege to plan and cannot be distracted."

Therri permitted himself a contemptuous glance at Gunthar, then pulled his father across the hall towards the stairs that led to the second floor. They had not mounted three steps before Gunthar stopped them again.

"Laurant." He followed them to the foot of the stairs and held out his hand. "Give me the braid."

Laurant hesitated. The anger surged back into his face. "You've no right to it," he said, clutching at the plait he still held.

But Gunthar's stare was remorseless. "Give it to me."

Therri cursed him, but even now Laurant had not the power to resist the earl's command. Reluctantly, with a sob of defeat, he placed the braid in Gunthar's hand.

Gunthar's throat tightened painfully at the vivid memories evoked by the touch of the silken strands against his palm. It lent a throb to his voice as he pled, "Laurant, you must understand. Were this matter solely between Rousillon and me, I would bare my own breast to his sword if it would win your daughter's freedom. But this threat reaches to the throne itself—"

"Come, Papa." Therri pulled his father away and up the rest of the steps. Laurant's loyal guard went with them, leaving Gunthar very much alone in the midst of his own knights.

"I will prove it to you, Gunthar, once and for all. I will lead this assault myself!"

Gunthar barely suppressed a shudder at the prince's enthusiastic offer. Heléne would not stand a chance were he to surrender this expedition into Richard's impetuous hands. The prince had shown promise during the war of one day becoming a brilliant strategist, but for now his youthful blood still ran too hot.

They confronted one another, as they had for twelve of the last sixteen days, on the plain outside the city of Poitiers, with the bishop, Jean aux Bellesmains, between them. Each stood flanked by his personal guard of a half-dozen knights—a suggestion, Bellesmains had owned, of Gunthar's vassal, Lord Challons, to eliminate any troublesome interference by the Count of Angoulême. The clever Challons held many useful talents, but they did not include swordplay, and Gunthar had left him behind at Pennault. That Challons' ploy had nearly delivered Gunthar into Rousillon's hands was a calamity his vassal could not have foreseen. And the decision had ultimately proved beneficial in removing the prince from Count William's virulent influence. Except for a few regressive flashes of pouting independence, Richard had proven much more tractable since coming to Poitiers.

The patient negotiations of the bishop had effected a tenuous truce between them. Richard had been made to listen while Gunthar laid down the king's demands. In response, the prince insisted that he *had* tried to enforce the terms of the Peace, but had been frustrated by his father's neglect. Richard reminded Gunthar how, immediately after the war, he had seized the castle of the rebel Arnold of Bouteville. He protested that the two-month siege might have been accomplished in a fortnight, had he only had the money to employ an adequate force of men and purchase the proper equipment.

When Gunthar asked, in exasperation, why the prince had not taken this complaint to the king instead of abandoning the remainder of his charge to unite himself with the likes of Angoulême, the prince turned sulky. He muttered that Count William was his friend and he would not turn his back on his former allies. He rejected any consideration that Angoulême's "friendship" might be less than sincere, and when Gunthar suggested that the count, with easy access to the uniforms of the prince's guard, might in fact have conspired with Rousillon to betray him, Richard flew into a rage.

Gunthar knew the futility of trying to check a Plantagenet temper once it had been roused. He exchanged a weary glance with the bishop and said nothing more until Richard had screamed himself hoarse.

"There is only one way to learn the truth," Gunthar had said then. "It is to ride to Vere Castle and fetch it from Rousillon himself."

To his dismay, the prince had leapt at the idea. Swearing that he would prove both his and Angoulême's innocence to Gunthar and the king, he insisted that he should take charge of the siege and proceeded to detail the tactics he would use to level Vere to the ground.

Gunthar was quick to see the merit of involving the prince in Rousillon's capture. There could be no surer way of returning the son to his father's favor than to have him play a part in unraveling the conspiracy. But the havoc Richard hoped to wreak upon the castle's walls would spell disaster for Heléne.

"I presume my father has sent the money to do the job properly this time?" the prince inquired. "I do not know if Angoulême will wish to quarrel with de Brielle. We may need to hire mercenaries."

"I am already arranging for that," Gunthar said, "and I have sent word to my men at Pennault to begin assembling the necessary engines of war. My men will join us at the walls of Vere, though I hope to avoid a pitched battle if I can."

Richard looked disappointed. "Surely Rousillon would not be so cowardly as to surrender without a fight?"

"On the contrary, I expect he will fight like a cornered rat."

"Well, then," Richard said, encouraged, "how soon will we be ready?"

"Soon," Gunthar said. "But, my lord, there is a difficulty.

"Oh?"

"Rousillon has a hostage, a young daughter of one of your 'former allies'. You recall the Baron de Laurant?"

Richard nodded. "His daughter's beauty is legend, even in the courts of Angoulême. Word is you mean to marry her."

"That is the Lady Clothilde. It is her sister, the Lady Helen, whom Rousillon has carried off in the mistaken belief that I hold her in some affection. It is absurd, of course, she is such a drab little thing, but I fear that Rousillon might do her some harm for spite. It was I who brought his crimes to the attention of your father's courts, and he has made no secret of the fact that he should like to deal me some injury in repayment. I have been blunt with Laurant, informing him that he must not hope for too much. Rousillon's defeat must take precedence over his daughter's safety. But she *is* the sister of my betrothed and daughter to my future father-in-law. If there were some way to rescue her—"

"Of course," Richard agreed, rather perfunctorily. The apparent vagueness of Gunthar's concern, coupled with his description of Heléne as 'drab', had squelched any genuine interest the prince might have held in her plight. "Then what do you suggest we do?"

At a gesture from Gunthar, one of his men handed him a map, which Gunthar proceeded to unroll in the grass. The prince listened, bending over Gunthar's shoulder to follow the sweeping lines traced by his finger. The prince nodded in reluctant respect of Gunthar's strategy, but when his own part in the scheme was named, he recoiled.

"Were I to consent to that, then *I* should appear the coward. Why can I not lead the assault, and you—"

"Because I am the one Rousillon wants," Gunthar said. "Someone bigger than he is undoubtedly at the heart of this conspiracy, but Rousillon is his agent and I suspect his reward is to have my head. It is my face he will be looking for, and if he sees you by my side he will know his master's intrigue is exposed and will be off to warn him—after he relieves his vexation on the Lady Helen."

The prince frowned. "You truly believe he would harm her?"

Gunthar thought of the severed braid. That, he knew, was a mild prelude to what he would be sent if he did not make some attempt to dance to Rousillon's tune. "If he cuts her throat, she will be fortunate," he said curtly. He rolled up the map and got to his feet. "We may have to do it your way in the end, my prince. But the Lady Helen's fate must rest on my conscience alone. If the walls of Vere are to fall, it must be at my command, not yours."

"And if I do as you say and you capture Rousillon, where does that leave me?"

"In your father's good graces," Gunthar said. "Rousillon shall be your prize. *You* shall deliver him to England and renew your father's faith. And see that you do not lose it again."

The prince considered all that Gunthar had said, then slowly nodded his head.

Heléne rubbed her sleeve briskly over the surface of the breakfast tray and held it up to her face. Her spirits sank at the blurred image that met her eyes. She had not had the courage to look before, and now she wished she had clung to her ignorance. Though the features reflected in the metal were indistinct, one attribute was clear—that fluffy halo around her head was all that was left of her hair. She had known by touch that the ends reached no further than her chin, but to see the reality of Rousillon's cropping revived her tears of shame.

She returned the tray to the table. Perhaps he would never have to see her. Perhaps in the confusion of his storming the walls, she could slip away, a pluckless squire trying to evade the carnage. These clothes of Etienne's would help with the deception. She had traded her brother's soiled tunic for them at Triston's leave, for she had refused to don any garment of the wicked Osanne's. Triston had told her that she might go into his father's wardrobe and borrow one of his late mother's gowns, but they had all been too small. In any event, it seemed ridiculous to try to reclaim her femininity with the Lady Alyne's beautiful skirts after Rousillon had shorn her.

Heléne rubbed a hand over the nape of her neck. Rousillon had ignored her since he had cut off her hair, but the terror he had inflicted on her that day had not paled with his neglect. He would come for her again, and soon. Gunthar's forces had surrounded the castle days ago, but Rousillon had laughed at every offer Gunthar had made to sweeten a surrender: a gentler, more merciful death for his treason; a commutation of his sentence to imprisonment for life if he released his hostage and yielded Vere without bloodshed; a shorter conviction if he would turn king's evidence and reveal the name of his master. Rousillon had rejected them all. If Gunthar wanted him, he said, he would have to come through the walls of Vere to get him, and woe betide his sweet lady if he attempted that.

According to Triston, Gunthar was steadfastly denying that she meant anything to him and had sent a clear message that his sympathy for her would not prevent him from doing whatever it required to bring Rousillon to justice. Heléne guessed these denials were meant to protect her, but Rousillon, Triston said, was not convinced. Rousillon was certain that his source at Pennault had not been mistaken, and he was quite willing to bet Heléne's life on it. Heléne did not doubt Gunthar's love any more than she doubted his resolve. She understood too well the quandary she had unintentionally cast him in, and she was not nearly as confident as Rousillon that he would subject his duty to his heart.

Triston had given her a key and warned her to keep the door locked, but they both knew that would not stop Rousillon from reaching her if he wanted her badly enough. If Gunthar defied his warnings and attacked the castle, he would need her to try to effect another escape. If Gunthar did nothing, Rousillon was just as likely to abuse her merely to torment his enemy.

She realized she could not depend on Gunthar to help her avoid either fate. If she were to survive this ordeal in one piece, she would have to find a way out of it herself.

A rapping fell on the door. She jumped and called out nervously for a name.

"'Tis Audiart, milady. I've come to clear away the tray."

Heléne always hesitated to let anyone in, lest Rousillon be at his or her shoulder, but the sound of Audiart's voice started the wheels turning in her mind. The servant was as unhappy at Vere as she. Perhaps—

She opened the door, pulled Audiart in, and locked it quickly again.

"Milady," the servant scolded on seeing the tray, "you've not touched your breakfast. You will make yourself sick if you continue this willfulness."

"Audiart," she interrupted, "are there any poppies in the garden?"

"Poppies?" Audiart echoed. "Are you having trouble sleeping, milady? I'm sure 'twould be no wonder if—"

"Audiart, you want to return to Pennault, do you not?"

Tears sprang into the servant's eyes. "Oh, milady, but I cannot. I helped Master Julian to set a criminal free, and he said if I were caught that I would be hanged."

"He was just trying to frighten you not to tell. If you were to help me to safety, Papa and the earl would be so grateful that I'm certain they would pardon you."

Audiart clasped her hands. "But do you truly think we can? Rousillon's guards are everywhere."

"That is why we need the poppies. We could drug a few of them to sleep and—"

She stopped as Audiart's face fell. "Even if I could get into the garden to look, they don't let me anywhere near the food or wine, save to hand me this tray each morning and send me up to you."

Heléne stood abashed for a moment, but quickly rallied. "Perhaps Triston will help us. If you could only find some flower or herb that would send the guards to sleep, or even make them sick, he might smuggle it into the wine for us."

Audiart nodded. "I will try, milady."

She picked up the tray and turned to leave, but Heléne caught her arm. "Wait, there is one more thing. Can you show me the way to Rousillon's chamber?"

Audiart gasped and shook her head. "Oh, milady, you mustn't go there!"

"I must. He has something of mine, and I'll not leave Vere without it."

"But milady—"

"Audiart, I am determined. Rousillon is not there, is he?"

"No, milady, he's on the battlements, watching the earl's camp."

"Then this is the perfect time. Leave the tray and come . . .

While Audiart searched the gardens, Heléne hunted through Rousillon's chamber, bent on finding her father's letter. He had not brought much with him to Vere. The room's furnishings were spartan, nothing but a bed without hangings, a trestle table with a pitcher and basin, and an old, scuffed chest on the floor. That seemed the most likely hiding place, so she knelt by the chest and threw back the lid.

She tossed out the tumble of clothes on top and explored the items beneath. Two pairs of shoes, some tangled jewelry lying loose, several leather bags containing silver coins . . . Her heart leapt when a pile of letters appeared. She picked them up and used her teeth to break the string that bound them. Each one bore a different heraldic seal, probably used, like her father's and Julian's, to blackmail the reckless souls who had affixed them to incriminating words. But though she found wax impressions of animals and flowers and at least a dozen variations of birds, the double-headed phoenix remained maddeningly absent.

She flung the letters down so they went scattering over the floor. Her father's letter must be somewhere. Surely fate could not be so cruel as to have left it on Rousillon's person? She dared not even consider that possibility until she had exhausted every other. She had not searched everywhere. Perhaps it was under one of these oddly wrapped bundles.

She took out the bundle on top, a hard, longish object shrouded in a woolen cloth. It was wider at one end than the other, and dark shadows suggested stains of some kind on an inner layer of the fabric. Prompted by impulsive curiosity, she unraveled it.

Her gasp nearly drowned out the clatter of it striking the floor. It was a dagger, still crusted with blood. But most horrific was the image on the hilt—a five-petaled rose, painted gold, with a blood-red center. The de Brielle rose. Triston's rose.

She did not even want to contemplate what this might mean. She pushed it hurriedly away, praying, at the very least, that it had nothing to do with John Lee's death.

The discovery cured her of wanting to know what might be in the other bundles. She could not help shivering a little as she removed them one by one. Still there was no sign of her father's letter. Another glance around the starkly furnished room assured her there was nowhere else it could be hidden. Unless she rifled through the bed. She supposed he might have stuffed it beneath the mattress.

With nearly extinct expectations, she lifted out the final wrapped object, and found herself greeted with one last hope. A small wooden box had been shoved into one corner of the chest. There was a tiny lock on the lid, but it was not strong enough to withstand her pounding it against the stones of the floor. Two strikes shattered it. She took a deep breath and closed her eyes, then opened them again and looked inside.

She stared at the contents, baffled. The box seemed to be filled with small circles of cloth, embroidered patches of a creature half-man, half-beast. No, not man. It bore a woman's figure on top, while the nether part swirled away into a twisting, serpentine tail.

Melusine. They were not patches at all, but badges, enough to have adorned a whole garrison of soldiers. She tumbled the circles out onto the floor, and found a letter beneath.

"No doubt you would like to know what it says?"

Heléne looked up at the dripping voice. Rousillon stood watching her from the doorway.

"Where is my father's letter?" she cried. This still was not it.

"Ah, your father." Rousillon sauntered into the room. "I fear that was a little deception, contrived for the necessity of the moment. I needed your eyes and ears that first night of the earl's arrival. Le Reynard refused to risk being seen with me, and he had not yet convinced young Parr of where his interests lay."

"You mean—" Heléne scarcely dared believe the implication of his words. "You mean there was never any letter at all? My father never—"

"—intended to betray his oath of capitulation to the crown? No."

Indignation mingled with relief to briefly flood out her fear. Her father was not a traitor. Rousillon had lied.

"You used me!"

"Of course I used you. You were not going to betray the earl of your own accord. And all this would have been over a long while ago, had my archer not failed on the road to Angoulême." The glitter in his eyes reminded her of her danger. "Did you think to redeem yourself for that at Michelet's castle? Or did you risk yourself only for love?"

Her heart thudded unevenly against her ribs. If she did not distract him quickly from that memory— "Triston says you killed his father."

"The erstwhile Sir Damian? Aye. The man was too soft. The moment his kin was threatened, he thought to go blabbing all to Gunthar. I could not have that."

"And Julian? Did you kill him, too?"

"Parr?" His lips thinned thoughtfully, but he shook his head. "The boy was little more than a messenger. It was le Reynard who obtained Sir Adam's letter and used it to secure the services of his son. Whatever happened to young Parr was done by le Reynard, not me."

Then there was still a threat to Gunthar among his own men. But who? If she could only gain a clue. "And how did you blackmail le Reynard? With one of these—" she picked up one of the letters scattered about her "—or one of these?" She pointed to the cloth-wrapped bundles, and shuddered when her eye caught Triston's dagger again.

"I did it with this." Rousillon scooped up a leather bag from the floor and tossed it into the air. Heléne heard a jingle of coins as he caught it. His lips twisted into a sneer. "But aren't you curious about what *that* letter says?" She followed his glance to the letter still lying in the box. "You'll find a good many of your answers there. Go ahead, take it up and read it."

She hesitated, but he seemed to expect her to comply, so she picked the letter up. She had already glimpsed that the seal bore some sort of flower, but she was not prepared for the recognition that now struck her. Her hands jerked as she pulled the letter open and her eyes absorbed incredulously the words inscribed within.

"You are mad," she whispered. "This could never succeed."

"It very nearly has already," Rousillon said. "Convenient, how it all worked out. I did not anticipate, when I was recruited for this task, that Gunthar would be in Poitou just when I stood in need of a catalyst. But nothing could better suit my master's needs, or my own revenge, than a princely assassination of that particular royal counselor."

Despite her shocked protest, Heléne perceived an ominous logic to their plot. But they had not succeeded yet. "Gunthar will learn of it. He has you surrounded and when he storms this castle—and he will!—he will find this letter and then he will know the truth."

"Then I shall have to burn it."

Rousillon reached down to retrieve the letter from her, but Heléne thwarted him by stuffing it down the front of her tunic.

He grinned. "Now there's a challenge I may not be able to resist."

He pulled her to her feet and meaningfully eyed the laces at the neck of her tunic. She tried to break away, but he held on tight to her arm.

"Gunthar will never see it," he said. "What your beloved does not know is that *I*, in fact, have *him* surrounded. Even now, the mercenaries I have hired are waiting in the woods for the signal that will send them swooping down on the earl's forces. When Gunthar turns to defend himself, I will open the gates and our garrison will attack his rear. Gunthar will be slaughtered—and all the world will know that it was done by the prince's guard."

Heléne tried hard not to show her horror. "But if he should attack first, before you are ready—"

"He will not, not while he fears what I may do to you in retribution."

"You are mistaken. It is my sister he loves and is going to marry."

"No, you are the one he holds in his heart, and that weakness will prove his downfall." Heléne shook her head, but Rousillon sneered. "Le Reynard is not wrong. On the road below Michelet's ruins, Gunthar spared you but a glance, yet that glance spoke volumes of the truth. Perhaps he will die with your name on his lips. It is more than you shall be able to do when I am through with you." He pulled free the dagger at his side.

"If you kill me, you will have no more hold over Gunthar."

"I am not going to kill you," Rousillon said. "But you have read the letter, and what would it profit me to murder Gunthar if you are free afterwards to blab about what you know?"

With a sudden, terrifying strength, he threw her across the room. She fell onto the bed. Before she could recover, he was atop her, the point of his blade pressed against her lower lip. The eyes that stared down into hers cut like the eyes of hell.

"One quick snip and it will be gone," he murmured. "The only question is—should I cut out your tongue before I ravish you or after?"

Heléne dared not move. His free hand fondled her throat while his blade threatened at her lips.

There was a click and a footstep. "Rousillon, I thought you would want to know that Gunthar has—"

Rousillon turned the dagger and pressed the flat of the blade against her mouth, stifling her cry at the sound of Triston's voice.

But Triston had seen. "What the devil are you doing? Heléne—?"

"Get out, de Brielle," Rousillon snapped. "This is not your concern."

"The devil it is not! Let her go."

Triston grabbed Rousillon's shoulder and pulled him up, but when Heléne tried to bolt, Rousillon clenched her arm so fiercely that she winced in pain.

"I'm warning you, de Brielle—"

"There is not time for this. Gunthar has begun the assault. His mangons have already loosed one volley at the walls, and his men are preparing to bridge the moat and attack the gate."

Rousillon swore. "Have the walls been damaged?"

"Not yet, but a few more hits and they—"

"Then there is not much time to teach him of his folly. Leave me to finish with the wench. When he learns the cost of his choice, he will draw off again to spare her further grief."

"I'm not going to let you—"

"*Get out.* Unless you wish her and the rest of the world to learn who wielded that knife on the floor and who lies dead as a result?"

Heléne followed both men's gaze to the crusted dagger beside the chest. Triston blanched. His tortured eyes caught Heléne's for an instant. Then he turned towards the door.

"Triston, don't go!" she screamed.

He paused, his hand on the latch. She saw the tremor that smote his broad shoulders. He would not leave her. He *could* not leave her! He glanced back, but his expression had gone abruptly shuttered. His dark eyes flicked from her to Rousillon. Then he wrenched open the door and went out.

Rousillon laughed and pushed her back onto the bed. Panic sliced through her disbelieving shock at Triston's betrayal. Rousillon's fingers groped at the laces of her tunic. She tried to slap them away, but he, too impatient to deal with the knots, slid his dagger inside the strings and cut them. He pushed the cloth aside, exposing the letter she had sought to conceal. He plucked out the folded parchment and set it beside her head on the pillow.

"Ah. A double prize."

She had threaded the key to Sir Damian's chamber with a ribbon and hung it round her neck inside her tunic. He cut the ribbon and set the key alongside the letter.

"Alas," he murmured, "Gunthar has left me no time to taste of your charms. But we will teach him to regret his rashness, eh?"

She twisted wildly away from the chill malevolence in his eyes, and for a moment thought she had succeeded in breaking free. His hold on her slackened. She wrenched herself from his grip and rolled onto her stomach. But before she could draw up her knees, his weight landed on her back with such force that it knocked the breath from her. She gasped for air, but her face drove down into blankets that threatened to smother her. Desperately, she rolled her head away from their stifling warmth.

"Ah!" Fire burst like a trail of lightning through her shoulder. Only as the pain ebbed did she realize that Rousillon had jerked her arm up behind her back.

"The hair was just a portent of things to come," he muttered. "Gunthar should have known that. He should have known *me*. Right hand first, my lady. If that does not persuade him to withdraw, then I shall send him the left."

She felt an edge of steel, cold as ice, press against her wrist. "No!"

"Lie still. I promise it will be over quickly. Providing your beloved cooperates, I may even give you back to him when I am done."

*No, no, no!*

"Milord!" A pounding fell on the door.

"Whoever it is, *go away*." Rousillon's command snapped out like a whip, carrying with it an implicit warning of retribution to any who dared disobey.

But the pounding persisted and the voice came more urgently than before. "Milord, you must come at once! The yard is in an uproar! Sir Triston has flung open the gates!"

Heléne gasped, then gave a shivering sob of relief as the blade withdrew from her wrist. Rousillon did not shift from where he straddled her back, but she heard his blasphemous oath.

"Come!" he called.

A soldier wearing the badge of Melusine burst into the room. "Sir Triston has opened the gates," he repeated, "and ordered the garrison not to resist the earl's advance. At least half of them are obeying, though Sir Oliver is doing his best to rally them back to your cause. But the earl's forces are streaming over the bridge, and there are not enough men—"

Rousillon sprang up. He slammed the dagger into its sheath. Then he pulled Heléne up and laid a blow across her face.

"You and he are going to pay mightily for this," he swore. "Brun, come with me. And get a torch from the corridor. We are going to need it."

The soldier obeyed. Rousillon snatched up the letter and the key and pulled Heléne out of the room.

With Brun on their heels, he dragged her down one flight of steps and up another until they reached Sir Damian's chamber. Heléne strained her ears for the sounds of battle and rescue, but Rousillon slammed the door shut behind them, cutting off any noise but that of her own pounding heart. He stopped to survey the room. His lips twisted up when he saw the wardrobe door.

"There, that is where we shall put her."

He thrust her into the small, windowless chamber and told Brun to block the exit.

"He will find me here," she panted.

"Not in time," was Rousillon's retort.

With a frenzied energy, he began overturning the clothing chests, snatching up the spilled garments as he went and strewing them over the floor. There were blankets, too, and sheets and other linens . . . He scattered them all, even pulling down most of the tapestries from the walls, until the floor was a sea of cloth. Then he walked over to Brun and took the torch out of his hand.

"Now we shall see whom Gunthar wants most—you or me."

Heléne stared into his evilly glinting eyes. "What are you going to do?"

He smiled. The wall opposite the door was still draped with a tapestry which Sir Damian or his former lady had stored away here. Rousillon walked across the room and calmly set the torch to one corner.

It flared up in a rich, red blaze so hot that Heléne recoiled and instinctively flung her arms in front of her face. Rousillon's laughter made her lower them again. She saw him drop the letter, take two paces back, and touch the torch to the cloth at his feet. Flames shot up, but he sprang away with the nimbleness of a cat and reached the door and safety in one bound. Heléne lunged for it as well, but he pushed Brun through and slammed the door in her face. She tugged frantically at the latch, but he held it fast. And then she heard the click of the lock. The key had worked both doors.

# Twenty-Four

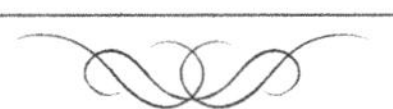

Gunthar shouted the command that sent his men over the drawbridge. Its lowering had been a surprise and was quite possibly a trap, but it was an invitation he could not ignore. Arrayed in full battle armor and astride his black warhorse, he thundered with his forces into the bailey, where they were met with such disorder that he was tempted to hope some fed-up squire had done away with Rousillon. Only a handful of knights sought to block their advance. Gunthar saw Sir Oliver and his lieutenants riding from one idle group of men to another, cursing and striking them in an attempt to prod them into action. One soldier came flying at Gunthar on foot, but Gunthar dodged his sword and felled him with a kick.

It was then that he saw the sign of Melusine sewn to his attacker's shoulder. A sweeping glance through the slits in his helmet revealed a like badge on the tunics of almost every soldier in the garrison. Richard's badge. He had been duped!

Gunthar had sent the prince to guard the forest road, praying he could trust in Richard's word. It had been his last hope to save Heléne, to let Rousillon slip through his ranks, knowing that Richard would be waiting. But the prince's protestations had been a lie. He was as guilty as Rousillon, and Gunthar's duty was clear. Closing his mind to the cost, he called out the order that would seal her fate:

*"Find Rousillon. Under no circumstances is the villain to escape again."*

Gunthar's men took up the cry, creating an echo that haunted him as he fought his way through the confusion of the yard. His forces spread out behind him, overwhelming the meager resistance of the castle's garrison. Gunthar's goal was the keep. The haste with which Sir Oliver abandoned his rallying efforts and rode to bar his way, told him that Rousillon must be holed up inside its towering stone walls.

Gunthar's memory kindled as he warded off a blow of the captain's sword. Sir Oliver's arm was strong, but Gunthar parried every thrust. There was not time to punish this cretin as he would have liked. He settled for a slicing arc that knocked the sword from the captain's hand, then slammed the flat of his blade into Sir Oliver's head. Having foolishly relied on a mail coif rather than a helmet, Sir Oliver tumbled off his horse like a sack of wheat.

Seeing their captain's fall, Sir Oliver's lieutenants fled with a small coterie of soldiers into the keep. Gunthar followed, flanked by his personal guard. The great hall became the new battleground as Sir Oliver's men turned and sought to block access to the stairs leading to the upper floors. Unlike the half-hearted struggle in the bailey, these men fought with determination and Gunthar found his guard initially beaten back.

Sir Roger lowered an opponent with a swinging blow, but Gunthar's shout failed to warn Sir Thomas in time to evade the bloody thrust that pierced his mail. Beset by two attackers of his own, Gunthar had no chance to avenge him. Precious minutes were sliding away. Surely Rousillon had heard the commotion? Even now the fiend might be slipping down some back passage in disguise.

Gunthar fended off blow after blow. He ducked a swing that was aimed at his head and with two moves that flowed together as one, drove his elbow into his assailant's ribs and rammed the hilt of his sword into the doubled-over man's jaw. The maneuver disposed of one opponent, but left Gunthar open to a smashing hit by the other's sword that sliced sideways into his shoulder. It staggered him, but the iron links of his armor held. He whirled around to parry a second thrust and dealt a blow of his own that sent his last opponent off his feet.

"Enough, my lord! Put down your sword and command your

men to do the same!"

Gunthar spun at the ringing voice. Rousillon stood at the top of the stairs, a leaping torch in his hand. Unlike the soldier at his side, he no longer wore the prince's badge.

"You are outnumbered, Rousillon," Gunthar said. "None but these fools remain to defend you, and in another moment—"

"In another moment," Rousillon replied, "your lady will be ashes."

Gunthar moved towards the stairs, but found himself blocked by Sir Oliver's guards. "If you have harmed one hair of her head—"

"That bird has already flown. Did you not receive my gift of her charming braid? It should have been a warning to you, Gunthar."

Gunthar choked back his dread. He gave a signal that caused his men to lower their swords, though they remained drawn and ready to resume the battle at a gesture from their lord.

"What have you done to her?"

Rousillon sneered. "She is locked in Sir Damian's wardrobe where, I fear, a small fire has been set. Here—" he held out his hand "—is the key. It is yours for a word."

"What word."

"I want safe passage out of Vere and the guarantee that none of your guard shall follow. Your oath on it, Gunthar, and the Lady Heléne is yours."

"My lord—" Sir Roger was at Gunthar's shoulder "—you saw the men in the bailey, the badges they wore. They belong to the prince. If you let Rousillon go now, Richard will be waiting, not to seize him, but to spirit him away. You will not have another chance to take him."

Gunthar knew that. His mind raced for an answer that would save her, but there was none.

"There is not time to dither, Gunthar," Rousillon called down. "The room is small. Even now the flames are licking at your lady's feet."

Gunthar's mouth was dry. "Give me the key."

Rousillon shook his head. "First your oath."

"I cannot let you go."

"Come and get me, then. There is no place for me to run. Of

course, by the time you fight your way past my men, your lady will be dead."

Gunthar swore at him, but a quick count of the guards defending the stairs told him that Rousillon was right. There were too many, too well armed, to force a quick break-through.

Rousillon laughed and tossed the key into the air. The tarnished metal gleamed in the light of the torch. "Make up your mind, Gunthar."

"Throw it down and I will give you your life."

"In prison? I thank you, no. My freedom or nothing."

"I cannot—"

"A pity. I understand the flames to be an excruciating death. Perhaps in the scuffle to seize me, you will not be able to hear her screams."

Rousillon was playing with the key, passing it in and out of the torch's flame. Gunthar knew his duty. His fist tightened on the hilt of his sword and he opened his mouth to give the only order he knew he dared give, but all that came out was a croaking groan.

For weeks he had forced himself to think solely of the king and the realm, and of John Lee's blood, but suddenly all he could see was her . . . Heléne, trapped in a blazing room, waiting for him to come to her, believing to the last that he *would* come, that he would not fail her . . .

"Is it worth it, Gunthar?" Rousillon called down in soft mockery. "The innocent's life for mine?"

Gunthar stared into the monster's pitiless face. Suddenly he knew it was not.

"Go," he said. "Give me the key and go."

"My lord," Sir Roger protested, "you said in the bailey—"

Gunthar seized his marshal by the front of his surcote. "Don't challenge me, Tollerton. I know what I said, and I will answer for it to the king, but Rousillon goes free *now*. He has my oath on it. Now get out to the yard and see that I am obeyed." He released him with a snap that sent the marshal stumbling towards the exit. Gunthar turned back to Rousillon. "Now, Sir Garoux—"

Rousillon laughed his hated laugh and ambled down the stairs. Not until he reached the bottom and touched two of his soldiers on the shoulder did they part to let Gunthar through.

"The key—"

Rousillon placed it in Gunthar's hand, but his smirk of triumph vanished when Gunthar slammed him against the wall with a mailed arm across his throat.

"This is not the end, Rousillon. If I am too late, there is no place the length and breadth of this earth that I will not find you and cut you down like the dog that you are."

There was not time for more. Gunthar hurled him out of his way and lunged up the stairs to find Heléne.

The door to Sir Damian's chamber was locked. In panic, Gunthar threw his shoulder against it, then forced himself to stop and think. Sometimes keys served a double lock. He slid the key into the hole and felt it turn. He lifted the latch and the door swung open.

The room within was grey with smoke. Gunthar saw it pouring out from beneath the wardrobe door. His mouth was as dry as the ashes he envisioned beyond it. If he were too late . . .

He fumbled with the wardrobe lock.

"Helen?" he shouted.

The wood of the door was hot. His hands began to shake when the key refused to turn. Had Rousillon tricked him? He struck the door, cursing in frustration. He tried it again, jiggling the key, wrenching at it, and finally heard a click.

"Helen? *Helen?*"

Smoke billowed through the open door, burning Gunthar's eyes and filling his lungs with a thick, acrid heat. He strained for a glimpse of her through the cloud and flames. The floor, even the walls appeared to be engulfed in the horrible, awesome conflagration. She could not have survived such rage. Still, living or dead, he would find her.

He stripped off his surcote, trusting to his armor to protect him, and stepped into the flames. The room was small. He should be able to search it before the heat overpowered him, before the fire could heat his iron links to roast him like an oven. The flames were not as high as he had thought at first. Most reached only to his waist, though a few lapped upwards towards his shoulders. But the blaze had spread over the entire floor, leaving no quarter for a trapped victim. The stone wall just opposite him seemed to be blanketed in leaping, orange-red tongues.

He strode a quick circumference of the room, stepping around the wooden chests, large and small, that had been toppled over and emptied of their contents. Some made of thicker, heavier wood were smoldering rather than burning, an indication that the fire had been but recently set. But there was no sign of Heléne. He rounded the room again. Even through the smoke, he should have been able to see her—unless Rousillon had lied?

*"Helen?"* he called again.

No answer came but the snapping and cracking of flames. Sweat streamed down his face inside his helmet. Unable to wipe it away, it trickled into his eyes, stinging and further blurring his sight, already wobbly from the heat-wavy air. The quilted gambeson beneath his mail hauberk offered some insulation, but he knew it was a temporary barrier, at best. He felt his chest tightening as he breathed in clouds of torrid air. She was not here. Then where had Rousillon put her?

Choking for breath, he stumbled back across the room. He had reached out one hand for the doorjamb when he heard the thin voice, so faint that he could not be sure a feverish desperation had not conjured it from the depths of his own despair.

"My lord?"

He spun about, but still saw nothing but smoke and a yellow sea—until it moved. At first, he thought it was a trick of the unsteady air. Then he saw it lift and fall back again. One of the chests, over by the wall. He plunged back into the scorching waves and heaved up the overturned box. She was there, cowering beneath it, her body pressed against the heated stones of a little island she had cleared for herself on the floor.

He dropped to his knees beside her. Her flesh was red beneath a layer of soot, her hair, cropped to the chin, smirched black as a raven's wing. She gave a small sob when he slid an arm around her shoulders.

"I knew you would come," she whispered.

"It's not over yet," he said. "I'm not sure how to get you out of here."

He glanced at the licking flames that surrounded them. He could make a dash for the door, but there was no way to shield her from the blaze. Even if he held her high, some flare might well catch her clothes on fire. Still, a few burns would be preferable to the risk of leaving her here while he sought her some protection. Smoke inhalation alone must have reached a dangerous point for her by now. The chest he had removed had already begun to kindle and the odds that she could continue to elude the flames, even on her little island, were too slim to even contemplate. Were a single spark to alight on her tunic—

There was no other way. He steeled himself against her inevitable pain and scooped her up in his arms.

"My lord? My lord Gunthar, are you there?"

"Challons?" Gunthar squinted through the smoke at the figure in the doorway.

"Aye, my lord. Have you found her?"

"Aye, but we're trapped. I need some device to shield her while I carry her out of the flames."

There was a pause. Gunthar could not see if Challons were conferring with others, or whether he was alone. In a moment, the voice called back, "A shield, you say? I think I see—"

"My lord, look out!"

Gunthar glanced up at Heléne's cry and saw the blazing wall collapsing. He dropped back to the floor and threw his body over hers. Sparks exploded around them, bathing them in a fireburst that crackled in his ears. His flesh tingled dangerously, but the crushing weight he braced for never landed on his back.

"It was a tapestry," she gasped. "Rousillon set it on fire."

Gunthar's muscles sagged with relief. He remained sprawled atop her for several minutes, until he was sure the worst of the sparks had burned themselves out against his mail or the stones of the floor. Then he pulled her back up.

"Are you hurt?" he asked. She looked dazed, but shook her head. "Not burned?"

"No, but—oh!"

"What is it?"

"Your helmet! It's on fire!"

Gunthar almost laughed and put up his mailed hands to douse his flaming crest. "Challons!" he called.

"Here, my lord. Are you injured?"

"Nay."

"And the lady—?"

"She is safe with me, for the moment. Have you found—?"

"I have an idea, my lord. Hold on."

Gunthar crouched beside Heléne and spoke a word of calm reassurance, but she was beginning to cough in a racking manner that alarmed him. He was having more trouble than ever breathing himself, and his skin felt as though it had been thoroughly scorched.

"My lord Gunthar—"

Gunthar pushed himself to his feet.

"—try this."

Gunthar stepped forward to catch the spinning object Challons tossed from the doorway and heard the hissing of steam as it sailed through the flames. Whatever it was had been thoroughly soaked in water. At least, the outer layer had. He retreated to Heléne's side and stripped off the cloth covering to reveal exactly what he had said he needed—a shield, this one bearing a gilded rose.

"Here," he said, "quickly, wrap yourself in this." He had recognized the wet fabric as a cloak, stretched out over the shield. He draped it around her and drew the hood over her head. Then he pushed the shield into her hands. "Hold it close against you. What it does not protect, the cloak will."

The shield wobbled in her grasp. He realized she was nearly too weak to obey, but after a moment she steadied it and he lifted her into his arms. He staggered with her back into the blaze. The flames were higher now, lapping about both their bodies. Steam swirled out from the wet cloak, but she hid her face against his breast and hugged the shield close. He stumbled over a chest he could no longer see and landed on his knees, but struggled up and pressed forward again. And then there was a hand on his shoulder, pulling him over the threshold into Sir Damian's chamber.

Gunthar lurched to the bed and fell with her across it. His lungs felt ready to burst. He released her to sit up, pulled off his helmet, and succumbed to a violent coughing fit. Heléne gasped against the pillows, with the shield caught beneath her. Windows had been opened to try to disperse the smoke pouring from the wardrobe, but the taste of it still stung in Gunthar's throat. Anxious voices echoed in his aching head. There seemed to be several people in the room, though he could not see their faces through his streaming eyes. Someone handed him a cup of water. He drew Heléne up and made her drink first. After several choking attempts, she succeeded in swallowing a few mouthfuls. Her dragging coughs that had frightened him earlier began to ease.

Gunthar took a deep swig of the water that was left, then splashed the rest of it into his face. At last, his vision cleared. A half-dozen men in blue and silver livery hovered around them. One of them refilled his cup from a pewter pitcher. Gunthar pressed it into Heléne's trembling hands. While she drank again, he turned his attention to the activity by the window. There were more men there, including Challons. One of the men removed a bucket from a rope, tied on another one and lowered it down the outside wall. He handed the first bucket to Challons, who carried it to the wardrobe and tossed its contents into the flames.

"Think you it can be put out?" Gunthar asked, his voice rasping through his throat.

Challons turned to answer. "We will do our best, my lord. We are lugging up water from the well. At the very least, we should be able to contain it so the flames do not spread to the rest of the castle."

Gunthar gave a curt nod. He pushed back the mail coif from his head and turned his face towards the widow, luxuriating in a gust of cooling breeze

"Helen?"

"I'm all right," she said, her voice gruff but reassuringly determined.

She refused to drink any more, but Gunthar gladly gulped down a second, and then a third cup. The activity from the window to the wardrobe was increasing, buckets being lowered and raised and rushed across the floor to try and douse the fire. Gunthar's whole body ached, but the unpleasant tingling in his flesh had faded. The links of his mail had been singed black. His helmet's crest, once a proudly charging stallion, had been charred to an unrecognizable clump.

Heléne began to cough again. He stripped the cloak off of her, stood up and scooped her off the bed, observing, as he did so, the way she clutched up a piece of scorched parchment that had lain beside her.

"Come," he said, "we will get you into some clearer air."

He carried her out of the room and was about to carry her down the steps to the hall when she tugged at the mail about his neck.

"No," she said. "Rousillon—"

"Rousillon is gone," he soothed.

"Then I must show you something. Take me there."

He hesitated, glancing in the direction of her pointing finger. "What is it?"

"Please—" She broke off with another choking cough. When she recovered she was so urgent that he carried her where she wished.

Her directions led him to a sparsely furnished bedchamber. The shutters were open, letting in the clean air from outdoors. She took several gulping breaths to clear her lungs. Then she pointed to the floor, littered with items from an open chest.

"Put me down there."

Gunthar dropped to one knee beside the clutter and set her down, but when she began to reach for something, he pulled back her hand. "No. Helen, first you must tell me again that you are all right."

The brightness of her eyes reassured him. "I'm fine. My chest doesn't hurt as much now. It was easier to breath on the floor, until the flames got so high. But I kept telling myself that you would come if you could." She fingered the fluff of hair about her face and her cheeks, still pink from the flames, grew rosier beneath the layer of soot that stained them.

Gunthar looked away, too appalled at the dreadful choice he had almost made to meet her earnest gaze. "I should get you outside."

"No, I must show you this, first." Her voice dropped to a more subdued note, but she gathered up a handful of fabric circles that lay scattered beside her and dropped them into his mailed hands. "Look."

He did so and recognized the badge of Melusine.

"They are not the prince's."

Gunthar lifted a skeptical brow.

"They are not. The French king made them and sent them to Rousillon. It was in the letter."

"What letter?"

"The one I found in this chest. Its seal was the fleur-de-lis, the royal symbol of France."

Both his brows shot up at that. "Where is this letter now?"

"Rousillon dropped it in the wardrobe before he set the room on fire. I tried to save it, but it was already caught in the flames." She held up the charred bit of parchment that she had let fall in her lap. "That was when I got trapped against the wall. I tried to clear a space on the floor and I dragged that clothing chest over, hoping it might slow the flames from reaching me. But then the smoke got so thick and I couldn't breathe, and somehow the chest toppled over and I couldn't lift it off—"

She faltered. He took her hand and squeezed it.

"—and then you came. And I kept this, hoping there might be something left that you could decipher."

He took the scrap from her, but there was not enough to make heads or tails of what might have been inscribed there. "Are you sure about the seal?"

"Yes. And I remember what it said, too."

He glanced up. "You read the letter?"

"Rousillon let me. He—he did not think I would be able to tell you afterwards." She touched her lips and shivered.

"*Can* you tell me?"

She took a deep breath. "Yes. It said that the King of France commissioned Rousillon to 'create some great disturbance' between the princes and their father, such as to 'divert the attention of our good cousin—' I presume he meant King Henry? '—from our just but previously frustrated ambition'. He sent these badges at Rousillon's request and a replica of Prince Richard's dagger. Rousillon was to be rewarded with a castle and estate twice the size of that forfeited to the English crown when he was charged with his father's murder."

She paused. She was acting very brave, but an occasional flicker across her smudged features betrayed the precariousness of her composure.

Gunthar said, "So that was why he wished to assassinate me and blame it on the prince. The 'great disturbance' France wanted was another familial war."

"Yes," she said, "and while King Henry and Prince Richard were locked in a struggle for control of Poitou and Aquitaine, King Louis was going to sweep into Normandy and claim it for the French throne."

Gunthar nodded. The Capetians had long sought for a way to dismantle the 'Angevin Empire' in favor of their vision of a 'Greater France'. The plot was not only plausible, it was brilliant.

"It might have worked," he said. "Henry's victory over his sons was expensive, both in money and energy. He might have found himself unable to defend two territories at once, again."

He hoped this meant that the prince was, in fact, guarding the forest road and would intercept Rousillon. But if he did not—

"Without the letter, we can't prove anything. Unless Rousillon left some other evidence here. Did you search everywhere? What is this?"

He reached for what looked like a dagger's hilt half hidden behind her back. Heléne stiffened. When he saw the dried blood and the gilded rose, he understood why.

He stared grimly down at Triston's dagger.

"It may mean nothing," she said, reading his expression. "Rousillon may have—"

"Helen, your loyalty is laudable, but it is time you stopped letting it blind you. Sir Triston is as guilty as Rousillon in this conspiracy to ruin the king."

"But Triston could not help himself. Rousillon forced him with horrible threats. But he did his best to protect me, and it was his command that opened the gates!"

"I don't care if he ran out to meet me with open arms. There are times when repentance comes too late."

It had for John Lee. Gunthar had not the slightest doubt that the blood crusting the blade was that of his friend. For that alone, he would see Sir Triston at the headsman's block. He put the dagger down and got to his feet, then pulled her up too. To his relief, she stood quite steadily in the circle of his arm.

"You are sure you are not burned anywhere?"

She shook her head. Her mouth trembled unhappily, for she had read his resolve against Triston and did not agree with it. Still, he was surprised to find himself rebuffed when he leaned down to kiss her.

"Don't."

"Helen—"

"No. Just don't."

Her voice was strained. Well, that was understandable. Her escape from death had been horrifically narrow.

He kept his arm around her, but said in studied, neutral tones, "I will send one of my men to search these bundles. Perhaps he will find something else to link Rousillon to the plot with France. Either way, the scheme will be frustrated now we know of it. And if Richard will only keep his word to return with me to England—"

"England?" She sounded dismayed, though her eyes remained fixed on her shoes. "You are leaving us?"

"Aye. I've had all of Poitou that I can stomach for a while. A day or two more should suffice to tie up loose ends, and then . . . But we will talk of this later," he said, seeing the droop of her shoulders. "It is time to get you home."

He touched her face very gently, rubbing the back of his mailed hand over her cheeks to wipe away the soot. It was then he realized the blackish stain near her eye was not the work of ashes. He did not need to ask whose blow had raised such a bruise, but if that was all the harm she had suffered at Rousillon's hands, he stood in eternal debt to the heavens.

He ignored her protests that she was perfectly able to walk. He swept her back up in his arms and carried her out of Vere Castle.

Heléne leaned back in her father's embrace, aware that the rhythmic movements of the horse were almost lulling her to sleep. She was glad now that Gunthar had refused to let her ride alone. He had held her perched up before him as far as the forest road. Laurant and Therri had met them there, together with the prince who was glowing with pride at his own military triumph.

While Gunthar had been besieging Vere, Prince Richard and his forces had flushed out of the woods a formidable band of vagabond knights masquerading as members of the prince's guard in counterfeit badges of his infamous ancestress. The prince's outrage at this presumption had half of the offending knights on their knees in terror for their lives when Therri's shout had alerted the prince to the approach of Rousillon. Rousillon, seeing his danger, had tried to flee another way. But, the prince boasted to Gunthar, he had anticipated every possible retreat and had stationed his men to block them. Rousillon had been brought to him, surly but bound.

Heléne caught the deadly look that Rousillon flashed at Triston. Poor Triston had been found in the gatehouse and dragged out to the bailey to await Gunthar's pleasure. Gunthar had ordered him stripped of his sword, but allowed him to mount his own horse and ride unfettered to his judgment at Pennault. Heléne winced at the abuse Rousillon let loose upon the unfortunate knight, and held her breath in dread when he swore that Triston would regret his treason "when his lady stood exposed for her crimes." Triston waited, grim but powerless to prevent the imminent blow.

That was when Gunthar deposited Heléne in her father's arms and ranged his horse in front of Rousillon's. The defiant grin on Rousillon's lips vanished when Gunthar drew his sword.

"Hold, de Bury! You said he should be mine!"

The prince's cry checked Gunthar's rage, but it did not extinguish it. He returned his sword to its scabbard, but the savagery with which he struck Rousillon across the mouth made Heléne shudder.

"That is for the Lady Helen," Gunthar said, " and this—" the second blow, struck with a fist, hurled Rousillon from his saddle " — is for John Lee."

Heléne tried not to think of Rousillon's bloody face as he had lain stunned in the road.

"The devil," Laurant muttered into her ear, and to her dismay she realized he meant, not Rousillon, but Gunthar. For miles as they resumed their journey, her father complained of the earl, of the coldness with which he had refused to allow her father and Therri to take part in the siege, of Gunthar's callous indifference to her safety, of the pitiless devotion to duty that had brought her so near to disaster. He would never forgive Gunthar, Laurant swore, fingering the cropped off ends of her hair. To her surprise, she felt a splash of moisture on her neck that might have been a tear.

Heléne had never known her father cared so much, but she was too exhausted to respond to his frank expressions of affection. She closed her eyes and leaned her head against his shoulder. She wished her father had not reminded her about her hair. She had seen Gunthar's shame, the embarrassed averting of his gaze when she had touched it in Rousillon's chamber. He had only tried to kiss her out of pity, and that had hurt more than all that she had suffered for him before.

An exhaustive numbness gradually dulled the pain, but it revived when they rode through the gates of Pennault and her father shook her awake. Young Brandon de Vexin was already in the bailey and ran to take Gunthar's reins. Therri lifted Heléne to the ground. Almost immediately her mother and Clothilde appeared, but when Heléne turned to look for Triston, she caught Gunthar's eyes instead.

He did not try to avoid her now, but his expression was impenetrable. He has mastered his consternation, she thought, but behind the veil she was certain there lay disgust. She looked away, pulling on the ends of her hair in a vain attempt to cover her neck. If Rousillon had disfigured her face, she could not have felt more ugly.

She was glad when Therri led her across to her mother. But the Lady Gwenllian's only reception was a shocked exclamation at her daughter's appearance.

"Dressed like a dirty squire, and shorn like one, as well! Why did your father not think to at least cover your head?"

While her mother scolded, Heléne heard Gunthar behind them, directing his guards to take Sir Triston to the tower.

"Etienne is to be released at once," he said, "but Sir Triston—"

*"No!"*

A sudden shove pushed Heléne into her mother. She saw Clothilde bump against Therri as well as she dashed across the yard towards her lover. Everyone turned at her shriek. Sensing her target, Gunthar moved to block her path.

"She's got my dagger!" Therri shouted, but it was too late.

Clothilde moved like the wind, and Heléne watched in horror as she slammed the blade twice into Gunthar's chest.

# Twenty-Five

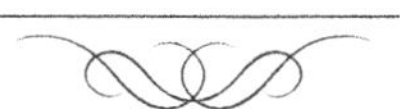

The blows threw Gunthar back against Triston's horse. Heléne screamed. The whole scene blurred before her eyes, but she ran after Clothilde and leapt for her hand to prevent another strike.

"No! Heléne don't touch her!"

Triston's warning, like Therri's, came too late. Clothilde whirled and lashed out at Heléne, just missing her face with the swishing blade. Heléne stumbled, her foot caught in Clothilde's skirts. She fell and Clothilde tumbled down with her.

At first, Heléne sought only to disengage herself from their tangled limbs. Then she saw Clothilde's face. Her delicate features had contorted into a hideous caricature. Heléne cried out her sister's name, but it failed to stay the thrust that landed in the dirt near her throat. The dagger flashed up and plunged down again. Heléne twisted away with a sob.

Somehow the blade missed her. She caught Clothilde's hand and tried to wrestle the weapon away but her sister's arm, grown frail from weeks of pining, now possessed an unnatural strength. Heléne felt her fingers slipping and saw the blade swoop downwards towards her breast.

She flinched, then gasped. Hands closed about her sister's shoulders, jerking her back. Clothilde swung about and thrust the dagger at the man who had seized her.

There was a grunt, and then a shriek so ghastly that Heléne shrank and covered her ears.

*"No, no, no!"*

Heléne saw Clothilde fling herself across Triston's crumpled body. The dagger was buried up to the hilt in his chest. Heléne scrambled to his side and felt at the base of his neck for a pulse.

"Is he dead?" a male voice asked.

"No, look, she missed his heart. But we must—" She gasped and stared up into Gunthar's face. "How—"

"The iron links held on my hauberk," he said. "At least, the first blow glanced off. The second blow broke the links, and had she had a chance for a third . . ."

He knelt beside Triston's body. She saw that the surcote, which he had redonned in the bailey at Vere, was torn, exposing the hole in the mail near his heart. Tears flooded into her eyes again, this time of relief and gratitude, but her impulse to throw her arms about Gunthar's neck was checked by her sister's moans.

"Triston—ah, Triston!"

Heléne reached for Clothilde and found Gunthar's hand on her wrist.

"Helen—"

"It's all right now," she said and pulled Clothilde into her arms.

"Triston . . . Oh, Heléne!" Clothilde collapsed, weeping, against her sister, the mad fury gone.

Heléne stroked the golden locks as she had so many times before. "Yes, love, I know. You must try to be brave. We will help him if we can."

"Well?" Gunthar said

Heléne leaned against the door to the room where Triston lay. A day had passed and she was still so weary that her very bones seemed to ache. A hot, lingering bath had washed away the grime of Vere and restored her hair to its natural color, if not its former glory. Mindful of her mother's chiding, she had changed into a serge-blue gown and tied a scarf around her head so that its tasseled ends draped her shoulders in a semblance of respectable tresses.

Clothilde was still sleeping under the influence of the draught that Heléne had mixed for her, while Triston now rested uncomfortably in Therri's bedchamber. The wound in his chest was deep, but Heléne's determined ministrations had finally slowed the bleeding. If no inflammation set in, she judged his chances of recovery were good.

"He ought not to be talking yet," she said.

"But *can* he talk?"

She hesitated, but she had left Triston conscious and lucid. She nodded, frowning at the flint-like cast of Gunthar's features. Was there no mercy in the man?

"Can't this wait?"

"No," he said, and reached around her to open the door. "You needn't come," he added, as she straightened her shoulders and turned to follow him.

"I have not saved Triston's life just so you can bully him to death. If you upset him too much, you shall have to leave."

Gunthar merely stood aside to let her precede him into the room.

At first glance, Triston appeared to be asleep. But when she cracked open the shutters, she saw the tension in his face, hinting of a pain too great to permit him the bliss of slumber. His cheeks were as white as the bandages she had wrapped around his chest, but the chalk-like lids fluttered open when she bent to touch his hand.

"Triston, the earl wishes to speak with you, but if you do not feel well enough, I will send him away again."

Gunthar muttered a protest at this, but Triston moved his head against the pillows.

"No, I knew he would come. Let us get it over with." His eyes followed Heléne as she seated herself in the chair beside the bed. "Have you told him?"

"I promised you I would not."

"Told me what?" Gunthar said.

Triston freed her from her vow with a nod.

"Are you sure?" she asked.

He groaned. "He will learn of it from Rousillon anyway. Tell him for me, Heléne."

She pressed Triston's hand, then looked at Gunthar and said, "You cannot marry Clothilde, because she is already Triston's wife."

From his startled reaction, it was clear this was not the revelation Gunthar had expected. "I beg your pardon?"

"I said, you cannot marry Clothilde because—"

"Devil take it, girl, I heard you. What the blazes has that to do with Sir John?"

"Why, it has nothing to do with—"

"Heléne." Triston stopped her as Gunthar strode to the foot of the bed and glared down at the prostrate knight.

"I don't give a snap about your sister," Gunthar said. "I'd not marry that hellcat now if the king threatened to have me drawn and quartered. What I want to know from *you* is—" he pointed a menacing finger at Triston "—where were you the night that John Lee died?"

Triston did not answer immediately. Lest he be considering some false reply, Heléne said, "We have both seen the dagger, hidden in Rousillon's chamber. Triston, it was covered with blood—"

"I was nowhere near the clearing when Rousillon attacked Sir John."

"Then where—"

"I was at the river with Clothilde—and Sybil." Triston sighed and rolled his head against the pillows to stare at the ceiling. "Rousillon knows about that, too. He forced Audiart to spy on us, then he took the dagger and said that if I tried to double-cross him— But after today, I can't protect her anymore." He closed his eyes. "The blood on that dagger is not Sir John's—it is Sybil's."

Heléne gasped.

Triston groaned. "I could not stop her. It all happened so fast. It was like today. One moment Clo was perfectly sane, the next she had seized my dagger and—"

Heléne rose halfway out of her chair. "Are you saying that *Clothilde* murdered Sybil?"

"Helen," Gunthar rounded the bed and pushed her back down, "she would have murdered you today had Sir Triston not intervened.

Your sister is clearly mad."

"I have only seen it manifested twice," Triston said. "Today it was when you threatened me with the tower. That night . . ."

"Tell us about that night," Gunthar said, "and this time hold nothing back."

Triston gave a defeated nod. "It was all arranged by Rousillon. He used Osanne to persuade you to visit the clearing, where he and his minions were waiting to do their bloody deed. But I swear I did not know beforehand what he intended that night. To keep me from learning of it, he distracted me with Clothilde. Through Julian Parr, he arranged for her to meet me down by the river. Parr contacted Clothilde through Sybil. The old nurse was devoted to Clo. She knew about our marriage and had sworn to help us be together. But I did not know until that night the lengths to which that devotion had already carried her—or how much it was tinged with guilt."

Gunthar said, "She must have seen my royally backed betrothal as a threat to you. Helen thinks it was Sybil who cut my saddle strap and tried to poison me by putting cowbane in my wine."

"Aye," Triston said, "she confessed it to Clothilde and me. I was horrified, but Clothilde bore the admissions as mild as you please until—until Sybil spoke of the child."

"Child?" Heléne said, but Gunthar signaled to her to be quiet.

"What happened then?" he asked.

"Clothilde began shrieking and the next thing I knew, she had my dagger. Sybil was dead before I could pull her away." Triston paused and frowned. "She did not seem to remember afterwards. I left her weeping but quiet beside the river while I dragged Sybil's body into the woods, and when I returned she asked quite innocently where Sybil had gone. Even after I made her tell me about the child and understood why she had turned on the old nurse the way she had, she still did not comprehend what she had done."

He stopped, catching his breath at some twinge of pain in his chest. Heléne rose in alarm, but he waved her back.

"No, let me finish. I did not tell you everything, Heléne. I did not know everything myself, until that night."

The discomfort passed in a moment, or at least became tolerable enough for him to continue.

He looked at Gunthar and said, "Clothilde's marriage to Merval was a sham. She was already my wife, but I left her behind to fulfill a vow to my mother. I knew that Clothilde loved me, and I knew she was weak. What I didn't know when I left was that she was carrying my child. When the Lady Gwenllian learned of it, she took Clothilde to their manor at Beaulac. There she tried every coercion she could think of to make Clothilde abjure our marriage. But Clothilde withstood it all with rare courage . . . until the night the child came forth."

A shadow passed over the taut planes of Triston's face and his voice grew more ragged. "Unwilling even then to lose the alliance with Merval, the Lady Gwenllian sent all the servants away save Sybil. And then, in an atrocity of nature beyond belief, heedless of her own daughter's tears and pleas, she ordered Sybil to take the babe into the woods and leave it there, abandoned to cold and wild beasts alike. It was a punishment, she said, for her daughter's shame. But our marriage was made before God. It is the Lady Gwenllian who sinned, and it is she who will suffer the flames of hell for it."

Triston's voice shook now, the depth of his anger overwhelming his pain.

Heléne felt herself paling with shock at his words. "Mama—I cannot believe it! I know that ambition is everything to her, but even she would not have done something so wicked as that!"

"She did not."

Gunthar's quiet voice startled them both. He said, "I gather it was that which unsettled the Lady Clothilde's mind? Thinking her child dead, and in such a hideous way."

Triston nodded. "It sent her into such despondency, Sybil told me, that they feared for her life for a time. When the Lady Gwenllian insisted on pushing through the marriage with Merval, Clothilde was too feeble from grief to offer any further resistance." He hesitated. "My lord, what did you mean, the Lady Gwenllian did not . . . ?"

"Your son is alive, Sir Triston," Gunthar said. "Or at least, I believe he may be yours. I saw him in a village on the road to Angoulême, a child scarce four years old, dark of hair and blue of eye, and wearing the de Brielle rose at his throat."

Triston looked incredulous. "But Clothilde said—"

"I don't doubt she was convinced of her child's murder. A cruel trick of her mother's to bring her into compliance with Merval. Or perhaps the Lady Gwenllian did give such an order, and the nurse took it upon herself to save the child. The boy I saw was residing with a clothier couple, too old, I judged, to be his real parents. A Master Guillem and his wife—"

"Not Mistress Jeanne?"

"I believe that was her name."

"My mother's seamstress," Triston said. "She married a clothier named Guillem just before my mother died."

"I will have them all brought to Pennault. We will learn the truth of this matter, Sir Triston."

Triston's eyes lit with an almost feverish glow, but the light died as quickly as it sprang up.

"No," he said, "leave them where they are. He will be better off a clothier's son than a traitor's orphan."

Heléne turned to Gunthar. "My lord, can't you—"

"No," he said. "Do not ask it of me, Helen. Sir Triston knew the price when he shielded Rousillon."

"But—"

"Heléne, he's right. I will answer for the choices I made. Only—my lord, what will happen to Clothilde?"

Before Gunthar could reply, Heléne whispered, "This will send her into complete madness. Even the restoration of her child will not save her, if you harm Triston."

After today's episode, there was little doubt in anyone's mind that she was right.

"It is a risk we shall have to take," Gunthar said. "Sir Triston must stand his trial. But I shall not pursue the old nurse's murder, if that is what you fear. I am not a persecutor of the mad."

Triston sagged against the pillows. "If only I could take her to Vere," he murmured. "I could keep her quiet and safe . . ." He closed his eyes again and let out a long, slow breath. "The Abbey of Maillezais. My mother left it a large bequest. The sisters will take

Clothilde in and care for her."

"I will see to it, Sir Triston," Gunthar said. They all knew that Clothilde could not remain at Pennault. With Sybil removed as the focus of her hatred for the loss of her child, the Lady Gwenllian might well taste her daughter's vengeance next.

Heléne saw Triston's exhaustion, and gestured firmly to Gunthar that they must leave. He followed her to the door, but paused there for one final question.

"Sir Triston, did Rousillon reveal to you the identity of the spy in my household known as le Reynard?"

Triston might have been a corpse, so still and white did he lay, but after several moments he gave a barely perceptible shake of his head.

Gunthar said nothing more until he and Heléne had left the room. He stood then outside the door and gazed broodingly at the passageway wall. Heléne knew he was reviewing in his mind every possible instance of betrayal by any of his men, but she was surprised by his conclusion.

"It had to be Challons."

"Lord Challons? But he saved our lives at Vere!"

"And thereby possibly hoped to save his own. But all evidence points his way. It was his recommendation that sent me to Poitiers without an adequate bodyguard, a journey he conveniently managed to avoid making himself. And I recall that it was Challons who brought me word of Bellesmains' arrival that morning I kissed you in the garden. I worried then that he had seen us. It must have been he who told Rousillon that I was in love with you."

Heléne did not want to believe it. Challons had always been kind to her, a generous and witty table companion . . .

"But are you sure? Rousillon said he betrayed you for silver."

Gunthar's brows swept up in a cynical arc. "The man is a spendthrift. I have seen him squander far more money than he could ever hope to recoup from his neglected estates. And those jewels he wears, I have known a long while that they were beyond his means. I have often wondered how he managed to maintain himself so grandly. This is doubtless not the first infamous alliance he has entered."

"What about Julian?"

"What about him?"

"Rousillon said it was le Reynard who persuaded him to betray you."

Gunthar thought that over, then said, "Challons and Sir Adam Parr hold lands near to one another in York and seemed more than friendly the last time they waited upon me at my court. They may have been involved together in the Norwich affair."

"Then Challons stole Sir Adam's letter and used it to frighten Julian into betraying you? But then he killed Julian. Why?"

"Because Julian was going to tell me the truth. He came to me after John's murder, but before he could speak Challons came upon us. I thought it was guilt that made Julian turn so white, but it must have been fear that Challons had overheard."

Gunthar fell into another reflective silence, until Heléne disturbed it to ask, "Will you plead Lord Challons mercy from the king, for what he did for us yesterday?"

"There have been two murders, Helen, one by Challons' own hand. None of his actions at Vere can mitigate those deaths, still less his treason."

"What if he will not confess?"

"Rousillon will give us what we need. If I am any judge of that snake, he will want to take his cronies to the gallows with him."

"Including the Lady Osanne?"

"No doubt. I have placed her under guard until she can be questioned about her part in the plot." He paused and touched a finger to the little crease between Heléne's brows. "Do not worry yourself about it. I will take care of it all. But you have a journey to prepare for."

"A journey?"

"Aye. You did not think I was going back to England alone?"

He reached for her hand, but she pulled away. "Don't. You don't have to do this."

"Do what?"

"What—what I think you are about to do." She glanced away from his probing gaze. "You think because Clothilde is Triston's wife, that I will now expect you to— But I do not. I saw the way you looked at me at Vere. I do not blame you in the least. I know I was never pretty, but now—"

"What the blazes are you talking about? How did I look at you?"

"Like—like you were ashamed. You admired my hair, and now it is gone and I look like a nun, or worse yet, a *boy*. You deserve someone prettier than me on your arm."

Gunthar gave a disgusted snort. "I don't want you *on* my arm, I want you *in* my arms, and if I have to wait one more hour to put you there—"

She evaded his attempt to embrace her, then stole a glimpse at his startled face.

"Great heavens, you're serious!" Before she could stop him, he seized her hand. "Come with me."

She had no choice, as he dragged her down the passageway to his bedchamber. Her heart thumped nervously when he closed the door behind them, but he left her standing beside it while he retrieved something from the table near the bed.

"Take this—" he thrust the object into her hands "—and look."

It was a circle of glass backed with some kind of reflective metal and set in a wooden frame. A mirror. Father Dominic called them the devil's tool, a window to the sin of vanity, and refused to allow them in her father's house. She shook her head and tried to hand it back.

"No." Gunthar pulled her over to a large, elaborately carved chair and pushed her down onto its cushioned seat. Her cheeks flamed when he snatched the scarf from her head, but he only repeated, "Look, and tell me what you see."

At first, her eyes were too blurred with humiliation for her to see anything clearly. But he dropped to one knee and caught her hands, forcing her to hold the mirror before her face until she blinked away the tears and looked.

It was not nearly as bad as she had feared. The eyes that stared back at her were wide and clear, not terribly striking in color, but pleasingly shaped. A bruise marred one of the high-boned cheeks, but the short little nose was respectable and the generous mouth curved in a way strongly reminiscent of her father's. The fluff of pale hair brushing level with her jaw softened the sharpness of her chin, but those cropped-off ends could not be ignored. Was it a woman's face she viewed or a prettily-featured youth's?

"Have you never seen yourself before?" he asked, as she tilted the mirror to another angle.

"In water sometimes," she admitted, "but Father Dominic says it is wicked to linger over one's reflection, and Mama said I would never be as beautiful as Clothilde and that I should not waste my time in wishing."

She bit her lip and put the mirror face down in her lap.

His hand brushed against her hair. "It will grow back, you know, as lovely as before."

"It will not be the same," she whispered. "It will never be the same." She could not bear to look at him.

He said softly, "It is not your hair that I am in love with, and if this is the only way to prove it . . ."

He stood and walked across the room. When he turned back round, she saw that he held a thick, looped braid, tied with a crimson ribbon.

"A night has not gone by that I have not slept with this in my hand, but now . . ."

He crossed to the fireplace and cast it into the flames.

"What are you doing?" she cried.

"Putting an end to this foolishness. Helen—" Suddenly he was kneeling before her again and the mirror was gone so that there were only his hands on hers. "I don't know how I looked at you at Vere, but if you thought you saw shame in my eyes, it was at myself, at my own stubborn, bull-headed devotion to a 'duty' that nearly got you killed. When I think how I might have lost you—"

She felt him tremble, but he tried to conceal his emotion. He bowed his head and immersed himself in a detailed study of her hands.

"Are you quite sure that Rousillon left you with all your fingers and toes?" He separated and fondled each fingertip, then lowered her hands and pressed his face into her palms. He gave a groan that ended in a muffled sob. "How can you forgive me?"

The shudder that ran through his body frightened her. "Oh,

don't. Of course I forgive you." She pulled one hand away and stroked his hair. "Why can you not forgive Triston, too?"

He asked without lifting his head, "Is that what it will take to win you, now?"

"No. If you want me—truly want me—I am yours without condition. But—" she ran her fingers through the waves that lay against the nape of his neck. "Papa told me of your resolve to take Rousillon at any cost. You broke it for me, you know you did. You risked everything to save me, Rousillon, the king's anger, even your revenge for Sir John. How was that any different than what Triston did for my sister?"

"It was your life—"

"As for him, it was Clothilde's." She told him then of Rousillon's murder of Merval and his threats against her widowed sister. "Had you been Triston, what would you have done?"

"Had it been you," he said, after a long, struggling silence, "I might have let a murderer go free." He looked up then. His eyes were dry, but his face was drawn, still haunted by the tragic choice he had almost made. "Very well. Rousillon I will see in hell, but Sir Triston—I will have him removed to Vere and allow him to recover of his injuries there while I petition the king on his behalf. Your sister may go with him, if you think it will be safe."

She lifted his face and kissed him. She could not ask more of him than that. "Do you think the king will listen to you?"

"He has Rousillon and his reconciliation with his son. There is just one more thing we might do to sweeten his temper."

"What is that?"

"Give him the alliance he wants . . . with the house of Laurant." Gunthar gave her a quizzical smile. "Marry me tonight and I can almost guarantee Sir Triston's pardon."

She laughed. "That sounds like blackmail. You are as bad as Rousillon." He did not look amused by the comparison. "What about Lord Heywood?"

"I'll persuade your father to sell him the Northumberland land, and throw in a bit of my own for good measure. That was all Heywood really wanted from the marriage."

"I do not know if Papa will agree. He does not like you at all after what happened at Vere."

"A pity," Gunthar said. "I find I like him a great deal since he seems to have found his spine. And when he sees how I adore his daughter, he will be happy that he gave me your hand. Or that I took it, for one way or another, you are coming with me to Poitiers and Bellesmains is going to marry us."

She smiled at this return of arrogance. "But why must it be tonight? Why can we not wait until—"

"Because I want you out of this house before your witch of a mother can try to interfere. I don't think she will be pleased at your becoming a countess in your sister's place, and if she is as ruthless as Sir Triston says—"

Heléne had no impulse to defend her mother now. The Lady Gwenllian would be livid at her ousting Clothilde as Gunthar's wife, and when she learned that Clothilde and Triston were to be reunited—

"You had better set guards around him," Heléne said, "until you return him to Vere. I hope Mama would not feel herself so desperate as to actually try to injure him—but then, I would never have believed she would try to harm her own grandchild, either."

"I promise Triston will be safe, and your sister, too. Now will you—?"

She anticipated his demand and said, "I do not think I should leave before you return them to Vere. What if Clothilde should need me?"

"I will bring you back in the morning," Gunthar said. "Once you are my wife, there will be nothing more the Lady Gwenllian can do. Your sister can endure one night without you."

"But—"

"Helen."

"Oh, very well. Will you give Triston back his son?"

"Yes, anything. I will do anything you ask, if you will only marry me now."

She hesitated and raised a hand to her cropped-off hair. How *could* he want her like this? "Perhaps we should wait until it grows out—"

*"No."* He pulled her hand away so hard that she tumbled out of the chair. His kiss left no further room for doubt that he found her charms quite powerful enough as they were.

"Tonight," she gasped when he freed her. "I will marry you tonight."

"Tonight," he echoed hoarsely, and pulled her back into his arms.

# Author's Note

Prince Richard reconciled with his father at Winchester Castle in the spring of 1176. At a family conference, Henry II called upon his eldest son and heir, Henry the Young King, to go to his brother's assistance and complete the subjugation of the Poitevin and Aquitanian rebels. Money was made available to the princes for the hiring of a large mercenary force, and by the end of the summer the last of the resistance was crushed with the defeat of Count William of Angoulême. His city and castles were surrendered into Richard's hands and Count William was sent to England where, the chroniclers report, he begged the forgiveness of Henry II on his knees.

That Richard boasted of the legend of Melusine, demon ancestress of the Plantagenets, is recorded by the chroniclers of the time. How-ever, Richard's use of the serpent-woman on badges his servants wore and on daggers he gave out, is purely the author's invention.

# *Thank you for reading*

I hope you enjoyed reading ***A Candlelight Courting***. If you did, would you please consider ~

Recommending this book to a friend.

Leaving a review on the website where you downloaded this book. Just a few words about what you liked about the story will help other readers find and enjoy this book too.

Subscribing to my newsletter at joycedipastena.com so we can keep in touch about future releases in this series along with other books I'm writing.

Thank you again for reading ***A Candlelight Courting***!

# Glossary of Medieval Terms

**Angevin**: One who hales from the Anjou region of present-day France; birthplace of King Henry II of England.

**Aquitaine**: A region of southwest France that was ruled by Henry II of England in the Middle Ages.

**Bailey**: The courtyard of a castle.

**Chemise**: A woman's loose undergarment.

**Coif**: A hood made from metal rings (i.e., mail) worn beneath a knight's helmet.

**Curtain wall**: The outer wall that lies between the towers of a castle.

**Dais**: A raised platform in the great hall.

**Drawbridge**: A bridge that can be raised or lowered to allow access across a ditch or moat into a castle's bailey.

**Fealty**: The loyalty sworn by oath by a knight to his lord.

**Fortnight**: Two weeks (from fourteen nights).

**Gambeson**: A quilted jacket worn beneath a knight's armor to cushion the blows of battle.

**Gatehouse**: A heavily fortified entrance to a castle complex.

**Girdle**: A belt worn around the waist by both men and women.

**Hauberk**: A long tunic worn of chain mail that covers the upper body.

**Hilt**: The handle of a dagger or sword.

**Keep**: The central tower and main residence area of the castle.

**Kirtle**: A long, one-piece gown worn by women.

**Mail**: A flexible armor made of small, overlapping metal rings.

**Mangon or mangonel**: A medieval siege engine similar to a catapult, used to hurl large projectiles at a castle wall.

**Marshal**: A high-ranking officer in charge of a prince's or lord's horses and stables and, during war, his military cavalry.

**Moat**: A broad, deep ditch filled with water that formed a defense around a castle.

**Oubliette**: A dungeon deep underground with an opening only at the top.

**Page**: A boy between the ages of 7 and 13 who served as an attendant to a knight, lord or lady; the first step in a male's training to become a knight.

**Parchment**: Material made from animal skins used for the pages of books and other writing.
**Poitevin**: A resident of Poitou.

**Poitiers**: The capitol city of Poitou.

**Poitou**: A region of west-central France ruled by Henry II of England during the Middle Ages.

**Pommel**: A counterweight, usually in the shape of a circle or ball, at the top of the handle (hilt) of a sword or dagger, often intricately decorated; derived from Latin word for "little apple."

**Portcullis**: A grated gate usually ending in spikes that dropped vertically to seal off the entrance through a castle's gatehouse.

**Postern**: A hidden door in a castle's curtain wall.

**Seneschal**: Official in a medieval household responsible for the supervision and management of a nobleman's estates; in England, called "the steward."

**Smock**: A loose, blouselike garment.

**Squire**: A boy between the ages of 14 and 20 in training to become a knight; a squire might be knighted at the age of 21, although some men never advanced to knighthood and remained squires all their lives.

**Surcote**: Also known as the surcoat or super-tunic; a secondary tunic worn over an under-tunic, usually more elaborately decorated.

**The hall or great hall**: The central living space of the castle inside the keep; the ceremonial and legal center.

**The Great Revolt**: A civil war that took place between Henry II and his sons in 1173-74; also called the Great Rebellion and the Great War.

**Trencher**: Large slices of stale bread, cut either round or square, and used as "plates" for medieval dining.

**Tunic**: A sleeved, loose-fitting outer garment worn by both men and women; could be worn alone or under a surcote; for a man, could be knee or ankle length.

**Vassal**: A man who owes military service to one of higher rank, in return for land and protection.

**Veil**: A linen cloth draped over a woman's hair held in place with a gold or silken band around the head.

**Vellum**: A thin, fine form of parchment made from calfskin; also known as "veal parchment."

**Wardrobe**: A room or (for a king or great noble) series of rooms in a castle that housed the lord's clothes, jewelry and other personal valuables, as well as cash and important documents.

# Discussion Questions

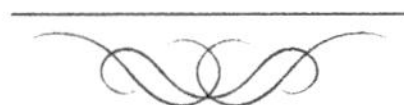

~ Why do you think the author chose the title, *Loyalty's Web,* for this book?

~ How can loyalty be both a positive and a negative trait? How are both aspects of loyalty portrayed by the characters in this book?

~ Decisions and actions always bring consequences. What were the consequences of some of the decisions and actions made by various characters in this book?

~ Which characters, if any, did you relate to the most? Why?

~ Did the characters change or evolve during the story? What circumstances contributed to their growth?

~ Did you agree with Heléne's decisions in this book? With Gunthar's? With Triston's? Why or why not? What decisions might you have made differently? How might your decisions have effected the outcome of this story?

~Did the setting enhance the story? If so, how? If not, how did it detract?

~ What did you learn about medieval society by reading this book? medieval politics? the role of women in the Middle Ages? How did you feel about the latter?

# *Join my Medieval World!*

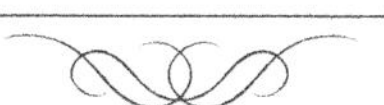

Sign up for Joyce's newsletter to receive announcements on new releases, special promotions and offers, participate in monthly giveaways, get subscriber-only glimpses into writing updates, book recommendations, historical trivia, and more! You are free to unsubscribe at any time.

Sign up at joycedipastena.com

# Acknowledgments

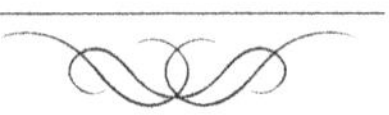

I would be most ungrateful if I did not express my deep appreciation to the following:

Sara Fitzgerald, my critique partner, for her boundless faith and encouragement.

Anna Arnett, for her eagle eyes and generous gift of time in proofreading this manuscript.

And the women of ANWACritique, who also shared their time and insights in improving important sections of *Loyalty's Web*.

# Suggested Reading List

(For readers interested in a further study of subjects addressed in *Loyalty's Web*)


### The Legend of Melusine

Costain, Thomas B. *The Conquering Family*. New York: Popular Library, 1949.

Kelly, Amy. *Eleanor of Aquitaine and the Four Kings*. Cambridge, Massachusetts and London, England: Harvard University Press, 1950.

Warren, W. L. *King John*, Berkeley and Los Angeles, California: University of California Press, 1961.

### Medieval Healing

Lust, John. *The Herb Book*. New York: Bantam Books, 1974.

McLean, Teresa. *Medieval English Gardens*. New York: The Viking Press, 1980.

Stevens, Serita Deborah, with Anne Klarner. *Deadly Doses: A Writer's Guide to Poisons*. Cincinnati, Ohio: Writer's Digest Books, 1990.

### Longbow vs. Crossbow; the Mangon; the Oubliette

Bottomley, Frank. *The Castle Explorer's Guide.* New York: Avenel Books, 1979.

### Conflict between Henry II and Richard Plantagenet

Barber, Richard. *Henry Plantagenet: 1133-1189.* New York: Barnes & Noble Books, 1964.

Warren, W. L. *Henry II.* Berkeley and Los Angeles, California: University of California Press,
1973.

### Norwich Castle

Warren, W. L. *Henry II.* Berkeley and Los Angeles, California: University of California Press,
1973.

### Jean aux Bellesmains (John aux Bellesmains); William, Count of Angoulême

Warren, W. L. *Henry II.* Berkeley and Los Angeles, California: University of California Press, 1973.

### Penalty for a Woman Poisoning Her Husband

Hanawalt, Barbara A. "The Female Felon in Fourteenth-Century England." *Women in Medieval Society.* Ed. Susan Mosher Stuard. University of Pennsylvania Press, 1976. 125-140.

### Child Abandonment in the Middle Ages

Shahar, Shulamith. *Childhood in the Middle Ages.* London and New York: Routledge, 1996.

## Poetry of Marie de France

Hanning, Robert, and Joan Ferrante, trans. *The Lais of Marie de France*. New York: E. P. Dutton, 1978.

# About the Author

Joyce DiPastena illuminates the Middle Ages for modern readers through heartfelt historical romance. However many changes a few centuries may bring, she believes that stories of love can unite people across time.

Joyce grew up in southern Arizona and can easily withstand summer temperatures of 115 degrees, as long as she's sitting in a restaurant, movie theater, or under a ceiling fan—inside an air-conditioned building. She can be bribed with chocolate chip cookies and enjoys attending the Arizona Renaissance Festival every year. She holds a degree in history, specializing in the Middle Ages, from the University of Arizona. Joyce currently resides in Mesa, Arizona with her black cats, Nyxie and Calypso, who bring her good luck every day.

Joyce loves to hear from her readers. Email her at joyce@joycedipastena.com.

Visit her website at joycedipastena.com.

Follow her on Facebook, Twitter/X, Amazon and BookBub. (Just search for "Joyce DiPastena." She's the only one there is!)

Made in United States
North Haven, CT
10 June 2024

53470507R00205